He wante
again
rule her

He pinned her against t
tried to duck, she fought until she was panting, but Simon
held her firm.

"Take your filthy hands off me, you slime-bitten
bastard!" Storme hissed.

He lifted a mild eyebrow. "Why, dearest. Could it be
only two nights ago you were begging me to put my hands
on you? Fickle, thy name is woman."

She spat in his face.

"Don't," he said very quietly, "ever do that again."

The light from the room poured over his shoulder,
etching him in stark relief. He was undressed to his white
lawn shirt and breeches, and she could see the light hair on
his chest. The strikingly perfect aristocratic face no longer
seemed a thing of beauty, but of force as well; the lovely
gray eyes were as hard as steel. There was an aura of danger
about him that Storme would have never suspected before.

It did not frighten her. It only made her heart beat
faster.

🐎

Also by Leigh Bristol

Amber Skies
Scarlet Sunrise
Silver Twilight

Published by
WARNER BOOKS

Hearts of Fire

Leigh Bristol

WARNER BOOKS

A Warner Communications Company

WARNER BOOKS EDITION

Cover illustration by Melissa Duillo Gallo

Warner Books, Inc.
666 Fifth Avenue
New York, N.Y. 10103

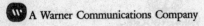 A Warner Communications Company

Printed in the United States of America

First Printing: January, 1989

10 9 8 7 6 5 4 3 2 1

To Sarah Jane,
who always insists we do our best

PART ONE

*

The Taking

* *Chapter One* *

Dead Man's Cay, the Caribbean
1720

It was nearing sunset in the islands, and no more beautiful sight was to be found on all the earth. Finger strokes of pink, magenta, and sulky violet washed across the sky, underscored by a brilliant orange that burst against the horizon like a startled gasp. Tangled hills of verdant green spilled toward the coast, topped by golden highlights of the sun's last rays and etched in the contrasting valleys of shadowed twilight.

Upon the beach dark-skinned islanders in bare feet and short breeches hauled in their nets for the day. Naked children chased the waves, and plump women in colorful, loosely fashioned gowns squatted upon the sand, digging for the clams they would serve for dinner. Seagulls circled lazily, and in the distance, sitting upon waters so clear they almost appeared to be suspended in midair, were the ships. Sleek, low, fast, armed with cannons, and reinforced with raised gunwales and sturdy timbers, they represented, separately or together, the single most terrifying force ever to sail the seven seas. But as eventide spread its dusky gold wings over the Caribbean waters, even the ships seemed to be affected by somnolence. They bobbed harmlessly upon the waters, sails lowered, prows darkened, looking more like some graceful, innocuous species of waterfowl than the fierce birds of prey they were.

Yet around the cove from the harbor the atmosphere of lazy indolence abruptly gave way to the clamor and activity of a busy port of call. Dead Man's Cay was boisterous and alert, its shell streets crowded with carts, livestock, and traffickers in all sorts of merchandise, its taverns bursting with noise, its alleyways sheltering conspirators in crime or lust.

From a second-story window a bare-bosomed woman leaned out to empty a chamber pot, laughing uproariously at the curses and threats issuing from the hapless victim below. A runaway shoat upturned a flower cart across the street, its furious owner losing the chase by several lengths. A herd of sheep blocked traffic to the south. A corner of the central boulevard had been circled off for a cock fight, and a knife fight broke out near the wharf, where a woman was selling her favors from a store window.

Dead Man's Cay was populated by adventurers and profiteers, criminals and renegades. It was a violent, colorful, constantly fluctuating society. There were places in the city where not even the bravest dared go.

One such place was a small, crowded tavern on the waterfront called The Blade. Its interior reeked of smoke, salted fish, and spoiled ale; its floor was sand and its walls scarred with the nicks of many knives—some thrown in anger, some in sport. More than one table still bore the stain of some unfortunate's spilled blood, and before the night was over similar stains would splash the walls and be ground into the sand by boot heels. Lard-soaked rags, twisted into torches, gave off a greasy, black-smoked glow from wall brackets. The men who shouted for service and reeled from drunkenness were seedy from habit, explosive from many months at sea. They had earned their reputations with skill, daring and cruelty, and each one of them had a price on his head. For The Blade was known throughout the Indies and beyond as a favorite gathering place of the Scourge of the Seas, the brotherhood of piracy, often called the Brethren.

Of all the well-feared faces gathered at The Blade this night, Storme O'Malley was the most notorious. At twenty-two, she had already captained her own ship, the *Tempest*, for six years, and commanded the roughest, most courageous crew on the seas. She sailed the route from the coast of America to the Indies, and her record of prizes was unsurpassed, her skill in battle legendary. It was well said that there was not a man alive, on land or sea, who was her equal.

But it was more than Storme's record on sea that had earned her the position of respect—and even awe—within the community of piracy. It was more even than her womanhood, for there were other women who had taken to the buccaneer life with notable success. Perhaps it was her youth, or even her comeliness, that had a disarming effect on victim and comrade alike. Some of a more superstitious bent claimed it was witchcraft that gave Storme her unnatural command over the sea and her unblemished record of captured prizes. Others, who knew her better, realized more concrete elements were at work.

Mad Raoul Deborte was one of the few who knew Storme well. He was a handsome man of, some said, noble lineage, and was as much of an oddity among pirates as was Storme herself. It was not only his exceptional good looks that set him apart—marred only by a rather dashing scar that ran from the tip of his hairline to his cheekbone on the left side of his face—but his education, breeding, and cultivated wit. He had earned the nickname "Mad Raoul" through a rather eccentric habit of wagering fingers and ears upon a hand of cards to ease the tedium of long voyages. So far, it was rumored, he had collected twelve ears and twenty-two fingers from erstwhile members of his crew.

Raoul had known Storme since she had inherited the *Tempest* upon her father's death. It was she who had given Raoul the scar on his face, which he wore with pride and fond reminiscence, for few could boast such a compliment from the infamous Storme O'Malley. He, among a very few, knew exactly the components of Storme's legendary success, for he had studied her and was not ashamed to admit he had learned from her. She had skill, cunning, and extraordinary intelligence and courage. But even more, she had passion—and it was the kind of passion that could not be imitated or manufactured. Storme loved the sea and she loved her life upon it; everything she did was performed with single-minded dedication and calculated triumph. She was a rare breed of man—or woman: one of those born to victory.

And because Raoul understood all of this, he could also see, as few could, the beginning of the ebb of Storme's power. He recognized the fact with a mixture of selfish pleasure and sentimental regret. No one in his profession could afford to become too supportive of the competition, of course, but it touched his Gallic sense of the tragic to witness the death of a legend.

Raoul said now, leaning back in the rickety ladder-back chair, "*Oui*, these are trying times for all of us, *ma petite*. The business is not what it once was."

Storme sat across from him, having positioned herself to allow a full view of the room and the outer door with her back protected by the wall. There was a battered tin mug of half-finished ale in front of her, and a plate of discarded mussel shells at her elbow. She sat with one booted foot propped on the table edge, as she casually pared her nails with the razor-sharp edge of her cutlass. She did not even glance up at Raoul's mournful pronouncement.

"Times are what you make of them," she replied without interest.

"I don't know," sighed Raoul. "Things have not been the same since the death of Blackbeard. Why, every day a new horror story reaches my ears. You heard, of course, that the *Vengeance* was taken, and poor Charles Blake swinging from the gibbet with his pretty wife looking on."

"Blake was a coward and a braggart," returned Storme shortly. "He deserved to hang."

A glass of wine hurtled across the room to crash on the wall behind Storme. Neither she nor Raoul appeared to notice.

"Sometimes I think," continued Raoul reflectively, "that a man would not be foolish to consider leaving this trade. Why, even our friends in North Carolina are beginning to turn against us, and word is we could be in for another scourge like the one Rogers brought us two years ago. There is fear among us, *chérie*, and it spreads like oil across the seas."

Storme knew there was a point to all this, and it was more than Raoul's overly sensitive flair for the dramatic. His voice was solemn and baleful, but she did not have to glance up to ascertain the shrewdness behind the eyes that rested on her, nor the speculation that lurked within the lines of his carefully composed face. Deliberately, she refused to rise to the bait.

"I fear no man," she replied, testing the smoothness of her nails on the rough weave of her doublet. Discovering a ragged edge on the nail of the third finger, she carefully applied her knife to it again. "And neither does my crew."

"Perhaps you should," commented Raoul, and though there was nothing but innocence in his tone, Storme could feel a sharpening in his gaze. "With great fame comes great danger in these waters. But of course you among all of us have the means of protecting yourself."

And then Storme smiled—a very faint, very secretive smile that barely caressed the corners of her lips. *At last*, she thought. *The point.*

"Ah, yes," she murmured, pretending disinterest. "Blackbeard's treasure. What many have found and none have sought. Is that, do you think, the secret of my power?"

He was hard put to keep the avaricious gleam from his eyes even as he gave a hearty laugh. "Treasure it is, and worth more than in gold to any captain on the seas! But a grand joke, *n'est-ce pas*, to those who dig up half the coast looking for a chest of jewels!"

Storme gave an enigmatic shrug. There were few secrets among the Brethren, and the nature of her treasure was well known. Not gold, not jewels, not plundered booty—but a plain parchment addressed to Edward Teach, Blackbeard, from the governor of North Carolina, listing in precise detail the nature of the governor's conspiracy with pirates and the price he exacted for it. Blackbeard had used that letter as blackmail against Governor Eden for years; when Storme inherited the letter, she had also inherited Blackbeard's power.

Raoul's tone was nonchalant, but there was a definite sharpening in his eyes. "Is it true you buried it, *chérie*?"

She turned her attention to the fingernails of her left hand, carefully trimming them down to serviceable length. "At the bottom of the sea, for all ye'll ever know. The man who has that letter is King of the Seas, and Blackbeard deemed me the only one strong enough to protect it. You can be sure I will."

"Aye, as long as you are able to."

"I have an able and loyal crew," she remarked. "And twice the skill of any captain who ever walked a deck. I see no reason why I should not be able to protect *everything* that is mine." There was a definite warning inherent in those last words that Raoul could not fail to notice.

A pockmarked serving woman paused to refill Raoul's mug, and he gave her buttocks an absent caress as she passed. The woman retorted, "The next time ye want to fill yer hands, ye'll put a coin in mine!" and Raoul chuckled.

"I'll fill something more than my hands for the price of a coin," he returned. The woman, ugly as she was, managed a provocative flounce as she moved off. Raoul sipped his ale and turned back to Storme as though their conversation had never been interrupted. "And that is only the point," he said, arranging his features into careful lines of concern. "Times were when your crew was among the ablest on sea, but of late I hear rumors of discontent. I speak to you only out of my great affection for you, *petite*, and your dear departed papa, and as a friend I must ask—what trouble is brewing on the *Tempest*? Perhaps you're holding back a bit more than your share of the booty? Cheating your sailing master?"

That got Storme's attention, just as he had no doubt known it would. Her eyes jerked up, flashing, and even as she felt her temper flare she knew she had only risen to Raoul's bait. "I've the fairest split in the isles. There's not a man with his sea legs who wouldn't kill to sail with me."

Raoul shook his head sadly, though his eyes were glinting

with unpleasant amusement. He was in a vicious mood tonight, for the way some men got their pleasures from whoring and drinking, Raoul took his from provoking discontent. Storme was not an easy person to provoke, which made her all the more an enjoyable challenge.

"Ah, *ce'st vrai*," agreed Raoul. "Or at least, so it once was." His eyes were alive with speculative malice, but his expression was bland and sympathetic. "But in these dangerous times one hears so many distressing tales of mutiny. It makes me ashamed to tell you this, *ma chérie*, but able-bodied seamen laugh behind your back, and even your own crew is beginning to refer to themselves as The Petticoat Brigade."

In an instant, Storme's booted foot swung to the floor and she was across the table, her eyes glittering inches from Raoul's face, the tip of her cutlass pressed into the thin flesh at the hollow of his throat. She said in a low voice, "Defend those words with your life, Captain. Better men than you have died for such calumny."

Raoul's gaze was steady and unafraid, but he swallowed convulsively. The movement brought a trickle of blood from the edge of Storme's blade. He murmured, *"Un moment, ma petite.* Calm yourself. You know I speak only from friendship, and repeat no more than I have heard."

"You hear," spat Storme, "more than is good for you. And you presume too much on our friendship." But the pressure on her cutlass eased infinitesimally, and Raoul took a cautious breath.

"If you please?" His eyes moved meaningfully toward the knife at his throat. "You are soiling my neckcloth. And I have something to say to you that can't be spoken with a blade at my throat."

"I should have cut your throat years ago," returned Storme sharply, and let him feel the edge of her blade once more, briefly, for good measure. Then she withdrew slowly, her eyes hard and her muscles alert, and resumed her seat. She did not sheathe her cutlass.

Raoul withdrew a kerchief and dabbed at the scratch on his throat. Storme took a long swallow of her ale, never removing her eyes from him. Finding the brew flat and flavorless, she spewed it out on the floor with a curse, then hurled the mug across the room. Raoul calmly replaced his kerchief and met her glowering temper placidly.

"And now, *petite*, will you listen to the words of one who has adored you near and far for all these many years? Who has defended you and praised you and admired and yearned for you through fair weather and foul? Who has—"

"Enough!" ordered Storme with a swift twist of her wrist. But the exaggerated flattery had had the expected effect on her, for it was difficult to remain angry with Raoul when he went to such lengths to amuse her.

Inwardly she cursed herself for being so fond of him, but friends were few and far between for a woman like herself. Raoul, for all his failings, was loyal to a point, and he must be tolerated. One never knew when he might be useful.

Raoul smiled as he saw the edge of her temper abate, but his tone was serious. He rested one arm upon the table and leaned forward slightly. "Herein is the problem, *chérie*, and any man with eyes in his head can see. It was quite one thing when you were a young stripling—an amusement, *n'est-ce pas?*—a thing of lore and legend. A child leading a ship into battle and emerging victorious—ah, what a tale it all made! What stirring stories to ease the tedious days at sea, what rumors to pass back and forth over ale in port. Those were grand and glorious days for us all." His eyes softened in a moment of fond reflection, but then sobered again as he looked back at her.

"You are a child no longer, *ma petite*," he said sternly, "but a full-blossomed woman ripe for the things of womanhood. Is it any wonder your crew is restless, with such as you flaunting your charms day and night and you with not even the decency to pick among them? Why, they're setting wagers to see who'll be the first to bed you, and fighting amongst themselves over the privilege."

Storme's delicately etched eyebrows drew together with the sudden ferocity of the wings of a hawk diving for prey. "And the first that lays a hand on me had best be ready to lose it," she shot back. "It's well known I'm not for any man's taking. Haven't I proved that point many times over?" She looked meaningfully at the scar on Raoul's temple.

But Raoul only smiled gently—pityingly, Storme thought. His condescension raised her ire to a new level.

"Ah, little innocent," he murmured. "So wise in the ways of the world, so ignorant of men and women. Do you not see that is the root of the trouble? You dangle your virginity like a charm before every man who sails the sea, and have you ever known one of us yet who could resist the lure of a prize not yet taken? It is not," he elaborated further, "that men object to serving a woman captain—but that some of them are beginning to wonder if it is indeed a woman they serve."

He raised a hand in instant self-defense as her color rose and her fist tightened on the cutlass. "Not, of course," he hastened to assure her, "that I am among them. No . . ." His lips spread into an expression that was half-leer, half-affection. "Mad Raoul Deborte, famed near and wide as a connoisseur of feminine delights, has never doubted the power of your abundant womanly charms. Have I not waited all these years to taste them?"

Emboldened by Storme's silence, Raoul reached out one finger and traced the sharp angle of her jaw with a lover's caress. His voice lowered in intimacy. "The time has come, *ma petite*, for you to embark on the most magnificent voyage of your life. You and I will sail the seas of love together, and as one command the mysteries of life."

Not a muscle in Storme's face moved as he drew his slender finger like a whisper over the texture of her skin. Her eyes, the color and clarity of a Caribbean sky, were impassive. Her voice was deceptively soft and honey-smooth. "How very fortunate you have been, old friend," she commented, "to have kept your own fingers and ears so long. Perhaps you've now grown tired of them?"

Raoul jerked his hand back as though he had been stung, for Storme's own fingers were still wrapped around the hilt of her cutlass.

With a shrug, Storme tucked the knife into her belt. Still her expression was mild, her tone matter-of-fact. "You are not only a swine, Raoul, but a fool as well. Truth be told, it's a lot more than my bed you're interested in sharing.''

Raoul hesitated, then conceded guilt with a lopsided grin and an expressive French lift of his shoulders. ''You must admit, you could do worse.''

Storme replied sweetly, ''Not by much.''

''The two of us, Storme, sailing together—we would sweep the coasts clean! With my expertise and your—er—friends in high places...'' He let the suggestion linger, judging her reaction for a moment, and then forged ahead recklessly. ''It is what your papa would have wanted—''

Like lightning on a summer day, Storme's placid blue eyes flashed. ''My papa,'' she retorted, ''would have carved up that piece of meat between your legs that passes for an organ and fed it to the gulls if he'd had a notion of what you just tried to do.''

And then, just as quickly as a summer storm, her mood passed. She pushed up leisurely from the table. ''Fortunately, he bred a daughter who is of a more tolerant temper. I think I will leave you whole....'' And she regarded him for a moment speculatively, as though reconsidering. Then she smiled, gave a curt nod of her head, and decided, ''For the sake of our friendship.''

Raoul, for a moment nonplussed, watched her push her way across the crowded room. Then, recovering himself just in time, he called after her, ''You mark my words, Storme O'Malley! You are headed for a fall, and you have just refused the finest offer you're likely to get!''

At the door Storme paused to shout back, ''I have had better offers from a rutting bull on market day! At least from him I know the source of the smell!''

A burst of raucous laughter and cheers followed as she strode out of the room, and Raoul turned away, covering his humiliation by calling loudly for a glass of wine. This was not the first time he had been bested by Storme O'Malley, and it would not be the last. But tonight, only tonight, he would have dearly loved to win.

* * *

Storme O'Malley shouldered her way past a drunk lingering in the doorway and stepped over a bundle of rags that might have been a man. Her hands were tucked into her belt in a manner that kept her cutlass within easy reach, and a heavy sword bounced against the top of her calfskin knee boots. A gunbelt, partially concealed by her gaily embroidered hip-length jacket, divided her bosom and supported a bayonet-equipped boarding pistol. A thin, expertly crafted stiletto was fastened to her calf by the garter that cinched her yellow silk breeches at the knee. Her hair, her only vanity, was wound into a rich honey-colored braid that swung across the middle of her spine as she walked.

Storme was tall, slender, and sinewy. Sun and sea had burnished her skin to a rich golden brown against which her eyes were a startling water-clear blue. Her features were small and feminine—except for her mouth, which rarely smiled except in cynicism or threat, and too often drew into grim lines of warning and authority. An artist might have found something of beauty in the unvarnished, wholly natural catlike grace and leanness of muscles, small, perfectly rounded breasts, proud neck, and high, aristocratic forehead—but most people, when looking at her, did not think of Storme as an attractive woman.

One looked at Storme and saw mastery, discipline, and willfulness. Hers were eyes that had seen too much to be innocent, hands that had done too much to be gentle. She was a girl-child raised in the world of men where only men were conquerors—and she had conquered. She was an untamed creature who had learned the price of survival and learned to enjoy it, and, like a jungle feline, whatever beauty she possessed was quickly set aside by the aura of power—and danger—she projected.

Raoul's words had disturbed her, and because it would have been a sign of weakness to let him see it she had reacted with anger instead. Long experience had taught her that men respected only two things: strength and force, and she had learned to use both to her advantage. But sometimes in her private moments, like now, she wished for the liberty to be simply a woman, and acknowledge—if only to herself—a woman's doubts and uncertainties.

There was truth in what Raoul said, for as keenly as she could smell a far-off storm or a shift in winds, Storme could sense the subtle changes that were creeping upon her and her kind. Nothing was simple anymore. It wasn't just her crew and their slow erosion of loyalty; it wasn't just defectors like Raoul who daily abandoned the glory of sailing beneath a free flag for the safety of a home harbor. It was a rising tide of unease throughout the Brethren, and Storme knew deep within her soul that the life the privateers enjoyed today would not last much longer.

A great deal of the trouble came from Lieutenant Governor Spotswood of Virginia and, indirectly, from England itself. With no more wars to fight, Britain had no need of the entrepreneurs who sailed the seas at will but who could be persuaded—if the price were high enough—to band together against the King's enemies when the time came. Piracy, which once had been supported in a small and secret fashion by the homeland, was now an embarrassment, and worse, a danger. The control Britain now held over its faraway Colonies was an economic one, and as long as ships like the *Tempest* continued to supply the Colonies with necessities and luxuries at a fraction of the cost, Mother England not only lost revenue but power as well. The King, therefore, had no choice but to exercise every possible incentive to rid the seas of piracy. Spotswood, whose loyalty to the Crown was exceeded only by his own personal greed, had thrown all his efforts behind this cause in hopes of discrediting Governor Eden, whose rule of the neighboring Colony of North Carolina was well known for its tolerance of piracy, and acquiring the vast Carolina lands for himself.

Storme understood the motivations behind the politics as instinctively as she read the needle of a compass, and in her darker, more solemn moments she had to admit that the Brotherhood could not hold out for long against such forces. And on a deeper, more personal level, she knew that she, Storme O'Malley, could not live this way forever. For two decades she had known no other life, but what would become of her in another score of years? When she was forty, or fifty, would she still be striding the decks of her ship, shouting the command to raise the black flag, divvying up plunder, waiting for the next battle? What would become of her when her arms were too tired to lift the sword, and her legs too old to climb the mast?

The prospect of losing power did not frighten her, for she had no intention of losing. Perhaps what really disturbed her was winning, and growing old and alone with nothing but a string of battles well fought to comfort her in her old age.

But what was there to do? There were no simple solutions, and even if there were she could not find them tonight. Someday, undoubtedly, she would have to deal with the future and make sense of it, but it was not Storme's way to borrow trouble from tomorrow; she generally had enough to deal with just staying alive for each successive day. It was only Raoul's maudlin philosophies that turned her thoughts down such a dark course, and she was angry for allowing his fool's ramblings to affect her.

Storme crossed the narrow, littered street toward the waterfront, her steps purposeful and her muscles taut. No one walked the streets of Dead Man's Cay, day or night, without some risk, and Storme made it her business to be prepared for risks.

From the shadows of a building a huge, dark form materialized and fell into step two paces behind Storme. Storme, aware of his presence, did not even glance back. She had other things on her mind.

Pompey was a six-and-a-half-foot-tall, three-hundred-pound mute eunuch captured off the coast of Africa. No one knew how he had lost his tongue, for when Storme had purchased him off a slave ship in Barbados he had been a shell of a man, much abused and near death. She had nursed him to health, given him refuge aboard the *Tempest*, and from the moment he could stand upright he had not allowed the young woman out of his sight. Storme, whether she desired it or not, had acquired a permanent bodyguard and devoted personal slave. No one was allowed near her without her protector, who possessed all the blind loyalty of a ferocious guard dog.

She walked with her head up, her eyes alert, and her brows drawn into a formidable scowl. She was thinking about Raoul, and she was furious. And the more she realized how angry he had made her, the more irritated with herself she became. Not because of what he had said. Because she had more than good cause to believe he was right.

For twenty-two years she had lived with the sea as her home and the *Tempest* her only family, her closest friend, and her chosen lover. For sixteen of those years life had been rich, uncomplicated and carefree. Then her father, brutally betrayed and murdered by the very government he served, had left Storme to make her way alone, the *Tempest* and her sharp wits her only weapons against the world. Innocence had turned to bitterness, peace to war, and overnight Storme grew from an amusing, precocious child to the captain of a ship with a dozen men in her charge.

At first her crew had followed her out of admiration for her temerity and a shared desire for vengeance. Later, as she proved herself in battle and forged her reputation, it had been a novelty—even an honor—to sail beneath the flag of the spirited girl-master. But Storme was not unaware of the building of discontent aboard her ship in the past year or so, the steady disintegration of morale, and she had turned a blind eye to the cause for too long.

As she drew nearer the waterfront, the cheap storefronts and market booths huddled closer together, forming dark narrow alleyways and blind turns. The odor of salt water and rotting shellfish was thick and foul, and careless driftwood campfires colored the night with orange and yellow shadows. Around those campfires the most disreputable of all the island's disreputable inhabitants crouched: the diseased, the mad, the filthy, and the savage. They scanned their surroundings with darting reptilian eyes, waiting for a likely prospect to rob or murder. Scarred and tattered women roamed the alleyways, boldly calling out their prices.

In the flickering glow of a fire not two paces from Storme a man and a woman were entwined in a grunting exercise of carnal lust. Storme watched with a faint twinge of disgust as bare buttocks pumped against flabby thighs, dirty fingers squeezed flaccid breasts to squeals of pain or delight. Everywhere she turned were reminders of mankind's unholy interest in mating, and the older she grew the more of a freak she felt.

God's teeth, she swore viciously to herself, *for this?* Abruptly she resumed her stride again, churning inwardly.

And yet . . . She sobered somewhat as she wound her way through the refuse that littered the waterfront. It was not only the males of the world who were afflicted with such urges, that she knew for a truth. The entire matter intrigued her, titillated her, fascinated her with hot and curious longings in the middle of the night. Virginity had become as much of a physical burden to her as an emotional one, and she was impatient to put it behind her. But she would boil in the seas of hell before she would ever submit to the services of any of the spraddle-legged, gap-toothed animals that sailed these waters.

Suddenly and intensely she wanted to be aboard the *Tempest*. Life was so much simpler with a deck beneath her feet and the rhythms of the sea soothing her blood. Surrounded by the familiarity of all she knew and loved, in command of all within her reach, she could put aside her doubts and discontents and concentrate on the only things that were important—the next prize, the next battle, the next narrow escape. Were it not for her crew and the necessity of taking on supplies, Storme would never make port at all, and the events of this night served only to remind her why.

She half-turned to command Pompey to bring up the longboat for the brief journey to the moored *Tempest*, and suddenly, from nowhere, three men appeared, forming a loose circle around her.

Their stance was unsteady with drunkenness, their eyes gleaming with lust. Said one, "Aye, and there's a likely lass, a-hungerin' for a good filling wit' what I have a-special!"

Another laughed wetly, slobber flecking his bristled chin. "She looks mighty hungry to me! 'Twill take more'n what you got to fill her!"

They crouched low, advancing slowly, their hands ready and their lips parted with avaricious anticipation. Two were small and scurvy, but the third was good-sized, silent and cruel-looking. None of them had noticed Pompey, who was well back into the shadows, and Storme was glad. Pompey knew better than to interfere when Storme had the matter in hand, and her blood was racing with a burst of heady eagerness for this fight.

"Come along," she murmured softly, and her eyes took on a disconcerting glow as they moved invitingly from one man to the other. Her hand was on the hilt of her cutlass but she did not draw it, preferring the swift and certain element of surprise. "Give me a reason."

The promise of a challenge intoxicated her, for there was nothing Storme loved better than a battle—on land or sea. This was what she needed, what she had been hoping for, unconsciously, all night. *Come on*, she thought again, and her fingers itched on the hilt of her knife. Storme was in her element, for no man would best her at a contest of skill.

The glitter in her eyes, caught by the flicker of a distant fire, must have seemed to her attackers like a gleam of madness, and two of them hesitated, uncertain. The third, the large one, pressed on, chuckling lowly in his throat as he flexed his big hands.

As swift as the strike of a snake, Storme's cutlass was in her hand, slicing an arc through the air. At the same instant one of the other men gasped, "Bejesus and be gone! It's Storme O'Malley!"

The big man paused, obviously startled, and his eyes narrowed as he took in her heavily weaponed figure, her crouched stance, and the blade of the knife shining purposefully in the firelight. Storme saw his moment of indecision and advanced. "I'll cut no man without cause," she warned, hoping he would ignore her. "If you fancy your face the way it is, be gone."

The big man shot his eyes around for support from his companions, but they had long since departed. With a soft oath, he, too, backed away, reaching the safety of the shadows before he turned and lost himself in the crowd.

"Coward!" Storme shouted after him furiously. "Scurvy droppings of a toad! A curse upon your bones!"

Pompey materialized beside her, calmly sheathing his own knife in the huge leather belt that spanned his middle.

With much less grace, Storme returned her own knife to its sheath, restraining the impulse to stamp her foot in frustration. Was she not even to be allowed the pleasure of proving herself with weapons any longer?

Pompey stood at a respectful distance from her, waiting for her temper to burn itself out. Storme looked at him, a hulking black giant with patient velvet eyes, and a rueful smile touched her lips. "Ah, Pompey," she murmured, as she had done so often in the past. "What secrets would you tell if only you could speak? Perhaps . . ." And she sighed, tightly, tucking her fingers once again into her belt. "You could tell me why it must be such a curse to be a woman."

But Pompey's infinite silence was her only answer, and Storme sighed again, shaking her head. Her eyes moved out over the darkened sea, picking out the smooth, sleek form of a graceful schooner silhouetted against the dusky sky, and slowly she felt the anger, the frustration, and the confusion seep away into a peculiar kind of contentment. The *Tempest* lay there, waiting for her, and what more in life did she need? Tomorrow they would weigh anchor and put to sea; there were prizes to be chased and challenges to be met, rough seas to navigate and daring escapes to be made. Her veins began to warm and thrill with the promise of the future, and suddenly she could not bear to be land-bound another moment.

"Come along, Pompey," she said, and briskly slapped a glove against her thigh as she strode forward. "Let's go home."

* *Chapter Two* *

*Cypress Bay Plantation, Albemarle County, North Carolina
Two weeks later*

In 1660 King Charles II, anxious to secure a stronghold in the New World and to reward his supporters who had been loyal during the Cromwellian conflicts, had established several generous land grants in the New World. He named eight of his most faithful followers Lords Proprietors over these tracts, which together came to be known as the province of North Carolina. The richest of these grants lay along the coastal bays and inlets, lush with hardwoods and riddled with waterways, abundant in dark bottomland where such crops as rice, tobacco, and indigo thrived to the profit of both the Crown and the proprietor.

Percy York had secured from the proprietors one of the largest portions of the Chowan River tract—thirty thousand acres of lush forests and arable meadows that stretched from the foam-flecked shores of the rugged coast to the dark tropical forests of the southern inlands. But it was the deep, still mystery of the moss-laden swamps that had most inspired Percy York, for which he had called his plantation Cypress Bay.

York was an old name in England, and proudly distinguished, so it came as some surprise when Percy's son William demonstrated a heretofore unsuspected talent for agriculture—and further, when he chose to emigrate to America to develop his Carolina lands with his own hands. Now Cypress Bay was one of the most profitable plantations in the Carolinas. Its fields were green with tobacco, its vineyards trailing with deep purple fruit, its swampy bottomlands converted to undulating seas of rice. Cypress Bay was a testament to one man's vision, a legacy of simple determination.

When William York met his death at the hands of Tuscarora Indians, who were driven to war by their treatment by the settlers, his son Simon—then barely seventeen years old and still in school in England—had not had an instant's doubt about returning to the land his father had loved, and continuing the dream for which William York had given his life.

Simon had been born on Cypress Bay, and to him Carolina had always been home. The ten years he had spent being educated in England had been nothing but time to be passed, days to be occupied while yearning for the tangled forests and foggy lowlands of his childhood. He had never once imagined that when he once again set foot upon Carolina soil he would be doing so alone. Simon was a boy abruptly thrust into manhood—abandoned with a vast estate, an infant sister and the heavy responsibility for the future his only companions.

Few people, seeing Simon now, would have guessed the struggle of those first few years or the strength of character it had taken to survive them. To all appearances he was an aristocratic young planter who surrounded himself with the signs of his wealth and indulged himself in the luxuries of his station. He was rarely seen hurried, frustrated or out of sorts; his bearing was easy and his manner convivial. In short, he represented everything that was most desirable in a high-born son of England, but no man—high-born or not—prospered long in this harsh land without a will of iron. Like most planters, Simon York was emperor, lord, and caretaker of his plantation and all it encompassed, and beneath the trappings of wealth and sophistication was the strength and determination of a born pioneer.

But for the past few years life had been peaceful on Cypress Bay. Dangers of Indian uprisings were past and his plantation was too far up the river for pirates. And on this warm June morning of 1720, the only thing that was troubling Simon York was how best to make his escape from the plantation without attracting the attention of two very vexatious young ladies, and the only thing that showed on his face was alarm as he heard footsteps—unmistakably feminine ones—determinedly approaching his office door.

The office was a separate building from the plantation house proper, and it was here Simon had sought refuge until his traveling bags and his horse could be brought around. Hearing the footsteps, Simon turned to the single narrow window, casting an anxious glance out just as the door opened. He turned guiltily, and then released a breath of relief. It was only his sister, Augusta.

Augusta stepped inside, closing the door behind her. The room was small and musty smelling, filled with ledgers and feed samples and a broken tool or two. A single shaft of dusty sunlight streamed through the window and onto the scarred oak desk. Generally the office was the domain of Simon's overseer, Peter McCollough, and Simon, elegantly clad and impeccably groomed, looked distinctly out of place in these rustic environs. The expression that crossed Augusta's face was as close to annoyance as it was possible for one of her generally sweet and retiring nature to achieve.

"Simon York, whatever can you be doing here? I've sent halfway to Bath and back for you. You know we have guests and it is most unlike you to be rude."

Simon stifled a long-suffering groan and busied himself with straightening some papers on the desk. "The estimable Mistress Trelawn and her charming daughters, I know."

"As well you should," replied Augusta, a note of puzzlement creeping into her tone. "Since this visit has only been announced for a fortnight."

Simon shot her a glance that was both sheepish and endearing. "Do me a favor, sweetings, and make my excuses? Tell them I've already gone, and I promise I will be the very instant Peter brings down my horse."

Augusta's eyes widened in genuine confusion. "And not even say good-bye? You would depart on a journey of six weeks without even sparing a moment to take your leave of guests? Simon, I must say I find your behavior most baffling. What have the Misses Trelawn done to deserve such treatment?"

Simon's lips curved into a smile that managed to be at once both rueful and indulgent. "You would not understand, innocent. Suffice it to say that Mistress Trelawn has made her intentions quite clear, and unless I mind my step I'm likely to find myself leg-shackled to one—if not both—of her lovelies before the summer is over. A discreet departure is the wisest course in such a case, I think."

But Simon was wrong. Augusta did understand, and she looked at her adored older brother now with a mixture of sympathy, amusement, and, very far below the surface—so far, in fact, that even she herself did not entirely recognize it—perhaps a touch of envy.

At thirty-two, Simon was not just a handsome man. He

was extraordinarily, one might say even exquisitely, formed. He was tall, athletic, and trim. His rich auburn hair drew back from an aristocratic forehead with the luxury of sable; his features were patrician and perfectly formed. His skin was smooth and unflawed by even the faintest pockmark or blemish, and even his eyebrows, a slightly darker tone than his hair, formed perfectly symmetrical wings over crystal gray eyes. His lips were full and prone to laughter, his teeth straight and white.

He was his tailor's pride and joy. It was impossible to cut a jacket that did not complement his shoulders nor hang perfectly from the hips, for he was neither too broad nor too slim. His waist was trim, his abdomen flat and muscular, his back straight. The current fashion of tightly cut breeches had been designed for men with thighs like Simon York's, and his calves were at an advantage whether graced by elaborately clocked stockings or molded into calfskin riding boots. He wore his clothes with an innate and careless grace few men could manage; his taste and style were impeccable.

When Augusta considered that in addition to her brother's striking physical beauty, God and the King had also seen fit to bestow upon him wealth, social position, and as little conceit as could possibly be managed under the circumstances, it was little wonder that all the designing females and ambitious mamas in the Carolinas had set their caps for him.

Augusta, looking at him now, could barely suppress a sigh. She tried to be sympathetic to her brother's plight, for she knew the hardships of being so well-favored must be many and trying. But, in truth, Augusta could barely imagine them and would have given a great deal to know—even briefly—a share of her brother's problems. For it was as though when the good Lord finished lavishing his bounty on Simon, he had made Augusta up out of scraps, and never had there been a brother and sister who resembled one another less.

She had the wide, deep-toned York eyes, it was true, and the distinctive mouth, but what looked balanced and artistic on her brother merely appeared awkward and out of place on Augusta. For Simon's graceful height she had been awarded dumpiness, and she was, quite frankly, almost as round as she was tall. Her mouse-brown hair was thin and frizzled, her lashes stubby, her hands fat and dimpled. At seventeen she was of an age most young women were making their final choices as to home and spouse, but Augusta felt she was destined to be a burden and an embarrassment to her brother forever. Sometimes, for all that she loved Simon and knew he returned the affection, she wondered how her brother could bear even to be around the ugly duckling that fate had saddled him with as a sister.

With a sudden rush of affection that shamed her for her previous scolding words, Augusta stepped forward. "Oh, I do wish you didn't have to go! Six weeks is such a long time and the islands are so far away. Life is so dull here without you, and I'll miss you so."

Simon grinned and drew his sister to him with an arm around her plump shoulders. When he grinned like that he was devastating, and no female within the range of his sparkling eyes could even begin to entertain a notion of denying him whatever he wanted. "Have a care, little one, or you'll have me thinking you mean it and I *shall* be impossible to live with! Besides, you'll have no end of fun without me, what with one ball and another garden party, and the Misses Trelawn will be fine company for you I'm sure."

A shadow crossed her face and she drew a breath as though to speak, but the words faltered at her lips. From the moment Augusta had graduated from short skirts, the rote had been the same: season after season, Simon dragging her to every party, dance and gathering the county had to offer, lavishing upon her expensive gowns and fripperies; bribing, she suspected, the most eligible young men to dance with her—and never understanding, no matter how often Augusta tried to tell him—that these exercises were sheer torture to her.

It was so simple for Simon. He was handsome, dashing, and witty, always the center of attention, whereas Augusta was shy, awkward, and embarrassed. She knew she could never live up to his expectations of her and certainly could never compete with him; long ago she had ceased trying. It was so much easier to stay at home with her books, her needlepoint, and her puppies. In these things she found security and pleasure with none of the challenges Simon was always tossing her way. Alone in the quiet company of her animal companions and sedentary pursuits, no one ever compared her to Simon, no one ever expected her to be more than she was, and she was content. But she simply could not make Simon understand that she would never be the bright, vivacious, beautiful woman he wanted her to be.

"Perhaps," she said in a small voice, avoiding his eyes, "I shall merely have a quiet summer at home."

"Nonsense." With a swift squeeze of her shoulders he stepped away, dismissing the matter and turning to more important things. "I've made certain you have scores of invitations to occupy you while I'm gone, for I won't have you languishing away for lack of entertainment. Enjoy yourself, my dear, and spare a thought for me once in a while, will you, as you go about breaking every heart in the county?"

A shaft of misery tightened within Augusta. It seemed to penetrate from the roots of her hair to the very pit of her stomach. Visions of herself flashed through her head—fat and dowdy in the elaborate silks and satins Simon provided for her, shrinking in the matron's corner, forced to stumble through the steps of a quadrille with ancient colonels and stammering boys of twelve, trying to avoid the snickering of girls her own age and the embarrassed pity of young men—and she did not know how she would bear it. At least when Simon was along he offered a measure of protection, and she could achieve some vicarious pleasure by watching him enjoying himself, but without him...

Her voice held the slightest note of desperation. "Truly, Simon, I'd much prefer to enjoy my own company this summer. Might I beg off—"

Simon turned away from the ledger he was depositing on a shelf, and his eyes held a shadow of puzzlement as well as an unaccustomed twinge of impatience. "Don't be absurd, girl, you just this moment finished telling me how dull you're going to be while I'm away, and I've gone to a great deal of trouble to make certain you're not. Now stop your silly female ramblings and perk up. You're behaving like a spoiled child."

Augusta blinked with the unexpected sharpness of his words and immediately retreated. It was so unlike Simon to be harsh with her that hurt was swamped by confusion, and she courageously swallowed the sting of tears. She lifted her small round chin with as much dignity as she could manage and replied quietly, "You're right, of course. Forgive me. I didn't mean to seem ungrateful."

The annoyance that had sharpened Simon's eyes was immediately mitigated by regret, and the impatience in his sigh seemed this time to be directed at himself. "I'm sorry, sweetings." He crossed to her and placed a light kiss upon her forehead. "I have a great deal on my mind and I shouldn't have been short with you. We shouldn't part with cross words."

Augusta managed a weak smile. Simon didn't mean to be autocratic, she knew. He was the kindest and most generous of men, and if occasionally he was short-sighted or insensitive, he meant to hurt no one with it. Besides, he was her brother and he always knew best.

She looked at him searchingly, hardly knowing what to say. "Simon—"

But at that moment the jingle of a bridle was heard outside, and Simon moved in a boisterous step toward the door. "At last! Escape is mine!"

He flung open the door, and then turned back, silhouetted for a moment in the bright square of sunlight. "You will give my excuses to the ladies, won't you, dear? There's my girl! Come give me a kiss."

Augusta flew to him, and hugged him with such ardor that Simon laughed, feigning breathlessness as he extricated himself from her clutches at last. His eyes twinkled indulgently as he looked down at her. "Be a good girl now, and I'll bring you something pretty from the islands. And I expect a glowing report on all the galas I've missed when I return!"

After squeezing her hand affectionately, he turned to Peter, taking the reins from him. Simon paused to clap the other man on the back before he mounted. "In your hands," he declared, "I leave all that I hold dear—my horses, my lands, and my beloved sister." But the note of jesting in his tone sobered just a fraction as he added with a smile, "I can't think of anyone in whom my trust would be better placed."

Peter's broad Scottish face softened as he looked at the man who had been more of a friend than a master to him for the past ten years. "Aye, and I'll do me part, sir, though"—and he cast a twinkling glance toward Augusta—"keeping this young baggage o' yorn in hand will take some doing!"

Simon laughed and swung into the saddle. "Your best, my friend—'tis all I ask." He saluted Augusta with two fingertips touched to his lips. "I'll be back before you know it, lovely. Mind yourself!"

He wheeled his horse and cantered off—around the outbuildings and the garden, away from prying eyes that were even now gathered at the front windows of the house—toward the road to Williamsburg, where a ship was waiting to take him across the seas.

Augusta listened to the sound of his retreating hoofbeats, unaware of how long she had been standing there with a half-pensive, half-sorrowful frown on her brow until Peter prompted gently, "You look like a lass with somethin' preying on her mind, right enough. Can it be that grave a matter, I wonder?"

Startled out of her reverie, Augusta looked up with a laugh that did not quite ring true. "Gracious me, you're right! Here I'm standing here with clouds in my head while guests are twiddling their thumbs in my parlor! What will they think?"

She lifted her skirts out of the dust and started toward the house. Peter, unconvinced, walked with her. "It couldna be you're worried about your brother, could it, princess? He'll fare fine, ye know, and be having the time of his life while you're at home a-mournin' him."

There were some who might have been shocked at the

familiarity that passed between Peter and his betters, but it was just as difficult for Augusta as it was for Simon—if not more so—to remember that Peter was an indentured servant, and not a valued peer and friend.

Peter was close to Simon's age, a big, dark, curly-haired young man who seemed effortlessly to hold the world between his strong broad hands. He had been a part of Cypress Bay from Augusta's earliest memory; she had grown up in his protective, indulgent shadow, and he was her best friend in the world.

Augusta knew very well it was useless to keep up a pretense with Peter, who knew her better than anyone—even Simon. With a sigh and a small droop of her shoulders, she confessed, "It is only—I do wish sometimes that Simon wouldn't try so hard to make me into something I'm not."

Peter's sensitive brown eyes flashed with sympathy and understanding. "Aye. 'Tis hard, sometimes, to see the people we love with another's eyes."

There was gentleness in his tone and a softening of his features as he spoke, but that was not unusual for Peter. Invariably when he spoke to Augusta it was with gentleness or teasing, affection or tenderness. The only unusual thing at all was how quickly he tried to hide his expression when Augusta glanced at him, and the faintest appearance of what might have been a flush edging the corners of his sun-burnished skin. He shrugged and continued, a bit more gruffly, "He only means the best for you, lass. He's used to takin' care of you, 'tis all."

Augusta sighed. "I know. It's just that what he thinks is best for me . . . well, he just doesn't understand how I loathe being dragged around from party to tea like a—like a tame piglet on a leash!"

Peter's eyes sparked quick anger and his tone was stern. "Now see here, miss, I'll not listen to you talk about yourself like that!"

Augusta flushed and caught her underlip between her teeth. "I'm sorry. My nerves are all frayed today. Oh, it's going to be just hideous this summer without Simon around!"

"Nay, you make much ado about nothing," scoffed Peter.

"You've plenty of friends and folk in the country, and you'll have a grand time, with many a young gentleman to squire you about."

Augusta gave a short laugh. "Like who?"

"Why, like your young cousin Christopher, for one."

"Christopher Gaitwood is Simon's friend, not mine," she returned with an impatient lift of her shoulders.

The glance Peter slanted her was deceptively mild. "Is that so? Seems to me you had a special fondness for the young buck."

Augusta's eyes flew to him in unfeigned astonishment. "Christopher? Don't be ridiculous! The only reason he's nice to me at all is for Simon's sake, and to tell you the absolute truth, I think he's rather a ninny."

Relief lightened Peter's face for the very briefest of moments. But when he spoke, his tone had taken on the familiar note of teasing. "As you grow more familiar with the ways of men and women, little one, you will find that most men *are* ninnies, and it's the sweet hand of woman-hood that steers the course of history true!"

Augusta joined his amusement with a wide grin of her own. It was impossible to stay vexed or worried for long in Peter's presence. Peter, familiar and strong, smelling of fresh hay and animals and honest labor, was the only man in the world with whom she ever felt completely comfortable— and he never failed, simply by being near, to make her feel better about herself and the world and all that was in it.

"Women can be ninnies, too," she confided now, mischievously, "and if you don't believe it, try spending an afternoon confined to a stuffy parlor with the chattering Trelawn sisters and their huge mama. She has a mustache, you know," she added, stifling a giggle. "She tries to hide it with rice powder, but all that does it make her look like a mean old man. No wonder Simon is afraid of her!"

They had neared the doorstep, and Peter, grinning, gave her a gentle tap of the chin with his knuckle. "Mustache or no, she's yours for the duration and you'd best behave yourself. Off with you now, for I'll be making no excuses for your behavior to your brother when he returns."

Suddenly lighthearted, Augusta swept up her skirts and started up the steps. "Oh, pooh! Simon's well on his way to Williamsburg by now and little does he care how I behave around the Trelawns—as long as I keep them off his coattails!"

And at the door she paused and sent back to Peter a beaming smile. "You always cheer me up, Peter," she said. "I'm so glad you're here!"

Peter stood at the doorstep until she had disappeared inside. The smile he had held so long for her benefit slowly faded and became laced with something very like sorrow— or longing. Suddenly, impatient with himself and his own fancies, he turned abruptly and went back to work.

* **Chapter Three** *

It was two days later that Simon arrived in the Virginia capital of Williamsburg. Alexander Spotswood's hospitality was, as always, exceptional, and when Simon was bathed and rested he was set before an elaborate supper table with the best in imported wines and culinary treats.

That Alexander Spotswood, by arranging this meeting at the newly completed governor's palace, was applying his own brand of political warfare was a fact that amused Simon but troubled him not in the least. The Dutch crystal, the draped and beaded chandeliers, the fine Irish linen and gold-etched porcelain appealed enormously to Simon's vulnerable sense of the aesthetic. It was impossible for him to maintain a sour disposition when surrounded by such beauty and refinement, and before long the lieutenant governor's generosity had its expected effect. Simon relaxed, forgetting his ill-temper at the autocratic summons, and set forth to enjoy the moment—but not without maintaining some measure of caution.

The governor of Virginia held the position as an honorary

title from the safety of his estates in England. Lieutenant Governor Alexander Spotswood was the real ruler of Virginia, and he used his power to its best advantage. For years he had actively discouraged settlers from going to North Carolina, persuading them instead to purchase lands in Virginia— some of which he owned. At one time he had even undertaken an invasion of North Carolina, complete with troops and weapons. And it had been Spotswood who, in desperate need of a political coup to improve his stature in Virginia, finally captured Edward Teach, the infamous Blackbeard, who until that time had been living under the open protection of Governor Eden.

Some said Spotswood was a true patriot whose only purpose was the good of the Crown. Others were more direct and claimed that he was a power hungry chieftain who wanted only one thing: North Carolina to line his own pockets. Simon suspected the truth lay somewhere in between, but in fact it made little difference to him. Simon had little faith in the efficacy of government, and he was unable to summon much interest for anything that did not directly affect the home or family of which he was so fiercely protective.

For all his political machinations, Alexander Spotswood was a genial host, and Simon found the conversation light and diverting. It wasn't until the table had been cleared and port and fruit were set up that the real purpose of this meeting was broached. By that time Simon was in a mood to deal with it.

"I do hope you know how much I appreciate your rearranging your travel plans to stop with me, my boy. I trust it was not too great an inconvenience."

Simon smiled into his glass of rich ruby liquid. Nothing in his tone or expression signaled the slight increase in alertness the other man's words had brought. "One can as easily sail from Virginia as from Carolina," he demurred. "And for the pleasures of your table, my friend . . ." He raised his glass in a small bow. "Any slight inconvenience is more than worth the effort."

But obviously Spotswood was done with the pleasantries.

Abruptly, he said, "I suppose you've an idea what it is I wished to discuss."

Simon took up the small paring knife at his plate and began, with fluid, leisurely motions, to peel an apple. "One would imagine it is the same issue we've discussed on many other occasions—your ongoing feud with Governor Eden, a subject that interests me not at all."

But if Simon's cavalier dismissal of the subject that had become Alexander Spotswood's driving passion in any way insulted or offended the other man, he swallowed his personal emotions for more pressing concerns. "Something has got to be done," Spotswood announced without preamble. "The deplorable conditions in North Carolina have gone on long enough, and Eden must be brought down before he brings the entire British rule in the Colonies to ruin. We've in mind to mount a formal—but insidious—political movement against him. You, sir"—and he leaned forward confidently, lowering his tone a fraction for emphasis—"are the only person in North Carolina I can trust to spearhead such an action."

Spotswood's piercing dark eyes met only mild disinterest in Simon's. "I hardly see what makes you think that. It's little secret that my influence with Governor Eden is hardly less than that of a scullery maid. As for politics . . ." He cut a neat slice of apple and popped it into his mouth, savoring the taste before finishing, "I leave such games to the experts." He smiled, charmingly. "You yourself, my old friend, pop immediately into mind."

"You are a respected man in Carolina," Spotswood insisted. "More importantly, you *are* a Carolinian. You practically live in Eden's back garden; you are close to him—"

Simon gave a desultory laugh and sliced off another piece of apple. "I barely know the man, nor he me—which is a situation greatly to my liking, if the truth be told. I have hardly made secret my opinion of the governor of North Carolina and his policies; consequently Eden steers me a wide berth. We maintain the civilities, no more."

But Spotswood would not be deterred. "Nonetheless,

Eden could hardly ignore your influence should you choose to make it known. And it is precisely because I know you are loyal to our cause that I so desperately need your help in North Carolina.''

''I have told you before, my lord, and with all due respect—I will not be caught up on your political wheel. It simply isn't my style.''

''Blast and confound your style!'' burst out Spotswood, and at Simon's mild lift of the eyebrow he took a steadying breath. ''Your family and mine have been allies for uncounted years,'' he continued more persuasively. ''Why, I counted your own departed father among my closest of friends. Were he here today—''

''He is not,'' said Simon shortly, and the sudden opaqueness of his eyes must have served as a warning to the other man, for he tried a different tack.

''Eden has completely run amok,'' Spotswood stated flatly. ''He is stronger now than he was the last time someone moved against him, and *that*, as you know, was an unforgettable debacle.''

Simon only shrugged and tossed the apple core onto his dessert plate. ''Which only goes to show what happens when premature moves are made by people who don't know what they're doing.''

Spotswood seized on that. ''Precisely the point. You *do* know what you're doing.''

''Quite so.'' Simon smiled. ''I am looking out for myself, and my own.'' His voice had a slight edge to it.

Spotswood's features hardened briefly. ''We are at war, sir!'' he demanded. ''An undeclared war, perhaps, against invaders unnamed and unallied with geographical boundaries—but these pirates to whom your esteemed governor so unabashedly gives succor are as deadly to the Crown as the French or the Spanish ever were! Have you any idea how much has been lost to these vipers in the past year alone? Soon we will be hemmed in at our own shores by this band of lawless, barbaric ruffians, and all we have struggled to bring forth on this continent will be to naught. Where is your honor, sir, your patriotism? Have you no conscience at all?''

The faintest trace of a smile curved Simon's lips. "My dear friend," he replied patiently, "I make no quarrel with your position. When you asked, did I not personally supply funds for the ship you sent against Blackbeard? And if it's more money you need to keep your ships in operation along the coasts, of course you can rely upon me. But it does occur to me to wonder, old man, whether or not these pirates of yours are becoming something of an obsession— and an unhealthy one at that. One ought to strive to keep these things in their proper perspective, you know."

"Blast it all, there *is* no 'proper perspective' for this perfidy! It's a matter of survival, man, can't you see that?"

A moment's silence filtered through the candlelit room, echoing in the aftermath of the outburst. On slippered feet, a wigged and liveried black servant moved to refill Simon's glass, which, until this moment, he had not noticed was almost empty.

Simon allowed a moment for his host to recover his temper, lifting his glass to his lips and tasting the liquid appreciatively. Then he commented mildly, "I am a planter, sir, not a soldier. I find I have my hands quite full with a house to maintain, crops to harvest, and a sister to settle. It is difficult for me to gather the . . ." He delicately searched for the right word. "The passion you display over events on the high seas, and I must confess I sometimes wonder if you do not exaggerate their importance."

Spotswood leaned back, a calm and rather shrewd contemplation coming over his face as he directed his gaze at Simon. "Do you know what your problem is, sir?" he said at last.

Simon granted his ignorance by lifting his glass and tasting the rich, warm port.

"You feel safe in that fortress of yours on the Chowan," pronounced Spotswood. "Since we took Blackbeard you've had no personal losses to piracy, and whatever threat you might once have feared seems to exist no longer. I shouldn't doubt that you are among those who think my patrols along the coast are a useless extravagance . . ." Simon started to form a polite protest, but Spotswood gave him no chance. "And so it may seem," he continued, "as every day pirate ships slip through the net and invade North Carolina. But let me assure you, sir, the fault is not mine. I am at this very moment tightening my patrol, and under great secrecy—the next pirate ship that thinks to find safe harbor with Eden will be *my* prize!"

He took a breath to subdue the fire that had begun to blaze in his eyes. "The fault lies not with military effort, but with apathy. You think the crisis is past, the danger is over—a common ailment among all of us, I think. We wanted the King to take some action against these barbaric plunderers of our coasts, and when he did, we were all lulled into a sense of false security. Oh, not that Captain Rogers' mission in Nassau was not a smashing success," he conceded. "He was sent to the Bahamas to clean out the filthy nests of pirates, and clean them out he did. A most laudable victory."

And then his eyes darkened as he leaned forward tensely. "What he *did*," he spat, "was to drive the louse-infested vermin out of the islands and onto our very shores! Their numbers have not diminished but increased, and they have found succor and safe haven in the bays and inlets of North Carolina, where they can be sure of their welcome by our good friend Governor Eden. And you, sir, by your simple indifference are as good as offering solace to the very monsters who will one day destroy all that you hold dear. I warn you, Simon, these pirates are as dangerous to the citizens of North Carolina today as were the Tuscarora Indians a decade ago."

Simon rose after a moment's silence, slowly and deliberately. His eyes were momentarily hard, his lips tight. "And you see how little politics availed in controlling that situation," he said. "It was left to the citizens to take care of themselves then, just as it should be now."

Spotswood was unperturbed by Simon's words. "The Tuscarora were a proud and warlike nation. They weren't easy to subdue."

"And perhaps that Indian war might have been avoided if the English had paid the Tuscarora for the land they took."

Far from being offended, Spotswood smiled and looked at

Simon thoughtfully. "Do you know, sir, I do believe there is a touch of the rebel in you. And despite your pretense of indifference, I suspect you have a far greater passion for politics than you would have anyone know. I wouldn't be surprised if you even harbored a secret admiration for these pirates. Sometimes you appear to be a bit of an anti-imperialist yourself."

Simon knew he was being baited. He bowed to Spotswood. "You are a trusted and respected family friend," he said, "and for that reason you will always be welcome in my home—as I hope I will continue to be in yours. But in the future . . ." He offered a small, conciliatory smile. "I would prefer no more talk of pirates or politics at our supper table. You serve such excellent fare it is a shame to have it spoiled."

The lieutenant governor got to his feet. "You will at least stay the night, and in the morning we shall meet with my advisors, and further discuss—"

"Thank you, no." Simon's tone was firm but unerringly polite. "My cousin Christopher is expecting me for cards, and I don't like to be late. My thanks for a most stimulating evening. I trust we will meet again soon under more congenial circumstances." He bowed again, and left the room.

Spotswood sank to his chair, a curious hint of defeat—however temporary—weighing on his stern features. "Ah, my naive young friend," he said softly. "So certain of your own way. You will discover the truth, of that I am sure. I only hope, for all our sakes, that by the time you do, it may not be too late."

* *Chapter Four* *

*The Atlantic Ocean, Near the Coast of North Carolina
Two Days Later*

If there was anything Simon York hated worse than sea travel in the middle of the summer, he would have been hard pressed to tell you what it was. The planter had, over the years, found it worthwhile to journey to the Caribbean every season or so in order to survey the foreign markets; however, those trips that had been taken during the cooler months seemed like pleasure rides in comparison to this one. Simon knew but didn't want to face the fact that his rather hasty retreat from Cypress Bay was not only badly timed but probably foolish as well. He stood on the deck of the *Valiant*, braced at the rail against the nauseating roll of the ship, and scowled at the merciless glare of the sun on the water. Beneath his brocade waistcoat and finely tailored broadcloth jacket the shirt was plastered to his body by a sticky layer of sweat that the famed sea breeze never seemed to reach. The queue of his hair was tangled and tousled, and his face, already a healthy golden tan from afternoon rides in the Carolina sun, was beginning to burn. His eyes felt scalded in their sockets, and when he thought of the days remaining before they reached port he all but groaned out loud.

The interlude with Governor Spotswood had left a bad taste in his mouth. He was far from being a coward, but he had no desire to step into another man's fight. As a matter of personal taste, Simon did not like Governor Eden; as a matter of ethics, he condemned that man's traffic with outlaws. But thus far Simon had remained untouched by Eden's machinations. There was little doubt that Eden knew of Simon's support of Governor Spotswood, but there was little Eden could do to threaten Simon, one of the most powerful of all the planters.

Planters were autonomous and needed little organization or governmental interference. Simon took care of his own and expected others to do the same. That was how he had managed his life since he was eighteen and had returned home to find his mother and father murdered by a band of Tuscarora Indians. Only the infant Augusta, hidden in a corn crib with her nurse, had survived the massacre.

The violence of the New World was no stranger to Simon, and he had, in the aftermath, enforced the only kind of justice available to him—killing his family's murderers. He had then retreated to Cypress Bay to establish his kingdom, making it safe for all that he deemed his.

He had achieved his goal: Cypress Bay was impenetrable; the savagery of the outside world did not penetrate its refined, civilized interior. For most of the intervening years the tragedy of Simon's past had been kept in the dark recesses of his mind, so utterly hidden away that it was almost forgotten. Perhaps it was this voyage—the sweltering heat combining with the brisk salt air—that put him in mind of another journey, a young boy eager to return home who all too quickly had to become a man. But it was a painful memory, and one he had spent many years trying to avoid. With a soft curse, he jerked his mind away from the dangerous course. Blast Spotswood anyway, for bringing back the past.

Overhead the sails cracked and timbers groaned. The bos'n's mate shouted out an order and a seaman in the crow's nest bellowed out an unintelligible reply. The *Valiant* was a small merchantman bound for the Bahamas with a load of fresh-cut timber for trade. Simon York was its only passenger.

Absently, he let his mind wander back to Cypress Bay when he departed. A rather rueful smile touched his lips as he thought of the Trelawn sisters, two of the most comely young ladies in all of Albemarle County. Simon had done nothing to encourage either of them—or, he had to admit honestly, at least not much—but Mistress Abigail Trelawn, their mother, had taken it into her head that the time had come for Simon to make one of them his betrothed. The older daughter, Lucinda, with her deep mahogany hair and cool green eyes, was very much to Simon's taste, and perhaps he had, over the past winter, paid more attention to her than was strictly proper.

Of course, the blonde Darien, with her luscious figure and bold flirtatious gazes, had a certain appeal as well, but the point was Simon was not about to be brought to the altar with either of them. But the more he demurred, the more determined Mistress Trelawn became—not to mention the determination of her daughters—and over the past month or so the situation had become untenable. Obviously, Simon had to find some way to extricate himself from their designs before the matter became embarrassing—or worse—but so far he had been unable to discover how to do so.

The ship pitched gently, and Simon almost lost his balance. Swearing softly to himself, he caught the rail in a firmer grip, and in the same moment attempted to regain a similar grip on his usually buoyant mood. Surely, in all the much-famed beauty of the Caribbean islands, he could find something more cheering to dwell upon than the troubles he had left behind. As for Mistress Trelawn . . . well, one thing was certain, he decided, with a slow surfacing of an irrepressible grin, she couldn't follow him here.

On the horizon, looking like little more than a cloud or a spray of water at this distance, the sails of another ship materialized. Simon studied it absently, finding something vaguely soothing in the graceful, amorphous form as it blended against the skyline. A man-made shape breaking up this godless monotony of blue; a sign of human life in this vast forsaken expanse of water and sun. He wondered if it carried passengers.

"Enjoyin' the sea air, are ye, sir?"

Simon inclined his head with the faintest of automatic smiles to greet the captain, who rested both forearms on the rail beside Simon. The little man smelled strongly of fish and sweat. "Indeed," Simon murmured. "Quite—ah—invigorating."

"Best thing in the world for the constitution," agreed the captain. "Sea air."

Simon saw the other man's eyes pick out the shape of the ship on the horizon, and he thought the captain frowned a little. But just as Simon was about to comment the captain turned to him again. "We don't get many passengers this time o' year."

Simon maintained his pleasant, rather implacable smile. "I can understand that."

They were interrupted by the appearance of the bos'n's mate. He murmured something to the captain that Simon did not hear, but instantly all traces of good humor were wiped from the other man's face. With a curt nod of dismissal to his mate, the captain took out his spy glass and directed it at the horizon.

Immediately Simon was alert. "What is it?"

The captain took a long time refolding his glass before he answered, carefully, "Too far to tell for certain. But if she's in these waters, she's up to no good and that's a fact."

Simon felt a slight, startled thud in the center of his chest. He looked back toward the shape on the horizon. "A pirate ship?"

The captain's expression was studious and abstract. "Likely."

There were over one thousand pirates patrolling the seas of Coastal America. The chances were one in five that an innocent vessel, sailing the route between the Colonies and the Indies, would encounter one of these infamous plunderers of the main. One part of Simon's mind was registering these facts, another was wondering idly how he had come by them and deciding, most likely, it was from that ever-present prophet of doom, Alexander Spotswood—while still another part of him, a dull and incredulous part, could only stare at the cloud upon the horizon and refuse, with all his might, to believe what his eyes told him.

At last, with an effort, he gathered his wits. "But we're carrying nothing of value. What would they want with us?"

"Aye," agreed the captain mildly. "Likely she'll pay us no mind." His narrowed eyes moved from the horizon back to Simon. "Still and all, if ye're carrying money or jewels, I'd hide 'em good. And . . ." His eyes moved meaningfully to the ring on Simon's finger. "I'd be shed o' that ring if I was you, and any papers you got sayin' who you are. Some of them bastards can read, you know, and if they had an inklin' who you was . . . well, hostages sometimes pay as good as cargo."

And at the volatile combination of alarm and objection that crossed Simon's face the captain hastened to draw a reassuring smile across his own. "But 'tis likely we're fretting for naught. We've nothing she'd want, like you said, and most likely she'll pass us by."

But Simon knew, with a heavy sinking feeling in the pit of his stomach, that she would not. It was as though destiny's capricious sense of humor had foreordained this moment long ago, and Simon—who took such pride in his well-ordered and secure life—had no choice but to meet it with as much grace as possible.

The captain raised his glass again and turned to track the progress of the innocuous-looking cloud on the horizon. Uneasily, Simon followed his gaze. The wind cracked loudly in the sails and the ship plunged on, and the two men at the rail waited in half-dread to see what fate had in mind for them now.

* *Chapter Five* *

The *Tempest* was a swift, light schooner of twelve guns, built specifically for one Charles O'Malley by Dutch craftsmasters. She was a rare ship, for the schooner design had been originated a little over fifty years ago in Holland, and the *Tempest* was one of the first of her kind to sail English waters. She was faster than a sloop, and more nimble, her square-rigged, two-masted design enabling her to outmaneuver most anything that sailed.

In her day she had fought proud against the enemies of England, inspiring awe and bringing in more than her share of bounty for His Majesty's glory. So fleet was she upon the waters that even then her enemies had begun to refer to her as a phantom, a witched ship that could strike like lightning and be gone before the flash faded.

She was a ship of shallow draft, but her sturdy construction and careful design enabled her to navigate the roughest seas. Her light weight and fleet sails could outrun most anything on the water, and her small size allowed her to maneuver narrow inlets and channels where larger, more heavily armed ships could not follow. In motion she was a thing of beauty—her graceful prow skimming the surface of the water, her tall sails billowing in the sunlight. In battle she was a thing of terror, able to draw up within leaping distance of an enemy ship and come about at an instant's notice, her powerful guns toppling masts and ripping hulls before the enemy could even arm itself.

Mistress and ship were of a kind, almost a reflection of one another: each shrewd, sleek, powerful, bold, and not a little savage. Together they had performed feats that awed the common man, building a legend for themselves upon a foundation of mystery and daring. It was their complete interdependence upon one another that made greatness, for the *Tempest*, without the crafty mastery and undaunted foolhardiness of Storme O'Malley, would have been only another ship, her beauty and her speed wasted upon some idle gentleman yachtsman, her sturdy timbers straining under the rigors of the English Channel as she transported lords and ladies across the way to France. And Storme, without the *Tempest*, was impossible to imagine.

In a day when sea commerce was at its peak and when the freedom and adventure of the life of a buccaneer was at its greatest appeal, piracy upon the high seas had been almost more common than legitimate trade—and easily more profitable. The Brethren of the Coast were the undisputed masters of all who passed their way, but among them all, the *Tempest* had the grandest record of prizes of any ship on the seas. The *Tempest*, in all her years of plying her trade, had never been captured, nor even cornered. It was little wonder that, among the hundreds of pirate ships that looted the coasts and prowled the islands, the *Tempest* alone had earned the reputation as the terror of the seas.

But aboard the *Tempest* today all was not well. Tempers had been shortened by their curtailed port call two weeks

ago, for one night ashore was not nearly enough to alleviate
the previous six-week restlessness that had been accumulat-
ed at sea. Worse, since setting sail again they had endured a
storm and lost a mast that took three days to repair, and had
not sighted a single prize worth taking. Tension crackled on
deck like electricity beneath the hot summer sky, and Storme
had been waiting for the explosion with the suspended impatience with which one might wait for the second shoe to drop.

It came swiftly and without warning. Alerted by her
bos'n's mate, Storme rushed belowdecks to the galley,
where she found Rafferty, her lieutenant, circling an overturned
table across from the cook. Rafferty was armed with a knife,
the cook with a cleaver, and both men had murder on their
faces. Half the crew were gathered there cheering them on,
and no one even looked around when the captain entered.

This, perhaps more than anything else, infuriated Storme.
She had prided herself on running the tightest ship on the
seas, but at that very moment she was forced to accept
graphic and indisputable evidence that Raoul had been right.
Discipline had deteriorated to an unconscionable level when
she, the captain aboard her own ship, was ignored in favor
of a knife fight.

"Come on, ye filthy whelp of a whore," taunted Rafferty,
crouched low to aim his thrust. "Ye'll be servin' no more o'
that p'ison ye call food at my table!"

"I'll be servin' up the fleshy part of you for tonight's
supper!" vowed the cook in a rumble and swung the
cleaver.

Rafferty kicked the table forward and the cleaver struck it
square on the edge, wedging there. A roar of encourage-
ment swelled up, and as the cook struggled to free his
weapon Rafferty moved in.

Long ago Storme had learned to compensate for physical
strength with the ingenious use of weapons, and in a contest
calling for balance and skill, the whip was the most efficient
of these. On board Storme was never without a whip coiled
in her belt, and in a blind fit of temper she reached for it
now. Six feet of vicious rawhide shot across the room to
wind itself around Rafferty's neck.

The knife clattered to the floor as Rafferty's fingers instinctively went up to claw at his throat. The cook lunged in with every intention of settling the matter without delay, and he would have succeeded had not Squint, the quartermaster and second in command, restrained him. A cry of outrage went up from the crew at this interference, and it all happened in such a flash of an eye that no one realized exactly *what* had happened until somebody burst out, "The cap'n!" Then, and only then, did a shocked, half-disgruntled and half-respectful silence fall.

Rafferty, his face reddened and his eyes bulging with surprise and anger, twisted around to face her. Clearly, he was past the point of common sense, and as the cook lunged against Squint's restraining arms he tore at the whip around his neck. "Let me go, woman!" he shouted. "This is between men, and I'll finish what I started or be damned!"

There had been a time when no man, on board or off, would have dared speak to Storme O'Malley like that without risking the wrath of an entire armed crew. But times had changed, and such insolence was a matter of course for Storme.

She returned sharply, "Then it's damned you'll be!" and she gave an expert tug on the whip, tightening the pressure until Rafferty gagged and his eyes went glassy.

The crew, subdued into a fascinated silence, warily watched the interplay between captain and subordinate, master and victim. It was moments such as this that relieved long days of tedium at sea, displays of power that were necessary every once in a while to reassert their purpose and their mission. Storme knew this and was adept at exploiting it, but today it took all the self-command at her disposal to restrain herself from tightening the whip until all signs of life seeped from Rafferty's sea-dog face.

With a very great effort, she gradually released the pressure on the whip, advancing step by step upon him as she did. A wise captain at that moment would have had two options then: to let the matter drop with a stern reprimand, or to release the two combatants and let them fight it out. But Storme was in no mood to be wise. Her eyes were hard and her face was icy, and even the most inexperienced among her crew could tell she was in a deadly fury.

"You scurvy scrapings of a barnacled seahorse," she said in a dangerously soft voice, "I ought to break your bloody neck." She spoke not two inches from his face, and then paused there a long moment, letting him read in her eyes the cold determination to make her threat a fact.

Not a breath passed in the stale, grease-filled air, and the only sound was the clink of a lantern as it bobbed against the wall. Then, with an abrupt snap of her wrist, Storme released the whip. Rafferty staggered backward, gasping and rubbing his bruised throat.

But Rafferty was an intractable one and hadn't served under Storme very long. Resentment still boiled in his eyes and he spat out, "A real captain wouldn't be afeard to see a little blood spilt on his decks! That's what comes of letting a woman in breeches, that I'll warrant!"

Only the swift narrowing of Storme's eyes presaged what was to come, but it was all that was needed. Rafferty saw he had gone too far. He took a small step backward.

With an impatient curl of her lips Storme barked, "Keelhaul him!" And turned to stride away.

Instantly four men were upon Rafferty, eager for this new excitement and proud that their captain had not disappointed them. Storme drew up shortly before the cook, who was looking a bit too pleased with himself for her liking, and spat, "You just be glad you're not as expendable as a lieutenant. I want this rathole you call a galley scrubbed down with vinegar and salt water, and I want to see *your* fat ass moving at it! Now!"

The humiliation of a cook being required to scour his own galley was almost worse punishment than keelhauling, and the man's face reflected his shock. All he did was swallow hard, though, and when Squint released him he lost no time in following his captain's orders.

Storme followed the rowdy crew on deck, pausing only once to advise the bos'n's mate not to let the sport get out of hand; she expected to have need of her lieutenant—sorry bit of scum though he was—before very long. When the men, shouting and cheering colorfully, carried the hapless Rafferty to the rail where, suspended by his bound ankles, he would be dragged through the water for a course of some minutes, Storme affected indifference and went to the quarterdeck. She was seething inside.

She felt Squint's presence beside her a long time before she acknowledged it. Deliberately, she focused her spyglass on the quarry ahead, disciplining her mind away from the incident just past and toward the challenge awaiting. But Squint, silent in his disapproval, stolid in his determination, would not be moved. Storme waited impatiently for what she knew was to come.

Squint—so named for his left eyelid, which had some time past been sewn shut over an empty socket—had been born Roger Mercer fifty years ago, son of a gamekeeper in North Kent. At age fourteen he had been inducted into the Royal Navy—the result of a careless stroll through a market town, where a blow from behind had rendered him unconscious. When he awoke, he was locked in the hold of a British ship with several other "volunteers," awaiting his orders.

He fared better than most, for the first mate aboard that vessel was Charles O'Malley, and almost at once a special kinship had grown between the two. O'Malley was barely ten years Squint's senior, and he took a special interest in training and protecting the young boy. Squint was quick and adaptable and soon learned the ways of the sea.

He fought with O'Malley through five years of the King's war against France, and while stationed in Jamaica he fell in love with an innkeeper's daughter . . . hopelessly, desperately in love. The night before the fleet was to pull out for deeper waters, Squint jumped ship—and the only witness to this act of treachery was Charles O'Malley. The two men's eyes met, the officer and the seaman, each knowing where his duty lay. The punishment for Squint's crime was death. The consequence of an officer's refusing to report it was court martial. Charles O'Malley turned his back.

For three years Squint lived in blissful paradise with his bride, making his living as a fisherman and helping in her father's inn. Then the war came again, and inside a year he saw his wife brutally raped and murdered by vengeful French, his unborn child ripped from her belly and paraded through the streets on a lance.

In 1695, Charles O'Malley returned to Jamaica, captain of his own ship. There he found a drunken and dissipated shell of his old friend, and did the one thing he could to save his life. Almost by force he dragged Squint on board ship, sobered him up, and put a sword in his hand. For years Squint expended his anger and his hatred in savage vengeance against the French, joining the force of slaughter and mayhem that exacted justice from the enemy just as justice had been exacted from him. He was young and filled with passion, and he lost more than an eye during those bloody years upon the seas—he lost all memory, or need, of any other way of life.

Squint had now been at war over twenty years, and war had almost become a habit to him. Like Storme, he had been born in the midst of conflict and knew no other way to exist in a savage world than to fight. And, with Storme's father, he had taught the young girl the arts of survival the only way he knew how, because the times had demanded it and he knew no other way.

Only recently had he begun to wonder if he had been wrong. Times were changing, and the passions of youth had died long ago. The things that once had seemed important no longer bore much merit, and he wondered if they ever had. Perhaps he was merely growing old. Or maybe he was just tired.

Standing beside the young woman now who had been like a daughter to him, he experienced a shadow of regret for all that had gone before. And he wondered if it were not too late—for both of them.

Storme had borne his silence as long as she could. With an impatient snap of her glass she turned to him, eyes narrowed, and demanded, "Well, Quartermaster? You have a complaint?"

Squint kept his thoughts from his face as he chewed complacently on a scrap of straw and directed his mild gaze toward the ship upon which they were closing at a leisurely pace. He answered her question at leisure. "Nay, Cap'n, not I."

The frustration that had been churning inside Storme evaporated into a self-defeated heap, for she could never keep up grandiose pretenses with Squint—not for long. By naval tradition his authority on board the *Tempest* was second only to Storme's; by virtue of affection he was Storme's good right arm. He was the only man in the world—aside from Pompey, who hardly counted—with whom Storme could ever let down her guard completely.

She released a breath through her teeth and lifted her face to the sun, letting the wind catch a few tendrils of her hair. "God's teeth and eyeballs, man," she swore tightly, "what was I supposed to do?"

Squint cast her a look deep with understanding. "Aye, it's getting harder for ye, ain't it, lass?"

Storme turned to him, her eyes clear and simple and filled with nothing but the honest need to know. "Why, Squint? What's happening to this ship, to my men? Why are they turning against me?"

"They ain't agin ye, lass. They're just testin' ye, 'tis all."

A perplexed and recalcitrant scowl hovered over her brows. "It didn't used to be like this. Time was I would have run the man through who dared question the loyalty of my crew. Now I half-fear to sit with my back at the door on my own ship. It's not right."

Squint thought carefully before he spoke next. "It ain't right," he said at last, "for a woman to be in control of men. Ain't natural. You got ye'self a strong crew, and loyal in their way, but they know what ain't right. And they're goin' ter fight agin it. Tis the way she be."

Storme drew herself up, her eyes flashing. "They knew I was a woman when they signed on. They don't like the captain, let them elect a new one—and I'll tear out the throat of every bleedin' bugger that votes against me with my bare hands," she added in a fierce undertone. Instinctively her hands tightened into fists at her sides.

Squint chuckled, his single eye reflecting affection and amusement. "An' don't think they don't know it, girlie."

"I force no man to serve under me," she challenged Squint, her eyes still churning. "But, my God, when a man comes aboard the *Tempest*, he'd better know who's captain or swim for it! So let them go, the whole bleedin' lot of 'em! I can dredge up a better crew with a fishnet!" She raised her voice with the last for the benefit of any who might choose to overhear, but Squint only shrugged.

"Aye, and there's the rub, ain't it? You sail a fine ship, your split is better than any afloat, and ye're not a coward like most. They come aboard to sail with the best, forgettin' what it does to their manly pride."

"Manly pride! ha!" She made an obscene gesture with her fist. "*That* for their manly pride!"

Squint, as was his way, turned his attention away from her and back to the face of the sea, letting her steam in her own froth. Every time he did that he made Storme feel like a child, but she couldn't be angry with him for it. He had too impressive a record of being right.

After a time, somewhat subdued, Storme lifted her glass again to examine the distant ship. "She's bottom-heavy," she announced with satisfaction. "Can't outrun us. And the wind's against her. She's floundering out there like a pregnant sea cow, waitin' for us to move in."

From the other side of the ship came shouts and cheers and sounds of violent thrashing, an indication the keelhauling had begun. Storme frowned, mentally cursing Rafferty and the trouble he'd caused. She knew discipline was necessary, but she didn't enjoy enforcing it and resented any man who made her do so. They all had better things to fight than each other.

Never mind, she assured herself reasonably, a little seawater would cool Rafferty's temper and he'd think twice before he misspoke his captain again. Besides, the sport would liven the men's spirits and energize them for the conquest that lay ahead.

She gave a little shrug and spoke out loud. "Who needs a

lieutenant anyway? The only thing they're good for is assassinating the captain so's they can take the ship."

Her attempt at levity fell short, and she knew there was no point in avoiding the issue, not with Squint. She said simply, without preamble, "It's because I won't bed any of them, ain't it? That's why the men are so bloody insolent with me."

Squint turned toward her again, and if there was surprise or disapproval none of it showed in his crinkled, weather-beaten face. "Mebbe," he agreed slowly. "Mebbe 'twould make a difference, were you a bedded woman. 'Twould get ye more respect, like."

Forcefully, Storme repressed a shudder. She'd almost expected Squint to argue with her. "I'd sail this ship alone before I'd let any one of these filthy animals take my maidenhead."

"Aye," agreed Squint soberly. "You go beddin' one of yer own crew, ye'll have the rest of 'em slittin' throats for who'll be next."

"Raoul wants me," she announced abruptly. "Pig that he is. What he really wants is the *Tempest*, him and every other like him." She spat forcefully on the deck. "Well, they'll not get her—*or* me."

" 'Tis time ye were a woman," was the only advice Squint would offer. " 'Twould make things easier on ye all around."

There was no clumsiness in reviewing the matter with Squint, for Storme had given it all a great deal of thought since the encounter with Raoul . . . and even before. Everything was changing around her, and she had no control over it. All she could do was to fix what she could, and if virginity was a problem, that could be fixed. It was a cumbersome and awkward business and she was tired of protecting it. What she needed was protection of a different sort—the unspoken code of the sea that stated her right to choose. And once she chose, no sailor would question the right of the man who had first taken her to claim her—until she tired of him and chose again.

The only trouble was, her choices were limited.

"If I take a man of my crew," she pondered out loud, her brow knitting, "I risk mutiny. If I take another captain, I risk treachery. Damnation and hellfire, why does it have to be such a bother to be a blessed woman?"

Squint shrugged. "It ain't womanhood that's a-botherin' ye, lass. It's that ye ain't usin' it right. A man's got to know that a woman can be ruled—even if it's only once, and only in bed. 'Tis the way of the world."

Storme thought about that, and it made sense. It didn't seem fair, but Storme knew enough of men and the rules by which they lived to realize that fairness was rarely a criterion. If all it took was a set of tangled and stained bed linens to restore her authority over her crew, there was no question but that it must be done. And besides, she *was* a woman, and she had lived in curiosity and deprivation too long. Her first love would always be the *Tempest*, but was there any reason she should not have other pleasures as well?

It must be done, she resolved firmly, and a twinge of excitement, as well as anxiety, began to curl in her belly once the decision was irrevocably made. The world that surrounded her attached such significance to the act of mating that she'd be damned if she'd be kept in the dark any longer. It was high time she found out what all the bother was about, and if it admitted her to the secret fraternity which ruled her crew in the process, so much the better.

Squint turned to her, his expression solemn. He spoke so abruptly, so unexpectedly, that there was no way Storme could have been prepared for what he was about to say. "Times be changin', girlie. The waters ain't what they used to be and you—well, ye're a full-growed woman now and it's no life for ye. Ye should settle down and be a wife to somebody, suckle babes and wear skirts. It's time ye was givin' some thoughtful prospects to the future."

Storme stared at him, hardly trusting her ears. "You're mad," she decided at last, and turned away, dismissing the matter.

Squint's hand closed on her arm, and it was such an uncharacteristic gesture that Storme's head jerked around to face him, startled. No man aboard was allowed to touch

Storme, and Squint had never made himself an exception. Even Pompey, who was standing his usual guard only a few yards distant, was alarmed by the deviation from the normal and took a step forward. He was stopped only by a glance from Storme, but Squint did not release her. That was when she knew he was serious.

"Mad I may be," Squint said sternly, "to let you keep on with this foolishness this long."

Storme jerked her arm away, insulted and incredulous. "As though you could stop me!"

Squint held her with his single unwavering eye, and his tone was quiet. "Couldn't I?"

Storme swallowed hard, and found she couldn't meet his gaze any longer. Squint had done more than his duty aboard the *Tempest* these past years, and they both knew it. He had advised Storme, guided her, trained her, protected her, and supported her. He had more power aboard her ship than any man ought, but she had never begrudged him it. And if at any time he had thought to speak against her, the men would have rallied around him and there would be a new captain aboard the *Tempest* quicker than a gull could dive.

Was that what he was talking about now—mutiny? Had the entire world gone mad? Something cold and clammy began to congeal in Storme's chest as she realized how vulnerable she really was.

She took a deep breath, and found it unexpectedly difficult to draw in enough air to feed her suddenly aching lungs. She stared straight over the rail. "Any man," she said quietly, "who thinks to take the *Tempest* from me had best do it by murder." And she looked at Squint slowly, her eyes somber and dark with hardly imagined pain. "Because without her, I would die, and it would be a kindness to kill me quick."

Squint's face softened, and his gnarled fingers patted Storme's arm gently. "Nay, girlie, I ain't gonna take yer ship. I vowed ter yer pa I would take care of ye, and takin' care is just what I'm doin'. It's time to leave the sea, me girl," he said earnestly. "Ye're a young lady now and 'tis time to put away childish things."

That choking, desperate feeling still hampered her breath. Squint had never spoken to her like that. Raoul, with all his conniving and melodrama, might moan about leaving the business and she could laugh at him, but Squint . . . Squint was serious. The very thought left her chilled.

"I cannot," she said firmly, and there might have been just the faintest undertone of a tremor in her voice. She closed her fists firmly about the rail, as though forcefully to prevent her ship from slipping away. "I cannot. I will not. This is my life, the only one I know or care to know. You remember what happened when Papa tried to keep me land-bound."

Squint smiled faintly. "Aye, you gave that fine lady Annabelle a turn or two, didn't ye, and was back in yer pa's arms inside a year."

Storme gave a grunt of derision at the memory. "Annabelle was nothing but a wet-nosed sniveling petticoat."

"But yer pa knew ye needed the touch of a woman. With yer own sainted mother gone and buried, ye'd never knowed what it was to be female. It was a good thing he tried to do fer ye."

"Women, bah! A worthless lot. Who needs woman things when you've got a good sword arm at your side?"

"Now, lassie, don't you go speakin' without giving yer brain a chance to work. Yer own ma was a woman worth knowin', and that's a truth. Would yer pa have loved her otherwise? She was a lady, a fine lady . . . like ye could be, if ye put yer mind to it."

For a moment something softened within Storme; a yearning and an emptiness came upon her as it always did when mention was made of the mother she had never known. What would she have been like, a fine lady? Beautiful and strong and gentle, a woman equal to stand beside Charles O'Malley, yet different from him. A woman who represented all that was good about womanhood . . . and all the things Storme would never know. What would she think of the daughter she had birthed now?

But because those wonderings made her uncomfortable, she answered shortly, "I've no need to be a lady. I've got a ship. I've got the sea and all the plunder I can take from it, and men obey my commands. Should I want for more? This is all I've ever known, and I'm content with it.''

Squint made a small grunt of agreement. ''Aye, and I reckon ye can't expect to miss what you don't know. From the time ye was a nursling, ye've had a deck beneath yer feet and nothin' but men for playmates. . . . Why, I remember when ye was barely a-walking, tyin' ye with a rope to the mast so's ye wouldn't fall over and be swallowed by sharks, and before we even know'd it ye was scrambling up that mast like a monkey as fer as the rope'd go. . . .''

''The sea is in my blood,'' Storme said simply. ''I was born to it and I will live out my days on it. I want nothing more.''

''But it's not meant to be, lass,'' Squint said earnestly, ''an' ye know it as much as me. Ye're a strong lass, Storme, and ye can change. It's dangerous times a-comin', for all of us.''

For a moment she was uncertain, for Squint's words reflected only too well her own worries and doubts about the future. But as always, the questions could be raised but no answers were forthcoming. And Storme had no time to waste on indeterminate problems of the future whose solutions were not hers to command.

She gave an impatient shrug. ''Danger! Pshaw! Since when has any hand aboard the *Tempest* feared danger? We thrive upon it. It makes us strong.''

''It can also make ye dead.''

Then Storme did laugh, and impulsively squeezed Squint's arm. ''You must be getting old, Quartermaster. You're turning sentimental on me.''

And, suddenly buoyant with new enthusiasm, she lifted her glass again, focusing on the ship that would be shortly crossing their path. ''A merchantman,'' she commented. ''Bound for the Indies, from the course she's taking.''

Storme could sense Squint's debate as he measured what success he would have in pursuing his cause, and was pleased when his common sense won out and he turned to the matter at hand. "She's got nothing we want. We just laid in supplies. Let her go."

Storme adjusted the glass, and she did not respond immediately. "The men need a diversion," she said at last. "The exercise will raise their spirits."

Squint gave a derisive grunt. "They've had their sport fer the day."

Storme shrugged, not lowering the glass. "I'll not give my crew a chance to grow lazy. Besides, I owe them a prize for cutting short their leave."

"Let her go. She ain't worth the trouble."

For a moment Storme seemed to consider the suggestion, but then she made a slight adjustment in the viewer, and the lines about her mouth went grim. "No," she said curtly.

She folded the glass and tucked it away with a single decisive motion. Her eyes were suddenly hard. "Run up the skull and crossbones," she commanded. "She flies the Union Jack. We'll take her."

* ## Chapter Six *

Aboard the *Valiant* chaos ruled as the now sinister white-sailed form moved ever closer. Crewmen hurried back and forth across the deck, dumping the meager supply of munitions and other valuables overboard, shouted orders and acknowledgments blurring in the wind. Simon watched in horror and incredulity as the Union Jack was hastily and unceremoniously lowered from the mast.

Simon grabbed the captain's arm as he passed. "You're lowering the flag!" he accused, outraged. "Are you out of your mind?"

The enemy ship was almost within boarding distance now. Simon saw the grappling hooks being hoisted into position and clearly heard the bloodthirsty cries of the pirate crew raised in threat and victory.

The captain cast a glance toward the approaching vessel and jerked away from Simon impatiently. "We're surrendering, you bloody fool! How're they gonna know it unless we lower the bloody flag?" He turned to shout another order, but Simon grabbed his arm again, more forcefully this time, staring at him in a paroxysm of fury and contempt.

"You treacherous, cowardly dog!" he roared, and his fingers dug into the other man's arm fiercely. "You're a disgrace to your command! This is your ship and you're responsible for all aboard. Fight, damn you, for the sake of your good name and Mother England—"

The captain returned a look filled with scorn and jerked away from Simon's grasp with surprising strength. "That's Storme O'Malley, you frothin' idiot! Now shut yer mouth and get below if you value yer hide!"

It took a moment for the name to register through the black cloud of anger and disbelief that assailed Simon. Storme O'Malley was as much a legend of the seas as the serpents that swallowed ships whole and the mermaids that lured men to their deaths—and this shivering, shrinking fool was abandoning his ship for the terror of a myth!

"Are you mad, man?" Simon cried, but the captain was already gone, shouting the order to raise the white flag—but too late.

Simon felt the thud of the grappling hooks; the ship lurched, and he was flung violently against the rail. A female voice rang strong and clear, "Ahoy there, you white-bellied sons of England! Leave down your arms and prepare to be boarded or we'll feed your skins to the sharks!"

Nothing even in Simon's imagination had prepared him for this. No sooner had he recovered his balance from the grappling hooks than the deck was aswarm with men, all wielding swords and knives and screaming the blood-chilling screams of angels of death. The crew of the *Valiant* cowered on their knees or on their bellies, hands covering their heads; they hid behind barrels or crawled under canvas, and, for a single brief moment while terror ran like ice through his veins, Simon's contempt for their cowardice was tempered by the strong urge to run and hide himself.

A wiser or even a more experienced man would have done just that. But for Simon York the thin thread that separated the familiar from the unimaginable snapped at that moment and he was cast adrift in a world gone mad; even while one part of him plainly and violently denied the evidence of his own eyes, another part had no choice but to act on instincts as old as the art of survival.

There seemed to be hundreds of them pouring over the deck, yelping like the dogs of hell, swinging bayonets, thundering obscenities and colorful, bloodcurdling promises of what would be done to any who dared defy them. They blurred around Simon with the slice of blades through air and the acrid singe of torches—filthy half-humans with long tangled hair and scarred faces and gleeful lust in their eyes. With his peripheral vision, Simon saw kegs of rum being hefted over the rail to the enemy ship; he heard the thud of a blade against a timber and heard a man's scream but could not see, in all the confusion, whether human flesh had also been victim of that blade.

One of the pirates clambered up from below, grinning like a hyena, with a squealing pig under each arm, and as Simon watched he tossed one animal over the rail and into the sea, drawing his knife in the same instant to slit the throat of the other. Hot fresh blood gushed over the deck and mingled with the cries of men and the squawk of galley geese and the debris of the ransacked larder that choked the air.

It could not have been more than an instant that Simon was held captive by horror and disbelief, but it seemed like a lifetime. He saw the crew cowering on deck beneath the onslaught of outlaws; he saw the gleam of blades and the flow of blood and heard the ring of mad, greedy laughter. Someone fired a pistol and the explosion was no more than the crack of a whip against the riot of clatter that shattered the air.

And in a surge, without thought or hesitation, Simon leaped forward, propelling himself into the back of the nearest buccaneer. With a surety of grace and skill, Simon whipped the other man's sword from its scabbard and sliced the air with it.

The other man whirled, knife drawn, and lunged at him with a roar.

Simon caught a glimpse of bared, blackened teeth and a jowly, grizzled face before he feinted and stepped lightly out of his enemy's path. A brief astonishment for this unexpected display of drawing-room swordsmanship registered in the other man's hesitation, and Simon grasped the advantage. He thrust forward swiftly and surely, but an unexpected rocking of the ship prevented the blow from being fatal. Simon heard the rip of material and saw a thin stream of blood appear on his opponent's chest and he saw a huge fist clenched around the hilt of a knife raised upward to plunge.

Simon drew back his arm to thrust again, knowing it would be his last chance, and suddenly his arm was gripped from behind. The sword was wrenched from his hand and a round of cheers went up as the buccaneers, momentarily distracted from their looting and vandalism, gathered round to watch the sport.

He heard the roar of victorious laughter that burst forth from his opponent's throat and saw the knife suspended in midair for an endless moment. He felt the warmth of the wood rail against his back and the sea breeze on his face with the curious detachment of one who knows he is about to die, and at the same time his mind was working with the swift sure logic that can only be triggered as the bars of the trap begin to close. A sudden lunge forward, using his head as a battering ram, might throw his attacker off guard. A swift turn and a leap would put him over the rail, where he might take his chances with the sea. If he dived for the deck, and the other man's feet . . .

"Avast there! Back with you!"

The voice that rang out was sharp and commanding and unmistakably female, and its effect was instantaneous. The howling ruffians who had gathered to watch immediately turned to more profitable entertainments, and the man who wielded the knife now just inches from Simon's throat paused, a war of fury and disappointment glittering in his eyes.

" 'E's mine!'' he shouted, turning. "The bleedin' bugger cut me, 'e did! Drew me blood! 'E's mine by rights!''

Simon twisted his head to catch a glimpse of the owner of the voice that had, momentarily at least, spared his life. But at that moment a shadow seemed to eclipse the sun and the biggest black man Simon had ever seen strode onto the deck.

His skin was purest ebony, his features sharp and aristocratic, his muscles bulging and gleaming with sweat. His head was shaved and his bare chest strewn with thick gold chains, some of them in links as wide as a man's fist, and studded with jewels that glittered like eyes in the sunlight. He said not a word. He placed himself firmly between Simon and his attacker, towering a full foot above both men, folded his arms, and awaited further instructions.

The other man swore colorfully. "Let me take 'im, Cap'n!" he asserted. "I won't kill 'im, then, just carve 'im up a little!''

Simon bolted. While the knife was lowered, the giant was waiting for orders and the black-toothed man arguing with his captain, Simon saw his chance and he took it.

He got almost three running steps before a huge black forearm closed around his throat, slicing off his breath and sending shards of dizzying, multicolored light to his head. When his vision cleared, Storme O'Malley was standing before him.

The Storme O'Malley of legend was a huge woman, with ponderous breasts, coarse, hair-growing skin, a hook nose, and broken knuckles. She was forty years old, large-hipped and raw-boned, with a voice like thunder and a countenance to match. She wore her skirts belted between her legs and her hair shorn raggedly at her scalp, and she was known to cook the private parts of men and eat them for breakfast.

The woman who stood before Simon now could have barely been twenty. Her slender legs were bare except for short breeches that clung to her taut thighs and pelvis in such a way as to set aside for all time rumors that she was anything but a woman. Her skin was smooth and the color of honey. Beneath a battered cocked hat a braid of burnished light hair trailed to her waist, and her breasts, barely defined beneath a turquoise silk jacket and two crossed powder-belts, were anything but ponderous. Simon had to blink, twice, to assure himself of what his eyes told him.

She walked forward slowly, a tall girl with the natural grace of one at ease upon the sea and the mastery of one accustomed to command. She held a sword in her hand and handled it as casually as another might a parasol or a walking stick. She stopped about three feet from Simon, who was still held in the paralyzing grip of a granite arm, and extended the sword so that its tip rested just beneath his chin. She applied a slight upward pressure on the blade that made him lift his face to hers.

Her eyes went over him coolly, measuringly, and there was a touch of merciless speculation there that made Simon's blood run cold. And then, abruptly, she lowered the sword.

"No," she said shortly. "I don't want him killed, and I don't want him marked." She gave a curt nod to the giant who imprisoned Simon. "I'll take him. Bring him aboard."

* **Chapter Seven** *

The hold of the *Tempest* was an inferno, dark and thick with the sour odors of rotting fruit and spoiled meat, underscored with the faint nauseating taste of the sweat and blood of other prisoners, long since departed. Simon was strapped to a heavy barrel on the floor, his arms stretched behind him around the barrel and lashed tightly at the wrists, his ankles so tightly bound together that his toes had grown cold. The aching in his armpits from the cruel position had receded some time ago to a curious tingling numbness which only flared into excruciating shafts of pain when he tried to move. Wisely, Simon remained perfectly still.

He could hear the chatter and scurry of rats all around him and occasionally feel tiny paws scamper across his legs or his boots. Strain as he would, he could make out nothing of his surroundings but shadows against blacker shadows, for the compartment was almost completely airtight. So far, he had managed to control his rebellious stomach, but only through great exertion of will and a certain knowledge that, should he once relax his concentration, he would surely strangle on his own vomit. But moment by moment, as the air supply became thinner and more fetid, the fight for consciousness grew more difficult, and he began to wonder whether it might not be preferable to suffocate in this filthy hold than to live to face whatever fate his captors had in mind for him.

He thought it would be ransom, for if they intended to murder him would they not have done so already? And if ransom . . . would Augusta have wits enough to raise it? How could she? Perhaps Peter . . . but Peter was only a servant, indentured for life and restrained by law from taking any action on his own or his employer's behalf.

The truths chased themselves over and over in Simon's mind. He might never be freed. He might die here. And then, dear God, what would become of Augusta? Simon didn't fear death, but if he couldn't extricate himself from this situation, what would become of his sister, and Cypress Bay, all that he loved in the world. . . .

But no. He wouldn't die. The matter simply was not up for debate. Somehow he would get out of here, somehow he would return home.

About an hour ago he had felt the hull scrape shoals, indicating landfall, and heard an increase of activity on the decks above as the crewmen tied off. He tried to focus his fuzzy brain as to their general position. He did not think they could be too far off the coast of North Carolina, and even in his desperate condition the irony struck him. That he should come to this on his own homeland, in all probability less than a day's ride from Cypress Bay... it was all too much to be absorbed, and indisputable evidence, if any was needed, of God's own cruel sense of humor.

And yet, if he could escape...

He heard movement above him, the creak of the hatchway, and a square of sunlight almost blinded him as heavy footfalls descended the stairs. Gasping gratefully at the briny air, Simon turned his head away from the painful shards of light, and when he focused again a shadow was standing before him.

"'Ere ye go, mate," a cheerful voice declared. "Supper for the prisoner. Ne'er let it be said we mistreat the highborn aboard the *Tempest*!"

Simon knew that voice; but worse, he knew the face. It was the same man he had wounded in battle aboard the *Valiant*, and he politely set a bowl of greasy gray gruel on the floor just out of reach of Simon's bound hands. Not that it mattered, for one look at the concoction almost caused Simon to lose his tenuous control over his stomach. The gruel appeared to be squirming of its own accord.

Simon let his gaze travel from the bowl on the floor to the man above him. His breeches might once have been a brilliant shade of embroidered gold, but now were so stained with filth and old blood as to be nearly unrecognizable. A wide turquoise scarf divided his midsection, and Simon recognized his own doublet—taken from him, with his jacket, shortly after capture—worn without a shirt over the man's naked chest. A paunch of belly, as white as the underside of a frog and studded with a few spiky black hairs, protruded through the lower open buttons of the doublet, and a blood-stained bandage decorated his upper arm.

The pirate squatted beside Simon, his lips parting over yellowed and broken teeth into a lascivious grin. He wore a gold hoop in one ear; grime beaded his neck and matted his unshorn hair. The smell of him was strong enough to overwhelm even the offal that rotted in the hold. Instinctively Simon shrank back.

"Eh, now, no need fer that. An' here I be tryin' to show

ye there's no hard feelings." The light from the open hatchway revealed a horrible glint to his eyes as he brought one stubby, dirt-encrusted finger to Simon's face and traced a lazy pattern from temple to chin. "Aye, and ye're a pretty one, ain't ye?" he said softly. "Too pretty to be languishing away down here all by yeself."

Simon tried to jerk his face away but succeeded only in wrenching his arm so painfully that he saw stars. His heart was pounding dryly in his chest, and the other man chuckled lowly. "The cap'n said I wasn't to hurt ye, but I don't reckon she'd mind if I turned ye over this barrel here and had a little fun. Ain't no harm in that, is there? Ye's too pretty—and too ripe—to waste like this."

And as he spoke he was tugging at the ropes that bound Simon's wrists, his foul breath washing through Simon's nostrils until he thought he would choke from panic and revulsion. His instinct was to struggle, and struggle he did, but his ineffectual efforts only brought forth gusts of lusty laughter from the pirate.

A shadow momentarily blocked the light, and they both heard the descending footsteps at the same time.

The black Colossus stood before them, crowding the small space with his bulk, and the pirate backed away, grinning. "Just feedin' the prisoner," he announced, and Simon thought he detected the slightest note of unease in his voice.

The black knelt and began to jerk ungently at the ropes on Simon's arms. The other man chortled, "Eh, that's the way o' it, all right. I ain't selfish. Let's take 'im on deck and all have a turn. 'E's a strong young buck, 'e can take it."

Simon's arms fell free with such a flare of fiery agony that he had to bite back a cry. The ropes on his ankles followed, and blood rushed back into his extremities like bubbling acid through his veins.

Roughly, he was jerked to his feet and pushed toward the hatchway. His feet, so long separated from the rest of his body, refused to obey any sensible command, and he stumbled and almost went to his knees. The grip of an iron hand tossed him upright again as effortlessly as though he were a puppet on a string.

Simon was aware of the stabbing rays of the setting sun, of green shadows in the distance that might have been trees, of cool, fresh air that rushed into his lungs like a potion. Flashes of color that skirted his vision were other members of the pirate crew, and he heard their whistles and their catcalls and their eager obscenities as though from a distance. Behind them trailed the man Simon had wounded, whining about being cheated.

He thought about running. He thought about turning and tackling the giant who would surely snap his neck with one crook of his finger; he thought about leaping the rail and striking through the wilderness for safety. But his arms hung like ribbons at his sides, his eyes burned so with the light he could hardly see, and his feet barely supported his weight even with the help of the giant. And by the time he regained control of his extremities and his sight, they were in a narrow passageway belowdecks, and his captor was pushing him through an open door.

Storme paused in her conversation with Squint when Pompey shoved Simon forward, and though she tried to keep her expression unrevealing she could not prevent a small quirk of inner triumph—and a sheerly instinctive catch of breath when she looked at him. God's wounds, but he was even easier on the eye than she remembered. His hair—a wonderful shade of dark russet—was rumpled, and his complexion a little off, but those were the only visible ill-effects of his confinement. Thank God, she'd stopped Harry before he cut him. To have that beautiful face scarred would have been a blasphemy even Storme could not have borne.

He stood at the door, rather absently chafing his wrists, his shoulders straight and his head held high, meeting her gaze straight on. That pleased Storme, for she could not abide a cowed man, even as the expression in those lovely gray eyes intrigued her. Curiosity, was it? Even a mild negligence? His shirt was stained with sweat and the grime of the hold and several buttons had been torn off, revealing, beneath the tails of his crooked neckcloth, a fine glimpse of chest. And a wonderful chest it was, too: lean and graceful, with finely defined muscles across the breast and ribs and the faintest powdering of light, almost golden hair. She wondered if the hair elsewhere on his body would be of like color.

All in all, from the curve of his shapely calves to the arch of his aristocratic cheekbones, he was a perfect specimen, and Storme could not have been more pleased with her choice—or with the fates that had brought him to her.

Suddenly aware of Squint's alert gaze upon her, she turned back casually. "Let the men ashore tonight, and divide up that cask of rum we took. But..." Her tone became severe. "I'll abide no drunkards on the morn. Tomorrow we careen and scrape the hull, and I want every man fit for the job. Now..." She turned away in what she hoped was a suitably casual dismissal. "You've your orders. I won't be disturbed again tonight."

Squint lingered stubbornly. "What o' him?" He jerked his eyes toward the prisoner. "What be your plans for him?"

Storme met his gaze evenly, every line in her body radiating quiet authority. By her silence, she answered Squint's question—as though he had not already guessed—but whether it was acceptance or disapproval reflected on his face she did not care to know. She said firmly, "That will be all, Quartermaster."

Squint looked as though he would have liked to say more—a great deal more—but wisdom deterred him. He cut one more sharp glance toward Simon, and then back to Storme, but in the end he merely turned and ambled toward the door.

Storme breathed an almost audible sigh of relief when he was gone. "Close the door, Pompey," she ordered, "and bring the prisoner in."

Simon did not wait for the rough shove that would send him sprawling, but politely stepped forward as Pompey closed the door behind them. The black man, expressionless, folded his arms across his massive bare chest and took up his stance at the door.

A cautious ease of spirit had crept into Simon as soon as he realized it was the captain's cabin to which he had been brought. She was the one, after all, who had ordered his life to be saved and he doubted she had done so only to satisfy the bestial cravings of her crew. Doubtless negotiations for ransom would now begin, and that prospect, however it rankled his sensibilities, was not nearly so distressing as the fate he had so narrowly escaped. He was safe here, at least for the moment. She was a woman, after all—despite whatever evidence there might be to the contrary—and there had not yet been born the woman Simon York could not handle.

With the confidence of this thought, Simon took careful measure of his surroundings for the first time. The room was small and neat, almost spartan in its furnishings, and utterly utilitarian. The dark severity of the mahogany walls was relieved only by maps and charts at intervals and along the stern a high row of narrow leaded windows that refracted the last rays of a dying sun into a burnished glow. The floors were uncarpeted and unpolished, the bed covered by a plain wool blanket and so tightly made it appeared to be constructed of wood. A single lantern swung from a chain overhead. There was a desk bolted to one wall, and upon it a compass and a sextant. In the center of the room was a table, and upon it he saw a platter of fragrant meat, dishes of fruits and vegetables, a round of bread, a generous wedge of cheese, and a bottle of spirits. The sight and aroma of these dishes were so succulent that Simon's mouth watered, and his stomach, so queasy only moments ago, protested its emptiness.

Storme O'Malley, having procured him, now appeared to forget his presence completely. The moment the door closed behind her quartermaster, she strolled over to the table and sat down, grabbing a leg of fowl, leaning back in her chair and swinging one foot up onto the table comfortably. Her legs were naked below the short, loose-fitting scarlet breeches she wore, and her bare foot rested only inches from the bread board. She attacked the meat in her hand like a lion going in for the kill, and Simon watched in part fascination, part distaste, the woman who was now his captor.

True, she was not the monster he had been led to expect, but Simon would not have, under the harshest duress, have ever called her beautiful, or even appealing. The sternness of her features and the severity of her form were too harsh; they sat uneasily on a girl of her years. Her hair, a honey-gold fall of silk and luxury, was the only softening of an otherwise hard and angular appearance, but even it was unrelieved by the smallest curl or wave, pulled back at the nape of her neck with a leather thong and hanging to her waist. Yet Simon had to admit that the very crudeness and savagery of manner that so repelled him also fascinated him, in some dim and primal way.

She wore a broad gold-tassled sash about her waist and a bright green shirt embroidered with peacocks. The lacings of the shirt were open carelessly to her cleavage, and he could see the faint beginning of a white curved breast when she bent to pry off a hunk of cheese with her fingers. In one ear she wore a large gold hoop studded with chips of rubies, and on her forearm a wide band of hammered silver. When Simon realized from whence these treasures must have come—up to and including the silks on her back—he felt a swift surge of anger coupled with revulsion. The breeches she wore had doubtless been plundered off a dead man's body. The shirt had been lovingly crafted for someone else. And the jewels . . .

In the process of pushing the cheese into her mouth, she suddenly seemed to become aware of his gaze. She shot him a sharp look. "What're you staring at?" she demanded around a mouthful of cheese and meat.

In the nick of time, Simon's natural good humor and slowly resurging confidence returned to rescue him. He offered her a small bow and smile. "Pardon, milady. If I had known this was a dinner invitation, I would have dressed."

She stared at him for a moment. "Didn't they feed you?"

He shrugged lightly. "I'm afraid my meal was—er—interrupted."

A trickle of amusement filtered through Storme's preoccupation with her own plans and she looked at him more closely. A highbred swell, of that there was no doubt, used to fine manners and silly talk and covers on the table. She knew what went on in those fancy houses with their silver dinner knives and separate plates for bread and meat and was certain he would find life aboard ship somewhat of a surprise. Doubtless he had never seen anybody eat with her fingers before, but if that was the only thing he found surprising about this night he might count himself lucky.

She looked at him measuringly for another space of breaths, and then abruptly swung her foot down from the table, kicking out the opposite chair. "Sit," she commanded, and reached for the bottle. Tearing off a hunk of bread with her other hand, she brought the bottle to her lips and gulped, narrowing her eyes and releasing her breath through her teeth as she set it down again with a thud.

Simon approached the table with equal measures of caution and grace, and she waited until he was seated before observing, "You talk fancy. A highborn gentleman, are you?"

Simon watched her small teeth rip off an overlarge chunk of bread with the same unwilling fascination with which he might have observed a carrion-eater diving into a carcass. Minding his composure, he replied offhandedly, "I'm merely a farmer, madame, who makes his humble living from the soil."

She gave a bark of laughter. "Farmer! Hah! Squirmin' dirt-grubs. I wouldn't take a dozen of 'em for one honest seaman."

Simon smiled politely. "Indeed. In your line of work, I imagine you'd give a great deal for one honest seaman."

She was suddenly still, staring at him, and it seemed to Simon at that moment that his entire future hinged on her turn of humor. And then, abruptly, the knife-sharp grip of her eyes relaxed, and she chuckled, lifting the bottle again. "Eh, you're a bright one! I like that."

With the heel of her hand, she pushed the platter of meat toward him. "Eat up. It's fresh-killed." She took a swig of the bottle and passed it to him. "Something to wash it down with."

The bottle contained French brandy, a fine distillation of one of the nobler houses. And she had been guzzling it like creek water. Simon found that, above all he had witnessed since entering this room, almost unbearably offensive.

Simon raised his eyes from the label, careful to keep his expression bland. "Might one ask for a glass?"

Her gaze was piercing. "What are you—some kind of petticoat? Drink, damn your bones, it's in a bottle, what more do you want?"

Simon murmured, "Thank you, I find I am not thirsty."

Storme stared at him a moment longer, then shrugged and reached for another haunch of meat, tearing into it savagely.

Simon began to contemplate his situation. They were on land. He had the freedom of his arms and legs now, and nothing but a woman stood between himself and freedom. A woman... and that huge black guardian at the door. His eyes wandered to the cutlass strapped to Storme's waist. If he could but put that weapon into his own hands...

Idly, he tore off a piece of bread. "What do you intend to do with me? I should think if murder was on your mind you would have dispatched the matter by now."

Storme made a disgruntled sound around a mouthful of meat. "Murder! Bah! You listen to too many tales. Killing is wasteful and takes time. We don't do it unless we have to."

Simon was not at all certain he found that reassuring. "Ransom, then?" he suggested casually, watching her. He took a delicate bite of the bread and swallowed. "I'm afraid you'll be disappointed at the price I'll fetch."

She lifted her shoulders and took another swill of brandy. "I've got no time for ransom."

Simon lifted a gracious eyebrow. "Then I can only assume I am to be your guest for the duration. Very kind of you, I'm sure, but unfortunately I'm not overfond of sea travel, and, frankly, I have other appointments. So, if you'll excuse me..." He made as though to rise.

Storme laughed, her blue eyes twinkling in a way that

made her look suddenly young and full of life—an effect that Simon could not help finding captivating, however briefly. "You are quick! My *guest*, by damnation, I like that! Yes, that's just what you'll be—my *guest*!" And she laughed again.

Simon settled cautiously back into his chair, knowing there was more. Storme popped a piece of cheese into her mouth, scraping the remnants off her fingernails with her teeth, and informed him without further ado, "I will put you ashore tomorrow, in more or less the same condition in which you arrived, if you serve me well tonight."

Simon, more than a little confused and hardly that gullible, nonetheless asked the only sensible question. "And how, exactly, am I expected to serve you?"

Storme leaned back in her chair, wiped the grease from around her mouth with the back of her hand, and regarded him frankly for a long moment. "You are expected," she pronounced at last, simply, "to bed me."

Simon could not have, though his very life depended upon it, prevented what happened next. He stared at her, her incredulous announcement ringing in his ears, and nothing in this world or the next could have convinced him to believe this sudden incredible turn of events. Helplessly, uncontrollably—and not a little hysterically—he began to laugh.

* *Chapter Eight* *

In a heartbeat, she was upon him, her eyes glittering dangerously, the tip of her cutlass pricking at his throat. "You mock me?" she demanded in a dangerously low voice.

Instantly, all mirth vanished. Simon felt the skin of his

throat grow rigid against the blade and he dared not even breathe.

She backed away abruptly, allowing Simon space for a half-breath, but his relief was short-lived. The hardness was back on her features now, reminding Simon that this was no precocious young girl to be trifled with, completely erasing all previous suggestions that she might be harmless. She was a killer, a savage, a conscienceless thief, and—if he had really heard her utter the words he thought he had heard— she was more than a little mad.

She took a step backward, regarding him through eyes narrowed with contempt, anger, and a bone-chilling hint of speculation. And then she made a sharp gesture with her knife-hand toward the door. "Strip him," she commanded shortly. "Let me see what I have bought."

So swiftly that Simon did not even hear him move, the black man jerked him up by the back of the neck. His shirt was ripped roughly from his back and his neckcloth left a rope burn as it was torn from his neck. Struggling for whatever shreds of composure might be left to him as the sleeves were jerked from his wrists, Simon declared, "So this is how you take the laundry aboard ship! I've often wondered."

Standing there before her with such careless dignity, naked from the waist up, his face composed except for two small spots of angry color high on his cheekbones, he was indeed beautiful. His hair was tumbled down over his forehead, and his eyes, she observed, lost their drowsy color when he was enraged, and became almost black. She found she quite liked them that way.

But when Pompey began to tug roughly at the buttons of his breeches, a trace of real panic crossed Simon's face and he began to struggle in earnest. Partly because she was afraid he would hurt himself fighting Pompey, partly because she felt a small and unaccustomed twinge of real pity for the nobility of his efforts, she signaled Pompey to stop. A broken man was worse than no man at all, and Storme was wise enough to see the disadvantage in that.

The African backed away, and Simon stood straight,

controlling the exerted pace of his breathing with an effort, every muscle in his body tense for another attack—and every sense he possessed focused with new alertness on the woman who could precipitate it.

Her fingers carelessly stroking the blade, she walked slowly around him, inspecting him with the thoughtful detachment of one who is contemplating buying a horse. And Simon, lacking many choices, endured it.

At last drawing up before him again she commented, "You are an exceptionally well-formed man. I imagine you've many women wishing to bed you."

There was no possible reply a gentleman could make to that observation, so Simon did not even try.

"You have experience in such matters?" she persisted, somewhat more sharply.

Simon could feel all that was sane and ordered about the world slipping slowly through his fingers, and the sensation left him somewhat dizzy. Still, he managed to demur, watching her carefully, "Some."

Storme gave a curt nod of satisfaction and made another gesture to Pompey. Simon stiffened, but the big man only resumed his station at the door, arms folded, eyes straight ahead.

Storme took her time about resheathing her cutlass, watching him all the time from the corner of her eye. To Simon the silence seemed interminable. Outside he could hear the raucous shouts and laughter of the men on shore, the lap of waves against the hull, the whip of breeze across the windows. Twilight was falling and the distant orange glow that flickered against the leaded panes must have been a bonfire.

At last Storme looked at him. "You asked my terms," she said calmly. "I have given them to you. You will make me a woman tonight; tomorrow you go free and unharmed. I will even supply you food and water, and a weapon. Few in your position could ask for more."

Simon managed, somehow, to hold her placid gaze. "And if I—refuse?"

She shrugged. "Perhaps I will kill you. Perhaps I will

merely turn you over to my men. It makes little difference to me.''

Simon let the space of two heartbeats pass. Then he murmured, ''Madame, if it will not trouble you too much—I believe I will have that drink now.''

The briefest of hesitancy showed in her eyes, and then she gestured him toward the bottle.

Simon resumed his chair with careful, deliberate grace. He lifted the bottle, wiped the neck with the palm of his hand, and brought it to his mouth. All the time he was thinking, rapidly, concisely. He felt as though he had fallen into one of those bizarre parallel worlds famed in sea-faring legend, where mermaids rode crystalline seahorses and serpents as long as a galleon glided across star-studded skies. He half expected Poseidon himself to stalk through the door at any moment, dripping seaweed and breathing fire, demanding his virtue.

Yet one thing was clear. The woman was serious. He might have fallen into madness, but even in insanity there was method, and it remained only to him to discover that method . . . to play for time.

The brandy stung his eyes and burned his empty stomach, but it did deliver a measure of false courage. She was still standing across the room from him, watching him with a mixture of idle curiosity and alert interest, and he returned her gaze. He made his shoulders relax against the hard back of the chair, his fingers absently toying with the label on the brandy bottle. He noticed there was no knife on her table, nor cutlery of any kind.

Simon said, ''Regarding your—er—proposal. Might I ask why?''

Storme lifted her shoulders, and Simon thought he observed, with that gesture, the release of a tension he had not even noticed was there before. ''I am a virgin,'' she stated. ''I've decided to dispense with the matter, and you will serve just as well as anyone else.''

Several things went through Simon's mind, then, not the least of which was astonishment. That, in the brutal, lustful world in which she lived she had attained maturity untouched—

if, indeed, she told the truth—was a matter worthy of notice in someone's book of miracles. But then he considered the huge beast who guarded her door and thought that perhaps it was not so unlikely after all—and when he remembered the way she had wielded that cutlass, her purity became a definite possibility. But all he said was, "Most young ladies would find that a highly desirable state, and not one to be prematurely ended."

She gave a rude snort of laughter. "I am not a lady, and I *do* wish it ended. So . . ." She strode impatiently toward him. "Let us put an end to this chatter and be done with it."

Simon rose, an instinctive gesture of self-defense which immediately made him feel foolish—as well as did the sudden, alarmed lurching of his heart. Recovering himself, he hid his growing impatience with the entire affair behind a small smile and gave an apologetic lift of his hand. "Mistress O'Malley," he said, keeping his tone as reasonable as possible, "given your inexperience, you doubtless don't realize—and, at the risk of being indelicate, I feel constrained to point out—that such matters as those to which you refer cannot be forced."

Her eyes narrowed swiftly, and Simon could not imagine what it was he had done to engage her anger. "Do you take me for a fool?" she spat, and her face was uncomfortably close to his. "I know how the thing is done and I've seen it often forced! Do not take my *inexperience* too seriously, whoreson!" And with that she spun away from him, muttering a curse to herself that Simon was glad he did not hear.

Once again Simon's head reeled—not with the impact of her words, but with the truth they implied. Hers was a world of violence, savagery, murder, and rape, as far removed from Simon's world of beauty and order as the fields of Cypress Bay were from the depths of darkest Africa. Storme O'Malley had been raised with brutality and was so deeply immured in it she could not imagine any other way. She, a child in so many ways, was older than Simon would ever be, and for just the moment—the briefest, wavering moment—he felt a touch of sympathy for her he could not explain.

He said gently, and as plainly as possible, "That may be true, madame, in some cases. But while it is possible for a man to force a woman, the opposite, I assure you, simply is not feasible."

She turned slowly, her anger giving way to a slowly dawning comprehension. "Ah," she stated at last, with perception and satisfaction. "You fear your organ will not rise."

Simon felt color—incredible and heated—creep up his neck and stain his jaw. Silence seemed the only dignified reply, and that was exactly what he gave.

Storme turned and paced the room, her brow knitting in concentration as she gave herself over to contemplation of this problem. Though some of her confidence might have ebbed, Simon observed, her determination did not seem to be in the least affected. She whirled abruptly and demanded, "Am I ugly?"

Simon blinked, once. "No. You are not."

"Scarred? Diseased? Unclean?"

Simon replied carefully, "Not that I can observe."

"Then . . ." She nodded with the satisfaction of accomplishment. "You have no problem." And as though to test her theory, she began to tug her shirt from her breeches.

Simon lifted a staying hand. "There are," he said quickly, "other considerations."

Her face contorted with impatience and distress, but her hands fell still. "What?" she demanded.

Simon released a small breath. "Perhaps," he suggested carefully, "we might sit down like civilized people and discuss them."

Simon waited, breath suspended, while she considered this, and felt he had gained an enormous victory when she stalked to the table, kicked out her chair, and flung herself into it. She swung her leg up onto the table again, leaned back with her arms folded across her chest, and pronounced with the benevolence of a dictator bestowing a great favor, "Very well, Farmer, I can be civilized. Talk."

Simon pulled out his own chair and sank into it gratefully, not at all sure what it was he had gained. He took up the bottle of brandy and passed it to her, and she took a healthy swallow. Simon watched in dim amazement. He had never seen a woman drink like that before; he had not even known it was possible.

"Talk," she commanded, and now there was a glint of unkind amusement in her eyes, sarcasm underscoring her tone. "Tell me what it is you require to cause this mysterious flesh of yours to swell."

Simon hid his shock for her crudity by bringing the bottle to his own lips again. He swallowed. Distractedly he cast about for some reply, and his eyes fell upon her bare leg, only inches before his face. It was quite a lovely extremity, at that: The foot was small, narrow, and graceful, the calf firm and well shaped, the skin a very light bronze covered with the faintest dusting of downy hair. Simon wondered what it would feel like to take that slim, silky leg in his hands, to feel the muscle and trace the curves. But he simply could not imagine doing such a thing.

He lifted his eyes to hers again, and he cleared his throat. "In general," he began carefully, "there is a brief period of—courtship, if you will, wherein the parties involved allow themselves to . . . become acquainted with one another."

Storme frowned, and her tone was skeptical. "This is necessary?"

"It is—desirable."

She considered this for a moment, reluctantly, and then seemed to store away the information for another time. "Go on."

"Well . . . atmosphere is important. A fine meal—"

"I've offered you food."

"Soft lighting, congenial surroundings—"

"Bah! You *are* a petticoat!"

And suddenly Simon had an inspiration. "And privacy," he stated firmly, and moved his eyes meaningfully toward the door. "Your slave—does he intend to watch?"

Storme followed his gaze briefly. "Pompey is not my slave," she corrected him acerbically. "He serves me by choice. And," she added, as though she could not in any way understand why Simon should take objection to his presence, "he is mute, and quite devoted. He will not disturb you unless I order it, but it is his duty to guard me."

Suddenly and without any warning at all Simon's patience broke. He pushed up from the table in a rush of inexplicable emotion and exploded, "Damn it, woman, this thing cannot be accomplished at knife point with a bodyguard breathing down my neck! Have you no sensibilities at all?"

It wasn't until the words were spoken by Simon realized by uttering them he revealed that he was actually considering her absurd bargain—and that, in fact, he had been considering it for some time. Of course, such could not be the case. He intended only to disarm her, to lull her with confidence, to dispose of the bodyguard, and then make his escape.

For Storme had been right about one thing. A lack of willing partners had never been one of Simon's afflictions; consequently, he had grown to be very selective. He had never paid a woman for his pleasure, nor had he been forced—even in his youth—to resort to serving girls or tavern wenches. His taste was impeccable and quite explicit, and it encompassed cool, voluptuous brunettes artful in conversation and sophisticated in technique.

He liked porcelain skin and silky fingers, soft full hips and pliable flesh. He did *not* care for feral honey-blondes with brown skin and glittering eyes, ragged nails and offensive mouths. Storme O'Malley was hard of body and wicked of tongue, abrasive, ill-dressed, and uncouth. There was nothing beautiful, artful or soothing about her; all that he held in esteem was missing in her. The matter was simply out of the question.

And yet . . . and yet there was something insidious inside him, something wicked and exciting and vaguely dangerous, that made him wonder what it would be like. . . .

Quickly, he quelled these unworthy thoughts, faintly disgusted with himself, and pronounced calmly and with resolve, "I see we have reached an impasse. There is no point in further entertaining the subject. What you ask, madame, is quite simply impossible."

The expression that crossed the girl's eyes as she looked

at him was strange and unfamiliar. It was a disappointment, a flickering waver of slipping resolve—a peculiar and unexpected vulnerability that completely caught Simon off guard. She sighed then, very softly, and dropped her eyes. She pushed up from the table, and walked away.

The slump of her shoulders seemed curiously dejected, and Simon realized with a start that she was not a very large woman after all. She was somewhat tall for her sex, it was true, but it was only her bearing and her mannerisms that gave the appearance of formidability. Now, with her head bowed and her back to him, in those ill-fitting men's clothes and the waist-length spray of hair, she looked very much like a child playing at grown-up games.

She turned, and surprised Simon with an expressive lift of her shoulders, palms open, a gesture of truce—or defeat. There was the faintest hint of a self-mocking, uncertain smile on her lips as she confessed, "You are right, Farmer. I am inexperienced. But I am not stupid. I can learn, and you will be my teacher. You will guide and I will follow, and we will cease these foolish arguments. Is that fair?"

A thousand objections sprang to Simon's mind, but he was too disoriented by her sudden change of mood to voice them. He merely nodded, hesitantly.

As though to prove her willingness to cooperate, she inquired in a much friendlier tone than she had used heretofore, "You have a name?"

"Yes." Simon watched as she pulled the lantern down by the chain and turned up the wick. The twilit shadows disappeared into a bright, serviceable glow. "It's Simon." Foolishly, he found himself on the verge of giving his full name, just as though he were introducing himself in someone's parlor, but caught the error just in time.

She cast a critical eye toward the lantern. "And does the lighting suit your fancy, Simon?"

Simon opened his mouth to protest that such pleasantries were redundant and inappropriate since there was no possibility—simply none—that he would engage in her game. And then he remembered that the primary purpose of this exercise was to so occupy her attention that he might effect an escape, and he said, "A little dimmer, perhaps."

Obligingly, she turned down the wick to a pleasant golden glow.

Simon took a breath, and an enormous chance. "It is necessary, you know, for there to be some amount of trust between us if this thing is going to work at all. Perhaps you could send your servant away, and—lay aside your weapon."

She hesitated, and Simon did not release his breath until her fingers went to the leather belt that held her knife. But Storme was no fool. She walked over to Pompey, placed the knife in his hand, and said, "Stand outside the door. You are not to enter until I summon you, and you will let no one pass. Wait." She bent, rolled up her one breeches leg, and extracted a small, evil-looking blade from the garter that held it against her thigh. This, too, she placed in Pompey's hand. "No one," she repeated, and dismissed him.

Simon tried to be philosophical. True, now that Pompey had taken the weapons he would not be able to arm himself—but at least now she was unarmed, too. The odds were closer to being equal, and Simon was certain he even had some sort of advantage . . . if he could only discover how to use it.

Storme returned to him. "And now. This matter of acquaintanceship—is it so very important to you?"

It struck Simon then, fully and perhaps for the first time, the full absurdity of the situation. He was literally living out a male fantasy as old as Adam, yet all he could think of was escape. What should have been a dream most men dared not even conjure up was in fact a nightmare with deadly undertones, for reality, as he was rapidly discovering, rarely made itself accommodating to one's conception of it. It was strange, how many harsh lessons of life he had learned in the few short hours he had been the prisoner of this woman.

He said earnestly, because now he really wished to know, "What is important to me is why. Why do you wish to do this thing?"

Storme spent very little time pondering the answer. "Because I have reached two and twenty years, and I grow bored contemplating the mystery. I would know what is this grand obsession that so occupies men and women, and I would know it well."

"You may not like what you discover."

She shrugged. "Then so be it. Ignorance is danger, Farmer Simon, and I can afford neither. And now." Full of authority again, she became brisk and commanding. "You are to be my teacher. Tell me how the thing is generally done."

She walked over to the table again and perched upon its edge, taking up a ripe plum. Her eyes were alert and curious as she began to peel the fruit, waiting for him to reply.

What a disconcerting woman she was! A terror one moment and an innocent the next. He looked at her soberly for a long moment, and his voice was quiet. "You are determined upon this course?"

She nodded impatiently, swiping at the plum juice on her mouth. "Teach me," she replied, and the command was so beguiling—and so utterly inappropriate—that Simon smiled.

He came over to her, hardly knowing where to begin. She tossed the plum pit onto the table and wiped her hands on her breeches, looking up at him expectantly. Simon took a breath. "In general, I suppose, one begins by creating a mood conducive to romance. A stroll through the garden, perhaps, a secluded portico, an evening of music and gentle conversation . . ."

She frowned a little, though whether in confusion or disapproval Simon could not be sure. His eyes wandered to the windows. They were too narrow by far for him to slip through, even if he could manage to reach them before she alerted someone of his attempt. The door, unmistakably guarded as it was, was out of the question. And even if he somehow managed to quit the ship, the woods were filled with pirates who already had promised to use him much less gently this night than had Storme. She had promised to release him on the morrow, but dared he believe her?

Did he have a choice?

Simon looked back to her. He could not do it. He simply could not. "Of course, most ladies make an effort to make themselves appealing to their gentleman long before this point.''

That caught her interest. "How?"

He racked his brain. What did he know of female fripperies, after all? Only that when it was done well, it was exquisite, and when it was not, he knew it. "Ah . . . many things. Face powder, hair ribbons, perfume. A pretty gown, a tasteful jewel. Many things.''

She seemed genuinely puzzled. "Why, when it must all come off in bed anyway?''

Simon chuckled. He couldn't help it. "An astute question, my dear. Would that I knew the answer.''

She dismissed it all with a grimace. "Bloody foolery, if you ask me." Then she looked at him narrowly. "You think I don't know about men and women and the power one has over t'other? I am not so ignorant as that, Farmer!" She gave a snort of disdain. "You think I don't know I could have you groveling at my feet if I took off my shirt or showed you my thighs—the matter is not so difficult as you make it appear, fine sir! Primping and pampering and sniffing around—that's for whores and tavern wenches. Storme O'Malley doesn't have to trick or connive to get a man. I *command*; I do not beg. So go on with your talk of games and pretty nonsense," she announced imperiously, "but do not expect me to be impressed.''

Simon realized, finally and without a doubt, that he had no choice. Escape was impossible, and any attempt would doubtless be deadly. What awaited him on the morrow he had no idea, but for tonight . . . he had no choice. Whether he be caught in a nightmare from hell or a touch of heaven, he must do the deed to the best of his ability and take his chances with tomorrow. The prospect was not quite as appalling as it once had been, but still he could not bring himself to look upon it with a great deal of relish. For if he failed . . .

He cleared his throat and gathered his thoughts. "Then, commonly, the lovers draw close, and say endearing things to one another. . . .''

"Like what?''

Simon could not think of a single thing.

Her face, tilted up to him in unabashed curiosity, was quite comely at that. Her features were a bit sharp for his taste—the nose too proud, the mouth too wide, the structure too angular—but all in all it was not an unappealing countenance. And her eyes, set off by her golden skin, were the purest crystalline blue he had ever seen. Not cornflower, not sapphire, but bright, water-clear blue, and the color alone was captivating. Her scent, he imagined, would be wholly natural, a little salty, rich in the things of womanhood.

Very slowly, he lifted his hand. She watched him, but did not object, as he reached for the thong which bound her hair. He was aware of a slight tightness to his breathing, but that was due more to trepidation than arousal.

Gently, careful not to tear any strands, he pulled the thong loose. With his hands he fluffed her hair forward a bit, and it framed her face like a silk curtain. Its texture was smooth and rich and heavy, just as it looked. He smiled a little, though whether it was as reassurance to her or to himself, he was not sure.

There was nothing but frank curiosity in her gaze. "You like my hair?"

"Yes. It's very lovely."

And then she smiled. It was an expression he instinctively knew was rare, yet it was wholesome and unforced, without artifice or contrivance. It was enchanting. "So, there is something of me that pleases, eh, Farmer? Mayhap your chore won't be as distasteful as you thought."

Simon dropped his hands, the brief tenuous moment gone.

Storme looked disgruntled. "Must there always be so much to it? Talking and touching and walking and crooning. Why do you spend so much time? I think you don't know as much of it as you pretend," she challenged.

Simon fought a battle with exasperation and lost. "You asked me to tell you how it's done. I assumed you wanted to know how it's *properly* done. I apologize if my methods don't meet with your approval!"

"*That* for proper!" She made a twisting upward gesture

with her fist, her color suddenly angry. "You try my patience, Farmer!"

"And you, my dear young witch, sorely try mine!"

They stood before one another, glaring and tense, for an interminable moment. And then suddenly, unexpectedly, Storme laughed. "You do have spirit," she observed, her eyes dancing. "I began to wonder!" Then, shrugging, "I said you might teach me. Touch my hair, if it pleases you."

"Frankly, whatever pleasure there may have been has completely dissipated," Simon muttered, and started to turn away.

She caught his hand, surprising him, and pulled him back. There was no anger on her face now, merely the childlike expectation and a hint of stubbornness. "Not for me," she informed him, and she brought his hand deliberately to her hair.

Simon let his hand trail down the silky length of her hair to her collarbone, and then, with his knuckles, he lightly, experimentally, stroked the curve of her neck, watching her intently. "Is it true then?" he demanded quietly, hardly believing it. "No man has ever touched you before?"

"Not like this," she answered simply, and there seemed to be a widening, or a darkening, of her eyes as he continued the gentle caressing motions against her neck. He could almost feel her skin grow pliable to his touch, and suddenly, inexplicably, he was moved to tenderness for her. She no longer seemed like a devil in man's clothing, no longer an enemy to be outwitted or outbattled. She was just a very young—and in her own peculiar way—very enchanting woman.

He could see the faint outline of her nipples through the material of her shirt, and realized with something of a shock that she was wearing no chemise. He found the notion wicked and intriguing, and was suddenly seized by a curiosity—and it was no more than that, he was certain—to know what her body would feel like, pressed against his.

Cautiously, almost hesitantly, he brought his hands to her shoulders, drawing her to her feet. She never took her gaze off his, and that patient, crystal-eyed expectation in her expression was almost his undoing. His voice was thick with nervousness and uncertainty as he asked, "Would you like me to kiss you now?"

She nodded.

The courage that simple act required amazed him. Careful not to hold her too tightly, or to make any moves that she might construe as threatening, he leaned toward her. Warily, and with the very greatest of care, he brought his lips against hers.

* *Chapter Nine* *

At first it was a pressing of the lips, nothing more, and Storme found the entire business distinctly disappointing. But then, because she was curious, and because it seemed an easy thing to do, she lifted her hand and touched the bare flesh around his waist. Since he had entered the room, that beautiful male torso had intrigued her; she had wondered what it would feel like to touch, to press, to caress. And the sensation now was even better than she had imagined.

His skin was warm and firm and strange, and perhaps it was the very strangeness that excited her. His waist was tight, and young and spare, his ribs firmly sheathed in hard muscle, his spine straight and strong. She moved her other hand then, dissatisfied by what she could discover with only one set of fingers, and then the kiss changed.

It was as though her touch had triggered a response in him, and there was something oddly exhilarating—as well as disturbing—about that. The give-and-take of human intercourse was alien to her, and for a moment she was so absorbed in the new sensations he was creating against her mouth that she almost forgot her own curiosity about his body. She felt a breath tauten his lungs, and his lips moved against hers, opening a little, pressing more firmly. At the same time his hands, which had been resting tenuously upon her shoulders, slipped to her back and drew her against him.

She felt his length from chest to thigh, strong and hard and warm. She could feel, through the silk of her shirt, the soft abrasive texture of his chest hair against her nipples with a sensitivity to touch she had never imagined she possessed before. And his mouth, now quickening upon hers, demanding—the sensation was heady. It made her pulse beat faster and her breath grow shallow, and a compulsion she could not define caused her to move her lips experimentally against his, just as he was doing to her. It was pleasant. Most pleasant.

So occupied was she with the newness of all of this that it was a time before she became aware of the knot of heat and hardness pressing against her thigh . . . and even a further moment before she recognized it for what it was. When she did, a surge of pleasure rushed through her and she jerked her mouth away. "There, Farmer!" she exclaimed triumphantly. "The matter is not so difficult as you supposed!"

A shadow of confusion crossed Simon's passion-bright eyes, and he moved away a little. He did not know how it had happened. Some said that danger was an aphrodisiac, that fear was arousing. Simon only knew that what had begun as a chore, a tenuous act of courage, had somehow, the moment he felt her lithe young body pressed against his, become incredibly exciting.

She tasted of honey and plums. She smelled of hot yellow sunshine and clear water. And her experimental, guileless response to him was a stimulant like none he had ever known.

Now the contact was broken, and the spell that seemed to have momentarily ensnared him should have evaporated. It did not. Her skin was flushed with victory—or excitement—and her eyes as bright and eager as a summer day. Her lips, rouged with fruit juice and the contact with his, were slightly parted and upturned. It was becoming more and more difficult to recall he was performing under duress—that he was performing at all. He waited for the frustration, the distaste, the ebbing of arousal—even the anger—but it did not come. Helplessly, hopelessly, he felt himself compelled toward her, and all he could do was smile.

"Perhaps, madame," he murmured, and there was a touch of indulgent amusement in his tone, "this would go more smoothly if you kept your observations to yourself from now on."

Storme was momentarily taken aback, and sullen resentment briefly flashed in her eyes. But, having gotten this far, she did not want to do anything to adversely affect his capricious physiology, and after a moment, she nodded meekly. She removed her hands from about his waist, not wishing to take any chances.

His smile—that slightly rakish, unbelievably enchanting smile—deepened a fraction at one corner. "That is not necessary," he said, and lifted her hands to his waist again. "In fact, one might even say that a certain amount of touching at such a moment could be beneficial."

It surprised Storme to realize that she liked him even better when he was smiling than she did when he was angry. She wondered if there was any way she could make him do it more often, or if that, too, was out of her control.

He lifted his hand and caught a strand of her hair, bringing it forward of her shoulders, stroking it with his long fingers. It was an innocuous movement, tender, soothing, pleasant. She liked that, too. And his eyes . . . the way he looked at her . . .

It was not until that moment that Storme really believed it would happen. With her customary single-minded determination she had set upon this course, giving little thought to the consequence or, in fact, the reality of it. But something had changed, in the past few moments. He had transformed from a reluctant bridegroom to a man of purpose, and she was about to undergo the most important, destiny-changing event of her life. She was frightened.

It was not the intimacy that disturbed her, nor even the strangeness of it. He would hurt her, she knew, and make her bleed, but that first and very real consequence of what she was about to do was not what made her suddenly feel like a skittish colt ready to bolt.

It was that for the first time in her life, she was placing her fate in the hands of someone other than herself. She, who would fight to the death any man who tried to set foot aboard her ship without permission, was about to allow her very body to be invaded by a stranger, her senses controlled, her will rendered helpless. She would prostrate herself beneath this stranger and allow him to commit acts upon her person which she may or may not desire. She would surrender.

Storme was not at all certain she could do that.

And yet she did not, even for the wildest, fleeting moment, consider stopping it now. Once her mind was set, it had never been changed. Reasons might change, circumstances might change, wishes might change, but Storme steered a true course. That was the sign of a good captain. She wanted this. She had determined upon it. And it terrified her.

There were soft lights in his eyes that made her uneasy even as they intrigued her. And the gentling motions of his fingers in her hair, as much as she liked them, seemed designed to put her off her guard. When he leaned forward and brushed his lips against hers in a series of light, almost playful motions, it took all the will at her command not to back away.

He curled his hand around her neck and pressed his lips against hers again, briefly. He seemed amused by her lack of response, but she refused to be disarmed by his smile. He brought his lips close again, toying with hers, and he murmured, "Open your mouth, dear."

She stared at him. "Why?"

His eyes crinkled at the corners, and his fingers threaded through the hair at her temples. "You will see." His lips touched hers again.

She arched her head back to look at him. "What are you going to do?"

He whispered, "Something pleasant." And his fingers tightened on the base of her neck, tilting her head back. His mouth covered hers.

There was a softness to his lips, a warm and enveloping

moisture that was gentle, not demanding. The sensation caught her unprepared, and her nerves, already drawn taut, betrayed her with a rush of pulses and catch of breath. Heat flooded her face and her eyes instinctively closed.

She felt his thumb lightly stroking the side of her face, near her mouth. His lips were drawing on hers, caressing and soothing, gently urging until hesitantly, almost unconsciously, her lips began to part beneath his.

The warm, wet invasion of his tongue was a shock. Her heart lurched, and then went wild. A fever rushed upward to her brain and left her dizzy. Suddenly she was aware of a place between her thighs to which she had never given much conscious thought before, and nothing in her imagination could have given her foresight into sensations like these. His tongue skated over her teeth, probed the surface of her tongue, tasted the recesses of her mouth. It thrust and withdrew and thrust again, possessively, with purpose. His moisture mingled with hers. Her nipples tingled and swelled, and the weakness of her limbs appalled her, but there was nothing she could do about it. The sensation filled her and paralyzed her, and the alien pleasure he was creating inside her held her captive.

When he withdrew she still could taste him—a masculine taste, faintly salty, laced with wine—for already he had left his mark on her in a way that could not be erased. Her breathing was alarmingly uneven, but it was some strange consolation that his was no less so. And her arms were still wrapped around his waist, for she was not at all certain, even now, that her tingling legs would support her.

It was a moment before she could open her eyes. When she did she saw his face, very close to hers, flushed and somewhat damp and incredibly handsome. His hair was tousled, shadowing his cheeks and his forehead, a few rich auburn strands clinging to the dampness of his brow. His eyes were dark, just as they had been when she had enraged him before, but he was not angry now. Hungry lights of some unknown origin played deep within their charcoal depths, and his heavy lids seemed to hide a powerful secret.

His lips curved faintly in a smile that was almost absent,

for his attention was busy on her face, her eyes. He said huskily, "Well?"

She leaned back a bit to better view him. "I think, Simon the Farmer," she said softly, "that you do this very well."

His smile deepened, his chest rose and fell softly with a chuckle. His hand caressed her hair again, and she knew the gesture for what it was—tenderness. How strange that something so completely unknown to her before this moment could come so quickly to be welcomed.

She said, a little hesitantly and watching him carefully, "Do women—ever do the same to men? With the tongue?"

Something flickered through his eyes; whether it be surprise, amusement, or pleasure she could not be sure. But he only murmured, continuing the wonderful, soothing motions of his fingers against her hair, "Occasionally. Would you like to try?"

She felt her throat grow tight in anticipation. She nodded and reached up toward him.

She tasted his lips first and then, tentatively, the smoothness of his teeth. He angled his head and pressed her close, making it easy for her. She let her tongue slip inside.

It was darkly exciting, powerfully thrilling. Even more than when he had done it to her, this discovery of maleness sent her blood to rushing and her heart to tumbling, arrhythmic poundings. And when he reciprocated, his tongue mating against hers, his mouth pressing hard, his body growing tight, there was such an explosion of delight within her that it left her weak.

She wanted to discover more of him, to claim more and know more. Her hands rippled up the smooth expanse of his back, spreading across tight, unyielding shoulders, defining the muscles of his arms. She caught his hair in her fingers, felt the dampness of his neck and the heat of his scalp. Her hands moved down, fingertips brushing the damp thatches of hair beneath his arms, and then slipping beneath their bodies to explore the breadth of his chest, silky hair and straining muscles, humid warmth and thundering heart.

His mouth left hers in a catch of breath and traveled to her neck, focusing every nerve ending upon the pressure of his lips there. Her head fell back in delight as his kiss traveled to her throat, and then to the sensitive lobe of her ear. She shuddered, adrift in fever and mindless pleasure.

His hands cupped her breasts, drawing a startled gasp from her, for never had she imagined a man's touch could feel like this. It was light at first, caressing, and then more firm, maddening. His thumbs found the engorged tips of her nipples and circled lightly, rubbing the material of her shirt into pliant flesh, and she felt a sharp arrow of desire pierce her lower regions. It was an ache that coiled in upon itself, a nameless need that was almost a discomfort, and it centered directly from the gentle massaging motions of his fingertips against her breast. She wanted to cry out for him to stop and thereby put an end to this torture, but before she could do so he stopped of his own accord and that was even worse.

He drew her against him tightly, covering her mouth with his. She drew from him greedily, helplessly, stretching her arms around his neck, instinctively pressing herself into the hard male part of him that pushed against her belly. She was trembling, she was dizzy, she could not think. And she knew the mystery now. She knew the obsession. She knew why men and women did this thing, and could not imagine why she had ever questioned it.

When he lifted his face from hers she was reeling, breathless, awash with sensations that were demanding and confusing and utterly unquenchable. His face was a blur of passion and masculinity before her, his eyes focal points of brilliant darkness. His breath left whispers of uneven heat across her cheek.

She said, surprised when her voice came out as barely more than a hoarse whisper, "Now?"

His fingers brushed across her lips with an unsteady touch. "Yes," he answered gently, on a catch of breath. "I think so."

He stepped away from her, and she watched in sharp confusion as he reached for the lantern. "What are you doing?"

"Turning down the light."

"Why?"

He looked at her, gentle tolerance mixed with mild amusement. "Because, my dear, such things as we are about to do are generally best accomplished in the dark."

But she rebelled at that. Her fears were back, an unreasonable edging forth of panic, and she seized on this small fingerhold of control. She would not be held helpless in the dark. She would see the face of the man who did this to her.

"No," she commanded, and the sharpness of her tone seemed to startle him. "Leave it be."

He hesitated for a moment, reflecting confusion and mild distraction, then he smiled. "As you wish."

He came back to her, and laid his hands upon the bloused waist of her shirt, pulling it upwards. Nervously, she stepped back. Her voice was barely on the safe side of shrillness. "What are you doing?"

He laid a calming hand upon her shoulder. "I am removing your clothes, dear, and that, I fear, is one process that is *not* negotiable."

Again she balked, unwilling to be stripped naked while he remained fully clothed. "Why?" she demanded. "Why must I be naked first?"

A small frown shadowed his eyes, dampened his desire-flushed features. "Customarily—"

"I care naught for custom!"

An odd sort of understanding seemed to come to him as he studied her, and with it a measure of frustration, even reluctance. "Madame," he said somewhat stiffly, "if you're having second thoughts—"

"I'm not having any such thing!" she returned, a shade too sharply. "But you will undress first."

The perception in his eyes made her uncomfortable; the patience with which he endured her outburst maddened her. A long time seemed to pass before he spoke again, and when he did it was very quietly. "Perhaps now is an appropriate time for you to take a moment to consider what it is you really want. If you persist on demanding this thing of me, there shortly will come a point when you will not be able to retract your invitation. You see, madame..." He smiled faintly, and his gentle mockery seemed to be self-directed. "I find, much to my surprise, that your allure is quite unmistakable, and is growing a bit more difficult to resist than I had thought."

Allure. He had called her alluring. He wanted her, and that was a potent, however unfamiliar, stimulant.

She half-turned, frustrated with all that was battling within her, and tucked her fingers into her sash tightly. Turn back? It was unthinkable. But why was she suddenly finding it so difficult to deal with the sensations, the emotions, the tangled thoughts that intruded into her usually very well-organized mind?

She burst out abruptly, "I don't know what I want! How can I know when I don't know—*any* of it!" She clenched her teeth, ashamed of the outburst and the weakness it revealed, and spent a silent moment battling with herself over matters she could not even define. When she turned at last, she knew she was crossing a line from which she could never retreat.

She lifted her chin. She said quietly, and with decision, "I want it to continue."

There seemed to be a flicker of relief—or perhaps not—in his eyes, she could not be sure. But the emotion, whatever it was, seemed to surprise even him, for he quickly lowered his lashes to disguise it. And without a word, he walked over to her sea trunk, where he sat to remove his shoes and his stockings.

Storme sat on the bed to wait for him, and she felt the sensations begin again—the sluggish thump of pulses, the tightening of breath, the slight dryness of her throat, as he stood and unbuttoned his breeches. He slipped the garment over his slim hips and stepped out of it, and all the while his eyes were on her. Her eyes were on him.

He was even more beautiful in his nakedness than he had been clothed. She could not prevent a small catch of breath, for she had never imagined before that the male body, plain and unadorned, could be called that. Beautiful.

His shoulders were broad and square, the indentations of collarbone and arms defined by lean, firm muscles. His chest flowed in a simple, unpretentious swell toward a flat abdomen and tight hips. His nipples were brown and flat, his ribcage lightly rippled with bone and sinew. She could see the muscles that formed his thighs, and the hard swell of his calves. The hair on the private parts of his body was the same dark golden color as that on his chest.

Storme had seen the male member before, of course—swollen and flaccid, old and young, diseased and healthy—and had never remarked it in particular except to observe that it was a slightly grotesque, almost comical, extremity and—it appeared to her, at least—not enormously practical. She could not recall ever having been so fascinated by its appearance before. Nor could she ever remember noticing how large it was, or how long. It seemed, in fact, at this proximity, enormous.

Staring at him, she blurted the only thing that was on her mind. "Will it fit?"

Simon laughed. It was a low sound, deep and full and delighted, and though Storme's eyes went to his in sharp suspicion, she saw nothing there but pleasure.

He lowered one knee to the bed to sit beside her, and he took her face in his hand. His eyes were clear and gray and dancing with laughter, and he said, "Storme O'Malley, you are . . ." He paused and shook his head a little, full and easy mirth still cavorting in his eyes. "I have no words to describe what you are."

When he laughed like that, when he held her face and looked into her eyes with such bemusement and affection, it was as though . . . it was as though she was a maiden and he was her gallant young beau, as though they were friends of long acquaintance, as though barriers had never existed and the two of them, together like this, were the most natural thing in the world. For that brief moment, Storme knew closeness, and though she knew she should guard herself against it, she could not. She did not even want to, for at that instant he kissed her.

How quickly the embers of passion caught and reflamed! For now it was not only his lips, his taste, his scent, his power that encompassed her, but his body, strong and lean and naked, surrounding her, enfolding her, awakening her.

Dizziness swelled and fever rushed, taking her breath, filling her pores, stripping her will. The world of reason and caution faded away with the opening of an entirely new world—one dominated by the senses, by amplified awareness, by need and desire.

Their mouths parted but their breaths did not. His, heated and moist and ragged, fanned her face; hers, gasping and uncertain, melted into his. Her fingers, impatient and clumsy and overlarge, fumbled with her clothes, and his were there to assist her, pulling her shirt over her head, tugging her breeches off her legs. And in an instant so potent and aware it was like the slap of a cresting wave, she felt the full length of his body against her own naked skin.

Her legs, so strong and powerful, felt small and smooth and delicate against his. She felt the roughness of male hair that dusted his thighs against the bareness of her own. Her arms, the lean essence of tightly muscled strength, were limp and flowing as they encircled his back. Her flat, spare belly became soft, pliant flesh against the weight of his rigid member, pressed against her.

He held her like that for an exquisite moment, touching her, feeling her, every part of his body covering hers. The sensations were so many and so intense that she could not even absorb them all. And then, relieving her of a weight she had barely noticed, he turned onto his side, drawing her close.

His lips were upon her face, lingering leisurely kisses that tasted rather than touched, and his hand stroked her body from shoulder to hip, making her shiver with pleasure.

Desperate with curiosity and need, her own hands began to explore. The thick silken luxury of his hair, the tight cords of his neck, the planes of his back, slippery with perspiration and sheathed in power and grace. The curve of his buttock was rock hard, and his thigh was muscle. She liked the way his breathing speeded when she touched him there. But there was more.

She stopped her hands, and she made herself shift away from the exquisite play of his tongue over her throat to look at him. "Can I touch it?"

A heartbeat passed, and his eyes were such a dilated mixture of hues of darkness and lights that she could not tell whether it was shock or reluctance that registered there. And then he whispered, huskily, "If you like."

Storme slipped her hand between their bodies and closed her fingers hesitantly around him.

She did not know what she expected, for her curiosity about the matter had never been great, but she had not imagined it would feel like this to the touch. Heated and mast-stiff, unyielding and firmly ridged. Yet the flesh was silky, slippery, and the length of it . . . the breadth of it . . . It filled her hand, and more. It frightened her, and it intrigued her.

She felt his sharp intake of breath when her fingers closed, and she glanced at him quickly. His eyes were closed, his head pressed back against the pillow, and his face was tightly drawn, as though in concentration, or pain. Cautiously, she explored further, discovering the bulging tip, the fragile, mobile sack at the shaft. Curiosity, trepidation, and delight mingled into a hard knot of excitement within her, and she gave herself over to this new adventure, imbuing herself with a knowledge that was strictly and secretly male until with a sudden deep groan low in his throat, Simon caught her hand.

"Enough, for the love of God," he ground out, and she thought she had angered him until he turned and covered her mouth hungrily with his.

She responded eagerly, arching against him, winding her fingers in his hair, drinking of him. There was a restlessness inside her, a building impatience, an expanding emptiness she could not understand or explain, and it was gradually taking over every part of her. She wanted . . . she *wanted* . . .

And she trembled, every part of her trembled, when Simon lowered his head to her breasts, and she felt the heat and moisture, the excruciating suckling motions, of his mouth there.

She thought it must be madness. The gentle, stroking motions of his tongue across her nipples, his hands cupping her breasts, his heat redoubling her own. The touch of his lips lightly on her chest, her ribcage, her belly. His fingers stroking her skin. The ache that wound tight in her belly, the swelling, tingling discomfort between her legs. It hurt. It was ecstasy. She writhed and she moaned against it, seeking surcease, but there was none. She wanted him to stop. She would scream if he stopped.

But when his fingers drifted downward over the thatch of hair low on her abdomen, some swift primal shaft of fear caused her instinctively to clamp her legs together. Simon brought his face back to hers. His lower jaw was coarse against her cheek, his breath very uneven. She could feel the heat of his skin even through the raw flame of hers.

"Easy, little one," he whispered, and insistently his fingers moved lower. "I just have to make you ready, so it won't hurt. Loosen your legs . . . there . . . let me show the place where I am meant to be . . ."

It seemed the hardest thing Storme had ever done to relax her muscles, yet at the same time the most natural, the most inevitable. It was surrender. And the rewards were worth the cost.

Delicate fingers played the moist folds of her most private flesh, bringing a sweet hypnotic pleasure that was so intense she almost cried out from the beauty of it. Her pulses grew molten and her body liquid, and all that she had ever known of herself faded away, leaving only a sharp knot of awareness that focused on the exquisite, aching need he was building inside her. And just when she thought the torment could not grow any more profound, he slipped one slender finger inside her, and it had only begun.

Simon was a skilled lover, though he knew no conceit in the fact. Generosity was instinctive with him, and he gave pleasure because pleasure was natural to him. He did not know at what point the pleasure of this slender young girl had become more important than his own, nor how it was that he had so quickly lost himself to the experience that was not of his making nor, presumably, of his desire. He knew only that at some point he had lost the reasons why and had become helplessly immersed in the unfolding moments.

There was something wild and alien about her strong, lithe young body, and perhaps its very strangeness was the intoxicant. She was sinew and muscle, straining passion and shuddering need, and he responded to her with the deep primal admiration and instinctive awe one might feel for a creature of the wild, wholly beautiful and unflawed. There was no artifice or design about her. Everything she felt she felt with all her soul, and Simon, drawn into the well of sensation she created, only wanted to make her feel more.

When she cried out with pleasure and need, twisting her head upon the pillows and digging her fingers into his shoulder, Simon was gripped by a fierce savage thrill and he knew he could not delay any longer. He moved above her, replacing his artful fingers with himself.

Through the hot blur of passion a thin thread of reason remained, and he half-expected her to struggle then, in panic and fear. It would not have mattered if she did, for the moment was far beyond the control of either of them. He felt the resistance of her membrane, and could not tell if the cry she gave was of pain or need. He brought a shaking hand to her face to soothe her, but with another fierce cry she wrapped her arms around him and arched her hips. He sank into her deeply.

Storme could not have said afterward whether or not there was pain. All she felt was the sensation, the stretching, the filling, the burning deep inside her that his entry both intensified and eased. The want that felt like rage, the rigid, intense awareness that felt like ecstasy. He pushed inside her, deeper, and then deeper still, until she thought she would burst with him. His shoulders were trembling beneath her hands, his breath barely a gasp against her neck. She could feel something within him—surprise?—and a ragged whisper seemed to be torn from him, "Storme . . ." His hands slipped beneath her hips, and he thrust more deeply inside her, so that she could feel the agonizing pressure of him at the very core of her. His head fell against her shoulder and he gasped hoarsely, "Ah, God, Storme . . ." And then he began to move inside her.

His thrusts were as strong as a heartbeat. She lost herself

in the rhythm, the struggle, the aching, blossoming need whose fulfillment was just outside her reach. She wanted to cry with frustration and weep with pleasure. Nothing existed except her body, this strange new awareness, this dark and whirling conflict of sensations and desires. There was not a series of moments, but one single intense everlasting moment in which she was filled and she was empty, she was wanting and she was exquisitely content, in which she realized, in a starburst of cognizance, that she had never known anything of life before now.

Her harsh, dry breathing became matched with his; the perspiration that swathed her body blended with his own. She clutched at him and she rose to him, and when his thrusts became faster she knew nothing but his movement, the glory that was propelling her toward the brink of something she could not quite reach, something terrifying and elemental, something that pushed aside all else in the world except Simon, and herself.

His muscles stiffened beneath her hands, his breath stopped, and she felt him shudder as he plunged deeply into her one last time. And then he was still. The harsh sound of his breathing filled her ears, a burning glow spread over her body, her head spun. But she could not prevent a small shaft of disappointment as he braced his arms and slid away from her.

She was trembling. Her hair was wet and prickly against her back, her skin raw and feverish, and she could not seem to catch her breath. Her heart beat so strong and hard that it hurt. His absence left an emptiness inside her, but his presence had filled her with such ecstasy that her head still roared from it. She wanted him, and, like a nursling seeking its dam, instinctively she flowed toward the source of her fulfillment.

She flung an arm across his chest, nestling her head against his shoulder, winding her leg around one of his. He brought one arm around her, and she could feel the trembling of the muscles there as he drew her close. His breathing was so harsh and uneven that it almost blocked the roar of her own, and his heart was like thunder.

He whispered, at length, and with an effort, "My dear . . ." And then, bringing his lips to her hair with a lingering motion, he finished simply, on a sigh, "My dear."

She turned her face to him. His hair, as wet as hers, clung to his forehead and his neck in dark waves; his skin was still bright with the haze of passion, his eyes deep and content, and in some vague way, astonished with pleasure. She inquired, "Is that all?"

He was momentarily startled, and then his eyes crinkled at the corners. She liked that crinkling when he smiled. "Was it not enough?"

She lowered her face to his shoulder again, inhaling the rich scent of him—and of her. Yet her forehead furrowed with a small frown, and she answered slowly, "No . . . I do not think so."

He chuckled, weakly. His torso shook with it and the sound filled Storme with a warm and easy pleasure. His fingers tightened in brief affection upon her shoulder, and she relaxed in the simple joy of lying with him like this.

And then he said softly, "Put your hand on me, love."

She looked up at him again, questioning, but he merely took her hand and drew it downward, between his thighs. She felt him, moist and heated and flaccid. And then, incredibly, as she touched him, he began to grow.

She cast an astonished glance at him. "Can it be done again?"

His eyes crinkled again as he moved slowly over her. "My dear," he murmured, "you have a great deal to learn."

And she did.

* ## Chapter Ten *

Simon awoke in layers, as he was accustomed to doing, for whether morning held joy or disaster, he had learned it was always best to face it a little at a time. The deepest and most abiding of these layers was the memory of the night before; it had been a real and cognizant thing to him even as he slept. Amazement filtered through as though on the wings of a fantastic dream, and the difficulty was not in convincing himself that it had really happened—rather, in trying to explain to himself how it could have not happened, given the very explicit nature of his recollection.

Simon had considered himself an experienced man; he realized now that before last night he had been a mere novice. He could not explain the chemistry of Storme's strong young body that set every pore of his on fire, yet it was unmistakably there. Women should be soft and rounded; she was not. Women should be pliable and submissive; she was not. Women should be as lovely to the eye and as gentle to the ear as a delicate spring garden; Storme O'Malley most definitely was not. Yet the feel of her sun-browned skin beneath his fingers, the taste of her pebbly pink nipples, the surge of wiry muscles . . . the rake of nails along his back, the nip of teeth on his shoulder . . . it was unlike anything he had ever known.

Yet there was more, for the act of lovemaking, to be truly memorable, must go beyond physical sensations. She frightened him, she enraged him, she enchanted him, and at last she brought him to tenderness. She was a demon and she was an innocent, savage and naive, wise and vulnerable. In a single evening she had brought him through the gamut of emotions and left him dazed and thrilled. She had taught him, for the first time in his life, the meaning of sensual adventure. She had opened doorways he was not sure he wanted to enter and was equally uncertain he could turn away from, yet the possibilities were maddening, tantalizing, exhilarating.

Even now, in the haze of sleep, he wanted her. However bizarrely this might have begun, he could not regret it now. What had happened between them last night had been outrageous, incredible, barely to be believed . . . yet it was the most real thing he had ever known in his life. He would hold it to him, he knew, like a forbidden treasure, for the rest of his days. He had been her first lover, and that was an awe-inspiring, almost sacrosanct, position for a man. And she, to him, had been . . . what? His awakening? His damnation? He knew only that something elemental had transpired between them last night, and whatever life might hold for him in the future he would never forget her . . . nor what he had known because of her.

A second layer of consciousness unfolded: desire, laced with sensation. He remembered the warmth of her tawny form curled against him, and then became aware of its absence. Instinctively he shifted his weight on the hard cot to where her body had been, and then became aware of a tautness in his arms. He tried to move his arms, seeking to embrace her, but they were raised above his head, stiff and paralyzed.

He lay still a moment, puzzled. He felt the gentle rocking of the boat, heard the muted twitter of a bird that signaled dawn. There were soft sounds of movement in the room around him, and there was something rough against his ankles. Experimentally he tried to move his arms again, and found he could not. He opened his eyes.

Storme was standing at the foot of the bed, fully dressed. Simon's arms were tightly bound to the bedpost above his head, and Storme was matter-of-factly tying his feet.

Instantly Simon was awake, all hints of physical lethargy whipped away even as mental disorientation descended upon him like a thundercloud. He bucked at the ropes, trying to free his arms. "What are you doing?"

Storme gave a final tug on the rope that bound his left ankle to the footpost and the rough hemp bit into his skin painfully. She straightened up, her eyes were distant in the gray twilight. "It ought to be plain," she answered briskly. "You are still a prisoner aboard this ship."

Simon fell momentarily still, staring at her. This could not be happening. The night that had passed he could accept, it was real, but *this* . . . No. It was part of a demented nightmare. It could not be happening.

And all he could say was, hoarsely, "Are you out of your mind?"

She checked the ropes on his right ankle.

Outrage seized him, and humiliation, a raw and naked fury like none he had ever known. After what they had done, what they had shared . . . He could never have imagined that treachery could be so dark and bitter, and could incite the madness of blind, twisting rage.

He arched up on the bed and pulled against the ropes. He flung himself forward and to the side and twisted his wrists until the skin broke; he struggled and he cursed her, and she observed him calmly. The bed creaked and the boards strained, but the ropes did not give way. He fell back again, sweating and exhausted, and he stared at her with a new kind of loathing and a horrid revulsion gradually creeping over his face.

"My God, woman," he demanded at last, hoarsely. "Have you no sensibilities at all? After what we shared? Last night—did it mean nothing to you?"

She merely looked at him, blank and uncomprehending.

A weariness seeped into Simon, tempering his incredulity, his hatred, his anger. Weariness and amazement, and—yes, regret. He looked at her, and he tried hard to understand. But he could not.

He said, in a low voice, "What kind of woman are you, that you can do such a thing? Who *are* you?"

Her head lifted a fraction; her eyes were cool and determined, and there was within them not one flicker of hesitation. She replied simply, "I am Storme O'Malley, captain of the *Tempest*."

And she turned on her heel and left him.

The coves and inlets of coastal North Carolina were myriad and labyrinthine, which was precisely what made them such preferred hiding places for pirates. Open sea melded into brackish swamps; clear sky became obscured by gnarled branches and heavy curtains of moss; sighing tide gave way to still, dark water that twisted inexorably inland, rounding a beach, cupping a pine forest, weaving its way into deep river or heavy marsh. Here a small, light schooner like the *Tempest* could hide for months if need be; here a skilled and knowledgeable captain like Storme O'Malley could lose the most determined pursuit. And here, well concealed by sloping land and dipping coves, a patrol ship had only to float at anchor, quietly, unobtrusively, and wait.

And that was precisely what the British sloop *Warrior*, flagship of Governor Alexander Spotswood's private patrol, was doing.

On a gentle slope above the cove, neatly camouflaged by pines and scrub grass, Captain Albert Fairbrother had a perfect view of his own ship below . . . and of the other ship, quietly anchored around the bend less than two hundred yards away. As a cloudy gray-gold dawn crept into the sky, dispersing mists and shedding dew, the two ships rocked in lulling twin motions, so silently they might have been ghosts. Captain Fairbrother raised his glass, almost as though to assure himself that his quarry was, in fact, real. His heart was beating very fast.

The *Tempest*. What an incredible piece of luck. A man might go his whole career without a prize like this coming into his hands. Dozens of men for half a dozen years had sought her, laid traps for her, plotted against her . . . but now she was his. His throat went dry with excitement, just briefly, and then he was in command again. This, after all, was the moment he had been trained for.

Fairbrother heard the movement and brought down his glass as his first mate drew up beside him. "Begging your pardon sir . . ." He spoke quietly, aware of the distance sound could travel over water. "But the men have been in position over an hour. They're wondering, sir, what we're waiting for?"

The captain fixed his eyes upon the *Tempest*, and replied mildly, "My orders."

The mate followed his gaze, hesitating a moment. "Sir, aren't we taking something of a chance? She's heavily armed, and known to be maneuverable. Why didn't we take her last night, when she first came in? We could've sunk her with a broadside before she knew we were about."

Fairbrother's voice was sharp. "My orders are clear. That ship is not to be damaged, do you understand? No fire is to be brought upon her under any circumstances."

"Yes, sir." The reply was quick and rote, and the mate straightened his shoulders, standing beside his captain.

Fairbrother raised his glass again, focusing on the *Tempest*, and silence went on while the two men watched the still ship from the shore. And then Fairbrother's shoulders tensed slightly, even as a faint triumphant smile curved his lips. He saw what he had been waiting for.

Storme O'Malley came on deck.

Storme approached the deck with her customary energetic stride, strapping on her knife belt, Pompey at her side. Anyone observing her would have remarked she looked the same on this morning as on any other, but inside Storme felt the difference. And the difference amazed her.

What a surprise it all had been. For all the bawdy talk and explicit knowledge she had gained of the act over the years, somehow something very basic about the entire affair had been omitted. She had never guessed the intense, all-involving levels of pleasure to which the human body could be taken, never imagined how muscles and skin and thoughts and breath could all be concentrated so completely and exclusively into a single network of sensation. And the dark, powerful explosion of release, the endless, cascading ripple of mindless, paralyzing pleasure . . . ah, that had been a surprise. A wonder. She could only marvel at her stupidity in not insisting upon discovering this miracle long before now.

And the farmer . . . A secret, satisfied smile brushed her lips as she thought of him. He had been the one, all right. She could have looked the world over and never found a better teacher. Strong, tireless, healthy, and exquisitely made . . . could she have done better, had she designed him herself, specifically for the task? What was more, he was . . . pleasant.

Afterward, when she was tired and lethargic and a little sore, he had held her in his arms as a father might hold a child, and they had slept together. She found, strangely, that she liked that almost as much as what had gone before. Sleeping with a man. She began to think how pleasant it would be to share her bed with another every night, to feel a strong naked form beside hers through the dark, to hear the sound of another breathing, to turn, in the still hours after moonset, and take those pleasures again. . . . Doubtless it would all grow troublesome after a time, but for now the prospect held a great deal of appeal.

It occurred to her, in some far-off secret part of herself, that this was what had been missing. Raoul spoke of changing times, Squint told her of abandoning her life on the seas for that of the woman she had been born to be. . . . But this, then, was the essence of it. This joining with a man and feeling a part of him, allowing something bigger than her ship and her daily responsibilities to rule her, to allow herself, in very secret fantasies, to imagine being two, not one, and to share her life with another. Not growing old alone. Having something more than the sea and its bounty to compel her, for however short a time. . . . That was what she had never known before, what she had missed. But now she knew it, and she thought that some part of her would never be the same for the knowledge. It was an unsettling truth, but at the same time a good one.

She wondered how long she could reasonably expect to keep him without bringing more trouble upon herself than he was worth.

And that was the real puzzle. She did not know how she had expected to feel the morning after—powerful? wise? older?—but it was not like this. She felt soft inside, a little dazed, distracted by daydreams, and far too concerned with the pleasures of the night—and those, perhaps, that were still to come—for her liking. Even the thought of him brought a fluttering low in her belly. She had thought it would be done and forgotten. The lingering aftereffects caught her unprepared.

It was a cool, still morning, gray mists just now dissolving into the low branches of cedar and tangled shrub. A faint damp hint of smoke tinged the air. They were well inland, but a residual back tide from the coast slapped softly against the hull and rocked the ship gently in its wake. The whispering slap of water, the faint rustle of leaves, and an occasional birdsong were the only sounds Storme heard as dawn faded into the sky.

Had she not been so distracted, so soft-minded over the farmer she had left in her quarters, Storme would have noticed the signs much earlier. As it was she almost stumbled over the loudly snoring body of one of her crewmen before she realized anything was amiss.

Her crew was sprawled out over the deck and on the banks below. Some slept with empty rum bottles in their hands; some were naked; the litter of spent kegs and uneaten food was everywhere. An occasional wisp of smoke curled upward from the charred remains of a dead campfire, and as the sun coaxed day from night, not one man of them stirred, except to choke on a rattling snore or shift in his drunken sleep.

Horror and amazement rose up in Storme like a cold wind. Where were her sentries? Who was scouting the land for camp, who was replenishing the water barrels, who was lighting the galley fires? Who had been guarding her ship while the crew engaged in drunken revelry and the captain was otherwise occupied?

She spotted the body of her quartermaster beneath the shade of the mainsail, and with a roar of rage she strode toward him. "On your feet, you rotting carcass of a dog! What the bloody hell is going on here?"

She delivered him a furious kick to the ribs, and Squint grunted, struggling to a sitting position. He stared at her for a second of open-mouthed disorientation, then got to his feet, mumbling, "It appears we got a bit carried away with the rum, Cap'n."

Black fury swept Storme and she turned to kick the nearest body, and then the next. "Damn your scurvy hide! Can't I turn my back for a bleedin' minute? Get off your asses, whoresons, before I feed your stinking corpses to the sharks," she roared. "Up with you!"

She turned on Squint. It was with all the will at her

command that she restrained from reaching for her whip, and when she found she wasn't wearing it realized it was just as well. She curled her fists tightly and commanded through clenched teeth, "Take a detail and go for water. The sun is high in the sky and we've got work to do. And..." She gestured furiously to the sleeping bodies near the campfires. "Wake the rest of those scurvy bastards on your way. Get moving!"

Squint hesitated, and Storme noticed a peculiar curiosity in his gaze. He wanted to ask about last night, she knew, and didn't dare. The reminder of her own part in this catastrophe infuriated her, and her temper rose. "Well?" she shouted at him. "Are you deaf as well as blind? *Move!*"

"Aye, Captain." And Squint shuffled off, taking several of the sluggish, terrified men with him.

The explosion of rage, coming so unexpectedly on top of the lethargy and contentments of last night's pleasures, left Storme with a headache and a foul taste in her mouth. And the worst of it was, she had only herself to blame.

The cloudy contentment left by a lover's embrace evaporated into the cool, clear light of dawn, and reality was a welcome, though bitter, sight. Why had she done this thing, anyway? For the sake of the *Tempest*, that was all, for the integrity of her command, and what had it gotten her? She had *deserted* her command, she had turned her ship over to the hands of drunken slobs who hadn't the sense to sight a whale, and she had endangered them all.

A few moments of thoughtless sensation, of convulsive rapture... no, it wasn't worth it. She was a captain, not a weak-kneed woman; she commanded *men*, not bedrooms; she was Storme O'Malley of the *Tempest*, and she had risked it all for one night of meaningless coupling.

In a sudden surge of rage and determination, she turned back toward her quarters. That cursed farmer. It was all his fault, *he* had brought her to this, and she had been a fool to think of keeping him a moment longer than she had to. She would loose him now, be rid of him once and for all, for the sooner she got back to the business at hand the better off they all would be.

Pompey grabbed her arm, but she shoved him off, still seething. She had wondered how soon before the farmer became more trouble than he was worth. The answer was the moment she had taken him aboard. She cursed herself and she cursed him, and the only thing that was on her mind was getting him out of her sight.

Pompey grabbed her arm again, this time with more urgency, and she turned, a ready oath upon her lips. Her gaze caught the direction of the mute's gesture, but it was too late. Her heart jumped at the faint but unmistakable outline of a ship's mast against the morning sky, just around the bend, and then the dawn exploded.

On a nearby knoll Captain Albert Fairbrother lifted his hand; a sharp whistle rang around. The woods burst open with uniformed men and the thunder of musket fire, and all hell's fury charged at the *Tempest*.

Squint was no more than a hundred feet into the bushes when he heard the roar of guns. As one, he and the three men with him dropped the leather buckets they had been carrying and ran back toward the clearing, stopping just short of revealing themselves.

The entire British navy seemed to be drawing force on the lone ship. The air was thick with smoke and stabbed with fire, pierced with the cries of rage and terror and death. The crewmen who had been sleeping on the ground, drugged with drink, half-dressed, and weaponless, were easy prey. They fell like flies or scattered like dust in the wind. The few aboard ship were fighting valiantly, but they hadn't a chance; the deck was red with uniforms.

In a paroxysm of horror Squint watched as two of his companions broke away, enraged at the thought of losing their booty, and rushed the ship. One staggered back beneath the force of a British sword, clutching his throat while buckets of blood turned the ground to red. Another made it halfway up the ladder to the deck, then toppled in the sea with a hideous cry as a musketball ripped away his arm.

Squint looked around to find himself completely alone. The dust and smoke of nearby fighting burned his eyes and choked his breath. The *Tempest* was lost in a misty shroud of death. Squint took one more furtive look around him, and then faded quietly back into the woods—away from the *Tempest*, and out of the line of fire.

It was a massacre. In minutes, only minutes, the deck was awash with blood, the air was choked with gunpowder and the dawn was as dark as night. Storme wielded her cutlass furiously; she felt it strike flesh twice, and a third time, but they kept coming, and all she could do was back away. Her sleeves were wet with blood, her face was streaked with it, her bare feet slid in it. She heard the fall of bodies and the screams of dying and she knew it was hopeless, but she could not stop fighting.

She shouted, "Man the guns! Every man to his post!" But there was no one to obey her command; each man was fighting for his own life. She ran toward the forward cannons, Pompey slashing a path for her with his sword, and struggled to free the binding ropes. One good blast into the thick of them as they came down the hill toward the ship . . . one solid shot and they might have a chance.

She got the bindings loose and struggled to swing the heavy cannon around. She felt a hand jerk on her hair, snapping her neck back and drawing an involuntary scream of rage and pain from her, but Pompey was there, his cutlass swinging. She heard a choked-off cry and the thud of a body hitting the deck, and her hair was free. She turned back to the cannon, and she cried, panting, "Pompey! Help me!"

The big man backed toward her, slashing his sword at those who threatened. The smoke was so thick Storme could not tell friend from enemy, but in that endless, nightmarish moment she was afraid there was no one left, no one but herself and Pompey. . . .

And then, out of the corner of her eye, she saw the red-coated officer leap at Pompey from behind a coil of rope. His blade sliced the air. It was an instant, only an instant, but it seemed to wind out forever. Pompey turned, but too late. Storme opened her mouth to cry a warning, and too late. The broadsword came down, blood spurted, and Pompey fell forward, heavy and lifeless, onto the deck.

Storme screamed, "*No!*"

She left the cannon; she rushed to Pompey. The blood-slick deck went out from under her and she fell near Pompey's body, her cutlass skittering from her hand. Of all of this she was little aware, for it was Pompey, Pompey who had loved and protected and given his life for her. . . .

She screamed again, wild and hoarse with rage, "*No!*" and whirled around, blindly searching for her cutlass. Surging to her knees, she found it. She swung around, mad with hatred and grief and revenge, and looked directly into the descending blade of a broadsword.

PART TWO

*

The Bargain

* *Chapter Eleven* *

Cypress Bay Plantation
July 1720

Barely a week had passed since Simon departed, but it seemed like a year. The hot summer days had crawled by interminably, and Augusta felt very much like a small brown mouse trapped in a maze with three ferrets.

The visit of the Misses Trelawn had not worked out at all. Daily Mistress Trelawn complained about the heat, the food, the slovenly servants, the barnyard smells. Her daughters complained of boredom, early hours, and lack of companionship. In truth, Augusta could not blame them. Now that Simon was gone the purpose of their visit had been foiled, and Augusta had very little to offer in the way of entertainment. They played cards, rode a little, improvised pathetic musicales at the harpsichord—Augusta was not much of a singer, and her fingers were clumsy at the delicate instrument—and they gossiped until they ran out of fresh material.

Augusta tried to be hospitable, but she was not a very vivacious hostess, and there were times when she found herself hard put to even be charitable with the two empty-headed girls and their overbearing mother. The highlight of the entire visit had come last evening, when Mistress

Trelawn announced abruptly—and with very insincere regrets—
that they must cut short their stay.

The wide hall of the plantation house was piled with
trunks and traveling cases; the coach horses were jingling
their harnesses in the bright morning sun outside. In the
morning room Augusta lingered over tea with the two
daughters, enduring their effusive good-byes and their impatient fidgeting as they waited for their mother to descend
and set them on their way—by God's grace, Augusta
thought wryly, to plague some other household for the
remainder of the summer.

Immediately Augusta was ashamed of the ungracious
thought, and said warmly, "I know that my brother will be
so distressed to have missed your visit completely. Perhaps
you'll stop by before your return to Bath?"

"Oh, our plans are so uncertain," began Lucinda, the
older, a little vaguely.

And Darien countered with a bright toss of her golden curls,
"Perhaps we will at that. I can scarcely wait to hear the tales
of his travels—Simon *does* tell such an entertaining story!"

Lucinda shot her sister a look sharp with jealousy beneath thick dark lashes, but her drawl was dripping with
forced indulgence as she replied, "My dear, you are such
an impatient child!"

She turned back to Augusta with a smile that would have
been warm had not the woman herself been composed of
ice. "Why, we will see you and your charming brother
again on the occasion of the governor's ball, and I'm certain
we'll have time for a nice long gossip. I'm sure you'll be
coming to Bath sometime this summer to have new gowns
made, and we'll have a fine visit then."

Augusta smiled. "Oh, that's not necessary. I have my
own seamstress here."

Lucinda returned a delicately condescending smile. "All
very fine for provincial life, I'm sure, my dear, but I do
have the most excellent dressmaker, and I'm certain she'll
be able to come up with something a bit more—ah, flattering,
to your special needs."

And Darien put in frankly, "Of course it won't be easy,

with your figure. I'm sure your girl does her best, but you really need someone with more expertise in problem areas. Your complexion is so—well—*unusual*, you know, you really should choose your colors more carefully.''

The Misses Trelawn were, of course, dressed to perfection, even for traveling. The light airy colors of the morning room, sunshine yellow and white brocade, were a perfect contrast for Lucinda's ice-blue calamanco and Darien's mauve linen, as though they had selected the colors precisely for the best effect against the background they had chosen—which, no doubt, they had. The girls changed four times a day—except when they went riding, in which case it was five—and each ensemble was calculated to show their best features to best advantage. Augusta despaired of ever becoming that fashion-wise, and was not sure she even wanted to.

Lucinda tilted her head with a thoughtful air, allowing the morning sun to catch a bauble of pink feathers on her hat in contrast against the burnished mahogany of her hair. ''Have you tried tighter corsets?'' she suggested.

''Oh no,'' objected Darien, ''the poor thing would strangle! I've just the thing for you—I received a clipping of it straight from France only last month. It's called a wrap gown, and it is *so* concealing. Not, of course,'' she demurred, ''that *I* would ever wear such a thing, but I'm sure it would be quite charming on—''

''Where *is* Mama?'' interrupted Lucinda impatiently, bored now that the conversation had been snatched away from her.

There was a discreet tap on the open door of the morning room, and it was with great relief that Augusta saw Peter standing there. She got to her feet.

''Excuse me, Miss Gussie, but I checked on that mare of yours. 'Twas a loose shoe, 'tis all, and she's right as rain now.''

''Oh, good!'' Her enthusiasm, and her pleasure at seeing him, got the best of her and Augusta momentarily forgot her guests. ''Might we go riding then, later on?''

What a joy he was, so tall and sturdy and comfortable, a gust of fresh air wafting through the miserable confines of the morning room. It was no wonder that she went toward him so happily, hands impulsively extended to greet her rescuer, her eyes alight with welcome.

Peter's eyes softened warmly as he answered, "And sure, Miss, if you want." And at the last moment she became aware of her interested audience and dropped her hands, blushing a little.

Peter winked at her, murmured softly, "Courage, lassie," then nodded to the two ladies who were straining for a glimpse of him. "Mornin', ladies," he said, and turned a formal nod on Augusta. "Miss Gussie." And he left politely.

Augusta felt like laughing in his wake. How *was* it that he could always contrive to make her feel so good in such a short time? She turned back to her guests filled with tolerance and good humor, but her spirits dived again as she saw the speculative, almost wicked, look the two girls exchanged.

"My, my," murmured Lucinda, fanning herself a little with a lace-edged pocket handkerchief, as though to rid the room of an unpleasant odor. "You are awfully familiar with your servants, aren't you, dear? I suppose it must be that way in the country."

Augusta resumed her seat stiffly. "Peter has been with us a long time."

Darien smirked, drawing out the words, "How fortunate for you." Then, with wide-eyed curiosity, "Does he sleep in the house with you?"

Lucinda raised an eyebrow with a twist of her lips that could be construed as nothing but lascivious. "No wonder you don't mind staying alone."

"What a *brawny* man," sighed Darien. "Scotch, isn't he? I adore that brogue." And then she giggled. "You know what they say about the Scotch, don't you?"

Lucinda inclined her head curiously. Darien brought her hand to her cheek to hide more giggles. "They say that—as a race, mind you—they are exceptionally... *large*." And she dissolved into a new onslaught of blushes and giggles.

Lucinda looked bored. "Nonsense. It's not the race, it's all that outdoor air. Why, I have it on good authority"—and she leaned forward, lowering her voice confidentially—"that

the servant class is far and away the superior in the—ah—
essentials. It's told that Lady Alcombe—and she's been
married ten years, you know—once came upon her groom
in the bath and nearly died of fright, his thing was so big!''

Darien's eyes widened. ''What did she do? Faint dead
away?''

Lucinda gave a superior little smile. ''I've no way of
knowing what she did, of course, but I can only say that
since that time Lady Alcombe has been a *very* happy
woman!''

Augusta thought she would sink through the floor with
mortification. The very thought of what Simon would do
should he find her listening to such talk made her queasy,
but more was the fact that the discussion had been generated
by Peter . . . as though he were a piece of livestock, or—or a
degenerate like Lady Alcombe's groom! She was furious,
she was embarrassed, and she wished more than anything in
the world that Simon would walk through the door at this
minute and put an end to this torment.

Darien, recovering from her feigned shock and quite
genuine lusty delight, advised Augusta playfully, ''Well, I
only know if I were you, Gussie dear, I should keep a sharp
eye out for that Scotsman of yours! They say their appetites
are quite insatiable!''

That was by far enough, and Augusta could not prevent
the hot defense that sprang to her lips. ''You surely can't
suggest that Peter would—''

''Mercy me, no.'' Lucinda waved a languid hand. ''Where
are your wits, sister? Gussie, of all people—why it's laughable!'' And then, with a pained sigh, she added, ''You
don't know how lucky you are, dear, not to have men
panting after you all the time. It grows so tiresome, don't
you know.''

Augusta did not know whether to be angry, hurt, or
relieved that the topic seemed to be waning away from the
explicit. And why, she wondered, with her thoughts in a
turmoil, should she feel anything at all? It was just that the
thought of Peter lusting after anyone made her feel peculiar
inside . . . disappointed and embarrassed and uneasy. And

the very certain truth that no man would ever have such an interest in her was hurtful, even though she should have long since outgrown such things.

And then she started thinking about Peter, and wondering if he had lady friends, and remembering what the Trelawn girls had said about insatiable appetites, she was miserable and ashamed and curious and piqued all at once. Of course he must have had women over the years, he was a man after all, it was just that Augusta had never thought much about it until now... until those dreadful Trelawn girls made her wonder... until for the first time she began to imagine what it would be like if Peter looked at her with desire in his eyes instead of brotherly affection....

The random thought, coming from nowhere, shocked and disoriented her. Her cheeks went scarlet and her hands went cold and she felt as though someone had punched her in the stomach. What an unseemly thing to think! Peter was her friend, almost as close as Simon, he would never... she would never...

She was saved at that moment from the disastrous onslaught of conflicting and unreasonable thoughts by the bustling entrance of Mistress Trelawn, pulling on her gloves and commanding briskly, "Come now, girls, don't dawdle, we must be on our way. Dear Gussie, so lovely of you to have us for a stay; if it weren't for that ball in Queen Anne's Town we'd love to linger—are you sure you won't reconsider and come with us? No? Ah, well, we'll make your regrets, dear, such a sweet girl." She kissed the air near Augusta's cheek and fluttered toward the door, her two charges in tow. "Do pass on our compliments to your charming brother and tell him he is a naughty, naughty boy to abandon us so.... Into the coach, girls—this heat, my lord, it's a wonder we don't all fall out from it! Who has my vial? Oh dear, I already feel faint. Thank you again, Gussie dear, so charming, we can't wait to see you again in the fall. Say good-bye, girls."

And in a flurry of veils, petticoats, and dust, they were away. Augusta stood on the steps and waved until the plume of dust disappeared down the tree-lined lane, and then she stood alone in the wash of morning sun, feeling peculiarly dazed.

She was annoyed and embarrassed with herself for letting the idle chatter upset her. Imagine, thinking of Peter in that way! Why, it was absurd, just as Lucinda had said—laughable. But how empty the house seemed now that they were gone; how much space there seemed to be for foolish, unwary thoughts. . . .

She sighed, looking down the empty drive. Everything was always so much simpler when Simon was here. Nothing ever seemed to go awry when he was around. She would never have felt so confused and uncertain if Simon had been here to take her mind off it.

At last she roused herself and went back into the house. At least the worst was over. The Trelawns were gone, and if she were very, very clever, she might be able to manipulate herself out of the remaining parties and picnics and evening sociables that the county had planned just as easily. After all, she had plenty to occupy her time, and Peter had promised to ride with her this afternoon.

The thought did not cheer her as much as it should have—in fact, it made her feel embarrassed and uncertain again, and she scolded herself for being a foolish child. She was a grown-up woman and too wise to be turned into a scatterbrain over one idle comment made by someone as addlepated as Darien Trelawn. She had an entire summer of freedom from such as they, and she should be delighted. She *was* delighted.

But she still wished Simon would come home.

Simon wanted only to go home. Almost fifteen hours had passed since he, dressed in a sailor's borrowed coat, had left the patrol ship in the dead of night and had been escorted unobtrusively to the governor's palace. He had eaten, rested, and even been brought a suit of clothes that fit, but he was utterly miserable. The only thing he could think about was putting the place behind him and retreating to the sanctuary of Cypress Bay.

He writhed with embarrassment every time he recalled

the look on the young officer's face when he had burst into the captain's quarters and found Simon York, stripped naked and tied to the pirate's bed. Of course, in the tradition of British naval aplomb, the young man had risen to the occasion, quickly freeing Simon and supplying him with clothes—pretending all the while that nothing unusual had transpired. Simon could only thank fortune that in the excitement of capturing Storme O'Malley, no one was inclined to pay him much attention and also that, landing at nightfall as they had, no one had recognized him getting off the British ship. But he knew without a doubt the story was now being told in every tavern and on every streetcorner in Williamsburg and he seethed with anger and humiliation. He felt filthy and debased and abused; he felt, in fact, as though he should be in church—but dared not even show his face.

It was nearing sunset when he was escorted politely into the governor's reception room, and a bitter sense of *déjà vu* compounded Simon's bad temper. Of course, the last time the two men had met the surroundings had been different, the spirits somewhat lighter, but the cause of their meeting had been the same. Simon would have given half of all he owned to avoid this interview.

Governor Spotswood put a final signature to a paper on his desk, deposited his quill in its stand, and came forward, drawing on his jacket as he did. Somehow he managed to strike a perfect balance between warm welcome, sincere sympathy, and smug superiority as he clasped Simon's hand in both of his. "Ah, my friend. What fortunate circumstances that bring you to me once again."

But Simon was having none of it. He returned sharply, "Fortunate, hell. If it weren't for you I should never have sailed from Virginia to find myself in these *circumstances* now. If I didn't know better, I might be inclined to think you plotted the entire debacle."

Spotswood chuckled, gesturing Simon to an ornate white brocade chair near the hearth. "Wish I had, my boy, I wish I had. Sit down, please. We have much to discuss."

Simon scowled, but not even he was immune from a

governor's order, especially after having accepted the man's much-needed hospitality during the night. He replied, "I don't see that we have anything at all to discuss." But he took the chair near the hearth, and the governor settled himself upon the settee near him.

Spotswood leaned forward earnestly. "It is God's will, Simon—accept it. As much as the burning bush or the handwriting on the wall—you have been shown a sign. You wouldn't take a stand before, but now a stand has been forced upon you. Each man must meet his destiny eventually, and yours began less than a week ago when you left my table with scorn on your lips to experience for yourself the danger of which I warned you."

Simon was too tired and too dispirited to try to unravel the logic in that. "Indeed," he replied stiffly. "And my destiny now is to be away from this place and toward my own home, where with God's good grace I shall proceed to forget this entire unfortunate episode."

"Hardly." Spotswood's voice grew sharp. "You are well into this my boy, and the time for turning your back has long since passed. You laughed before but now the matter does not seem quite so amusing, does it? Had it not been for my new system of patrol boats in North Carolina waters, you might at this very moment be God-knows-where with no one the wiser to your plight."

Simon inclined his head in a small bow. "Thank you, sir, for rescuing me. Now might I go?"

Spotswood endured his sarcasm as he might tolerate a temper tantrum from an overwrought child. His smile was gentle and sympathetic—and masked a torrent of secret amusement behind it. "I can understand, of course," he murmured, "how you must be feeling. The circumstances under which you were discovered were—ah, most indelicate. But never fear my boy, I've no intention of interrogating you on that aspect of your adventure. I can only imagine what distress it must cause you to even recall it."

Simon felt his color rise, and his lips tightened against a rude retort. But as angry as he was with Spotswood's obvious delight in his discomfiture, he had to admit the treatment was deserved, in part. If it hadn't been for Spotswood's good judgment in keeping him cloistered here all day, his disgrace would doubtless be scrawled all over the next edition of the *Gazette*. When it came down to it, the man was right—if not for Spotswood's patrol, Simon would still be captive of that vicious, murdering wench, or worse. . . . He was behaving ungraciously, he knew, and though events of the past two days had almost rendered him beyond the ability of polite behavior, Simon resolved at least to try to go through the motions.

Spotswood, having succeeded in putting Simon in his place, relaxed into reflection. "What a curious thing, this." His dark eyes narrowed thoughtfully, and he shook his head a little, as though in regret. "So long I've dreamed of such a victory, and never guessed it would present as well a dilemma."

Simon answered stiffly, "I hardly see the dilemma, sir. You've captured Storme O'Malley, the most infamous of the pirates since Blackbeard. You are once again a hero to law-abiding citizens everywhere. You have what you wanted."

Spotswood looked at him oddly. "Indeed. I have what I wanted. The opportunity to be recorded by history as the first man to hang a woman pirate. Somehow the notion doesn't sit as well with me as I'd thought it might."

For a moment Simon was nonplussed. In the helter-skelter events of the past twenty-four hours he had barely given a moment's thought to the woman's fate, except for the flashes of fury and brief exhausting lapses into vengeful gratification that he had been freed and she had been taken to justice. It had not occurred to him that justice, for the likes of her, meant death.

He said, carefully, "You will hang her?" And even as he spoke he remembered the thunder of musket fire as he lay helpless in her quarters, the scuffle of feet, the cries, the acrid smell of smoke. He had thought about dying then, but he had thought it would be he who met his end, and he had never known a greater terror than that of lying bound and stripped and impotent over his own fate while the world came to an end about him. After all he had suffered, why should he pity her now?

Spotswood got to his feet and walked toward the window. "I don't suppose you've chanced to venture outside today?"

He pushed aside the drapery and opened the casement. A rabble of cheering voices floated through and, curious, Simon got up and looked out. Outside the palace gates a sizable group of citizens had gathered, men and women, servants and freeholders, merchants and statesmen alike. The activity among them increased when they saw the figure at the window, and they began to shout and wave their fists enthusiastically. The words, at this distance, were indistinct, but to Simon's dawning horror he realized that they were all calling for the blood of Storme O'Malley, and cheering the man who would give it to them.

The governor closed the window. His voice was very sober. "It's worse at the gaol. The crowds have been near to rioting all day; they want her hanged on the morrow and will stand for nothing less. So you see my dilemma." He gave a small helpless lift of his shoulders. "After all the attention I've given to the piracy issue, I'd look a fool if I backed down now. As the matter stands now, the esteemed Captain O'Malley has two choices: to die of legal hanging, or be torn to shreds by the mob outside the gaol. It's a sorry day," he mourned, "a sorry day indeed when womanhood should come to this."

Simon turned away slowly, feeling peculiarly hollow inside. How strange it was. She was a wicked, lawless woman, without shame or conscience or the smallest shred of moral fortitude and doubtless deserving of whatever fate brought her. Yet he remembered her laugh, and her quick, earnest intelligence, and blast it all, he remembered the childlike eagerness and forthright determination, and the thought of her neck twisted upon the gallows made him feel sick inside. He had slept with the woman, he had surely shared one of the most singularly important experiences of his life with her, and now she was to be dangled from the end of a noose and her body left for the birds in a public square. How was he supposed to feel about that?

He spoke softly, as though from a great distance, and was hardly even aware of his voice. "I never realized it would come to this."

Spotswood was watching him alertly, but when he spoke it was with studied casualness. "Of course, there might be a third choice." And he paused briefly. "We could use her."

Simon looked at him sharply. "What do you mean?"

The servants came in just then with long tapers and silently lighted candles against the fading light. Spotswood walked over to a handsome walnut buffet and took his time pouring two snifters of brandy. Simon could feel his nerves tightening with impatience like violin strings ready to pop.

When the door closed discreetly behind the servants, Spotswood brought the two glasses back to the hearth and resumed his seat. Simon, accepting his glass, did likewise. And at last the other man began to speak.

"You recall, of course, what happened when last we tried to bring charges against Eden for conspiracy with pirates—I believe we discussed it the last time you were here."

Simon nodded impatiently, and Spotswood sipped his brandy before continuing. "We were able to find some documents, of course, but few people know that what we were really looking for was never found. There was a letter, you see, that Blackbeard often boasted of, from Governor Eden to him, setting forth the exact terms of their agreement— what percentage of the pirate plunder was to go to Eden in exchange for his protection, what measures he was prepared to take to encourage piracy, all that sort of thing. Blackbeard was very proud of having gotten it all in writing, as well he should be, for whoever possessed such an incriminating document against Eden held the governor of North Carolina in the palm of his hand." He paused there, shaking his head a little in disgust, and commented, "A stupid, stupid man, Eden. He deserved to be outwitted by an outlaw.

"At any rate," he continued, "after Blackbeard's death we once again searched for the letter—tore the ship apart from stem to stern—to no avail. It had utterly disappeared.

"Mind you," he said with a sudden harshness to his tone, "I've no intention of making the same mistake with this evidence as I did with the last. The letter, when we have it, will go straight to the King, and Eden will be dismissed. This is our final weapon against him, our last chance. The man has been a thorn in my side ere he set foot on Colonial soil, but we have him where we want him now. Yes indeed,'' he murmured, and an avaricious gleam came into his eyes as he sipped his brandy again. ''Just where we want him.''

Simon struggled to conceal his impatience. ''An interesting supposition, sir, but I fail to see . . .''

''My informants tell me,'' Spotswood interrupted mildly, ''that in the last days of Blackbeard's life, when his trust for Eden had begun to waver—or perhaps it was due to some precognizance of his own imminent demise—he passed the letter on to a fellow pirate for safekeeping. Among the 'Brethren,' as they like to call themselves, there is a peculiar hierarchy of sorts. Blackbeard, king of the pirates, knew he would one day be abdicating his position to the next in line—and that that captain would have need of the same protection he had enjoyed from Eden. So he passed the letter on to his successor, as it were. And that captain was none other than Storme O'Malley.''

He paused for a moment to let the implication sink in. Simon availed himself of a sip of the governor's excellent brandy, hoping it would clear his muddled thought processes. It did not.

''Of course,'' continued Spotswood, ''our case at that point seemed hopeless. O'Malley was not only the most daring of pirates, but the most elusive, and our chances of catching her . . . well, suffice it to say, it seemed a lost cause. And so it was . . . until now.''

Simon said, ''You have the letter?''

Spotswood shook his head. ''It was not on her person, nor in her strongbox. I dare not try to bargain with her for it, for if she had a clue as to what we wanted it would never be ours. My men are at this moment going over every inch of the ship, but there remains a chance we might not find it there. And if we do not, we need her alive. That, dear boy, is where you come in.''

Everything within Simon went abruptly still. He paused with his glass halfway to his lips. "What do you mean—me?"

"I would like," announced Spotswood mildly, "for you to effect the woman's escape from prison, and take her to Cypress Bay, where she will be safe until we need her."

Simon was stunned, so much so that for a moment the full implications of the governor's proposition did not even register. He burst out incredulously, "Are you out of your mind? You expect *me*—to aid and abet—to take that filthy renegade into my *house*?"

"For a variety of very excellent reasons," agreed the governor calmly. What astonished Simon was that the man actually seemed to be serious. "For one thing," Spotswood continued, "Cypress Bay is isolated—difficult to find and difficult to escape from. It is also well defended, you have seen to that, and your men are well trained. For another, it has the most particular advantage of being just across the Chowan River from Governor Eden's plantation. Furthermore, you do actually know the woman. Perhaps she would be inclined to trust you a bit more than a stranger."

Nothing but a choked bark of half-hysterical laughter escaped Simon's lips. "Hardly!"

Spotswood's expression was very grave—frighteningly so. "Providence has brought us this far, my young friend," he said soberly, "but my plan hasn't a prayer without your cooperation. This is a chance that will come but once in a man's lifetime; you cannot fail to see the importance of what is at stake."

But Simon hardly heard him. His head was still reeling from the possibility . . . the utter improbability. . . . "It's out of the question," he declared, as firmly as he could possibly manage. "I won't entertain the notion for a moment. I'm appalled that you should even think to ask such a thing of me! I have a sister to think of—"

"All to the better," smiled Spotswood confidently. "She can be your chaperon."

Simon stared at the governor in growing horror, rapidly becoming convinced that the good man had lost his mind. His obsession with pirates had finally taken its toll, for there could be no other explanation for this insane scheme. "The woman is a criminal—a vicious killer! You would have me take her into my home like a—a long lost relative? Upon my oath, sir, it's beyond all reason!"

Spotswood chuckled. "Come, come, my boy, surely you exaggerate. She's but a woman, after all; how fearsome can she be?"

Simon's jaw tightened grimly and he set his glass down on the small cherrywood table at his elbow with a click. "This," he pronounced, "is ridiculous. I won't listen to another word." He got to his feet with all due dignity and turned to go.

Spotswood spoke heavily behind him. "Very well. I confess I hoped you would think differently, but I suppose one can't blame you. I'll begin proceedings for her trial and hanging, although"—he added sadly—"I doubt she'll make it to the gallows."

Simon stopped still, a chill inevitability creeping through his blood and churning in his insides. For that was it, then. She would swing from the end of the noose or be murdered by angry citizens exacting justice, and if he walked away now he would be the cause of it.

A fury with Spotswood for putting him in this position combined with his own horror at the situation and a turmoil of conflicting emotions battered at the secure defenses he had built for himself and his world. He turned, his eyes cold and his face tight, but he said nothing.

Spotswood, his expression softening, got to his feet. "Look, my boy," he said gently, spreading his hands, "I don't want to go to my Maker with this woman's blood on my hands any more than you do. There's something indecent about the entire prospect. Aside from that, she is of no use to us at all dead—but alive, she can accomplish a great deal . . . perhaps even enough to justify an amnesty when it is all over. There is a way out of this sticky situation, for all of us. Come, let's at least discuss it."

Simon knew he was beaten. He had known so from the moment he entered the room. Perhaps Spotswood was right at that—there was no point in trying to escape destiny.

He walked back over to his chair, however reluctantly, and picked up his brandy glass. He stared into it with concentration. "You keep talking of her 'use' to you. I assume all this has something to do with that letter you want so badly." And suddenly he looked at Spotswood. "You surely don't think she'll tell *me* where it is?"

Spotswood smiled, and it was doubtless meant to be a reassuring gesture. "Certainly not. Your role in all this need not be nearly so active. All there is for you to do, Simon, is keep her alive, and under observation. She will do the rest herself."

Simon was too weary, and too dull with shock from the events of the past hours, to even try to reason that out. He spoke flatly. "So I am to effect the escape of the most notorious outlaw living from a gaol surrounded by guards and a bloodthirsty mob, transport her somehow out of Virginia and into North Carolina, where she will have immunity from prosecution and—assuming that she does not murder me and my family in our sleep—you then expect her to deliver this letter of yours miraculously into our hands. Has it not occurred to you, sir, that Governor Eden might have some interest in the matter? He knows full well I am a friend of yours, and have worked with you against him in this matter of piracy. Won't he find it somewhat suspicious that *I* am sheltering the most infamous pirate of them all?"

A gleam of smug satisfaction came into Spotswood's eye. "That," he replied, "is precisely what we want. Don't you see, my boy? Eden has been after this letter as long as we have, and with equal determination. As long as O'Malley roamed free he was as helpless as I, but now that she is within his grasp... he will try to contact her, never fear. And the more he worries about what bargain she has made with us, the more reckless he will become. He will try to extract the letter from Storme O'Malley, and when he does, he is ours."

"So," replied Simon slowly, "she is merely the bait for the trap."

"Or the trap itself. She will not bargain with me, but

without her ship, helpless in the middle of a North Carolina plantation, and with a death sentence hanging over her head, I daresay she will bargain anything with her good friend Eden for her freedom.''

Simon swirled the liquid in his glass thoughtfully. ''It seems . . . cruel.''

Spotswood returned harshly, ''Crueler than the gallows?''

''No.'' Simon's voice was low.

''Cheer up, my boy, it shan't be for long.'' Spotswood's voice was exuberant, and he laid a bracing hand on Simon's shoulder. ''Why, my men may find the letter in a matter of days, and all shall be for naught. All you have to do is keep her safe in the meantime. Now . . .'' He turned Simon toward the settee. ''Let us go over the plan for getting her out of the gaol. It's quite clever, if I do say so myself. . . .''

* *Chapter Twelve* *

The cell was small, windowless, and filthy, but at least Storme had it to herself. The thick stone walls gave off a sour, fetid odor, and the straw on the floor was matted with the refuse of a dozen others who had gone before her. A torch made of old rags and lard shed meager light and a great deal of foul black smoke high upon the wall. There was a narrow cot covered with a rotting wool blanket, a chamber pot in the center of the floor, and a shallow fireplace. Storme wondered how she had been accorded the honor of a cell with a fireplace, and then realized that they did not expect her to be here long enough to use it.

She could hear the mob outside. There was a window somewhere along the corridor, and their voices broke through clearly. They chanted for her death, they screamed vulgarities; someone had made up an obscene song about the lady who went a-pirating, and occasionally the crowd broke into a new chorus. At first Storme had shouted back, flinging herself against the thick wooden door and cursing them all until she was hoarse, but she had no more energy for displays of bravado. She was barely even capable of anger anymore.

She had lost her ship. She had been stupid, careless, wallowing in her own selfish pleasures while a trap was neatly laid around her, and she did not deserve to live. They had taken the *Tempest*, they had murdered Pompey, and she had let it happen. Far better to have died in battle, but she was not even allowed that dignity. She had been taken at sword point, dragged by the hair off the *Tempest* and into the dank and airless hold of the other ship, and though she fought and bit and screamed taunting obscenities at them, they would not kill her. They were saving her for this.

The *Tempest*. What would become of her? Would they burn her? Sell her at auction to the highest bidder? Induct her into the Royal Navy so that she might skulk through the coastal waterways, lying in wait to take a sister pirate ship? An agony rose up within Storme that was so intense she had to bite her lip against it, for she would never see the *Tempest* again and the *Tempest* was what she loved best in the world.

And Squint. Had he been killed, too? Squint, who had been nanny, friend, teacher, and protector to her from her earliest memory—was she to die without even saying good-bye to him, without ever knowing his fate?

One more time, she thought bleakly, leaning her head back against the rough stone wall and staring emptily across the room. *If only I could have felt the wheel beneath my hands, the spray on my face, the deck beneath my feet one more time, it wouldn't be so hard. Am I so evil, that I deserve a fate such as this?*

Storme let her legs fold beneath her until she was sitting against the wall, her knees drawn up to her chest, her arms linked loosely about them. *It is over,* she thought, and tried with all her might to meet the knowledge bravely. *The sea, the wind, the endless sun . . . it's over.* She leaned her head back against the wall and repressed a shiver as the cold stones dug into her shoulder blades. It was over, and she had lost.

When she was little, her papa had taught her a prayer, a singsong child's rhyme about little lambs and angels' wings. He was always teaching her things, for he was determined to send his daughter into the world prepared for whatever she might meet there. As a child, the prayer had chased away shadows from under the bed and demon thunderclaps that tossed the ship across the tide like a feather in a whirlpool, but when Storme struggled for the words now, they wouldn't come.

"Oh, Papa," she whispered, and closed her eyes. "I never thought it would be like this. You never told me it would be like this. . . ."

Yet she should have known. Raoul, Squint, even her own unacknowledged thoughts had warned her that the end was near. She had refused to deal with it because she *couldn't* deal with it, but she had always known that it would eventually come to this. For a brief, fierce moment she wished she had listened to those warnings, taken the advice, that she had somehow managed to snatch for herself some sort of life whose inevitable end was not a noose. Yet what choices had she had? What could she have done differently? Could she have turned her back on her men and her ship and all that her father had stood for to save her own skin? Could she have dressed herself in fancy gowns and taken to the landlubber's life, perhaps hooked herself a high-speaking husband like the Farmer and settled down to breed babies?

All fine notions, to be sure, but at no time in her life could she have pictured herself doing any of those things. There would be no life for her on land, and a man like the Farmer would never have looked twice at her without the persuasion of her knife point. She had had no choices. She had done the best she could with what she had, and if this must be its end then so be it. It was a foolish waste of energy to rail against fate.

The mark of a good soldier was to die well, and Storme had been trained to be a good soldier. But she was only twenty-two years old, and she did not want to die at all.

She heard the clang of an outer door and heavy footsteps along the corridor. As she had every time she had heard movement along the hallway, she clenched her muscles, willing her heart to be still; previously the steps had passed her by.

But not this time. The click of boots against flagstone stopped outside her door, and she heard a key grate in the lock. Her heart gave one magnificent lurch, stopped in terror, and then resumed a slow, painful thud again. So, this was it, then. It was time.

She got to her feet, unwilling to meet the instrument of her death cowering like a dog, and the door swung open behind her. "Though I wasn't certain it would do any good," a smooth voice drawled behind her, "I have brought you a priest. No one, however depraved, should meet the gallows without a chance to cleanse her soul."

Storme knew that voice. She whirled. "Farmer!" she gasped.

He stood before her, as cool as an autumn day, as powerful as a sail at full wind. Not one hair on his handsome head was disarranged, not a speck of dust bespoiled the accent of lace at his wrists, and his boots were as bright as glass. A heavy traveling cloak adorned his shoulders, and he wore it with careless grace, flipped back over one shoulder to show the scarlet lining. In his hand he held a pair of kid gloves, and under his arm a cocked hat modestly adorned with a scarlet plume.

He looked for all the world as though he were just stepping out for an evening fête. Why should her heart jump so to see him? Why this joyous racing of pulses, the quick and instinctive rush of relief, the totally unpreventable urge to fling herself into his arms? *He* had been the beginning of her downfall, he and his stinking fellow Englishmen had taken her ship and killed Pompey and brought her to this place, and he had come now only to mock her.

He swept her a lazy bow and murmured politely, "At your service, madame." She did not miss the sardonic gleam in his eye as he straightened, and she wanted to spit at him, but lacked the wherewithal.

The gaoler slammed shut the door, and Storme noticed the slim young man in priest's cassock and hood standing beside Simon, nervously clutching a prayer book. As the door closed, the priest opened the book and began to stumble over the words. Storme thought he couldn't be over seventeen years old.

Storme jerked her eyes from the priest back to Simon. "What are you doing here?" she demanded. "I don't need some pebble-faced sky pilot mumbling words over *my* soul, and I for damn sure don't need you laughing while he does it! Get the bloody hell out of here!"

Simon moved quickly to peer through the barred grate on the door, and the sudden briskness of his manner surprised Storme. He said to the priest, "Keep mumbling, boy, but while you're at it, kindly divest yourself of those robes and hood and..." His eyes swept in a casual study over Storme, resting briefly on her bare feet. "Your boots, if you will. Be quick about it, please."

The young man, struggling to keep his eyes on the words while he fumbled with the sleeves of the cassock, did as he was told. Storme only watched in astonishment.

"In answer to your question," Simon said, catching the priest's robe that was tossed to him. "I have come to help you take your leave of this place—although I must say this environment suits you quite well and I don't doubt you've come to feel at home. Put this on, and quickly." He shoved the cassock at her and went to retrieve the boots. "Keep praying, boy."

It was happening so quickly Storme barely had time to comprehend it, much less question. She pulled the cassock over her head and tucked her hair under the hood, then sat on the floor to tug on the oversized boots. Her thoughts were whirling. He was going to take her out...he was going to free her...could it be a trick? What did it matter? What could he trap her into that would be worse than death at the end of a rope?

She got to her feet, stamping down the boots, and she couldn't help it. She had to ask, "Why are you doing this?"

Simon looked at her and for just a moment there was

something in his eyes that reminded her of the way he had looked the first time he touched her . . . a little reluctant, somewhat uncertain, yet—gentle. Immediately it was gone, however, and the familiar glint of lazy mockery was back. He murmured, "Madame, I have asked that question of myself more times than I can count these past hours."

He turned and banged loudly on the door. "Gaoler, if you please!"

He turned back to her at the sound of shuffling footsteps and jingling keys in the corridor, and pulled the hood lower over her face, casting a quick critical glance over her form. "You'll do I suppose. Keep your head down and don't say a word." He grabbed the prayer book from the boy and thrust it into her hands. "You," he told his companion, "get on the bed and pull the blanket over your head. Someone will be along for you shortly."

The boy scrambled under the covers, facing the wall, and the key turned in the lock. Storme stepped into Simon's shadow, keeping her head well down.

Simon said, "The lady doesn't seem to be interested in spiritual consolation. May God have mercy on her soul."

"Don't come as no surprise ter me," the gaoler replied. "The bitch's a spawn o' the devil hisself. Make her touch the Good Book, you'll see. She'll turn to ashes afore yer very eyes."

"Yes, well." Simon stepped through the door, and Storme, her heart thumping loudly, followed him. "As a Christian man, I felt it only my duty to offer her a chance for salvation. I'm saddened to have failed."

"Wastin' y'time, I told you. Hangin' won't be enough for such as that. We'll have to cut out her heart with a silver blade and p'ison it, then burn the rest of her with cedar wood for three days, elstwise she'll come back to ha'nt us all with her evil ways . . ."

And so it went, the droning voice, the jingling keys, the clattering footsteps, the beat of her heart. The smell of dampness and sweat and the grave, the flickering light of tallow torches, the shifting of Simon's cloak with each long stride and the echo of the one word with every step they took, *freedom, freedom.* . . .

She did not know why, she did not care. She only knew the taste of night air on her face, the slam of the gate behind her, and Simon's hand, hard upon her elbow, urging her toward a closed coach waiting in a shadowed alleyway. With the coming of night most of the mob had dispersed to their homes and families, but a fair-sized crowd still remained, and Storme could hear their ugly voices clamoring in condemnation. And as Simon pushed her into the coach, she caught a glimpse of something burning. Twisting her head around she saw a straw figure hanging by its neck from a noose near the gaol. Two men were putting torches to the pitiful effigy while the crowd cheered them on, and Storme realized with a start that the straw figure represented her. She felt ill for just a moment, and sank heavily onto the seat of the coach.

Simon climbed in beside her and slammed the door as the coach lurched into motion. They circled the crowd, and Storme could not help staring out the window, watching herself go up in flames. Simon noticed the direction of her gaze.

"What's the matter, my dear?" he drawled smoothly. "Do you find the sight of your own future so disturbing? I should think you would be prepared for it by now."

For another moment of horrid fascination Storme let her mind dwell upon the very graphic evidence of the fate that had awaited her, and then dismissed it with a snap. They did not have her. They could burn all the straw women they liked but they *would not have her.* She was free!

She tossed back her hood and turned to Simon on a surge of triumph, her eyes flashing and her face alight with victory. "We did it!" she exclaimed. "By God, Farmer, you are a clever one! I chose well when I chose you, I knew it from the first! Where is my ship?" she demanded quickly. "Are you taking me to her? My crew—are they free as well? By the Lord's sweet vengeance, Simon, what a pair we'll make! That fat pig Spotswood thought to take Storme O'Malley, did he?" She laughed out loud. "By *God*, we showed him! And we'll show him more, that we will! There'll be scourge upon his coasts like none he's ever seen when the two of us are under sail again!''

At some point she became aware that Simon was very quiet, his muscles bunched tensely beside her in the close confines of the coach. It was full dark and the coach had no running lights, so she could not see his face, but something about his silence disturbed her. Could it be that he did not want to join her? Was he such a fool that he didn't realize what a chance she was offering him? And why else would he have engineered her escape except on hope of her gratitude?

Impatiently she demanded, "Speak up, Farmer! Where's my ship? Is she in shape? Those bastards didn't hurt her, did they? Where are we going?''

And then Simon replied, very cooly, "I haven't the faintest idea where your ship is, nor do I care.'' As he spoke he took a silk handkerchief from his pocket and shook it out idly. "As for where we're going . . . you need know nothing more than that wherever it is, it will be at my direction, and as far away from the sea as possible. You see, my dear . . .'' And before she knew what he was about, he had grasped her wrists and begun to bind them tightly before her with the handkerchief. "You are now *my* prisoner.''

* *Chapter Thirteen* *

Christopher Gaitwood was spending a quiet evening at home. That was not a usual circumstance for a young man-about-town such as he, but with all the rabble on the streets tonight it hardly seemed safe to venture out, and besides, he had overindulged a bit the evening before and thought a brief period of abstinence would do his constitution good.

Except for the unexpected excitement over this pirate business, very little was going on in town these days, anyway. Most people were preparing to leave Williamsburg for the summer, and Christopher looked forward to a very dull season. He had toyed with the idea of going to the country himself—his father owned one of the lush plantations that lined the banks of the James River—but the prospect of spending the summer in the company of the old man, listening to lectures upon the merits of various breeding stock or irrigation methods, made a season spent sweltering in town seem like paradise in comparison. His stepmother was sweet, though, quite diverting at times, and always glad to see him, and he wondered if she might not arrange a party or two for the sake of making him known to some of the more presentable young ladies in the county. He weighed the matter, and decided that even the possibility of filling out his social calendar was not worth a summer of purgatory in the provinces.

Christopher Gaitwood was a bachelor of thirty years, blonde, pleasant-faced, and considered quite eligible by most of the matrons of Williamsburg. After reading law he was elected a member of the House of Burgesses and also maintained a rather desultory private practice in his spare time. Christopher practiced his profession as he practiced everything else—when it suited him. He loved making stirring speeches in the House and was eloquent in his delivery, but the intensity he brought to his subject was due more to an enjoyment of the sound of his own voice than to any real passion for his cause.

When he brought a case to court, one could be sure of three things: that the client was underprivileged, unable to pay, and, in most likelihood, guilty. It made no difference to Christopher; he enjoyed the pomp and spectacle of the courtroom more than he cared for the workings of the justice system, and in most cases he would pay his client's fine out of his own pocket, pleased to have gotten in on the sport.

Christopher liked cards, prizefights, horses, and women of all kinds. He did not care for sermons, debates he could not win, or excessive solitude. His philosophy of life was quite simple—to enjoy every moment of it to its fullest, and so far he was succeeding in doing so quite well.

The blue-shuttered brick house on Francis Street was settled in for the night, its lamps lit, its curtains drawn. In the drawing room Christopher, comfortable in a silk night robe and morocco slippers, was partaking of a light supper while idly perusing a copy of *Tales of a Woebegone Maid* and debating whether to invite Miss Jennifer Wright on a picnic tomorrow or attend the horse races outside of town. The knock on the front door surprised him, but he did not bother to get up. He was certain his man would tell the uninvited caller Christopher was not at home.

He was wrong.

He looked up in irritation at the sound of heavy strides approaching the drawing room, then sprang to his feet. "Cousin!" he exclaimed, and went forward.

Simon and Christopher were not technically cousins; Christopher's widowed father had married Simon's aunt when Christopher was but an infant, and the two boys, so close in age, had been raised like brothers. The relationship, though not of blood, had endured through adulthood and was closer than familial kinship. Christopher's pleasure—and astonishment—at seeing Simon now was unfeigned.

"What in blessed creation are you doing here? Didn't I wave good-bye to you at the pier scarce a week ago? I thought you to be in the midst of the tropical isles by now!"

Christopher was almost upon Simon before he realized his cousin had not come alone. Simon reached behind him and thrust forth a woman—at least Christopher thought it was a woman.

"Holy Mother and Babe," he exclaimed softly, staring. "What have you gotten yourself into now?"

She was without a doubt the most disreputable-looking creature Christopher had ever laid eyes upon. She was swathed from head to toe in some sort of rough-weave dark robe and wearing boots twice the size of her feet. Her hair was matted and tangled and glued to her scalp in places with grime of indefinable origin, and her face was streaked with filth. But she held her head high, and there was such a flame of hatred and fury in her ice-blue eyes that Christopher took an involuntary step backward.

His expression changed from shock to amused curiosity as he returned his gaze to Simon. He could never resist teasing his older cousin, and the possibilities this situation evoked were beyond anything he had ever hoped. "I say, old man, this is going a bit too far. Have you sunk so far into perversity that you've taken to gathering your pleasures from the gutter—and then you have to tie them up to get them to come with you?"

But the thunderous look on Simon's face all but discouraged further levity, and he roughly undid the knots that bound the handkerchief around the girl's wrists. "Do you still have that big woman?" he demanded. "The one who's built like a cannon?"

"Maude?" Christopher was growing more and more intrigued—and delighted. "Yes, but—"

"Get her down here," Simon commanded brusquely, "and have her get this one into a bath. She smells of a barnyard and is probably riddled with lice. And don't put her in the kitchen—one of the attic rooms, without a window. You'll have to find some clothes for her, and some shoes. Perhaps one of the serving girls will oblige. And for God's sake don't get too close to her," Simon advised as Christopher moved toward the hallway, far too fascinated by the proceedings to object to this autocratic disruption of his household. "She'd as soon claw your eyes out as look at you."

Christopher, casting a sidelong glance at the woman who stood fiercely chafing her wrists and shooting daggers of fire from her eyes, decided Simon was probably right.

The next few moments were a flurry of activity and excitement far beyond anything Christopher could have hoped for to enliven this night or any other. Maude was roused, objecting indignantly to the scurrilous creature Simon had brought into her parlor, much less the idea of heating and carrying water to the attic, all the while sending scullery girls and groomsmen to the kitchen to perform the task for her. At one point the waif who was the object of all this upheaval broke away and made a dash for the butter knife Christopher had left carelessly on his supper tray but Simon, prepared for just such a move, grabbed her short of her goal and thrust her into Maude's arms. The poor creature never had a chance. Maude, six feet tall and two-hundred-fifty pounds of country-bred determination, pinned the girl under the armpits and dragged her, struggling fiercely and screaming oaths of such a colorful and explicit nature that Christopher could only stare in openmouthed admiration, from the room and up the stairs.

In the wake of her departure Christopher looked around his drawing room, which only moments ago had seemed so cozy and tranquil, in the same manner one might look upon the aftermath of a cyclone that had destroyed everything in its path but, miraculously, left one swatch of habitation untouched. Then he fixed a pleasant smile on his face, straightened a disarranged pillow on the couch, and demanded cheerfully, "So, cousin. How have things been with you since last we met?"

Simon stalked over to the supper tray, picked up Christopher's half-finished glass of Madeira, and drained it in a single swallow. Then he loosened the ties of his cloak, tossed it over a chair and sank down heavily, leaning back his head and absently rubbing his hand. The small wound there still stung, and with the pain came a renewed surge of anger.

Overhead came a heavy thump and the sound of breaking glass. Christopher ignored it. He refilled Simon's glass, poured one for himself, and sat across from his cousin, pausing to offer a plate of sweetmeats. Simon, his usually tranquil brow knotted darkly, did not respond, so Christopher shrugged, selected one for himself, and settled back.

"Such a run of hot weather we're having," he commented after a time. "It's going to be a devil of a summer."

Simon glowered into his wine and said nothing.

Christopher finished his sweetmeat, wiped his fingers on a napkin, and crossed his legs, sipping his wine in an easy silence for a while.

After a time he asked, with no more than proper cousinly concern, "What happened to your hand?"

Simon took a gulp of his wine, and replied shortly, "She bit me."

The effort it took to swallow a bark of laughter almost caused Christopher to choke on his wine. He disguised it with a discreet cough and focused intently on the painting of a fox hunt over the mantel.

Another crash sounded overhead. Christopher politely pretended not to notice. "It's not, of course," he began conversationally, when he could trust his voice again, "that I am not always glad to see you, but whenever a man storms into my house at this hour of the night, dragging along a female bound with a silk handkerchief and demanding that I give her a bath—well, I trust I am not being unreasonable, but in all such cases, I feel more or less compelled by conscience to ask why."

Simon sighed, and slowly seemed to come out of his black reverie. He took another strong sip of his wine. "Have you ever heard of Storme O'Malley?"

Christopher's eyes widened. "Heard of her? Why, I've heard nothing else all day!" And he chuckled, leaning forward a bit. "There's the most outrageous story going about town, have you heard it? They say that when they took her ship, they found a man stripped naked and bound to her bed—"

He stopped short, staring at Simon's face. It all came together in an explosive burst of enlightenment. "Jesus Christ and Mary!" he gasped. "It was you!"

Christopher had to stand up, to walk a few paces away, keeping his back to Simon while he brought his incredulity and hilarity under control. Simon spoke quietly behind him. "I have known you since the cradle. I have paid your debts, nursed your wounds, heard your confessions. I would trust you with my life. But as God is my witness, if one word of this ever leaves this room—"

Christopher turned quickly. "Upon my honor, sir!" he assured him earnestly, though his eyes still danced with a torrent of mirth. "I'll take your secret to my grave. You

always were a better shot than me, anyway," he added
practically.

And then he cast his eyes wonderingly toward the ceiling.
"So that is Storme O'Malley. I must say, she's not much
like I thought."

Simon leaned back and closed his eyes wearily. His voice
was heavy. "She's not much like I thought, either."

Simon took a series of slow, deep breaths, trying to force
some equilibrium back into his tumultuous inner thoughts,
trying to relax the muscles at the back of his neck, which
felt as though they had been caught in a vise, and trying,
with very little real hope of success, to put the worst of this
night's events behind him.

Damn and blast the woman. She had actually expected
him to come with her. She had used him for a fool, tied him
up like an animal and left him to die, cursed him like a dog
when he came to her cell, and then merrily began to plot
their future together on the high seas once she was free.
What in the *hell* was he supposed to do with a woman like
that? How much could Spotswood expect him to endure in
the name of Christian charity and political intrigue?

And the scene in the coach . . . Simon almost groaned out
loud when he thought of it. She had tried to fling herself out
onto the hard cobblestones twice, then had begun to scream
imprecations at the top of her lungs—doing her best to alert
the entire garrison to their furtive escape—and had almost
taken his finger off when he tried to silence her. From her
most welcome friend, he had become her most hated enemy
in an instant, and there was murder in her every thought.
How could he endure another week of this? Another day?

"Ah, Christopher," he sighed softly. "I used to be such a
happy man."

Christopher fought another quick and stern battle with
rising mirth, but was unable to manage any more than a
sympathetic, "Hmm."

He cleared his throat with a taste of Madeira, and had to
wait another moment for the urge to laugh out loud to pass.
Curiosity finally won out over his sense of the outrageous,
and he said, "I'm sure the entire situation is very distressing

to you, of course, but I confess I don't understand what you're doing with the wench now. Or, more to the point, why the most infamous pirate of them all is at this very moment shut in my attic, doing her best to demolish the place brick by brick?''

Simon explained, "I've just helped her escape from gaol. We are on our way to Cypress Bay."

That announcement, at last, had the power to render Christopher speechless.

Simon sighed, and gathered himself to explain. He had had no compunction about bringing Storme to his cousin's house, and thereby making him privy, at least in part, to Spotswood's plan. Christopher, along with much of the Assembly, was no great admirer of the governor, and he was empowered as a lawmaker to cause a great deal of trouble over the affair, but Simon did not for a moment worry that he would do so. For one thing, there was the matter of loyalty, and for all his faults, Christopher was the soul of discretion where it counted. For another, Christopher would never risk his own enjoyment of so outrageous a development for the sake of mere politics.

However, Simon saw no point in embroiling his friend in this debacle any more than was absolutely necessary. He said merely, "The citizens of this town, it seems, were a bit more excited over the prospect of hanging a woman pirate than was deemed healthy. There was some doubt whether she would survive to have her day in court, and Spotswood asked me to remove her to a safer place until she could be brought to trial."

Christopher's expression was alert and mildly speculative. "And you agreed, of course."

Impatiently, Simon tossed down the last dram of his wine. "What was I supposed to do, let her be torn to pieces by the mob?"

Christopher murmured, "No, certainly not," and hid further skepticism by focusing on the contents of his glass.

Simon was not surprised. Christopher had never been accused of being slow-witted, and naturally he would realize there was more to the story than Simon was telling. The important thing was that Christopher, being Christopher, would take no action on his suppositions, and would allow Simon the courtesy of saying whatever he pleased.

Christopher glanced up again. ''It's occurred to you, I suppose, that you'll hardly be the most popular man in Virginia when word gets out that you've helped the vixen to escape. Has it occurred to you you've committed a crime, too?''

Simon shrugged uncomfortably. ''In Virginia, but not in North Carolina. I doubt if the people of Williamsburg will mount an attack on Cypress Bay.'' He hoped, of course, that word would never get out, but he knew it was a chance he would have to take.

Christopher lifted an eyebrow. ''Forgive me, cousin, but I can't hide my surprise. It's not much like you, you know, to risk your good name and your standing in the Colonies for a lowly criminal.''

''I don't see that I'm risking so much,'' Simon countered without much interest. ''The citizens of North Carolina have been sheltering pirates for decades, as you well know. The shops are filled with merchandise from pirate ships, a circumstance that many have come to applaud. The general feeling is that without the boon of piracy, the economy of North Carolina would be in dire straits. Far from objecting to harboring a fugitive like Storme O'Malley, the people of North Carolina are more likely to welcome her with a drum-and-fife parade.''

''But you've never been known to be a friend of the pirates,'' Christopher pointed out. ''And surely a man of your good sense can see that—as much as I loathe to admit it—Spotswood is right on this point. Now, mind you, I'm no lover of our illustrious Lieutenant Governor or his methods, but one does owe some loyalty to Mother England, after all. And if you shelter this pirate girl, what you are committing, my dear friend, is nothing more or less than treason.''

Simon looked away uncomfortably. ''That may well be, but what is done is done. I can hardly back out now.''

Christopher considered this thoughtfully, and could find

no argument. But he felt compelled to add, "You realize, of course, that this could be the very spark that lights the powder keg. Spotswood and Eden are on the verge of war over this piracy business, and now you have placed yourself directly in the middle. Who do you think is going to feel the full blast of that first explosion?"

But Simon was too tired, and too overwhelmed by the events of the past forty-eight hours, to deal with future consequences tonight. "The matter is well in hand," he told Christopher briefly. "I have a plan, and I can guarantee the wench will be off my hands within a fortnight—and back in the Williamsburg gaol."

An interested gleam came into Christopher's eyes, and he tapped one long finger against the stem of his glass, caught in an exciting prospect. "The General Court doesn't meet again till autumn," he murmured. "I don't suppose she'll need a good barrister when her case comes up?"

And then Simon laughed, softly, a bit tiredly. It felt good to do so. "Ah, Christopher, you'll never change, thank God." Then, lifting his glass, "She might at that. I'll ask her to keep you in mind, if . . ." And he quirked a dry eyebrow. "You think you're up to it."

Christopher's eyes snapped gaily. "Without a doubt, my liege, without a doubt. I'll give her the grandest trial this Colony has ever known! They'll be talking about it for years!" Then he sobered a fraction. "Simon," he put forth, the shadow of the newly realized thought crossing his eyes, "do you really think it's wise to take this woman into your *home*? What about Gussie, the servants—your neighbors?"

One neighbor in particular, thought Simon, but he only shrugged. "I shall have to make up some story. With luck it won't be for long."

Christopher was just about to comment that luck was a commodity that Simon seemed to have in short supply just now when they were both alerted to a presence at the door.

Maude stood there, a great hulk of a woman in no small temper. The front of her bodice and petticoat were dark and soaked, her apron dripping. Straggling threads of graying hair clung to her neck and chin and perspiration shone on her florid face. But in her eyes was a gleam of savage triumph, and she folded her arms across her formidable bosom with an air of grim accomplishment.

"Master Christopher," she announced crisply, "I been taking care of you for nigh on to twenty years and it's been no mean task, let me tell you. I done all in my power to bring you up right and make you a decent home, but I stand to say now I draw the line at scrubbing down the filthy creatures you drag in off the street and I'll take it kindly if you don't ask me to do it again!"

With a great effort, Christopher masked a renewed attack of amusement with quickly assumed chagrin. "Did she give you a hard time, Maudie?"

"The wretched creature threatened to slice up my gizzard with a broken bottle, that she did! Said she weren't about to sit in a tub o' muddy water for the likes of us! Called *us* heathens," Maude exclaimed indignantly, "for swimming in the waste of our own juices! And she, looking like something I'd be ashamed to let sleep in the stable!"

"I take it," murmured Simon, unwillingly amused and surprised at himself for being so, "the young lady is not a great proponent of the healthful benefits of cleanliness."

Maude made a hissing sound in the back of her throat. "Said that washing in a tub's no better than swimming in the gutter! That even rats know enough to swim in the sea! Daft is what she is, if you ask me. I fixed her, though," she assured them with a precise nod of her head. "Dumped a bucketful o' suds over her and pushed her in the tub, clothes an' all. She's clean now!"

Christopher choked on laughter and, as his host was momentarily incapacitated, Simon rose to the occasion. "Maude, you are indeed a jewel beyond price. There may be a sainthood in this for you. Now, if I could have the key . . ."

Maude sniffed at him, unplacated, and gave the key to Simon. She turned back to Christopher. "Will there be anything else, young sir?"

Christopher wiped his streaming eyes. "No, dear lady, I think that will be quite enough for tonight."

Maude huffed from the room, and Simon enjoyed the unexpected lightening of spirits her tale had brought for a moment longer. Too soon, however, reality descended again and he got to his feet, however reluctantly.

"We must be out of the city before dawn," he told Christopher. "I'd best try for a few hours' rest before the journey." And at the door he paused. "Come to Cypress Bay this summer," he invited impulsively.

"Cousin," returned Christopher, his eyes still dancing, "you may depend upon it. I shouldn't miss the outcome of *this* tale for all the tea in China!"

But then, as Simon prepared to say his good nights, Christopher's expression grew oddly troubled, and his tone was serious. He extended a hand to delay his cousin. "Simon—I know we've disagreed upon the subject before, but do be careful of Spotswood. He's a wily man with too much power and he doesn't much care how he uses it. You may find you've gotten more than you bargained for before this is all over."

Simon's smile was dry, and he shook his head slowly. "Thank you for your concern, Cousin, but I fear the esteemed Lieutenant Governor will be the least of my problems in the weeks ahead. From where I stand at the moment . . ." And he cast his eyes reluctantly toward the attic stairs. "It appears I have already gotten more than I bargained for."

The attic room was small and airless, obviously the quarters of a low-ranking servant. There was a rope bed and a washstand and chest of drawers of yellow pine; everything that was breakable inside the room had already been broken. The vile Amazon who had pushed Storme into the filthy tub of water had taken the candle with her when she left, and it was very dark.

The treachery and abuse Storme had suffered this night had left her normally volatile spirits at their lowest ebb, and she lay upon the narrow cot, staring sightlessly into the dark. The burning need to murder the woman Maude in her sleep no longer plagued her, and hatred for the man who had brought her to this had receded to a dull and bitter ache. She was thinking about the *Tempest*, and remembering hurt her inside as she had never imagined anything could.

They were good men, those she had led to their deaths. Aye, there had been squabbles and insolence, but it was no more than could be expected for the life they chose, and when tally was taken there wasn't a fitter crew around. They had fought beside her through calm seas and gale, they had defended her in word and deed, they had trusted her. . . .

She remembered Pompey, lying lifeless in a pool of blood, and the empty pain that flowed through her was so intense that she had to press her hand against her middle to try to quell it. The silent, loyal giant who had never harmed anyone, whose only purpose in life was to protect the mistress to whom he was devoted . . . he had died protecting her. The murdering, lawless bastards had killed him, struck him down before her eyes with no more thought or regret than one might swat a fly or drown a rat.

Hotness swamped her eyes and choked her throat and Storme wanted to cry. She wanted to bury her head in the pillow and sob out loud in sorrow and pain and despair, for it was gone, all that she had ever known or loved, and she was trapped here in this place awaiting a fate she could not guess. But no one had ever taught Storme how to give up, and she could not cry.

She heard voices on the lower stairs—the two men saying good night; she stiffened, abruptly alert. The sound of Simon's voice—low, desultory, strangely melodic—did something uncommon to her pulses. It felt like a stab of rage or a seizure of anxiety, but it was neither. It was enough to whip her out of despair and make her remember who she was and how she had come to this place.

She listened, breath suspended, and heard distant footsteps ascending. One door closed, and then two. She released her breath cautiously. So, he wasn't coming for her. Not yet.

She did not know why he had brought her here. She did

not know why he taken her from the gaol to make her his personal prisoner or what his plans were for her in the future, and she did not care. Long ago she had realized the futility in trying to understand the peculiarities of the working of the male mind and had learned the only way to deal with them was to beat them. She knew only that for one night the man called Simon had shown her secrets and unveiled mysteries; he had lain with her and made her feel things she had never guessed she was capable of feeling, and with him she had felt the brief beginnings of a closeness that both terrified and intrigued her. She had even liked him. Now he had betrayed her, and she hated him.

And Storme O'Malley was never meant to be any man's captive.

Upon the chest lay a serving girl's homespun bodice and petticoat—poor recompense indeed for her own ruined clothes, which had been soiled and stained beyond repair, but they would have to do. Silently she slipped from the cot and pulled the garments on, grimacing at the rough weave against her naked skin. Impatiently, she knotted the petticoat between her legs for greater freedom of movement, and crept to the door.

It was absurdly easy. The latch opened without a sound, and Storme, her eyes as sharp as a cat's in the dark, crept down the narrow stairway. Her plan was simple. First out of the city and to the river landing. From there she could steal, bribe or threaten her way onto a boat that would take her to North Carolina. Once there she would have no trouble at all raising a crew, and as soon as it was done she intended to pay a personal call upon Governor Eden. She would need his help in discovering the whereabouts of her ship and her men, and as long as she held the letter in power against Eden, he would not dare to refuse her. Besides, the opportunity she could offer him for revenge against Spotswood was not one he was likely to *want* to refuse, and together they would visit upon Virginia a plague the likes of which had not been seen since the Black Death. . . .

She heard the creak of a door, and an arm shot out of the dark to grab her. "Thank you," drawled Simon, "for not keeping me up too late, waiting. I was afraid this might take all night, and I'm rather tired.''

Storme struggled, and his hands clamped down on both of her shoulders, hard; he pinned her against the doorframe and got his knees against hers so that she was virtually helpless. Not that Storme surrendered that easily. An instinctive surge of primal instinct surfaced and she kicked, she tried to duck, she twisted and bared her teeth and fought until she was panting, and he held her firm.

"Scream the bloody house down if you want," Simon said quietly. His eyes were dark and his hair had become somewhat disarranged in the struggle, shadowing his forehead. But his tone was calm, almost nonchalant, and he wasn't even breathing hard. His hands were like iron on her shoulders. "No one will help you. Kick and bite and punch to your heart's content; it will avail you nothing. You see, my dear, whether you like it or not, I am stronger than you and *I* have the advantage this time."

"Take your filthy hands off me, you slime-bitten bastard!" she hissed.

He lifted a mild eyebrow. "Why, dearest. Could it be only two nights ago you were begging me to put my hands *on* you? Fickle, thy name is woman."

She spat in his face.

Very slowly, Simon lifted one hand to wipe the spittle from his cheek, using the other to exert a warning pressure on her chest, near the base of her throat. Not the slightest alteration of expression crossed his face. "Don't," he said very quietly, "ever do that again."

The light from the room poured over his shoulder, etching him in stark relief and placing Storme in darkness. He had undressed to his white lawn shirt and breeches, and she could see the strength of his throat, and fine sprinkles of light hair on his chest where the shirt opened. The strikingly perfect, aristocratic face no longer seemed merely a thing of beauty, but of force as well; the lovely gray eyes were as hard as steel. The power in his muscles was coiled and subtle, and there was an aura of danger about him Storme never suspected before.

It did not frighten her. It only made her heart pound faster.

And, more to break away from the sudden inexplicable uncertainty that threatened her than out of any real hope of escape, she lurched against his hold once again, furiously. "What do you think to gain from this, Farmer?" she jeered. "You're a bigger fool than I thought if you think you can hold Storme O'Malley! What do you intend to do with me?"

Her eyes were flashing, and an undertone of angry color glowed on her golden skin. Her hair, once again flowing down her back like fine silk, had been tossed around her shoulders during their struggle and a few shiny strands clung to her face. Simon, looking at her, thought in that instant of a great many things to do with her.

Her breasts were heaving, and he remembered how they had felt beneath his hands, small and firm like the rest of her. Her hands were clenched into tight fists and he remembered how they had felt on his back, and his thighs, and his buttocks. He wanted, for the briefest instant of almost blinding savage need, to crush her against him, to cover her mouth with his and rule her with his power. He wanted to thrust his hands through her hair and tilt back her head; he wanted to subdue her with his mouth and weaken her with his touch; he wanted to take her right there on the stairs.

His fingers tightened painfully on her shoulders, but his voice was very even. "I intend," he told her, "to take you to North Carolina on the morn. So if I were you I'd not be wasting any more time creeping about the house. It's a long journey."

Storme stared at him. North Carolina! Was it possible? Had he not betrayed her after all? He was taking her to safety, to . . . "Carolina!" she gasped, and her eyes searched his, wary in joy and disbelief. "To Eden?"

Simon felt a shaft of disappointment that was out of all reason. So Spotswood had been right. The plot was working already.

And his voice was unexpectedly harsh as he returned, "I'm taking you to my plantation, where you may safely await trial. Upon," he added, for no exact reason, "the request of Governor Spotswood."

Spotswood . . . trial . . . Her disillusionment, the second in one day, was so acute it seemed to tear through her very inner workings like a blade. He had saved her only to bring her to trial. He had given her hope and snatched it from her. He was taking her to Carolina only to return her to the vile clutches of Spotswood. . . .

"You pig!" She spat and began to struggle again, wildly, furiously, wanting only to bite, to kick, to scratch, to hurt him in any way possible. "You filthy, stinking son of a pox-ridden whore! I'll be damned and cursing your soul from hell before I set foot on your louse-bitten plantation! You'll not send me back to that gaol, I'll slit your throat first, and that's a bloody vow! You lying, pustulant, flea-breeding dog!"

Her sudden resurgence of rage had caught Simon off guard and he almost lost his grip on her. He caught her shoulders swiftly again and shook her hard, his face very close to hers and as dark as a swift thunderclap on a bright day. "You little fool!" he thundered. "I just saved your bloody life! Is this the thanks I get?"

"I don't need your kind of saving!" And in an instant, Storme wrenched her arm free and raised it to strike him.

Simon caught her wrist in midair and twisted it behind her, catching the other arm and binding them both against the small of her back with a single hand. He was breathing hard now, though more from furious, exhausted emotion than from exertion. He shoved her roughly toward the stairs, and when she continued to struggle, despite the pain it must be causing her, he lifted her and carried her bodily up the stairs.

He tossed her inside the narrow attic room, leaving her so off balance that she fell on the floor. Stunned and momentarily robbed of breath, she watched as he turned on his heel and strode toward the door. At the threshold he paused, ran an easy hand through his disheveled hair, and advised, quite mildly, "We leave at dawn. I suggest you get some rest."

He closed the door behind him, and in a moment Storme heard the turning of a key in the lock.

* *Chapter Fourteen* *

In 1720 most of the province of North Carolina was still wilderness. Within the memory of many living, the fertile banks of the Chowan had been hunting grounds for the Indians; rough-hide tipis had lined the inland creeks and streams. Less than twenty years ago a final, brutal battle had established the white man's authority in this part of the country, but renegade Indians still roamed, separately and in bands, striking out without warning against the encroachment of the newcomers.

The woods were filled with game and predators; sheep fell prey to wolves and man to bears. On the outer edges of the province buffalo still roamed, large and shaggy and stupid, though their numbers were dwindling now. Sanitation conditions were primitive and disease was common. Death came in the form of snakebite or fever or fire or flood, indiscriminate of age or rank. No man over sixteen left his home unarmed, for the threats to his safety and that of his family were many and varied.

Cypress Bay was a fortress of civilization set in the very midst of this wilderness, a testament to man's optimism or perhaps merely a symbol of hope. Its roads were wide and well tended, its fields broad and orderly. Cultivated shrubs and flowers lined its paths, fruit trees shaded its facade, and a flock of sheep kept the lawns trimmed to meadowlike neatness.

Just as Simon appeared to be a gently raised, graciously educated, indolently wealthy young man, Cypress Bay on the surface was a genteel estate, as carefully ordered and painstakingly cultivated as any of its stately British counterparts. But on Cypress Bay the servants not only worked the fields but weekly drilled in arms. Every man among them was issued weapons according to his ability: swords and muskets, knives and nets. Even the Africans carried spears and trained in battle. Between them they composed a small but formidable army, each one of them sworn to protect with his life Cypress Bay and all who dwelled there. Advance men patrolled its borders, and vigilant guards kept watch over its vulnerable areas day and night. Once before Simon had seen his home invaded by violence and all that he loved destroyed; he vowed it would not happen again.

The house itself was a simple design, for English lines had been modified for the sake of practicality in the Colonies. It was a sturdy square structure of mellowed rose brick, ornamented on both the first and second floors by galleries for shade. A wide front hall, designed to catch the breeze, bisected the house on both floors, each story containing four large rooms. There were a multitude of large casement windows and doors that could be flung open to the air in the summer, and large fireplaces in every room for the frequently inclement winters. Standing as it did at the end of a long drive, surrounded by ancient oaks and flowering crepe myrtles, it was a stately home, beautiful in its simplicity and inviting to the eye.

But its outer visage was where simplicity ended. Simon York, with some help from his father before him, had furnished his home with all that was most artful and coveted of the day. The furniture was from the most valued craftsmen, every piece personally selected and supervised. The walls were covered with silk, the tiles upon the hearths imported from Italy. A Renaissance tapestry from the York ancestral home adorned the front hall, and paintings from every century found their orderly and appropriate place in each room.

Upon his table were fine porcelain and heirloom silver, and crystal from the finest makers in England. His library was filled with leatherbound books, and was considered one of the finest collections in the Colonies. The curtains were of damask, the chairs and sofas rich brocade. Each lamp, vase and ornament was one of a kind and the best of its kind, and every portion of every fixture within the house combined to form an overall picture of peace, loveliness, and endurance. Outside the gates the wolves might bay and the cougars might stalk, savagery in every form might nip at the very heels of passersby, but within the stronghold of Cypress Bay there was only order, artistry, and civility.

For Peter McCollough Cypress Bay had been his only life for so long he could barely remember another. He was twenty-nine years old, and at fourteen he had been deported to the Colonies. The days in Scotland as a poor stableboy on a vast highland estate had not been happy ones, and he did not miss them much. His father died young of poverty and hard work; his mother bore a stillborn infant and followed him to the grave.

Peter pursued the only life he could until the day he came upon the overlord, a brutal, greedy man, raping his sister. Peter's crime was murder, and his indentureship was for life. He knew his sentence would have been death had not the high courts been experiencing some difficulty with rioting serfs at the time and inclined to show mercy. He knew also that without the good fortune that had brought him to Cypress Bay, he might have preferred death.

Simon had bought him fresh off the boat, and Peter remembered the irony of addressing a boy who was scarcely older than he as "master." But in a matter of hours Peter's attitude toward the fancily dressed, stuffily mannered young man had turned from contempt to admiration—within mere days it had grown to real friendship.

Simon York had arrived home to fallow fields, runaway slaves, crumbling fences, and dwindling livestock. He had the care of a rosy-cheeked baby sister who hadn't yet broken in her first pair of walking shoes, and Simon never went anywhere without the infant in tow—upon his hip, in front of his saddle, or riding on his shoulders. That was the first thing Peter admired about him.

The second was Simon's refusal to give up. He had a vision for what Cypress Bay could be, and when he spoke of it he made it real inside Peter's head. He asked for

Peter's help. Simon loved the land and what it could produce, but what he did not know about agriculture could have filled a whole shelf on his library wall. Peter knew how to work the soil and tend the stock, but he had no experience whatsoever in the management of a large plantation. They needed each other. Together they had built Cypress Bay into what it was today, and the three of them, together, had become a family.

And it was for that reason that moments such as this were so precious. They did not come as often as they once had and, Peter knew with a sorrowful insight, must grow increasingly rare.

They were in the stables, he and Augusta. Peter was currying the little mare, Syrabelle, while Augusta fed her handfuls of hay and crooned to her. Syrabelle, who was ready to foal any day, was one of Augusta's favorites.

"I still say she's awfully small to have been bred to that monster Zeus," said Augusta. "Do you think she'll have any trouble?"

"Nay, lass. She's a strong little mare, and sturdy." Peter gave a light affectionate pat to Syrabelle's swollen middle. "We'll get a colt out of her that'll be the best in the county, with his sire's speed and his dam's disposition. He'll be the start of a whole new line for Cypress Bay."

"And what if 'he' is a she?" demanded Augusta impertinently.

Peter grinned. "Then we'll just have to turn her out and try again."

"Heartless creature!" Augusta flung her arms around Syrabelle's neck and hugged her comfortingly. "Don't you listen to a word, my darling. We won't let him do any such thing." The mare nuzzled Augusta's cheek affectionately, causing Augusta to draw back quickly or be knocked off her feet. Peter laughed, and so did she.

Augusta never was more comfortable than in the stables or the barnyard, dealing with the animals she loved, enjoying with Peter the things she knew best. Now, looking into Peter's sparkling dark eyes, she was aware of a new dimension to the moments she spent with Peter . . . and it all went back to that dreadful morning with the Trelawns. Suddenly embarrassed, she broke the eye contact, reaching for another handful of hay. Syrabelle had had enough, however, and turned her head away.

Augusta wiped her hands on her apron and came out of the stall. Peter was turned away from her, replacing the currycomb on its shelf, and she thought she might not have the courage to broach the subject again. As casually as possible, she asked, "Do you have a lady friend, Peter?"

Peter could not hide his astonishment, and was glad his back was to her. Of all the questions for Gussie to ask . . . Gussie, who was no longer his "little darlin'," but who filled his days and his nights with her gentle laughter, whose smiling eyes haunted his dreams, and whose gentle ways broke his heart with wanting. Gussie, a highborn lady and his master's sister. Gussie, who had no place with him.

His voice was stiff and he replied without turning, "That's not the kind of thing a lady should be askin' a man, Miss."

"Oh." There was hurt in her voice, and Peter had to turn.

Her eyes were downcast, her fingers wound into her apron, and there was color in her cheeks. Everything within Peter softened, like sugar melting in the rain, and he couldn't help it. He reached forward and chucked her lightly under the chin, coaxing her eyes to his, forcing a semblance of his old teasing smile to his features. "Now how could I have a lady friend," he asked her, "when ye know you already have my heart?"

But her eyes were wide and her face was beautifully flushed, and her voice was a little breathless as she replied, "Have I, Peter?"

It was one of the greatest efforts of Peter's life to turn away just then, and to make the movement seem natural. "And sure," he replied easily. "Ye've been breakin' it since ye were a wee bairn."

A silence fell then, and for all Peter's attempts to lighten the mood, it was an uncomfortable one. Sunlight sifted through the log building and caught in spider webs and dust motes; the air was rich with the smell of hay, and there was no sound except the restless movements of the horses and the jingle of metal as Peter fussed with a bridle in need of mending. Augusta, desperate for the moment to continue, cast about in her mind for something to say. She glanced at Syrabelle, as though for inspiration.

"You'll call me, won't you, when it's time for the foaling?" she said. "I want to be here."

Peter chuckled, selecting a strip of leather from among those hanging on the wall. "Nay, Miss Gussie, you know your brother'd have my hide for a thing like that."

"Why? I've always been allowed—"

"That was when you were little. You're a young lady now, and Simon expects you to act like one."

Augusta frowned. "Oh, bother Simon and what he expects. I hate being a young lady. Simon is so protective, so concerned with all that is proper, so *determined* to make me behave like someone I'm not. . . ."

"He's only thinking of your future, lass." Peter brought the bridle and the leather over to the work table near where Augusta was standing. "After all . . ." He glanced at her, and he did not know what prompted the next words, unless it was a form of self-punishment, a grim reminder as to what her future held, and his, and how different they must always be. "You'll be marrying soon, and startin' a family of yer own."

Nothing was reflected in Augusta's eyes but absolute astonishment—and perhaps a measure of self-derisive mirth. "Peter, you can't be serious! Who would marry me?"

Peter's throat went tight, and he wanted more than anything in the world to reach out and take that sweet, adored face in both his hands and kiss it, ever so gently, and then more fiercely . . . but he was caught in her eyes, helpless with wanting, and all he could say was, huskily, "Any man in his right mind."

He looked at her, and it was an endless moment of cautious truth, barely defined hope. . . .

Neither of them could have guessed what might have happened then had not the sound of carriage wheels and harness intruded into the moment. Peter was the first to break away, looking embarrassed and uncertain, and he went to the door. Augusta followed him, her heart clamoring in her chest.

"Were you expectin' visitors, Miss Gussie?"

"No." Disappointment thickened her voice but residual excitement left it a little quivery. "But this time of year people are always dropping by—"

She stopped, shading her eyes against the glare of the sun as the driver got down and opened the carriage door. "Good heavens! It looks like—it's Simon! What in the world—"

"He's got a woman with him," said Peter. "He didn't say anything to me about bringing back a new serving girl."

"What on earth could have happened?"

"Whatever it was, he doesn't look too happy about it." And the two of them hurried forward, to find out for themselves.

If ever anything could have crushed Storme's spirit and left her beaten, it was the grueling two-day journey over broken roads and humid swamp. The heat and the dust were enough to make her physically ill; the jostling coach had left every inch of her body black and blue. During the day she had been bound hand and foot, at the mercy of the movement of the coach and the cold indifference of her silent companion. At night they had stopped at the Border Inn, where everyone had taken her for Simon's servant and she had been confined to a small anteroom adjoining his. She had been too exhausted to even eat, much less plot her escape. She had fallen onto a straw mattress and slept without dreaming until dawn, when the torture began once again.

As they approached the long drive that led to the house, Simon had wordlessly removed her bonds, but long hours of motionlessness had almost robbed her limbs of sensation. Her legs barely supported her as she climbed out of the carriage and stood there in the bright glare of the sun, rubbing her wrists. The big house, the fertile lawns, the outbuildings, and the curious, staring servants barely registered. She was so numb with exhaustion she could scarcely think.

A plump, florid-faced young woman rushed up, followed closely by a dark-haired workman. The woman, her eyes alight with pleasure and surprise, flung herself into Simon's arms. "Simon!" she exclaimed. "What are you doing back so soon? What happened?"

Something changed within Simon as he returned the woman's embrace, and Storme wondered dully if she might be his wife. The absurdity of that didn't even strike her.

"Hello, sweetheart!" Simon's face transformed with joy and his eyes sparkled as he shifted to a one-armed embrace of the woman and extended his other hand to the big, dark-haired man. "Peter, you old son of a goat! By God, it's good to see you both!"

The man laughed. "You sound like you've been gone a year, instead of a fortnight! What happened?"

And Simon replied with a grin that was only half amused. "I feel as though I have been away a year, believe me." He hugged the woman again and kissed the top of her frizzy hair, and Storme, watching, felt a dull stirring of resentment. She was not accustomed to anyone being happy when she was miserable, and Simon's pleasure now was a victory he did not deserve.

With his arm still around the woman's shoulders, he explained easily, "I had a change of plans, I'm afraid. I stopped by Williamsburg on the way and Governor Spotswood..." He looked in Storme's direction then, and there was a sharp edge of warning in his gaze. But he released the plump woman and wrapped a firm hand around Storme's upper arm, drawing her forward.

"This is Spotswood's niece," he lied smoothly, "and she's had a rather bad time of it, I'm afraid. She lost her family some time ago and has been more or less fending for herself...." His eyes fell then on her bare feet, and Storme could sense his displeasure as well as the increased pressure on her arm. He added dryly, "She's not entirely accustomed to living in society. We must be patient with her. The good governor asked me to bring her here, as she needs a time of tranquility and country air to recover her health...." There the fabrication seemed to run out, and he finished abruptly.

"Her name is Storme. My sister, Augusta York, and Peter, my overseer."

Augusta's eyes widened and her mouth flew open as though on an exclamation, but something—good manners, or perhaps another quick glance at her brother's face— stopped her. Her expression changed to a rather hesitant smile, and she extended both hands to Storme. "Welcome, Mistress—" She cast an uncertain glance toward Simon, then finished, "Storme. We'll do all we can to make you comfortable."

Storme ignored the gesture as easily as she ignored Simon's lies. She was beyond caring about much of anything at the moment.

Augusta withdrew her hands awkwardly, and Simon's fingers dug into Storme's arm. Another time she would have kicked him, but her muscles ached too badly to move.

"You must be exhausted from your journey," said Augusta quickly. "Let me show you to your room."

"I'll do that, dear," put in Simon smoothly. "Why don't you go to the kitchen and ask them to make up a tray?"

Augusta looked uncertainly from Simon to Peter, and then smiled. "I'll do it right away," she said, and Storme was left alone with the two men.

Storme looked for a moment at Peter and thought without much interest, *He knows*. She would have to be wary of him, for he didn't look like a man to be gotten around easily. The fat sister must be stupid to believe such a tale, but none of it made much difference to Storme. All she wanted to do was lie down.

Simon's easy manner changed when Augusta was out of sight, and he looked at Peter. "This is not," he explained simply, "Governor Spotswood's niece."

"Somehow I didn't think so," drawled Peter, and there was the faintest glint of amusement in his eyes.

Simon merely nodded, and something unspoken seemed to pass between the two men. He said, "Wait for me. We have some things to discuss."

He jerked Storme's arm roughly and half-led, half-dragged her up the steps. Once inside the great hall, he stopped, turned her so that she must face him, and bent uncomfortably close. He spoke very softly, but his eyes were stone-hard. "All right. You are here. I want you to know that I will be watching you every minute and whatever tricks you have up your sleeve had best be discarded right now. There are no weapons within your grasp, and every piece of silver will be counted before you leave the table. If you behave yourself, we shall get on quite well; if you do not, you'll suffer the consequences."

Storme looked at him, utterly unimpressed, and his fingers tightened once again, viciously, on her arm. "And another thing. You may rail and rage at me all you like, you may spit and claw and kick and try to strangle me in my sleep—but if you touch one hair on my sister's head," he vowed, "I will personally cut your throat."

For whatever else he had said to her, for all she knew or did not know about him, on this one subject Storme knew he was serious. She tried to summon anger, disdain, or even fear; none would come. She merely raised her chin a fraction, looked him in the eye, and with the very last of her energy said flatly, "Go to hell, Farmer."

She jerked her arm away and marched toward the stairs, hitching her skirts above her knees for climbing, and Simon was right behind her. If he had anything else to say she did not hear it, for the moment he opened the door Storme went to the bed there and was asleep before her head touched the pillow.

* *Chapter Fifteen* *

Storme awoke at twilight, alert, refreshed, and ravenous. On the table by her bed was a napkin-covered tray, and without getting up she uncovered it. There was sliced ham, bread, some cheeses and a cluster of grapes; there was no cutlery of any sort, and with a small grimace she decided the Farmer had checked her tray before it was brought in. One thing could have been said about him: he learned fast.

She grabbed a handful of ham and a couple of slices of bread, sitting cross-legged in the middle of the bed and eating quickly. She took the opportunity to study her surroundings and consider her situation, and the food that was rapidly filling her belly made the outlook much less dreary than before.

The room in which she found herself was pleasant, light, airy, and attractively appointed. The walls were whitewashed, the dark wood floors spotless. The counterpane and bedcurtains were white, and the draperies covering the three large windows were a rich blue print on a white background.

There was a washstand with a procelain pitcher and bowl, a standing pier glass in an oval frame, and a clothes press, as well as two pretty chairs embroidered in scarlet and blue. On one wall was a framed artwork made of seashells, on another a collection of landscape paintings that Storme found boring. There was a table before the window that held a pretty vase of some sort, and on the hearth was a collection of colorful dried flowers. Little shelves and shadowboxes held useless procelain knickknacks of various descriptions. All in all, the room did have something to recommend it over the Williamsburg gaol.

She finished the ham and reached for a wedge of cheese, taking a bite out of it. She sniffed the glass of pink liquid on her tray, but it smelled like wine so she took a sip. It was quite good. She drained the glass and finished the cheese, thinking.

Perhaps the situation wasn't as impossible as she had first assumed. Obviously the Farmer was stronger than she was, and without a weapon she hadn't a chance of overcoming him physically. That other man, the dark one, was a possibility. She didn't know much about him, and on first glance he had seemed both a formidable opponent and strictly loyal to Simon, but one never knew what might develop. Now the fat one . . . she was the real possibility, the weak link in the chain. Simon seemed fond of her, and if Storme could only find a way to use that...

Directly across from her was a set of floor-to-ceiling windows that opened outward onto the gallery. They were opened a fraction to admit the afternoon breeze, and Storme, plucking off a handful of grapes, went over to them and stepped out.

From the top floor she had a vista of sweeping meadows, neat, curving furrows, tall haystacks. There was movement in every direction—black men, white men, mules, horses, cows grazing, plows plodding—there must have been two dozen workers in one field alone. "Farmer!" she muttered derisively under her breath. "Ha!" Why, he was as rich as any one of those fat arrogant landlords in England, and doubtless just as corrupt. Her father had told her stories about the stupid, overbred aristocracy who worked their tenants to death and lived on the fruit of their labors, and if there was anything Storme despised more than a farmer, it was a rich one.

She spat a grape seed over the railing, and then she stopped, staring.

It lay there before her, still and wide and sunwashed, a broad, beckoning avenue lined with trees and undulating banks, a highway to freedom... the river. Her escape. She stared, and she could hardly believe it; she looked again, and she wanted to laugh out loud. The river! How could she not have known how close it was? Its banks were within five hundred yards of the very house—she could *walk* to the river, steal aboard a boat, and be on her way to the sea before anyone knew she was gone. What an idiot the farmer was! And how thoughtful of him to locate her prison mere steps from the avenue of her escape.

She turned quickly and went back into the room, chuckling to herself over how easy it was going to be. Of course, she would not be hasty. Doubtless she would get only one chance at escape, and she must plan it thoroughly. She absently washed her sticky hands in the water pitcher and dried them on her skirt, plotting the best way to proceed. Of course, it would be no problem whatsoever for her to climb over the galleries and leap onto the ground—if the Farmer thought the mere matter of a second-story room would deter her, he obviously had never climbed the rigging to a masthead in a blowing gale—but she needed to know what awaited her when she escaped the room. First, she must discover the lay of the land, as it were, and, with luck, she might even be able to put her hands on a weapon. . . .

She went over to the door and tried the handle without much hope. To her ultimate surprise, it opened easily, and she did not waste time questioning why. She stepped out into the hallway.

Her bare feet made no sound on the hardwood floors as, assuming correctly there was nothing on this story except more bedrooms, she moved toward the staircase.

Augusta could hardly credit this turn of events. From the lonely, rather dreary summer she had anticipated, the weeks ahead had suddenly turned into a season filled with possibilities; the plain but lovely sameness of life on Cypress Bay had abruptly become exciting and fraught with adventure.

A female guest was something to celebrate in itself. As much as Augusta disliked the Trelawn sisters, she did appreciate the companionship of other women, for it was something rare in her life. And the young woman Storme . . . well, one thing could be said already about her: She was nothing like the Trelawns.

Storme O'Malley. Who would have ever thought? Of course, Simon had not said that was who she was, but there simply were not that many women in the Colonies called Storme, and Augusta was a bit puzzled by the fact that Simon did not think her clever enough to figure it out. She was, however, a great deal more puzzled by other things— how Simon had met her, why he had brought her here, how long she intended to stay, where she had gotten those *awful* clothes . . . all questions that Augusta was too polite to ask, of course. Obviously, Simon did not think she needed to know, and she must trust his judgment. But it was all incredibly exciting.

She did wish Simon would come in, though. He had been

cloistered with Peter so long Augusta was beginning to worry. And perhaps once he thought the matter over he would decide to confide in her—a possibility that she would greatly welcome.

Augusta was sewing in the parlor, a somewhat frivolous occupation when so much of importance was going on around her, but it did calm her impatience. She looked up when she heard a sound in the library, and, thinking Simon had returned without her noticing, quickly crossed the hall.

But it wasn't Simon after all. It was their guest.

"Well, good afternoon!" Augusta said warmly. "Did you rest well?"

Storme turned quickly on the balls of her feet. She had been examining the guncase—a veritable treasure trove of muskets, pistols, and swords, all very carefully chained and locked, unfortunately. The voice shocked her nerves into preparation for battle, but when she saw it was only the sister, she relaxed a bit.

"I was just looking around," she said warily and wondered if Simon would take the precaution of locking her in her room after this.

Augusta smiled. "I'll take you on a tour of the house later, if you like. This is a lovely room, isn't it? Simon spends most of his time here."

Storme saw nothing particularly lovely about it. The walnut paneling was dark and oppressive, the massive desk pretentious, and the books that lined the walls smelled musty. The only thing of interest at all was the weapons cabinet, and as she had no tools to break the locks, even that was of limited interest to her. She shrugged.

"Come into the parlor," invited Augusta. "Simon will be in shortly, I'm sure, and we'll have tea. Until then we can just sit and chat."

Storme had little choice but to follow her, her sharp eyes noticing every detail along the way. The great door that opened onto the gallery and the front steps, the drapery that was tied back across the hall—a good place for hiding, if need be—the shadow of the dining room, from which the sounds of servants moving about came clearly. The hallway seemed to run straight through the house and give way to a back exit, and Storme marked that fact down for future reference.

The parlor, in comparison to the library, was bright and pleasant. Pale mauve draperies were drawn back over a wide front window, and little chairs upholstered in lemon brocade were drawn up before the fireplace. There were settees and footstools in gay embroidery, and the tables were a delicately carved fruitwood. A pale gray silk covered the walls, and the ceiling was an elaborate fresco of loops and furbelows, whitewashed to reflect the light.

There was a harpsichord in a lovely inlaid case, and lamps of the sheerest painted porcelain placed in all the right places. Storme thought that Simon the Farmer must be as rich as any English lord who had ever ruled, but she was little impressed. She was rich, too, but she didn't waste her hard-earned gains on silly frivolities like painted lamps and carved ceilings.

Augusta sat upon the high-back settee, spreading her skirts around her in a very ladylike fashion, and with a smile she gestured to Storme to join her. Storme preferred to be on her feet, and she wandered around the room, inspecting its accoutrements with a desultory interest.

Augusta's voice sounded shy, breathless, and a little tight with repressed excitement behind her. "Pardon me, but—you're Storme O'Malley, aren't you? The pirate?"

Storme cast a quick wary glance over her shoulder. "That's right."

"Oh . . . my." The exclamation was faint and demure, and Augusta quickly lowered her eyes as though to hide the eagerness there.

There was a silver tier of confections on the table near Augusta—sugared plums and candied citrus peels, glazed nuts and molded meringue. Curiously, Storme picked up a bit of white confection topped with a walnut half and popped it into her mouth. It was pure sugar, and the ultimate sensual delight. She took another.

Augusta blurted out, as though unable to restrain her excitement a moment longer, "Forgive me, I don't wish to be rude, but—I've heard such stories! Have you really done half the things they say?"

Storme glanced at her. Her temperament was much softened by the pleasures of the candy dish before her, and it was difficult to remember that this dowdy young woman, with all her earnest, wide-eyed curiosity, was allied to Storme's greatest enemy. She tried a sugared orange peel. "It depends on what they say."

Augusta blushed and seemed to decide not to pursue that topic. Her voice grew hushed, almost reverent. "Did you know Blackbeard?"

Storme filled her hand with a selection of candies—plums, almond meringues, and glazed nuts—and wandered over to the window. The fare aboard ship was plain, nourishing, but not very exciting—the breads were hard or moldy, the meats rarely fresh, and the occasional keg of molasses they captured too valuable to waste in cooking. Sweet candy was an entirely new experience to Storme, and discovering it was almost worth the time she was wasting here.

She answered, biting into a plum, "I knew him. A right gentleman he was."

Augusta's eyes widened. "But the tales about him—they're so fierce! Why, it's said he used to set his beard on fire to board a ship, and he was such a devil that he never once got burned!"

Storme chuckled. "He just did it to scare people. Used tapers, he did, stuck in his beard, that burnt out before catching his hair. We used to laugh about it." She licked the lingering sugar from the palm of her hand, and then she saw Simon, crossing the lawn in conversation with the dark-haired man. The Farmer's head was bent, his brow locked into a preoccupied scowl, his hands clasped behind his back. The wind ruffled his russet hair and the dying sun shadowed his face, and he looked, to Storme's everlasting annoyance, as handsome as he had the first moment she laid eyes on him—and infinitely more challenging.

Augusta was saying, "But . . . all the murders, the—the depredations of women . . . weren't you afraid of him?"

Storme turned, her irritation with the sight of Simon

darkening her eyes and all but souring her pleasure in the taste of his candy. "Edward Teach," she told Augusta shortly, "was a gentleman, just as much as Stede Bonnet or Calico Jack Rackham or any of the others you have such foul notions about. I never entered a room but what he didn't get to his feet and kiss my hand. He spoke as well as any of your pretty poets, and at *his* table nobody was ever slighted. He was every bit as well bred as that fancy brother of yours, and for my part, a far better man than his murderers will ever be!"

Augusta looked away, momentarily disconcerted. "I—I didn't mean to give offense, I'm sure," she murmured. "It's just that this all is so alien to me, you understand."

Storme looked at her, curiosity overcoming her hostility for a moment. What a peculiar wench this was, and more different from her strutting brother than even appearance would allow. Storme had very little dealings with women and hardly knew how to react to them at all. In Storme's world there were two kinds of people—those she could use, and those she could conquer, and there was no doubt that Simon's sister fell into the former category.

Storme walked back to the candy dish and scooped up the last three pieces of candy, regarding the woman through slanted eyes. "What'd you say your name was?" she asked abruptly.

"Gussie," Augusta replied. The shy uncertainty faded from her eyes as she added with a smile, "Actually, it's Augusta, but Simon is the only one who calls me that. I believe he feels that by addressing me by a regal name he will somehow be able to make me live up to it—as though overnight I could become tall, statuesque, and beautiful." And she laughed a little, gesturing to indicate her dumpy figure, frowsy hair, and ill-suited features.

Then she sighed, and a look of distant sorrow came into her eyes. "I know it must be difficult for him, to have such an awkward sister to take care of, and I do try to be what he wants me to. But it's so difficult. I never seem to get it right, and I always feel as though I am on the outside looking in. I never seem to belong anywhere."

Storme, through a mouthful of candy, only grunted. But it took her aback, the strange sense of kinship she felt with the girl. Storme, too, knew how it felt to not quite fit in, to struggle constantly to make a place for herself, and she had never heard anyone else voice her feelings before. It was sympathy she felt for Augusta, Storme realized slowly, and that was an alien emotion. Not, she assured herself quickly, that she wouldn't feel sorry for anyone who had to spend her life with an arrogant, pig-headed fool like the Farmer riding roughshod over her.

And then Augusta blushed and smiled apologetically. "But what am I thinking of? You don't want to hear my problems. I forgot myself for a moment."

Storme was surprised to see Augusta's face suddenly transformed with a radiant smile. "Please don't think I'm too forward," the girl said, getting to her feet impulsively, extending her hands, "but it is so good to have another woman around. I do hope we will become friends."

Storme was too nonplussed to even withdraw her hands from Augusta's affectionate clasp. What a silly, innocent ninny this sister was . . . but how strangely appealing it was to be treated with such unrestrained warmth. To be welcomed as a *friend*. Storme's friendships, if such they could be called, were based sheerly on a balance of power, backed by threats and underlined with treachery—and all of them were with men. She had never imagined what it would be like to have a woman as a friend, and for no other reason than that she was liked.

And then Augusta, pressing Storme's hands in brief reassurance, added gently, "I shan't pry into your reasons for being here, but I do beg that while you are with us you'll make this house your home, and know that you are most welcome. And whatever troubles you may have, you musn't worry yourself, because Simon is the brightest, most worthy champion in all of Carolina, and he will put them to rights in no time!"

It was only Storme's startlement that choked back an incredulous bark of laughter, and it was just as well, for at that moment Simon came in.

A black scowl marred his features when he saw the two women in such close confidence, but he erased it like magic when Augusta turned. "Well," he drawled smoothly, "I see the two of you are becoming acquainted."

"Oh, yes," replied Augusta brightly, giving Storme's fingers a last squeeze before releasing them. "We're getting along famously. We've been having the most pleasant little chat."

Simon murmured, "I can well imagine." He slanted a dark look at Storme. She kept her expression blank.

Simon turned back to Augusta with a small bow. "I thought perhaps our guest might enjoy a stroll about the grounds while it is cool. If, of course"—and he turned to Storme politely—"you're not too tired."

Storme hardly knew what to make of this. It was no doubt some trick, but trick or no, she was in no position to refuse such an opportunity. She arched her eyebrows at him. "I'm not tired at all."

Simon smiled at Augusta and took Storme's arm. "Excuse us, my dear."

They had reached the shaded front gallery before Simon dropped Storme's arm—and his pretenses at politeness. He said flatly, "You told her who you are."

Storme shrugged, her eyes scanning twilit, tranquil surroundings for various avenues of escape. The shepherdess was busily herding her sheep toward shelter for the night; in the distance wagons creaked and mules plodded toward the barn; the slaves were singing some strangely haunting tune as they came in from the fields, shovels and picks thrown wearily over their shoulders. All was lazy, relaxed, and open. This was going to be absurdly easy.

"I didn't tell her nothing," replied Storme to Simon's question. She went down the steps and he kept casual pace with her. "She ain't a idiot, you know."

At that moment Storme noticed a surreptitious movement behind a box shrub to the right—a gleam of metal, a brush of cloth. They were so well concealed that no one without an eye trained for the unexpected would have noticed, but Storme knew immediately what the movement represented.

Guards! she thought in some astonishment, and not a little disappointment. No wonder he didn't lock her room. He had armed guards with instructions to monitor her every movement, and that meant nothing except that she would have to rethink her plan for escape.

She cast a glance toward Simon that was laced with resentment and challenge, but he did not seem to notice. He was walking beside her, his hands clasped easily behind his back, his stride casually matched with hers. The only expression on his face was a slight hint of a preoccupied frown. "I don't want you around my sister."

Storme laughed sharply and unpleasantly. "Afraid she'll decide to go a-pirating with me? That I'll blacken her soul and send it to hell? That's your problem, Farmer, not mine. I've got no concern with the girl."

Simon said fiercely, "See that you don't."

They walked in silence for a while, and Storme was far more concerned with what she saw around her than what might be going on in her captor's head. Once she looked back, and though she caught no sign of the guards, she knew they were still there. She could feel them.

Storme's bare feet, accustomed to the smooth plank of the deck, were tender on the grass and shell drive. Once she stepped on a pebble and swore softly, and this seemed to amuse Simon. "You'd best get used to it," he advised. "This is not the high seas, and most people in the civilized world have learned there is a reason for wearing shoes."

Storme scowled and said nothing. She had left the servant's shoes back in the inn where they had stopped, and as much as she hated to wear boots, it was obvious she was going to have to find a pair if she intended to do any fast moving.

Storme had quite cleverly guided Simon's steps toward the river as they walked, without his noticing. Now they were only a few hundred feet from its banks, and she had an unobstructed view of her path to escape. She stopped, her eyes lighting as she saw a barge, large and heavy and fully functional, lying innocently awaiting its passengers in a cove.

Simon followed the direction of her gaze. "Ah, the Chowan," he commented easily. "Lovely, isn't it? We Carolinians think it's quite as magnificent as the James, and are just as proud of it."

Storme knew all about the Chowan. It was wide and deep and fully navigable, running from this point inland directly into Albemarle Sound, and then clear and free into the Atlantic Ocean. Elation swelled within her, but she disguised it with a slanted glance toward Simon. "Is this where you do your bathing?" she inquired innocently.

To her very great surprise, a twitch of mirth attacked his lips which he quickly subdued. "No," he responded reasonably. "Unlike the savages who formerly claimed this land, we bathe indoors, near the fire, in a tub."

Storme snorted. "That's filthy."

"Another thing to which you will soon grow accustomed."

Not, she thought with secret grim certainty, *if I have anything to do with it.*

"You've doubtless noticed the barge anchored there," Simon continued conversationally. His hands were still arranged properly behind his back, his shoulders tall and straight, his head held easy and proud. "That is the most common form of transportation upon the Chowan, used to ferry tobacco and other goods into city ports—and sometimes passengers as well. I feel compelled to point out, however, that it takes eight strong men to pole a barge, and even then it can be easily overtaken by a fleet sailing ship or even a canoe. That particular barge," he concluded with a gracious smile, "belongs to me, and nothing you can do or say will persuade even one of my servants to touch it without my express permission. They are frightfully loyal, you see. Furthermore, there are no other boats, canoes, sloops or schooners on this plantation—I don't much care for water travel and never saw the point in maintaining a fleet. However..." And he inclined his head to her most politely. "I shouldn't in any way wish to detract from your enjoyment of your stay with us, so please, feel free to try your luck with the river. My men need a good drilling, anyway, and no doubt we should all enjoy the sport."

Storme's hands clenched in tight fists at her sides, but she said nothing, staring straight ahead. Simon took her arm, and she kept her muscles rigid as he gestured her to turn.

"Now on your left," he continued conversationally, "you'll notice an impenetrable forest, complete with wild boars, bears, and wolves. Of course, you can't see it from here, but on the outer edges of the plantation lies the beginning of the Great Dismal Swamp. You remember the swamp, don't you? We passed through it on our way here. Quite a collection of interesting wildlife there, too—moccasins, cougars, alligators—all most deadly, I'm afraid, and not the least bit hospitable to visitors. Of course," he added helpfully, "you could always cross the fields and pastures on horseback—you do ride, don't you? No? Well, perhaps you could try it afoot; it shouldn't take you more than a day or two. And there you will find a very nice road that will lead you right back into Virginia, which is, I'm sure," he concluded with a smile, "exactly where you want to be."

Storme was silent for a very long time. She seethed inside from his mockery, she churned with the frustration of her plans, but she could not prevent a very reluctant surge of grudging admiration. When she looked at him there was resentment in her eyes, but also a sly measure of respect. "So, Farmer," she said thoughtfully. "You are smarter than I thought."

Simon smiled and tilted his head to her, gesturing her toward a promenade between rows of sculpted shrubs. He dropped his hand behind his back again and they walked in silence for a while.

And then Simon said, "Of course, we're not as isolated as it may first appear. We have some rather interesting neighbors. Edenhouse, for example, is just across the river." And he glanced at her with what Storme thought was exceptional shrewdness. "Perhaps you're familiar with it."

So. There was obviously more to this entire situation than first met the eye. He brought her to this godforsaken place, made certain she knew there was no escape, and then tempted her with the proximity of Governor Eden, the one person in the world who could be counted upon to free her.

She could not fathom what, exactly, was his game, but she knew she must be wary.

It was no longer a battle of daring and strength, but of wits and will, and the Farmer was a worthy opponent. She found, with a strange sense of rising excitement, that she was actually looking forward to the challenge. But her wits were sharper, her will was stronger, and she had no doubt that she would prevail.

Storme glanced at him through lowered lashes, noting the ease of his stride, the confidence in his manner. How different he seemed now than the night he had been brought to her cabin . . . taller, stronger, more powerful. Almost from the moment he set foot on dry land he had begun to change. This was his world, this alien, fertile place, and he was in command. She barely recognized him at all.

She had known him naked. She had explored every inch of his private body and had allowed him to do the same to her. He had been inside her, and yet . . . it almost seemed as though it had never happened. This man was a stranger to her. She could not believe she had ever lain in such intimacy with this strong, controlled man; that the hands that had stroked her so lovingly now held her captive; that the lips that had whispered such sweet and welcome endearments were now the author of her destruction.

She frowned a little, puzzling over it, and at last demanded curiously, "Is this the way it always is? After a man and woman lie together it's forgotten, just like it'd never been?"

At last she seemed to have caught him off guard. She felt him stiffen, and he didn't answer.

Storme shrugged. "I knew it was that way with the pirate lot. I guess it's so with the gentry, too."

Simon said carefully, "It depends on the circumstances." He did not look at her, and his tone was very formal. "At any rate, it is not something we discuss in polite company."

Storme raised an eyebrow. "Why not? Are you ashamed that you do it?"

"That, too, depends on the circumstances."

Storme kicked aside a worrisome pebble, scowling. For all his fine talk about the proper way the thing was done, it did not seem to her there was much difference, in the end, between his behavior and that of the rutting pigs she had seen in the alleyways. Not that it mattered to her, of course. But she would like to know the truth of the thing.

"It was pleasant, wasn't it?" she demanded abruptly.

Simon looked straight ahead. His jaw was tight, and he said nothing.

"It *was* pleasant," she insisted. "Else you wouldn't have wanted to keep doing it."

Simon said stiffly, "I think that is quite enough—"

"Ha, fine Farmer!" she exclaimed in disgust. "For all your fancy airs, you're no better than any of a dozen men I could scrape off the wharf at any waterfront on the coast! You put your pants on the same way they do, you take to bed the same women they do, and you're just angry because it's so!"

In a movement so swift Storme did not even see it coming, he turned, hauling her against him with fingers that dug into her upper arms and so forcefully that her breasts felt the buttons on his coat. His face was close, his eyes were blazing, and there was anger there, but there was more—something raw and naked and hungry that made her heart pound and her muscles seem momentarily liquid. She felt his gaze on her lips and his thighs hard against hers and she thought, *He's going to kiss me. He's going to put his mouth on mine and his lips will be hard and his tongue will be strong, and when he does . . .*

When he did, she did not know what she would do. She only knew that the pressure of his body was making her breasts ache and her breath shallow and she could not seem to break away from the fire in his eyes. She did not even want to.

And then, as though with a great struggle, something began to change within him. His fingers tightened, then slowly, stiffly, loosened. He dropped his gaze. He said lowly, "No. That's not what makes me angry." And then he let her go.

But Storme did not move. She looked at him, and made him look back. She was still breathing heavily. She demanded quietly, "Where is my ship, Farmer? What has become of my crew?"

He met her gaze steadily, and for a long time. For a moment, just a moment, she thought he might tell her.

But then, with a light touch upon her shoulder, he gestured toward the house. "I think it's time to go in," he said simply, and then he smiled. "We wouldn't want you to catch a chill, now would we?"

* *Chapter Sixteen* *

The day was endless for Simon. After he had dispatched the pirate girl to her room, Simon had looked forward to a quiet dinner of the kind he was accustomed to having at home . . . candlelight, wine, silent servants bringing and removing warm dishes; refined, gracious conversation with his sister; a chance to forget the horror of the past weeks. He was to have none of it.

Storme's arrival had upset the household to such a degree that dinner was late; the meal was cold, and Augusta, far from her usual reserved self, could not stop chattering. And all she wanted to talk about was Storme O'Malley and her pirating ways.

Simon could tell that Augusta was far too interested in the pirate girl, and after only one afternoon in her company. Nothing but problems could develop if limits were not set now, but he didn't feel up to dealing with the situation tonight. He wished Augusta would simply be quiet.

Finally he could stand it no longer. In the midst of Augusta's transported monologue about the legends of the sea Storme had shared with her, Simon set down his wine glass with enough force to make his sister break off in the middle of a sentence.

He met Augusta's startled eyes with a short, calming

breath. "Augusta," he said deliberately, "perhaps we could find a more palatable subject for the table, for be forewarned— if I hear the name Storme O'Malley once more this evening, I will be forced to ask that you finish your supper in your room."

Augusta's eyes went even wider. "Why, Simon! What a strange thing for you to say. After all, the young lady is our guest, and I quite enjoyed my visit with her this afternoon."

Simon felt a knot of tension grab his shoulders and travel toward the back of his neck. He kept his voice very calm. "Augusta, I'm going to have to ask that there be no more such occasions. Mistress O'Malley is quite unlike any other guests we've entertained, as you may have already ascertained, and I cannot say that I approve of her as company for you. Perhaps it would be best if you curtail your contact with her as much as possible."

Augusta looked hurt. "Simon, that's unkind. You know how dull I get here all alone, and she is by far the most interesting person I've ever met. I was so looking forward to—"

"Augusta," he said curtly, "this matter is no longer open for discussion. Please do as I ask."

Augusta was uncharacteristically argumentative. "You're being unreasonable and insensitive. What bad company you think she would be for me, I cannot imagine! Will you have me protected from life forever? Why, you even thought to deceive me about who she was—do you think I am so silly? I am a grown woman, Simon; I don't need you to guide my every thought."

Simon's jaw clenched, and his eyes narrowed as he got to his feet. "You can't imagine what bad company she is, can you? Already she has brought dissension into my house, and I will have none of it. You are my sister, and you will do as I say, do you understand me?"

"But Simon—"

"*Enough!*" he shouted. "You may think you're a grown woman, but you're not so old you couldn't benefit from a little old-fashioned discipline, and I will be happy to administer it if you do not desist this moment!"

To his horror, her eyes flooded with tears of humiliation and hurt, and too late Simon realized how harsh he'd been. Before he could stop her, she leaped from the table and ran upstairs, sobbing softly.

With a smothered oath, Simon threw his napkin on the table. He stalked across the polished floor, flung open the library doors, and reached for a bottle of brandy.

Simon came to breakfast the next morning in a foul mood. He had a headache from staying up too late and drinking too much, and he felt tired and blurry-eyed from a restless night. No matter how he had tried to put thoughts of Storme O'Malley out of his head, memories of her, anger with her, notions of her, and imaginings of her invaded his rest and chased away sleep.

It had shocked him, what she had brought him to as they walked by the river. Was it anger, or was it desire? Or perhaps, most frighteningly, a combination of both. He only knew that in that moment he had never wanted anything as fiercely as he had wanted to crush her mouth to his, to cover her body with his—and that, for just an instant, he was as close to losing control as he ever wanted to be.

And then later, with Augusta...he was ashamed of himself. Already Storme had brought divisiveness between them, caused him to shout at his sister and send her away in tears. How much worse lay in store?

Through the night he had lain awake, remembering Storme's long, perspiration-slick limbs entwined with his, her slim body straining with his, her firm young breasts and her hair, tousled and tangled on the pillow. Thinking how close she was, lying in her own bed just across the hall, how easy it would be...and despising himself for the thoughts. He remembered, and he was ashamed. He wanted, and he hated himself for it. But nothing he could do would keep the low insidious thoughts from creeping back into his consciousness.

He had never imagined, when he agreed to this insane assignment, that among the many problems Storme O'Malley's presence in his house would bring, this would be the most tormenting.

He came to breakfast that morning half-hoping that Storme would have escaped during the night, thus putting an end to all their problems. But Fortune did not seem in the mood to smile on Simon York of late, and she was there.

Augusta was sitting at her customary place, her napkin unfolded, sipping tea as she waited for the head of the household to arrive. Storme was moving around the room with the restless stealth of a long-legged cat, peering into cupboards, appraising the silver service, examining the texture of the draperies. She had wound her hair into a long braid that fell like a rope across her shoulder, and even in the dowdy servant's clothes that were half again too big for her, with her bare feet and tattered sleeves, she looked regal, commanding, and not a little dangerous. And the sight of her, for whatever reason, added a new edge to Simon's temper.

Simon pulled out his chair and snapped open his napkin. "Call your woman right after breakfast and set her to making some suitable clothes for Mistress O'Malley," he commanded Augusta shortly. "I want her in a proper frock before teatime."

Augusta, shocked at this unorthodox greeting, merely turned startled eyes on him, and Simon added more guilt to his list of afflictions. "I'm sorry, my dear," he said more gently. "Good morning." And then, forcing the politeness to extend to his guest, he added, "Mistress O'Malley? Would you care to join us for breakfast?"

Storme gave him a look which was neither welcoming nor polite, but she was not about to miss a meal simply to spite him. She pulled out her chair.

Storme had not had a much better night than Simon's. She had never gotten used to sleeping on land, and she was too old to begin now. But she was even less accustomed to having so much to worry about, and her busy, determined mind would not let her rest until she dealt with all of it. And among all of her perplexities and difficulties, the Farmer stood out: a singular, frustrating annoyance that simply could not be ignored.

Simon waited until Storme was seated to comment mildly,

"In the future we shall make it a policy in the household that all members shall come to the dining table fully clothed." He returned the teapot from which he had been pouring to its stand, and did not glance at Storme. "That includes shoes."

Augusta widened her eyes in surprise at his rudeness, but Storme ignored both of them. Just then the door opened and three black women filed in, each one of them bearing a tray of food.

Heaping platters of pork, venison, breads, cakes, and cheese were placed upon the table—along with an appropriate and extensive selection of jams, syrups and preserves. Storme's eyes widened as she watched. "God's balls!" she exclaimed in a mixture of contempt and awe. "All this food for just us? Don't you people eat more than once a day?"

Simon ignored her remark as beneath comment, and placed a slice of ham on his plate, passing the platter on to Augusta. Storme did not wait for such amenities, but plucked a couple of hotcakes off the platter nearest her, eating them with one hand while she tore off a piece of glazed cake with the other and dipped it into the butter dish. The hotcakes were made with cornmeal slightly sweetened with molasses, and she finished them off greedily, grabbing up a piece of ham before Augusta could set the platter down. The cake was glazed with almonds and sugar and was the most utterly delicious thing she had ever tasted. Whatever else could be said for the Farmer, he did set a good table.

Storme was unaware of the silence that had fallen, nor of the gazes that were riveted on her—Augusta's embarrassed and somewhat shocked, Simon's cold and disapproving. Even the servants who were standing against the wall in readiness for an order were staring at Storme with wide eyes and slack jaws. Storme stretched across the table to get a sweet roll, slathering it in the butter dish, and tore off a piece of ham with her teeth. The ham was salty, though, and she reached for the pitcher of what she assumed was water near her. She gulped from it greedily and almost choked, spewing out buttermilk everywhere.

Augusta gave a muffled cry and jumped to her feet,

brushing at the milk droplets that had sprayed from Storme's mouth onto her bodice, and Storme slammed down the pitcher.

"Great Lucifer's horns!" she gasped in disgust, scrubbing her mouth. "What the bloody hell is *that*?"

Simon was on his feet so swiftly that she could only interpret the movement to imply violence. Her hand closed around the butterknife but his hand was quicker, his fingers wrenching her wrist until she was forced to release it. In her other hand Storme still held the buttered roll, and she had no choice but to throw it at him, for the black anger in his face left no doubt that this was a situation that called for self-defense. The roll grazed the side of his head and bounced off the opposite wall, leaving a greasy stain on the rose-colored covering. Simon's fingers tightened on her wrist until she thought the bones would snap.

Simon said quietly, "Augusta, will you excuse us, please?"

Augusta cast an anxious, worried look from Simon to Storme, but neither combatant dared release the other's gaze. Augusta, remembering the argument of the night before, murmured somewhat distractedly, "Yes, of course . . ." and hurried out. The servants followed on more stealthy feet.

Storme exploded, "By the Virgin's womb! What mad dog bit you this morning?"

Simon spoke with such low and deadly force that the walls practically vibrated with it. "You will *not*," he told her, "turn my home into a cave dwelling for godless barbarians."

He released her wrist so abruptly that it hurt. "*This*"—he picked up the plate before her and set it down again with such force that a small crack appeared in the fine porcelain—"is a plate. One puts food upon it. This"—he thumped her empty glass—"is a glass. One drinks from it."

Storme thought in distant fascination that she had never seen his eyes so dark, yet so fiercely alive at the same time . . . except, perhaps, once. And remembering that last time did not frighten her at all. It made her feel excited, and curiously powerful.

"This," he continued tightly, taking up the knife, "is used for cutting food, not people. As for the contents of that pitcher which you've utterly contaminated, it is called buttermilk, and one drinks it. One does *not* regurgitate it at the table all over one's dining companions!"

"Cow dung," replied Storme contemptuously. Simon slammed the knife down on the table. The china rattled.

Storme folded her arms over her chest and regarded him thoughtfully for a moment. She could see that her silence infuriated him, and was pleased.

"Why, Farmer?" she asked at last, in a reasonable tone. "Why all these rules and orders? Does your food taste better off a plate than mine does from my hand?"

He seemed, for just a moment, at a loss for a proper answer. Then he recovered himself abruptly and returned without compromise, "Yes. This is my house, and we are civilized people. As long as you are under my roof, you, too, will behave in a civilized fashion—I don't care if it bloody well kills you!"

Storme snorted. "You Englishmen and your civilization! A bunch of filthy, lying murderers, that's what you are—"

"And you're not?"

She turned on him, eyes blazing. "I ain't a murderer! Not like your mad-eyed redcoats!" Her fists went tight and so did her voice and she cried, "They killed Pompey! He was defending me—he never did anything but defend me, and they hacked him down like an old tree! I sat in his blood and I held him, but it was too late because they'd *murdered* him!"

Simon was startled out of speech—first by the venom in her tone, and then by what he was certain was a flash of tears in those crystal-blue eyes. It took him a moment to connect the name with the big black beast who had been Storme's bodyguard aboard ship, and when he did he was even more disoriented.

She *was* capable of feeling, then. He had never thought of that before. She was more than a half-wild child, more than a cold-hearted criminal . . . she had held affection for the black giant, and when she spoke of him tears came to her eyes. The whole of it made Simon feel strange—in the wrong, somehow—and it took a while for him to gather his thoughts again.

He forced a harshness into his tone that he did not entirely feel. "I didn't kill your friend," he said curtly. "I never wanted any part of any of this, and I'm hard put to it to feel sympathy for you now. *You* chose the path of criminality, madame; you made your life what it is today, and now you must face the consequences."

"You sound like a bloody preacher!" she returned contemptuously.

All traces of former vulnerability were wiped away so quickly that Simon might easily have imagined the flash of tears he had seen before. Her emotions, like her mind, leaped like quicksilver from one target to the other, leaving Simon somewhat stunned by the effect.

Her quick disdainful eyes swept the room, lighting in a moment upon the lace cloth on the table. She gave it a scornful brush with the back of her hand and demanded imperiously, "Where did this come from?"

Simon drew a short breath through flared nostrils, exaggerating his patience. "That, madame, is fine lace. Presumably, it came from France."

"Like bloody hell it did!" There was a gleam of defiant triumph in her eyes. "It came straight off a pirate ship, and you were glad to pay the price for it!" Pursuing her point with grim delight, she thumped the teapot with a click of her fingernails. "And that fine Dutch tea you're so fond of, and them pretty clothes your sister wears, and . . ." Her eyes were brilliant with satisfaction as she reached forth her hand and flipped the linen cravat he wore out of its neat knot. "Even them elegant frocks you strut around in—if it was bought in a store, you've got pirates to thank for it! Ed Teach or Jack Rankin or *me*—we brought every scrap of bleedin' frippery onto these shores, and you don't ask where they come from when you go to market, do you?"

She settled back, the faintest hint of a victorious smile lighting her contemptuous features, and she declared magnanimously, "You like pretty things, Farmer, and I was most happy to bring them to you. No thanks are necessary."

Simon felt the back of his neck grow hot, more in irritation for her temerity than for whatever truth her words might have contained. Damnation upon the woman, anyway! Did she never give that agile brain of hers a rest? And why should he allow himself to be so annoyed by her incredible facility for being right?

He straightened his shoulders and replied coolly, "Madame, I've no intention of standing here and debating the economics of piracy with you. We were on a quite different subject altogether."

She gave a short bark of laughter, her eyes glittering gleefully. "It don't sit so well with you when it's put like that, does it? Get off with your pompous airs, Farmer! You and every other weak-kneed gent in this province owes us a living, and it's about damn time you admitted it. As for me . . ." She lifted her chin a fraction, that faint mocking smile still on her lips. "I'm the best in the business and bloody proud of it. You should be honored to even know me."

Simon's eyes grew stern, a hard slate gray, and Storme knew with a secret delight the fury he was battling. God, but he was magnificent-looking in a temper. She wanted to see those long muscles clench, those dark eyes crackle with anger . . . or with passion . . .

And she liked the way his lips tightened and his voice went very smooth as he replied, "Indeed. How very remiss of me. Perhaps you would be good enough to explain to me exactly why I should be honored by the presence of yet a common thief, a renegade savage whose manners, I beg to point out, barely rival those of my sister's pup!"

Now Storme's temper flared. "You ignorant ass! I commanded the best crew in the Caribbean! Your noble fleet trembled with fear when I raised my flag! There never was a stronger crew or a fleeter ship than mine, and I ruled them all! I'd like to see you do half as well, *Farmer.*" The last word was spat out like a bad taste, and she sat there, her glittering eyes pinning him and her fists curled against the arms of the chair as though she would hurl it at him if he said another word.

Simon knew he was being drawn in, but he couldn't stop himself. She never failed to bring out the very worst in him, and he was angry with himself for that as much as he was with her.

His lips curled in cool mockery. "Ah, yes. Your gallant crew. A bunch of filthy, cowardly dogs, if you ask me. For where is that noble, loyal lot now?" he challenged. "Half of them taken in their drunken sleep and the other half skulked off in the woods like the whimpering fools they are!"

That struck like the fine edge of a blade, for it was true. *Even Squint*, she thought and it hurt too much to think further. She had been alone against overwhelming odds before; she was not afraid to be so again.

"We brought *you* to your knees," she flung back at him. "You and every other arrogant jackass who crossed our path!"

"Save one," he pointed out, unperturbed, and she wanted to throw something at him. The only reason she did not was because she could tell by the hard glitter in his eyes that he was just as angry as she was, despite his ever-so-cautious pretense at coolness.

She lifted her shoulders grandly. "Laws were made to be kept by fools and ignored by the brave." And then suddenly her expression changed; the crystalline eyes slanted at him speculatively, almost coquettishly. "Shall I repent my wicked ways, Farmer?" she inquired innocently. "Is that what you want? And if I do, will you plead for my poor sorry hide before the great General Court? Or perhaps . . ." And a hint of malice came into the sugar-sweet tone, backed by a warning glint in her eyes. "If I were a *respectable* woman, you might do one better and favor me with a turn in your bed."

Simon wanted to hit her. In that single surge of red rage his hand even clenched for the blow before he caught himself, and then he was appalled. He had never wanted to strike a woman before. But he had never known a woman like this before, nor imagined the emotional depths into which she could plunge him.

He said distinctly, and with a very great effort, "Madame, I frankly don't care what you do. You can plunder every waterway from here to the Thames if you like. You can march into Windsor Castle and take the bloody *King* for ransom and I won't turn a hair trying to stop you. But as long as you're in my house, you're my responsibility, and you will bloody well do as I say."

He turned sharply on his heel to go, afraid to say more, afraid even to linger in her presence lest he be pushed beyond the bounds. But before he had taken a full step her arm shot out and closed about his wrist. She had a strong grip for a woman, and he was surprised. He looked back at her.

There was a speculative curve to her lips, and her eyes, lightly shaded by dusky lashes, held a dangerous confidence. She released his arm slowly. "You must think me a fool, Farmer," she said quietly. "I know why you really brought me here."

Simon's heart stopped.

"So many noble principles, such a brave martyr," she scoffed gently. "Save the helpless woman from a murderous mob, will you? Come off the hero? If the truth be known . . ." A grim, triumphant gleam sparked her eyes. "You just like having me your prisoner."

Simon's heart started beating again, slowly, heavily. She sat there before him, smug in victory and bright-eyed in defiance, her hair gleaming golden in the morning light and her face flushed with challenge, as proud as any queen who ever tossed aside a suitor or scorned a peasant. Simon did not know why it was—perhaps a remnant of anger, perhaps a wicked recognition of the truth she spoke, perhaps nothing more than the thrill of looking at her, so arrogant in her manner and wild in her beauty—but his blood began to thicken, slowly and unpreventably, gathering in his loins, congesting his chest, heating his skin.

He brought one hand to rest upon the back of her chair, and he leaned over her, very close. He saw her chest rise with breath, and her eyes quicken with alertness as he did so. He said softly, "Maybe I do."

He looked at her lips, close enough to kiss, and the thrusting curve of her breast beneath the baggy folds of material. He felt a strand of her hair brushing the back of his hand. He wasn't going to touch her. He was certain of that. "Maybe I should like it even better if you were bound hand and foot, and kept naked like an animal." He felt a breath on his cheek, and her eyes widened just a fraction. "Does that frighten you?"

She held his gaze boldly, steadily. Her lips parted to reveal the tip of her tongue, very briefly, moistening them. Simon thought, *I could have her . . . now . . .*

Storme said, "No, Farmer, you don't frighten me. You won't beat me, or kill me, or even tie me up." And she smiled with faint superiority. "You ain't the type. And besides . . ." Now her voice softened a fraction, though her eyes still held his firmly. "I don't think you really want me scared of you at all."

Simon slowly released his hand from the back of her chair; he made himself straighten up. With all the command at his possession, he made his face a blank and replied with the greatest possible restraint. "You are right. It matters little to me what you do or do not think of me. The only thing I insist upon is that you know this one thing: This is my home. I—and my father before me—have built it, protected it, cleared and planted the land, and put our sweat and blood into every acre. We have fought off flood, drought, and invasion from our enemies and we have kept this place firm. I will *not* have it threatened now by a bad-tempered criminal with a grudge against the world. I will fight to protect what is mine, do you understand?" His fist clenched at his side and his voice went tight. "When it comes to my home and my family, I give no quarter. I will *fight*."

Storme looked at him thoughtfully. Strangely enough, she did understand. The house, with all its fineries and fripperies, was his ship, and she was as much an invader into his world as the uniformed Englishmen had been into hers.

Once he had been the alien force to be bound and imprisoned; now she was. She was a threat to all that he held dear, and she knew exactly how she would react were the positions reversed.

She looked at him silently for a long moment, and she felt, as he did, the significance of a bond—tenuous and uncertain, but a bond nonetheless—that was just beginning to grow. And then she demanded quietly, "Where is my ship, Farmer? What have you done with my crew?"

There was a flicker of something in his eyes, very brief, and very faint. Then he said firmly, "When the time comes for you to go, no one will be happier than I. In the meantime, I am in command and you will do things my way. Is that perfectly understood?"

Again, no answer. But there had been that moment... that slight weakening in his eyes. She smiled. "You have butter in your hair," she told him mildly.

Simon's jaw tightened, and his muscles bunched. He turned on his heel and without a word stalked away.

Storme waited until he was gone, then helped herself to another stack of corn cakes, with syrup this time. She ate with her fingers because it was easier that way, and because she knew it would make Simon angry if he could see.

* *Chapter Seventeen* *

Simon was in the west field, stacking summer hay. Three of his slaves worked beside him, and half a row before them Peter led another crew with scythes and knives, cutting the grass for fodder. The field was a sea of rippled and tangled gold, not half of it yet mowed; the summer sun was hot and the insects vicious. Simon's shoulders strained and he was sweaty and itchy with chaff and dust, but he did not grate against the discomfort—he almost enjoyed it. Every muscle was working, every sense alive, and there was neither time nor inclination to focus on anything but the job at hand. At times like these he was reminded who he was, and why he was here, and life was beautifully simple.

Storme O'Malley had been at Cypress Bay a fortnight, and Simon's life had almost begun to regain some sense of equilibrium. Almost. At least he now felt safe in letting her out of his sight and going on about his business—although he still found himself returning to the house too often and on too many shallow excuses, and hours out of his day were wasted. As like as not, he would find Storme engaged in some harmless activity with his sister, for Augusta found the woman enchanting and Storme—much to Simon's surprise—actually seemed to enjoy his sister's company. Realistically, he found that there was no way to keep Storme and Augusta apart; he couldn't lock them both up—all he could do was hope that Storme would be gone soon.

On one occasion he had come in and found Storme engaged in intimate conversation with Augusta—regaling her with tales of a Caribbean island where all the natives went naked, the women painting their nipples bright colors and the men adorning their privates with peacock feathers. Augusta meekly accepted Simon's shocked scolding, but Storme merely laughed in his face.

Another time he found Storme sitting on the floor cross-legged, her skirts hitched up to her knees, teaching Augusta to dice. Storme had already won from his sister a pearl comb and a pair of jet earrings, and when Simon, outraged, objected, Augusta gaily advised him not to be such a bore—she would win it all back when the game turned to whist. And she did.

Simon paused now to wipe his sweaty brow, thinking, *I must find a husband for Augusta. I've put the matter off too long, and if she had something else to occupy her mind, she would not be so utterly enamored of every word that spews forth from that pirate-girl's mouth. . . .*

But that observation brought with it another, eminently disturbing question: How much longer could this impossible situation be expected to last? Already she had been here longer than he had ever expected, or would have agreed to, had he known. And his feelings about the situation were mixed.

There were times when Simon felt that his life, and all the careful control he so diligently maintained over it, was being wrested inexorably from him—and other times when he was amazed that, given the circumstances, disaster of immeasurable proportions had not already occurred. Storme was incorrigible—an irritant, a disruptive, a threat to everything he held dear, but all in all, matters could have been much worse.

Her language was still abominable, and so was her temper when given the slightest provocation. She still refused to wear shoes and shocked Augusta with a similar disdain for corsets and hoops. Simon secretly found her attitude on such matters amusing and oddly sensible, but, of course, he went out of his way to voice disapproval wherever Storme was concerned.

Her table manners had improved, but Simon did not flatter himself to imagine he had been the cause. Storme, he had observed, was not only intelligent and quick, but very adaptable—as, of course, she would have to be to survive this long in the life she led. If it was expedient to her to adopt some of the ways of country life, she did so without undue debate, but just as quickly and decisively discarded those mores she found absurd. There was something rather admirable about the way she had handled the entire matter. Simon wondered if he could have done half as well were the situations reversed.

Generally speaking, Simon made it a practice to spend as little time in Storme's company as possible. He had taken to having his breakfast in the kitchen before the rest of the household was awake, and he very often stayed in the fields till sundown, partaking of his supper alone and in blessed peace. But that did not keep Storme O'Malley from invading his thoughts with more persistence than he could possibly find comfortable.

Simon dug his pitchfork with particular viciousness into a pile of hay, trying to exorcise the images of her that followed him even into the hot fields and took his mind from the work he loved. How could a man help being fascinated by a woman like that? Whether striding across a deck in men's breeches or moving through the hallways of Cypress Bay in bright silks and taffetas the seamstress had done up for her, Storme was a presence, a magnetic glow of color and force that could not be ignored. Her voice, the robust ring of her laughter—usually mocking, usually delivered with arms akimbo and blue eyes snapping and usually directed at Simon—those were sounds that invaded every inch of a room and lingered long after Storme had departed. Her swift, decisive movements, the purposeful way she had of walking, the swing of her tawny hair—which she refused to pin up no matter how plainly it was suggested—those were sights to make a man's eyes linger, and to haunt him in the restless hours of the night when other memories, more explicit and more demanding, crept forth to entice him no matter how hard he tried to put them aside.

"Curses and damnation," Simon muttered now, causing one of the slaves to turn to him questioningly. Simon scowled and applied himself with renewed vigor to his work. He couldn't get away from her, even here. He had always prided himself upon his discipline, his self-reliance, his total control over himself and his environment. But he was helpless against the insidious hold this girl was gaining over him and his senses.

Sometimes, watching her stalk about his house with her skirts switching, issuing orders this way and that as though she owned the place, Simon had to repress a smile of indulgent amusement. When she sent his servants cowering for cover and his cook into a temper, he wanted to throttle her, and when he witnessed unobserved the covert delight she took in slipping candy to Augusta's puppies, he was touched by wonderment and confusion.

And sometimes, in a rare moment when he came upon her unawares, he noticed a hint of solemn contemplation on her face, a trace of forlorn yearning in her eyes. It was then he wanted to go to her and stroke her hair and draw her to him in comfort. . . . He was never unmoved by her. Everything about her sent his emotions into tumult and his reason into conflict, and he did not know how much longer he could hold up under the assault.

Blast Spotswood, anyway. Simon wiped his face on his sleeve and paused, his sun-narrowed eyes unconsciously hardening as he gazed toward the river. How could he ever have allowed himself to be talked into such a thing? It was a foolish scheme with little chance of success, and might one not think that the governor would have at least contacted him by now? How much longer was he supposed to wait?

Obviously, they had not found the letter. And just as obviously, Storme O'Malley was not inclined to go about shouting its location from the rooftops. Simon was certain that Eden had heard of her presence at Cypress Bay by now, but he had made no move to contact her. If Storme was plotting any method to get a message to him, Simon could find no evidence of it, and the suspense was wearing sorely on his nerves.

He had expected to receive further instructions from Virginia by now. He had hoped that Eden would have at least given some indication that he was aware of the threat Simon held against him. What the devil could Eden be thinking of? Was he fool enough to ignore the situation and hope it would go away? How long must they wait for him to rise to the lure?

Slowly, Simon let his eyes wander back toward the direction of the house, expelling a small and weary sigh. He would wait, he supposed, as long as necessary. But it was not going to be easy.

At Government House in Queen Anne's Town, Tobias Knight, secretary to Governor Eden, paced tautly back and forth, his hands clasped behind his back, his eyebrows drawn together in a frown. He was a slender man, high of brow and lazy of eye, in most appearances cool, collected, and competent. But when wrestling with a puzzle he took on the tenacity of a sea-turtle, and there was nothing smooth or negligent about him now.

"I weary of this game," he said impatiently. "O'Malley

has been here over a fortnight and we know less than we did at the beginning. It's useless to try to get into Cypress Bay; York keeps the place tighter than a frontier stockade. We've nothing to go on but rumor and speculation, and not one whit of it is helpful to us. We must know what Simon York is up to.''

Charles Eden smiled carelessly and without mirth. "Perhaps nothing. Perhaps the good man has merely decided to take himself a mistress.''

Tobias Knight stared at him, unable to see the humor in the situation at all. "Your lordship,'' he began carefully, "I think you may have underestimated—''

"I underestimate nothing,'' interrupted Eden calmly, yet there was an undertone of steel in his voice that drew Knight up short. His eyes were fixed and cold. "You, sir, however, are wrong about one thing. It's not Simon York we have to puzzle about, it's his unfortunate choice of friends in Virginia. This is obviously all some trick of Spotswood's, and *he* is the one we must guard against. It does concern me incidentally, however,'' he mused, "how York came to be involved. He is generally so careful to stay detached from affairs of state.''

"Perhaps he has had a change of heart,'' suggested Knight. "And not for the better.''

Eden made a noncommittal sound that dismissed more than acknowledged his secretary's comment. He was silent for a time, his heavily lidded eyes shielded in thought, his slim fingers absently toying with the quill upon his desk.

Charles Eden was a handsome man. His full-bottom russet wig curled to his shoulders, his long nose was possessed of the proper aristocratic tilt, and his lips perpetually upturned with the faintest hint of a proper cynical smile. Everything about him bespoke wealth and rank—his elegant tailoring, his impeccable taste, his arrogant bearing. He was a man born to rule and proud of it, and it was precisely for this reason, he knew, that the Carolinians he had come to rule despised him so. For the most part only the dregs of society had settled on these shores—criminals and runaways, indentured and impoverished; what could they know of what was good for them?

But Simon York . . . he was another matter altogether, and York's immutable antipathy toward him never failed to perplex Eden. Charles Eden and Simon York were two of a kind, cut from the same mold; they should have been the best of friends and strongest of allies. Both knew the way of the world belonged to the ruling class, both shared a common heritage from that class, both valued the privileges it brought. Yet Simon ruled Cypress Bay with the same solitary autocracy with which Governor Eden maintained his own Edenhouse, and more than a river separated the two plantations. York consistently rejected overtures of any but the most superficial social nature, and as for a political alliance . . . Simon York had always maintained nothing but an amused indifference toward all things political. Until now.

With a small dismissing frown, Eden turned back to his secretary. It mattered not why Simon York was involved in this, nor, indeed, how deeply he was involved. What did matter was that something must be done about it, and as quickly as possible.

Eden said thoughtfully, "This situation could be turned to our advantage, you know."

Tobias Knight looked up with interest.

"Spotswood may have done us a favor, though I'm sure it's the last thing he intended," Eden went on. "Since Blackbeard's death, Storme O'Malley has been a threat to us. As long as she was at sea, there was nothing we could do about it, but now the esteemed lieutenant governor from across the border has delivered her right into our hands."

Knight frowned. "It smells of a trap to me."

"Of course it is a trap, dear boy." Eden smiled tolerantly. "But that does not mean we must fall into it, does it?"

"Spotswood knows about the letter," insisted Knight. "If she uses it to bargain for her freedom—"

"We merely must make certain that she does not. But" —and his own eyes grew dark beneath lowered brows— "we'll not make the same mistake we did with Blackbeard.

First, find out if she has told anyone else of the location of the letter. If she hasn't . . .''

And he looked up, a complacent expression clearing his face and smoothing his brow. "If she has not," he finished simply, "I think it should be no trouble at all to be rid of her." His eyes met Knight's in a moment of explicit understanding, and he smiled. "After all, one good turn deserves another, don't you think? Spotswood brought her to us; we shall save him the trouble and expense of a public hanging. All in all, it should work out quite well for all concerned, don't you agree?''

Relief and eagerness lightened Tobias Knight's expression, although he was too well bred to share the familiarity of a smile with a superior. He merely straightened his shoulders with the confidence of a problem well solved, bowed formally, and agreed. "Yes, sir. I shall see to it straight away."

But once in the corridor he let the smile break through, and it was all he could do to keep from chortling with enthusiasm as he began to set in motion the investigations that would determine Storme O'Malley's fate.

In a wooded cove some seventy miles away, Squint crouched low over a campfire, warming a tin cup of blood broth and strong herbs over the flame. Occasionally he cast an anxious glance at the big man stretched out under the shade of a tupelo tree, but Pompey was sleeping naturally now. It wouldn't be too much longer before they were able to travel.

It had been rough going for a while. Knowing that Storme would need him more after the battle than during it, Squint had hidden in the bushes while his compatriots were slaughtered and the *Tempest* ransacked, while Storme herself was dragged like an animal into the hold of the filthy British ship . . . and every fighting instinct within him grated and railed against the common sense that told him to be still.

He had watched while bodies were dumped overboard— the filthy British pigs hadn't even the decency to bury the dead—and prisoners were taken away in chains. Then the ship was looted for cargo and looted again—bedding ripped, the galley dismantled, bulkheads slashed and scarred with swords—and watching it was like watching the rape of a fine and proud woman. It sickened Squint, almost more than the battle itself had done.

At sundown they had sailed away, the *Tempest* in tow, and Squint alone was left to survey the aftermath of the destruction, and to bury the dead. That was when he found Pompey, lying on the beach with the tide licking at his ankles, and discovered the big man was not dead.

Squint took the cup of broth over to Pompey and gently shook him awake. Weak as he was from his injuries and the fever that had plagued him the past fortnight, the African awoke in an instant, his arm instinctively going for his sword. Squint smiled and sat back on his haunches, offering the cup. "Aye, that's the way of it. A fightin' man to the end, and ye'll not forget it."

Pompey sat up slowly and took the broth as Squint observed him. The jagged wound that slit his bald head from crown to neck was red and puckered, but healing well from Squint's careful administration of poultice leaves. His bones had been too thick to break, and he had been free of fever for two days now. Squint nodded approvingly. "Aye, ye'll do. We'll be movin' out of this hellhole in a day or two, for by the Virgin's blood, I can't take it much more'n that."

He nodded toward the cove that glinted a cerulean blue in the distance. "There's a fisherman what comes most every day. 'Tis a small craft, to be sure, but it'll serve our purposes, and the fisherman's old. We'll have no trouble relieving him of his vessel."

He looked back at Pompey, his expression set and determined, but mildly confident. He had had a lot of time to think this through. "They'll be holdin' her in the Williamsburg gaol, for they can't hang her till fall. We'll get her out of there, don't you worry, and then we'll find the *Tempest*. We'll be back on the high seas in no time at all."

A measure of immense relief crossed Pompey's face, and he leaned back against the tree. Squint chuckled. "Ye didn't figure I was gonna let 'em hang her, did ye? Hellfire and brimstone, I'd like to see 'em try!'' And then his tone went serious, his grizzled jaw set grimly. ''No, they'll not kill that little girl, not while I draw breath. I owe her pa too much to let his seedlin' wither away in some filthy English gaol.''

He gave Pompey a bracing slap on the arm, and the big man responded with a wide grin, draining the cup. ''We'll get to her,'' Squint said. ''All she has to do is hang on till we do.''

* *Chapter Eighteen* *

Storme was going out of her mind. She had never been landbound this long in her life, and she did not like it any better than she had imagined she would.

The heat, the smells, the insects, the noise, the unerring sameness of every day . . . Everywhere she looked there was greenery, so much that the air practically seemed to be dripping with it and there were times she thought she would choke from the multitude of odors that lingered in the air with no sea breeze to cleanse them. Cooking smells, barnyard smells, grass and flower smells—even the earth itself had a heavy, decaying smell that penetrated every pore. The days were sticky with humidity and summer heat, and the occasional inland breeze was a pathetic relief.

And it wasn't just the common noises of a large household that grated on Storme's nerves, but the incessant background sounds that could drive a saint to swearing. The chatter of cicadas, the squeal of crickets, the snuffle and moo of barnyard animals, and the click of harness; the high-pitched creak of the well wheel and the clatter of wagons; squirrels scampering across the roof and fruit dropping to the ground . . . What Storme wouldn't have given for the rhythmic snap of sails and moan of timbers, the undulant sigh of waves and a cool salt breeze across her cheek! How did people live like this? Why would anyone do it from choice?

The worst of it was, nothing ever *happened*. One awakened every day in the same room, looked about, and saw the same trees, the same lawn, the same buildings. One moved around, ate meals, and went to bed again. What was the point in that?

And it was so blessed *hot*. Storme was accustomed to the sun, the baking rays on her face and the radiant heat rising up from the deck, but always there was a steady breeze to refresh it, and never had she endured it wrapped in so many clothes. This wet foul air trapped the heat, the walls and beams of the house held it, and she thought she'd strangle to death if she had to take one more breath.

Abruptly, and with an oath, Storme jerked off the wide lawn kerchief that swathed her neck and shoulders—Augusta called it a modesty piece—and flung it on the floor. That exposed her breasts almost to the nipples, but she didn't care. She jerked at the long sleeves of her red taffeta bodice, but they were firmly attached with expert stitches and she did not even succeed in loosening them. Storme liked fine materials and gay colors—the red bodice, yellow petticoat, and purple overskirt she wore today were testament to that—and Augusta had been very generous with her store of fabrics. But Storme had never realized how many yards of material went into the making of a fashionable frock, nor how hot taffeta could be when worn in layers. It only went to show what idiots these landlubbers were. In a climate where even the animals shed their furs in the summer, these people insisted upon covering themselves head to foot in not one, but several, thicknesses of fabric. They even wore clothes to bed!

With a derisive snort for the foolishness of it all, Storme flung herself onto the brass-studded leather couch, swinging her legs over its back and letting her heavy skirts fall back beyond her bare knees to catch the breeze from the open window. Discontentedly, she reached for a bowl of bonbons on the table near her head and, propping the bowl on her stomach, began to eat, scowling. The only good thing this place had to offer came from its kitchen, but even the joy of sweets was beginning to wane for Storme. She was growing soft, her muscles lax and her flesh slack, and she would soon be as round as Augusta.

It was midafternoon, traditionally the quietest part of the day, and for Storme the most frustrating. Augusta was napping in her room, the servants were engaged in quiet occupations to conserve their energy during the hottest part of the day, and Simon was in the fields. Storme was in the library, for it had grown to be her favorite part of the house. She did not know why, unless it was because looking at the weapons stored there gave her some sense of power, even though she could not reach them. Or perhaps it gave her pleasure to know how it would irritate Simon to find her here. Perhaps it was simply that being here, in this room he called his own, made her feel close to him, in an intimate, secretive way, and there was an advantage to studying the enemy.

Storme bit into a creamy pink confection, but the taste did nothing to sweeten her temper as she thought about the Farmer. What kind of man was he, to behave as he had done? It made no sense, and nothing irritated Storme more than a puzzle. He held her in his arms and murmured sweet endearments, and then he looked at her as though she were a stranger. He had saved her from mob execution and taken her into his home only to ignore her. He brought her within mere miles of a safe haven and then surrounded her with guards so she could not reach it. What kind of man *was* he? What did he want from her?

She had admired his courage when he fought off her men on the *Valiant*. She was amused by his cool wit when he was brought to her cabin, for not many Englishmen could have handled so uncertain a situation with such aplomb. And she was ever amazed by the unfolding layers of intelligence, foresight, and confidence that lay beneath the handsome exterior—amazed and puzzled.

She liked to see his eyes flash with anger and his fists clench with outrage. She liked the fancy words that rolled off his tongue with such cutting expertise, and she provoked him into scolding for just that reason. She liked the snap of unexpected humor that he tried so hard to repress, but mostly she liked the way he had looked at her, and smiled at her, that night aboard her ship, when his eyes were as soft as a lighthouse banked in fog and his lips, upturned just faintly at the corners, seemed to speak without words of things she couldn't imagine. No one had ever looked at her like that before. She wanted him to look at her like that again.

But the trouble was, he did not look at her at all if he could possibly avoid it. Since the morning at breakfast they had not exchanged half a dozen words alone, and she did not even have the satisfaction of provoking him to anger anymore, since he was rarely ever at home. Those brief fiery encounters were the only thing that had made the boredom of her captivity bearable, and now he had deprived her even of those. What the bloody hell did he want from her?

In a sudden fit of temper she tossed the bowl of bonbons aside. It skated along the floor and made a satisfying crash against the leg of a table, scattering candy and shards of porcelain everywhere. Storme swung to her feet and paced angrily over to the window, her hands clasped behind her back.

It was not, of course, that Storme's mind had been idle these past weeks. What Simon the Farmer wanted or did not want was basically irrelevant to her, for her future was clear: She must get out of this place and on with her life. But patience was a virtue any good soldier must learn, and Storme was a seasoned veteran who knew the value of timing.

She would not waste energy or risk her life in foolish deeds of derring-do, not unless she could guarantee at least some measure of success. She did not care to be shot in the back by one of Simon's ever-vigilant guards, nor to become lost in the swamp or eaten by animals in this strange and unfamiliar country. She would have but one chance for escape, and it must be plotted with care.

And, as the days went on and she grew calm enough to

consider her situation, Storme realized something else: Escape was not enough. She must have vengeance.

Her plan was simple and direct. With Blackbeard's legacy to her in one hand and a common hatred for Alexander Spotswood in the other, she would go to Governor Eden. Together they would raise an armada against Virginia, crippling its navy and plundering its shores. Virginia and all attached to it had been a scourge against piracy for too long; it was time to put an end to it once and for all. And Storme O'Malley, with Charles Eden's backing and a fleet of brave pirate ships behind her, would lead them all to victory. Once again she would be the Queen of the Seas, her honor restored.

The way to vengeance was Eden. And the only way to Eden was the river. Here, landbound, she was helpless. But the time would come when the moon failed to shine, when the guards grew complacent, when the Farmer snored in his bed and a ship passed close to the landing. . . . Until then all she could do was wait.

Day by day she studied the household and their habits. She allowed herself to fall into a routine, and the guards, expecting no surprises, grew lazy. She saw them more often now, recognized their footsteps and their habits. She made an ally of the sister—though, Storme had to admit, that pressed no difficulty on her for the woman's company was diverting and helped pass the days—and even made a point of acquainting herself with the Scotsman, Peter.

She watched the ships go down the river—tall sailing ships, barges, lean shallops, and swift canoes—and listened to the servants talk about what kind of vessels docked at Cypress Bay and how long they lingered. Her plan was shaped and reshaped, refined and solidified, and as much as she knew she must be patient, day by day the waiting grew worse. She was afraid she would do something foolish if she couldn't do *something*.

The depth of her brooding had brought her forehead to rest against the deep maroon velvet drapery, and the thickness of the pile tickled her nose. She slapped irritably at the drapery, but the rustle of fabric and the creak of rods was distinctly unsatisfying. In a surge of temper she turned for the nearest available object upon which to vent her frustration, a heavy leather-bound volume lying open on the desk, and hurled it across the room. The book knocked over a small table and a vase with a magnificent crash, and suddenly Simon flung open the double doors.

He was apparently not long in from the fields, for he had washed and changed but had not yet donned the fancy waistcoat and jacket that he liked to wear around the house. His hair was bound loosely at the neck, and his billowly white shirt was open at the throat and cuffs. The muscles of his legs were taut beneath the butternut breeches, a display of lean power held in check as he paused in the doorway, angry eyes sweeping the room.

He saw the broken candy dish, the overturned table, Storme standing defiantly at the window. A flame was banked in his eyes, and his jaw went tight. He drew in a short breath, deliberately forcing back temper. "What the bloody hell," he demanded distinctly, "is going on in here?"

Storme did not know whether it was the break in the routine, the satisfaction of having engaged Simon's anger, or the mere sight of him, half-dressed and in a smothered rage, bursting through the doorway with flames licking his eyes. But she felt a thrill of something—power or triumph—and she whirled back to the desk, lifting a tin of sealing wax and letting her eyes meet his defiantly before she hurled it against the opposite wall.

Simon did not move, and to her ever-growing frustration, he even managed to erase the anger from his eyes and look perfectly implacable.

Simon had not expected to come home to this, but then he never knew what he was coming home to these days. With a very great effort he restrained the urge to snatch her by her hair and shake her until her teeth clicked, for he had already learned that nothing gave Storme O'Malley more pleasure than to see him lose his temper.

She reached for an inkstand, and paused for a moment with her arm drawn back to throw, her eyes glinting challenge as she settled her aim on him. She looked magnificent in a temper, her eyes sparking white lights and her golden skin rouged with emotion. She had tied her hair away from her face with a ribbon, and it rippled down her back and flowed around her shoulders with a peculiarly childlike innocence that was at odds with the brash gaiety of her taffeta bodice and petticoats. Her refusal to wear a corset caused the material to cling softly to her breasts and slim torso and left half her chest bare. Her skirts flowed over her hips and legs and swayed around her bare ankles and she was a daring portrait of something half-tamed, free and defiant, and exhilarating to watch.

She threw the inkwell, and Simon ducked easily. It was empty and didn't even stain the wall as it splintered against the doorframe where he stood.

Simon lifted an eyebrow. "Surely you don't think I'd leave my inkwells filled with you about?"

Storme stalked to the library shelf and pulled out a volume, letting it thud on the floor. Simon merely commented, "Running out of things to do, are you? Well, we can't have that."

And, as she watched in arrested suspicion and sudden wariness, he strolled over to the weapons cabinet and opened it with a key on a fob. He casually extracted two swords. "Pray, don't expend your energy on my furniture. Some of it is quite valuable and a chore to replace." And, before Storme knew what he was about, he turned and tossed a sword to her. She caught it instinctively by the hilt.

"Let your anger work for you," he advised. "In a *civilized* fashion."

Storme could not believe this turn of events. She weighed the sword in her hand, testing its balance and its mettle. Simon sat down on the couch to remove his boots, and Storme was mildly impressed. No good swordsman would trust his balance to such tricky things as shoes, and the Farmer obviously knew what he was about.

She looked at him warily. "I won't kill you, Farmer," she warned.

He glanced up, a brief mixture of surprise and curiosity in

his eyes. But he merely said politely, "Thank you," and removed his second boot.

"But . . ." And a wicked glint came into Storme's eyes as she began to appreciate the significance of her position. So he wanted to play, did he? "I wouldn't mind cutting you a bit."

And to prove her point, she stabbed at the smooth leather of the chair behind her, and then stared in dismay as the point of the sword bounced back, leaving nothing more than a dent in the upholstery. "It's blunted!" she accused him. "You give me a damaged sword!"

"It's called a foil," replied Simon, and got to his feet, checking the tip of his own instrument. "It is the way gentlemen"—he stressed the word slightly—"engage in the sport."

And then, without another word of explanation or warning, he stood before her, feet spread, arm slightly upraised, sword in readiness. "Defend yourself, woman!" he commanded and swung at her.

* *Chapter Nineteen* *

His thrust was so swift and unexpected that Storme had no chance to object to his foolish game. She countered instinctively, and blade met blade with a ring of steel before Simon made a half turn and thrust again. She hadn't expected that, and only a split-second movement kept his blade from nicking her torso. Angry to have been caught off guard, she struck back with a vengeance, slashing downward and thrusting forward and slashing again until she forced him to retreat a step.

"You fence like a barbarian," he taunted, parrying her blows with instantaneous timing. "That's a sword you wield, not a meat cleaver!"

"Good enough for the likes of you!" she returned, color blazing. She bore in on him, graceless and determined, for to her swordsmanship was a matter of survival, not recreation. He parried every thrust, standing his ground, and then unexpectedly feinted back, causing Storme to miss her target. In the same instant he delivered a low upward thrust, and the blunt tip of his foil caught on her sleeve. Storme jerked back and, momentarily off balance, gave him the advantage.

She found herself then in the position of parrying his thrusts, retreating as little as possible, but retreating nonetheless. She had admired his courage when the *Valiant* was taken but had never realized that he was skillful as well, and there was a strange sense of exhilaration to be matched with so worthy an opponent. He was quick and cunning, feinting to take her off guard and then thrusting when she least expected it, testing her to her very limit. Her skin glowed with the heat of battle; the thrill of challenge pumped through her veins and tightened her muscles. He held back nothing, and her sword arm ached from meeting his blows; the ring of metal against metal was near deafening.

"You're strong, Farmer," she complimented him grudgingly and made a swift downward jab at his belt line. She was breathing hard, but so was he.

He parried her thrust and forced her backward with a series of swift, relentless cross-blows. "And you, madame," he returned between thrusts, "are quite good yourself."

With a sudden unexpected twist of his wrist, he lunged forward, and Storme felt the blunt tip of his foil press into her ribs. "First blood!" he declared triumphantly, and there was a wicked, almost vicious gleam of satisfaction in his eyes.

Storme was furious. She jerked away, returning such a blow against his sword that he was almost disarmed, and she spat, "It is last blood that counts in this game, Farmer!"

Storme felt the press of a piece of furniture against the back of her knees and, without glancing around, she snatched up her skirts and leapt onto the sofa, balancing herself on the soft cushions with feline ease as she ruthlessly rained down blows. Simon was at a disadvantage now, for the weight of his sword pressed his arm down and the angle of his thrusts was hampered. Storme concentrated on wearing him down, on weakening his arm until, with a single well-calculated turn, she might snap the weapon from his hand. His face grew grim and his eyes narrowed with effort, and the game by measures grew less and less of a sport.

It was a battle of wills, a fight for power, for domination, for mastery. It was strength against strength, skill against wit, daring against determination. The air was filled with the fast, harsh clang of metal and the hiss of uneven breaths, and neither opponent gave an inch. More was at stake here than a simple exercise, and both of them fought as though for their lives.

Storme's face was flushed and wet, her breasts heaved, and her muscles strained. Her arm ached magnificently and her lungs burned for air, yet her pulses sang with the swift sure thrill that can come only from the edge of conquest or surrender; her veins swelled with fire and glory. She felt Simon's power, the heat that rose from him and enveloped her; she saw the dark fire in his eyes and heard the harsh scrape of his breathing. Perspiration tangled the lock of hair on his forehead and glinted on his chest and throat; lean muscles bunched with every thrust. There was something primal in the air, savage and instinctive and completely beyond control. It consumed them and propelled them, it burned between them and seared them together, yet they fed upon it, hungrily, eagerly.

With a sudden fierce cry low in her throat, Storme leaped down, landing on the balls of her feet in a low crouch. Simon instinctively feinted backward, and she brought her foil up in a swift certain thrust that planted her sword in the vulnerable flesh just below the notch of his hipbone. In the same instant he lunged, and she felt the tip of his foil lodge firmly against her ribs just below her breast, over her heart.

They stayed there, locked in stalemate, their eyes ablaze and their chests heaving, for a moment that went on forever. Neither would back down, neither would press further. The room was taut with the static charge of energy that surged between them.

Simon's blood raged with fierce and unfamiliar emotions; the taste of danger, the leap of passions unbridled, the electric thrill of soaring power. It was heady, it was urgent, it was a touch of exhilarating madness that dared him toward the edge of control. He had not intended it to go this far; he could not have explained how it had happened, but he was in the grip of something basic and unfettered and as old as the first desire, and it was too late to back down now.

He looked at Storme, her blue eyes snapping with challenge, her wild hair tangled about her shoulders, her half-naked chest gleaming with perspiration and thrusting with every breath against the damp material of her bodice. He heard the blood thrumming through his veins and felt the fever searing his skin. He wanted her, as he had never wanted anything before.

He lifted his sword until it pressed against the curve of her breast. He held her eyes. Slowly, very lightly, he moved the blunted tip to encircle her nipple, and saw it grow erect against the damp material of her gown.

For Storme there was no definitive line between the passion of a challenge well met and the passion of desires aroused. She saw the change in him, the darkening of his eyes and the quickening of his muscles, but before he moved her own body was responding. Her heart had pounded with exertion; now it caught with anticipation. Her muscles had ached; now they strained with need. The intense sensory awareness of battle now blossomed into a new kind of awareness, and every pore was flooded with the presence of him, the promise of what she knew must come.

Her sword arm dropped, and, slowly, so did his. They came together as though drawn by invisible threads, slowly, certainly, measuring their flow toward each other by the beat of their hearts. The swords slipped from loosened fingers and fell crossed upon the floor.

Storme thrust her fingers into his hair as his hands closed upon her waist; her head tilted back to accept the power of his kiss. His mouth was hot, and hungry, infusing her with liquid fire and devouring her senses. Her fingers dug into his scalp, and she pressed herself to him, meeting strength for strength, greed for greed.

His hands traveled the length of her from breast to hip, exploring, memorizing, cupping, and pressing. The fastenings of her bodice gave way to his clumsy fumbling fingers, freeing her breasts to the humid air that surrounded them and the pressure of his touch. Storme trembled now, with fire and need, clutching him close, drinking from the recesses of his mouth, pressing into the muscles that strained against hers. She thought fiercely, possessively, *Yes ....* and again, triumphantly, *Yes ...*

Simon tore his mouth from hers, bending his head to taste the salt on her skin, the firmness and the softness of her upthrust breasts. Her head fell back and she moaned, deep in her throat, her fingers digging into his sides. He felt her knees weaken and, as though giving way to a pressure greater than their combined strength, he lowered her to the floor.

He wanted to stop. He wanted to slow his passion and bank his desires, he wanted to explore with leisure and savor every moment. But he was swollen and throbbing for her, every nerve in his body burned for her, and he could not stop. Through a haze he saw her face, flushed with passion and alive with need, those brilliant crystal blue eyes sparking with the hypnotic lights of a thousand fires, and he could not wait. He could not even think.

He gathered a handful of her hair and drew it across his face, inhaling of the rich sweet woman scent of her. And, with her hair still clinging in strands to the dampness of his face and tangled with his own, he took her mouth again. He was absorbed by her and absorbing her, her scent, her heat, the perspiration from her body blending with his own. He wanted to bury himself in her.

His hand pushed up her skirt, molding the slim shape of her leg, the firmness of calf and knee and thigh. She wore no underclothes at all. He was bursting.

He smothered her mouth with his, crushing her to him, unable to get enough. She made a sound in her throat of ecstasy or triumph; her arms around his shoulders were twin bands of steel and fire. She moved beneath him until her legs were on either side of him, one bare foot caressing his calf and winding about his knee. Her fingers threaded through his hair, touching his ears, his neck, slipping inside his shirt ... urgent, hungry, demanding. And the madness could be restrained no longer.

He tugged his shirt out of his waistband and tore at the buttons of his breeches. He kissed her face and her shoulders and her breasts. And then she shifted against him, welcoming him to where he was meant to be. In a movement as natural and as inevitable as breathing, he sank inside her.

He felt her long soft draw of breath, suspended wonder and paralyzing sensation, and it was a reflection of what was happening to him. A breath, a movement, an enfolding, an intense and concentrated wonder that flooded every pore and startled each nerve with starbursts of fire and pleasure. He was inundated with her, filled with her; his mind and his body echoed with her. No one had ever affected him like this. No one.

He opened his eyes and looked into the brilliant blue orbs below him, the eyes of a stranger, yet eyes more familiar to him, more wonderful and enchanting than any he had ever known. They were wide with surprise and pleasure, dark with the intensity of sensation, flicked with flames of passion. Everything she felt was written in those eyes and reflected back to him, and just looking at them blinded him with a surge of ecstasy so great it could not be controlled.

He began to move within her, great, powerful, unrestrained thrusts, and she rose to meet him. Her mouth sought his; her hands impatiently pulled at the material of his shirt and sought his bare back, clutching, exploring, demanding.

In Simon's mind were colors rich and vibrant and all-consuming—violent scarlet, royal blue, brilliant yellow—and there was Storme. Storme, who was a presence, a sensation, a force he could not resist. Storme, who was woman and all woman was meant to be, uncomplicated, unadorned, unashamed . . . who met him with greed and hunger and passion that matched his own, who knew no lies and no constraints . . . Storme, whom he had made a woman. Storme, who was his own. And when she tensed beneath him with a smothered cry, glorying in the power of her own pleasure, the explosion of his own release seemed to strip him of his very soul. It went on forever, he and she melded together by the searing pinnacle of pleasure, until at last he could do nothing but collapse, trembling and helpless in her arms.

How long he lay there he did not know. He felt her breathing, her hands against his skin, the perspiration that slickened their flesh at all points of contact. Her heartbeat was a small rhythmic thud against the thunder of his own. He was dazed by her, saturated with her. She was all he knew in the world.

At last he forced himself to slide from her, and she made a small sound of protest at the movement. He couldn't let her go. He drew her onto his shoulder; he kissed her face and her neck and stroked her wet tangled hair. *Madness*, he thought through a dim and distant haze. *It must be madness*. And he was helpless against it.

For the longest time Storme knew nothing but what her body told her: the hardness of the floor against her hip, the firm warmth of his shoulder beneath her head; a rustling breeze from the open window cooling the perspiration on her face, the heavy pounding of Simon's heart beneath her ear, the warmth he had left inside her, the strange tingling sensation that glowed all over her skin, the dazed dizzy feeling inside her head. Happiness. Wonder. Strength. Weakness. He had done this to her. How could she have forgotten what it was like?

Being with him was like coming home again, and the intense wonder of familiarity was all-consuming. His movements, his touch, his kiss, the strong hard pressure of him inside her—they were familiar to her, they *belonged* to her, yet the exhilaration of renewed discovery was intoxicating. She could fight with him, she could mock him, she could tease him and enrage him, she could day by day grow in knowledge of him and frustration with him . . . yet, when he was inside her something happened, something strange and rich and all-encompassing and totally inexplicable.

Before he had taught her the act, she had thought it somewhat peculiar, however pleasurable. She had never suspected that the nature of what they did—a man and a woman joined together—might have meaning. She felt as though she were on the brink of some grand new discovery, and even as the possibility exhilarated her, she was a little frightened to try to explore it further. She knew only that before he had invaded her body and changed it permanently; this time he seemed somehow to have touched her mind. Before, he had left her sated and exhausted; now he left her wildly happy.

Suddenly Storme wanted to talk to him. She wanted to tell him how it had felt with him inside her, how even now she could feel the tingling emptiness of where he had been, as though a part of her own body had been pulled away. She wanted to tell him how his skin tasted and how his eyes glowed and how beautiful and intense and even dangerous his face looked, poised above her. She wanted to tell him how he made her feel with every touch and movement, but mostly she wanted to tell him how she felt now. But she wasn't sure words had ever been invented for that feeling.

And she wanted to tell him other things. How the sea looked just before a gale, dark and angry and surging with power, or how the sun seemed to rise by inches on a clear morn, smearing the sky with color like a child's painting, or that peculiar taste in the air that presaged a thunderstorm before the clouds appeared. She wanted to tell him about the porpoise that once had followed her ship for six months, how she had named him Pierre, and how he had learned to recognize her voice and would jump out of the water when she came on deck . . . and how she had wept, secretly and alone in her cabin, for two nights when he had lost a battle with a shark and came no more.

She wanted to tell him her secrets, her joys, her hopes. She wanted to tell him how frightened she had been in prison, and how her heart had leaped when he came through the door. She wanted to laugh with him, she wanted to tease him, she wanted to touch him and kiss him and provoke him to passion again. She saw no reason why they should not stay like this forever.

She touched his face lightly, tracing its hard damp curves and planes, and he opened his eyes. They were gray and lazy and tender, and she loved them that way. She smiled. "Ah, Farmer," she said softly. Her finger traced a curve around his eye. "My pretty Farmer. Why do we spend so much time fighting when we could be doing this?"

Simon couldn't help returning her smile. She lay against him, flushed and bright-eyed and unabashed in her contentment, her clothing disarranged and her hair in wild disarray, and he wanted to embrace her hard, to laugh out loud, to kiss her and adore her and make love to her all over again. She made him forget himself, she made him feel unfettered, she made him careless of all but her, and when he held her in his arms, when he looked at her, nothing else mattered except the moment.

But it was a moment that could not last. Through the slow reorientation of his breathing and his heartbeat he heard a distant sound—a servant's voice, the rattle of china, the creak of the well—an ordinary sound, a household sound. He felt the cool hard boards of the floor beneath his back, and his eyes fell upon the open door where anyone, at any time, might walk in. . . . Reality seeped back, and with it a slowly dawning horror.

He sat up somewhat shakily, pushing his hair back with his fingers and drawing in an unsteady breath. Puzzled, Storme followed him, her hand resting lightly upon his shoulder. He couldn't stop looking at her. Her hair streamed down her back, her bodice was bunched at her waist, her skirts tangled about her slim thighs. He had never known a woman whose thighs were so lean and smooth, flowing perfectly into firm, narrow hips. Her breasts were like ripe peaches, small and round and colored cream and blush.

There was a triangle of golden skin from her shoulder to the cleavage of her breasts where the sun had found its way to the opening of her shirt, and he could see the fine definition of her ribs and collarbone. He wanted to touch her, to taste her. He wanted it so badly he ached.

He began to fumble with his clothes, stuffing his shirt inside his breeches, pulling the buttons together. "Cover yourself," he said hoarsely.

Storme hesitated, then gave a little shrug and did as he advised, buttoning her bodice and straightening her skirts. After one quick glance, Simon could not look at her again.

He couldn't believe what he had done. How had it happened, and so quickly? How could he have lost control so thoroughly, so irretrievably? He tried to be angry, with her, or with himself, but all he really felt was a sense of numbness, of shock . . . of fear.

This woman was his prisoner, not his consort. Had he forgotten so quickly what had happened the last time? Had he forgotten who she *was*? She was supposed to be under his protection, a guest in his house, yet he had taken her like an animal in heat, here on the floor of his own library where anyone might see . . . where *Augusta* might see. He wanted to blame Storme, but how could he? *He* had wanted this, *he* had done it. He, Simon York, had groveled on the floor with a woman in lust-crazed greed like a common streetsweeper, and he had no one to blame but himself.

He stood, looking for his boots, and he kept his back to her. He found his boots and sat to tug them on, keeping his eyes away from her. He said in a low voice, "I'm sorry. It shan't happen again."

All he wanted to do was leave the room, but her voice, curious and somewhat hesitant, stopped him. "Why? What makes you sorry about it? This is the best thing we do together."

She was sitting on the floor, her arms looped casually around her upraised knees, her skirts billowing with gay abandon about her. She was looking at him with her head tilted in slight puzzlement, her small brow furrowed and her eyes shadowed with concern. Her lips were still swollen with his kisses, her face chapped from contact with his. She wasn't even annoyed with him.

Simon took a breath, and closed his eyes briefly. *The best thing we do* . . . Everything about her disoriented him, took him off guard. She should have been angry, she should have been mocking, she should have been crowing her advantage over him or despising him for the moral deficient he was. Her simple, straightforward observation caught like an arrow in his chest. How should he argue with that?

He got to his feet, and said stiffly, determinedly, "This cannot continue."

She felt her cheeks grow hot, and her voice was harsh as she demanded, "You don't like lying with me, Farmer? Is that it? Well, nobody was holding a knife to your throat this time!"

He did not look at her. "No. No one was."

How curiously flat his voice sounded, how stern and immobile were his shoulders squared against her! She wanted to leap to her feet and whirl him around, to demand the truth from his eyes. She had done nothing, yet he was angry. It wasn't fair.

She clenched her fists against her skirts; she struggled to keep still. She wanted to rage at him, but pride would not let her. That did not make sense, but it was how she felt.

She had to fight to keep her tone even. "Then what's the matter with you? You liked it enough a minute ago; now you say it can't go on. What are you mad about?"

He released a soft breath, but did not turn around. "I'm not angry. It's just—not right, that's all."

"Bah!" Her exclamation was terse and disgusted, an impatient dismissal of what she did not understand. Relief rushed through her that this was just another one of his foolish notions. She supposed it all had something to do with being English, and civilized. "What do I care for right? I do what I please."

Simon looked at her. He still wanted her. He felt it in the pit of his stomach, a pull, a pain, a hungry urge to take that tousled head in his two strong hands and kiss her rouged lips until they cried out for him again . . . to trace the planes of her smooth slender body and feel it grow taut with yearning against his . . .

He tightened his lips against the ache inside him, and his

voice was harder than he had intended it to be. "That's your trouble; you've been pleasing yourself too long. If you hadn't been, perhaps you'd not now be awaiting execution at summer's end." He had not meant to say that, and with a silent oath of self-disgust, Simon added cruelty to the list of his crimes.

But Storme did not seem to be offended—nor even much concerned. She laid a thoughtful finger beside her mouth and inquired innocently, "Are you really going to let them hang me, Farmer?"

Simon felt his face grow hot, and his throat convulsed. He returned tightly, "That is not the point." And then he tried, with all the might at his command, to inject reason into this most unreasonable situation. "In this world there are certain rules and forms of order, and we must abide by them. We can't simply go around doing whatever we want to. There are certain things that—just aren't right."

Storme laughed, a sudden rush of bright carelessness into the suddenly stuffy room. "How pompous you sound, Farmer!" Her tone was mocking but her eyes were dancing, and Simon had to struggle to remain stern. He wanted to get away from her. No, he wanted to draw closer to her. . . .

Storme stopped laughing, and that was when Simon knew her mirth had been forced. He felt in that moment so many things—regret, confusion, anger with himself, pain for what he had done to her and admiration for how well she dealt with it—and he could not sort any of it out. He was handling the situation very badly.

Storme looked up at him through lashes that shaded her eyes and hid whatever real emotion might be there. She inquired simply, "And so what of these rules and orders of yours? They don't seem to bother you much. From what I can see, you do exactly what you please."

Simon drew in a breath that was startled and uncomfortable. How could he argue with that? He lived by his own rules, regardless of others, and she knew that very well. His jaw tightened, and he could manage only, "That's different."

"Is it?" A shrewdness came into her tone, and those

sea-blue eyes were filled with an uncanny perception that went right to his bones. "I think, Farmer," she observed softly, "that we are more alike than you'll admit."

Simon's fists tightened at his sides, and for a moment he didn't move. Storme saw him swallow and his chest expand for air. And then, without a word, he turned on his heel and left the room.

Storme brought her chin forward to rest on her knees, the forced smile fading and leaving her only confused, forlorn, and somewhat dejected. She listened intently as his footsteps disappeared down the hallway, and was irritated with herself for letting it matter so much that he was walking away. Why should she feel so betrayed? She had known worse than this. Simon the Farmer was nothing to her—nothing except her captor and her tormentor, and she should be glad he was leaving her alone. Blast him anyway for making everything so complicated. He was a fool, and when she left this place she would be well rid of him.

It was probably for the best. He made her weak when he lay with her, and foolish and vulnerable. She could afford none of those things, especially not with a man in whose hands her very life rested, and who had already proved himself to be cold and treacherous and utterly incomprehensible. Yet . . . he was weak in her arms, too. Perhaps that was what frightened him.

She sat there for a long time, brooding over it, but at last she gave up and, with a sigh, got to her feet. It didn't matter. Nothing about the Farmer made any sense at all, and it probably never would. She would not waste time brooding over inconsequentials when she had more important things to concentrate on—like how to get out of this place and return to a life she understood.

Yet she knew that from this day forward it would be much harder to put the Farmer out of her mind. And that was what really worried her.

* Chapter Twenty *

"Peter?" Augusta called softly as she stepped across the threshold of the stable. It was the dead of night, and the light from the stable had awakened Augusta. She had not even paused to dress, but merely flung a shawl over her nightdress and rushed out, knowing immediately what must have happened.

The yellow light spilling from a lantern on a peg over Syrabelle's stall told her she was right, and she hurried to the mare's enclosure. "Peter, why didn't you call me? I told you I wanted to be here—"

She stopped as she reached the stall, and a glance told the story. Syrabelle was down, and Peter, stripped to the waist, was at her head, soothing her. The straw was churned and littered with birth fluids, and in a corner, half-covered by Peter's soiled shirt, was the lifeless bundle of Syrabelle's foal.

Augusta smothered a horrified gasp, and Peter rose quickly. "Miss Gussie, you shouldn't be here. What can you be thinking of—"

Augusta ignored him, her eyes transfixed upon the foal. "Peter, it's not dead? What happened? It can't be—"

"Nay, it's not dead yet, lass, but soon will be." He came toward her, blocking her view of mare and foal. His naked chest gleamed in the lamplight, and his eyes were dark with sympathy and tenderness. "There's nothing you can do here. Poor little laddie never had a chance. Let me take you back to the house."

He took her arm gently as though to turn her away, but Augusta jerked free. "No! You're not going to leave him— he moved, I saw it! There has to be something we can do to help him!"

218

And before Peter could stop her, she pushed past him, falling on her knees beside the failing newborn. Working quickly, she used Peter's shirt to wipe the mucus from the infant's mouth, then delivered a series of gentle slaps to its chest, murmuring encouragingly all the while.

Peter hesitated, torn between the heartbreak Augusta was inviting and the unpreventable rush of pride and tenderness he felt for her. Nothing daunted Gussie York, nothing defeated her, and if anyone could bring life from death it would be she. He tried to remember why she should not be here, and how angry Simon would be if he knew, but none of it seemed to matter just then. He could not let her fight this battle alone.

He went back over to her quickly, murmuring, "All right, lassie, we'll give it a try." He caught the slippery hind hooves and lifted the foal in the air, giving it a fierce shake to clear the airway and keep the blood circulating.

"Again!" Augusta cried, for she knew as well as he that time was running out, and she refused to believe that it was already too late. She slapped the colt hard on the withers with both open fists, commanding, "Again!"

Peter tightened his lips grimly and gave the colt another shake, and another, determined now to win for Augusta's sake as much as for that of the foal. There was something about her that just wouldn't let a man give up, and Peter knew that more acutely than ever in the next few frantic moments as they fought side by side to rekindle that desperate spark of life.

The minutes seemed like hours, and hope turned into despair. There was the sound of Augusta's exerted breathing, and his own, and the exhausted sympathetic whinny of Syrabelle as they worked frantically and futilely over her colt. Peter saw the grim courage in Augusta's eyes, the determined set of her lips, and he could not let this go on anymore.

He said painfully, "Gussie, enough. It's no use, lass." He pulled the colt away from her, and laid it on the straw. "I'm sorry—"

And on the echo of her stricken, pleading look, there was a stirring in the straw at their feet. Both pairs of eyes flew to the little colt as it struggled to its wobbly legs.

Augusta, her hand flying to her throat, gave a cry of delight, and even Peter was hardly able to believe his eyes as an involuntary laugh of joy was torn from him. "By the good Lord above, lassie, you did it! You worked a blessed miracle!"

"*We* did it!" cried Augusta, half-laughing and half-crying, and she threw her arms around him.

They hugged each other hard in the triumph of the moment, a joyful and innocent embrace like so many others they had shared over the years. They were laughing and exclaiming, and Peter lifted her off her feet and whirled her around once, exuberantly. When he set her on her feet again her face was tilted up at him, flushed and laughing and framed by her tumble-down hair; her eyes were sparkling, and her arms were looped about his neck, and he bent his head and kissed her.

Not until the moment his lips met hers did Augusta realize how badly she had wanted this, and how long, and how natural and beautiful and unpreventable was their coming together. Joy exploded inside her and then dispersed into something too intense, too all-consuming and blissful even to be called by name. She felt the strong, naked muscles of his chest and the soft mat of masculine hair pressed against her breasts. She felt the smoothness of his skin and the strength of his arms, and she knew she should be alarmed, or ashamed, but she was neither. She kissed him back, as instinctively and as fully as though this were the moment she had lived all her life for, and nothing filled her but happiness, and the complete rightness of a truth at last known. *Peter* she thought, and that was all. Peter, whom she had loved with all her heart for all her life.

It was a moment without beginning or end, in which all the secrets of hidden hearts poured out in a flow as inevitable as the rushing of the river toward the ocean, or the rising of the sun upon the horizon. Love, as natural as a breath, as powerful as a prayer, engulfed them and sealed them forever within its folds.

When his lips left hers at last, reluctantly, Peter stood looking down at Augusta with adoration and dazed longing in his eyes. Augusta saw in his face all she had ever wanted to know, more than she had ever dared hope, and everything that was right and honest about the world. He looked at her, and he saw beauty. She looked at him, and she saw everything in her life that had been missing before this moment.

A happiness so sweet and poignant that tears misted her eyes filled her, and she touched his face gently with a trembling hand. "Oh Peter," she whispered. "I love you so!"

A shaft of agony went through Peter that he could not disguise, and as great had been his joy only a moment ago, so was the depth of his pain now. For the truth was upon him, and it was a truth that could not be borne.

He said hoarsely, "No. You mustn't say that." And with the greatest of efforts, he fastened his fingers around her arms and removed them from around him.

"But it's true! You know it is! It has been so for so long I hardly know when it began, only that you are all my life and I cannot pretend any longer."

Peter knew it was true. He saw it in her eyes, and knew it in his own heart, which had ached for her so long he had thought at times to go mad from it. But he couldn't look at her—the confusion and the pleading and the utter goodness in her eyes—any longer. He couldn't bear to hurt her further. He turned away. "You should go inside now," he said stiffly. " 'Twouldn't do for your brother to find you like this."

She touched his arm. "Peter—"

And as though her touch had burnt him, he whirled. His eyes were ablaze with pain and his voice was harsh. "No! You go inside and forget this ever happened, for it canna be! Do you see that? It canna be!"

"No!" cried Augusta, and the tears spilled over now, tears of confusion and fear where once there had been only joy. "No, I don't see that! All I see is what is in your eyes, and what was in your arms when you held me, and I know you feel the same!"

"It doesn't matter what I feel!" The words were dragged from him in torment, and his face twisted with an inner battle as he looked at her. "Look at you," he commanded, and grabbed her arms, so tightly that it hurt. "And look at me! I am *owned* by your brother, lass! I've no right to love you, and you none to feel for me! Can ye be blind, then? This is wrong, and there is nothing for us!"

He gave her arm a little shake, and then released it abruptly. "Go away," he commanded tersely, through clenched teeth. And his eyes closed in agony as he turned away. "For the love of God, go away and *leave me be.*"

Augusta looked at him for another moment, the eternity it takes for a heart to break, but he did not turn. She picked up her skirts and, blinded by tears, turned and fled toward the house.

Simon couldn't sleep. Or perhaps he was afraid to sleep. The events of the afternoon played over and over again in his mind, haunting him, mocking him. Sleep would offer no escape, and he was afraid of what he would see if he closed his eyes.

He sat at the escritoire in his sleeping chambers, the lamp turned low, a quill in hand. He was wearing his dressing gown, for he had intended to be abed an hour ago. His hair was rumpled from many passes of a tense hand through it. He frowned at the paper, and at the crumpled sheets surrounding him. He wrote for the third time:

Lt. Gov. Alexander Spotswood
Willmsbrg, Virginia

My dear sir,

I have waited in vain and must confess my disappointment that you have made no effort to contact me regarding

With a muffled oath he struck through the words and tried again.

Sir—

I've no news to report to you, but do sincerely
hope you've some for me. It occurs to me that
this plan has been ill-conceived from the first,
and as there has been no progress

"Damnation," he muttered, and crumpled that paper, too, beneath an angry hand. Ill-conceived, indeed! That was at best an understatement.

Simon tossed down the quill and leaned back in his chair, pushing his hair back from his forehead with the heel of his hand. Something had to be done. This could not go on much longer.

He tried to remember what Spotswood had hoped to accomplish from this. Did he really believe that Eden would be so foolhardy as to come to Cypress Bay to negotiate with Storme? And if so, what was he, Simon, supposed to do about it? Simon could not believe he could ever have agreed to this. How could he have been so foolish?

He remembered the afternoon and his neck went hot; his throat convulsed. He wanted with all his might to blot from his mind the events of that frenetic half hour, to pretend it was someone else who had taken Storme O'Malley in blinding lust on his library floor . . . but he could not. It had been he, and there was no forgetting it.

He stood and paced over to the window, hoping the deliberate, measured steps would calm his mind, that the night air would cool his heated skin. He pushed aside the drapery and leaned on the sill, but there wasn't even a breeze.

This cannot continue, he told himself firmly, and clenched his fist against the sill. Every day she stayed was only that many more moments he would spend listening for the sound of her voice, watching the sway of her hips, remembering the touch of her fingers on his face and his hair and his naked skin . . .

Another curse escaped him, and with a breath he stiffened his shoulders, dragging his fingers through his hair. Something had to be done. Somehow, he had to get his life back.

He glanced at the desk and the remnants of unfinished appeals to Spotswood. He remembered then, with a surge of frustration and anger, that he was involved in intrigue, and if he wrote directly to Spotswood what guarantee did he have that the good man—in order to protect himself—would not simply ignore Simon's missive? What he really needed to do was to go to Williamsburg and meet with Spotswood personally, but that was, of course, out of the question.

He strode over to the desk and picked up the quill again. The time for waiting was past. He had to do something to put an end to this torment before it was too late. If it was not already.

With bold, determined strokes, he wrote:

To the Honourable Christopher Oliver Gaitwood,
Esq.
10 Francis Street
Willmsbrg, Virginia

Then taking no chances, he added,

Or to be found at Carrington Plantation
On the River James,
Near Suffolk, Virginia

Dearest Cousin,

Not knowing whether this missive might find you
in town or at your father's house, I nonetheless

must prevail upon you for a favor which will result in no small inconvenience to yourself. I know you won't like me for it, but I must ask you to intervene with Gov. Spotswood on my behalf regarding a certain package he left in my care, and please do so with no delay. The situation has become intolerable. . . .

* *Chapter Twenty-one* *

Storme twisted restlessly in her bed, tangling the hot sheets, thumping the knotted pillow. Outside her open window a bird chirped and trilled with determined cheerfulness. Sleeping on land was hard enough, but who the devil ever heard of a bird that sang at night?

It was a warm night, and humid, but so were all Carolina nights. That was not why Storme couldn't sleep.

She was angry, but that wasn't what made her skin burn. She was hurt, but that was not the cause of the hollow feeling low in her stomach. She couldn't stop thinking about the afternoon, and every time she thought about it her restlessness only increased.

The merry chirping of the bird made a mockery of her misery, and she flung the pillow over her head, trying to blot it out. She had to get out of this place. She was going mad.

She emerged from the suffocating folds of the pillow with a growl of rage and fumbled on the bedside table for the candleholder. Like everything else in the Farmer's house, it was elaborate. It was made of heavy crystal, decorated with prisms, and covered with a clear globe to reflect the light. Viciously, Storme hurled it through the window. It crashed on the outer gallery and splintered magnificently, and there followed blessed silence. She hoped she'd killed the wretched bird.

Satisfied with the expenditure of temper as much as the cessation of the chirping, Storme thumped her pillow into shape and settled down. She had barely closed her eyes before the door was flung open, and Simon stood on the threshold, silhouetted by the light from the hall.

"What the bloody hell," he demanded, "is going on now?"

Storme sat up, her heart thumping unaccountably. The sheet fell down to her waist, leaving her torso completely naked, but she did not notice. Simon did.

She lifted her chin defensively. "Didn't you hear that blasted bird? I threw a candlestick at him, is all. Think I hit him, too," she added smugly.

Simon released a breath, and ran his fingers tightly through his hair. "Madame," he said, with a great show of patience, "it is not permissible to murder nightingales with my crystal candleholders. Kindly restrain yourself in the future." He tightened his lips against further imprecations, his eyes glittering like smoked crystal in the moonlight, and he half-turned on an angry step as though to leave.

Abruptly, he seemed to change his mind, and his angry eyes swept the room until they alighted on a scrap of clothing at the foot of her bed. He scooped up her nightdress and tossed it at her. "Cover yourself," he snapped. "You are not a pagan, and this is not a brothel."

Storme had never worn clothes to bed; the thought had simply never occurred to her. Every night the maid diligently laid out a fresh nightdress for Storme; every night Storme carelessly kicked it away as she crawled naked under the sheets. But when Simon brought up the subject, she felt suddenly self-conscious and exposed.

She ignored the nightdress, but drew the sheet up under her arms, glaring at him. "Get out of here, Farmer. You've got no business with me."

Simon's eyes were like iced fire, and there was such tension in his bearing that Storme felt her own muscles tighten in response, or self-defense. He said abruptly, "What would happen if you escaped this place? Now. Tonight."

Storme's breath caught, and she was careful not to let him see. She searched his face intently in the dimness, but there was nothing to be found there. "Are you going to let me go, Farmer?"

He repeated, tightly, "What would you do?"

She answered without hesitation, "I would go for my ship, and my crew. And then . . ." Her fingers curled into a small fist upon the sheet; her eyes narrowed. "I would contact the other captains and we would bring a fleet upon the shores of Virginia, a wave of looting and rioting and bloodshed that wouldn't stop until I personally paraded Spotswood's head on a pike down the main boulevard of Williamsburg. *That*," she finished with vicious determination, "is what I would do."

Simon lowered his eyes. "So," he said softly. All the tension left his body, and he sounded rather tired. "You leave me no choice."

He sank down on the edge of the bed beside her, and Storme cautiously drew up her legs so as not to touch him. She replied sharply, "Did you ever have one?"

Simon looked at her, his eyes narrowing intently. If she knew just how much of a choice he had . . . if she knew what was really at stake, was there any possibility she might tell him where the letter was? Couldn't she be persuaded to bargain with him for her freedom, and thus put an end to this torment?

He said carefully, "If I could arrange for an amnesty . . . I am not unknown to Governor Spotswood, you know. If you would give me your word—"

"I won't take no bloody amnesty from a pig like Spotswood!" She spat the words out like an oath, her eyes snapping. "And I don't need any help from *you*, Farmer!"

Simon met the proud curve of her profile, the stern and distant set of her jaw. Her eyes were but darker lights in a darkened room, and accusation and bitterness were written plainly there. Her words did not surprise him; it had been a frail hope at best. And her anger was no more than he deserved.

"Storme, listen to me." His voice was quiet, his expression serious. She returned his gaze warily. "The life you knew is over. You cannot return to it even if you were able. The time of Captain Kidd and Calico Jack is gone, and piracy is a dying art. We Colonists are too many in number and too strong in determination to continue to bow meekly to attack. We're too used to fighting for every scrap we possess to allow ourselves to be pushed aside—whether on land or on sea. Can you understand that? Our ships are growing faster, and our laws harsher. Your hiding places are fewer and your friends disappearing fast. There is no place for the life you knew in these times. It's *over*, and to try to hold on to a dying time is an exercise in futility. There's no point in thinking you can go back, for it has passed you by. And you are a fool if you don't realize it."

For a moment Storme hesitated, struck by the eerie echo of Squint's words . . . and even Raoul's. Could they all be wrong? But what was left for her if she believed them?

She lifted her chin and looked him straight in the eye. "You're the fool, Farmer, if you think to take me in with your fancy words. And we'll just see what lives and dies once Storme O'Malley takes to the seas again!"

He shook his head slowly, but his smile was not so much defeated as resigned, and a little curious. He looked at her thoughtfully. "What a woman you are, Storme," he said, and her eyes quickened suspiciously. "Have you ever thought of it? In all this world you are one of a kind—you have done things and seen things and mastered things most men would envy, let alone every other of your gender. You're intelligent, powerful, somewhat educated in the ways of the world—you have ruled *men*. You could be anything you want to be. I've no doubt that you have won several fortunes in your lifetime, you've traveled to places few have ever seen before, you have literally had the world at your feet. And look at you now. Your ship is gone, your army has deserted, and you're helpless in the hands of your enemies."

"I'll show you helpless!" she flashed at him, but Simon merely smiled, rather sadly.

"It is a great pity," he said simply. "You could be a wealthy and independent woman by now, a person to be admired. Instead you've wasted your youth and your skill in reckless adventure, and it's availed you nothing."

Storme regarded him with narrowed eyes. "Don't be stupid, Farmer. *I* didn't fritter away my fortune on pretty baubles! I *am* a wealthy woman, and a landowner, too. My plantation in St. Thomas makes this place look like a tenement farm!"

Simon's brows flew up in astonished laughter. "So then! You are a farmer too!"

Storme scowled fiercely. "Don't vex me, Farmer!" she warned, and then, hesitating, she shrugged. Her voice was a little disgruntled. "It wasn't of my doing. The place was my father's."

"Oh?" The interest in his voice surprised even himself. "Who was your father?"

He saw then the first hint of a cautious relaxing in her reserve, the faintest trace of daughterly tenderness in her face. She replied simply, "He was a great sea captain. He wanted to retire and build a home for my mother. He was going to grow and ship his own sugarcane and suchlike, so he bought the place on St. Thomas."

The farmer in Simon was intrigued. "Sugar? Is it very good land, then?"

She shrugged. "It must be. People say so. What do I care for sugarcane? The fields are all grown up now, with nobody to work them, but the house is nice."

Her expression softened, remembering. "It sits atop a green hill, with steps leading down to the sea that would take a lame man half a day to climb. From the front gallery I can stand and see every ship coming in and out of the harbor, and every man that passes my gate or goes in the village below. It's built of stone, for Papa knew something of island gales, and stands three floors from the ground, with sturdy galleries all around, and high ceilings that waft the island breeze. It could use some fixing up, I don't wonder, but I've often thought...." She stopped, catching herself on the verge of confessing something that felt like a secret. But Simon looked interested, and not in the least censorious, so she shrugged and finished carelessly, "that I might live there, when I'm old, or crippled."

"Why don't you live there now?"

She answered frankly, "Because I'd rather be at sea."

Simon was aware, all at once and yet as though it were an insidious thing, how easy he felt, being here with her like this. It was dangerous, for the memories of the afternoon were still too fresh with him, and she was much too close. The tangled sheets were evidence of her restless night, and where he sat was warm with her body heat. He could smell her smooth, womanly scent. He knew he shouldn't stay here.

And he could not quite make himself go.

He inquired quietly and because he very much wanted to know, "What in the name of heaven ever persuaded you to piracy?"

Storme drew up her legs and wrapped her arms about them. She looked at him for a long time, as though weighing the merits of responding. In fact, she was thinking that in all her years no one had ever given her cause to answer that before, and how strange it felt to put the story into words for this man. And yet, how wholly natural. Almost inevitable.

She said, "My father was a captain in the Royal Navy. He retired, and took it into his head to bring my mother to the house he'd built for her on St. Thomas, where they were to live out their lives in peace. She was already big with me, but wouldn't hear of putting off the journey—said she wanted her child to be born in her new home, so it's told. Anyways, they got becalmed, and the voyage took longer than expected, and she was old for childbearing, and took ill. A gale blew up off the coast of Bahamia, and I was born, and she died." This part of the story Storme related dispassionately, for she could have no sorrow for a mother she had never known.

She continued, "My papa's heart was near broke, I

guess, for he couldn't bear to set down in St. Thomas after that. And they say it was a touch of madness, too, because he wouldn't let me out of his sight. He took on a Haitian nurse till I was weaned, and he went on about his merchant-man business, ferrying light cargo back and forth between the islands. I grew up on the *Tempest*, tied to the rail so I wouldn't fall off, climbing the rigging as soon as I could stand upright, taking the wheel by the time I could reach it.''

Simon felt a sharp twinge of horror for this unnatural rearing, which he was careful to disguise from her. Still, as though reading his thoughts, Storme added, ''Oh, Papa came to himself right enough and tried to put me ashore to be reared by a proper English nanny, but it wouldn't do. I near died from missing the sea, and him, and soon was back aboard again.

''Then, with the time of the war, Papa was pressed back into service again—only this time as a privateer. The *Tempest* was perfect for it, you know, being one of the few of her kind on the seas, and though Papa pretended not to like it, I think he was really glad to be back in service again. The whole thing was very secret, though. A Lord Templeton gave him his letters of marque, and we had free rein to plunder the enemy, as long as we split the profits with the British navy—which we did. It was a grand service, me and Papa fighting side by side, sailing our ship in and out of coves and inlets where rowboats dared not go. . . .''

The glow of memory on her face, the rapture of memory in her eyes faded, and Simon saw her fists clench together on her knees as her face grew tight. Her voice now was low, and peculiarly flat. ''Then the war ended, and Papa was arrested—for piracy. They held the trial right there in the islands, with fancy British officers in their polished jack-boots and braided coats looking down their long noses. . . .'' Her voice caught there, and Simon felt something unexpected wrench inside him. He guessed the end of the story before it was told.

''Lord Templeton stood right in the witness box and swore he'd never met Papa. Them letters of marque—they'd disappeared, right out of his strongbox. They hanged my papa at sunrise and sailed back to Mother England.''

Simon's gorge rose at this, yet another cruel example of the efficacy of politics. He could feel her misery, her bitterness, and her rage radiating toward him as though in waves, and he could not condemn her for it. How could he fail to understand her, after this?

"And so," he said slowly, "you are in effect doing nothing but what was done to you. There is no law under British law."

She looked at him, surprised for a moment out of her black memories. "Yes," she said simply. "I'm doing what the British trained me to do with their war; only I'm doing it better now."

He looked at her studiously. "And there was no reprisal against Lord Templeton? No one ever knew the truth?"

She gave a laugh that sounded dry and forced. "The worst of it is, the old bugger died on the voyage back to England. I didn't even have the satisfaction of killing him myself." She lifted her shoulders, stiffly, and let them fall again. "So me and my crew, we stole back the *Tempest* and set sail. I make a fine living off of British pigs, and I'm proud of it." Her eyes grew hard with a glitter of defiance. "So it's plain why I'll throw any amnesty you offer back in your face. I don't want to be forgiven for what I'm proud of doing."

Simon looked at her and was moved by such a tangle of emotions that for a time he could not speak. *Ah, Storme*, he thought in a wash of tenderness and regret. *How proud you are, and how innocent. Don't you know that the dangers lie not in the forest and swamps around you, upon the high seas or in the courts of Virginia, but that they are here, in this room with you now?*

He said quietly, "So you will spend your life taking vengeance on the seas for a crime long since forgotten."

Her eyes flashed. "It ain't forgotten by me! I'm only doing what's right, what my papa would've done in my stead, if he'd had the chance!"

"Would he?" enquired Simon carefully, thoughtfully.

"The man you described to me was gentle and sound. He dreamed of building an estate on a tropical island, of living out his life in tranquil trade and agriculture. He built a sturdy home for his wife and child, and plotted no future except to bring them there to live with him in gracious peace. He sounds to me like a man who was tired of fighting, and done with the sea. I wonder, Storme," he queried gently, "if he would be proud of you now?"

The very newness of this notion caught Storme off guard and hit her like a lump in the center of her chest. She remembered her father, the tiredness in his eyes sometimes, the sadness of lost dreams, the reluctance that almost seemed like dread whenever they engaged in battle . . . She had thought it was widowhood, or age. She wondered now if it could have been something more.

Her chin jerked up, and she responded sharply, "Of course he would!" But there was uncertainty in her voice, and in her mind, and she did not like it. This notion of Simon's was treacherous, unconscionable. If it were true, then all her life had been wrong, and how could it be wrong? She knew nothing else.

As though sensing her confusion, Simon's eyes softened. He lifted his hand and caught a strand of her hair, pushing it back over her shoulder. Storme's heartbeat caught with the touch, and then her breath. His fingers lingered against the side of her face. He said softly, "I only know that if you were mine, this is not the life I would ever wish for you."

If you were mine . . . The words hung in the air, caressing it, like a promise. His eyes were like smoky velvet, and Storme could not seem to take hers away. She wanted to lay her head against his chest, and feel his arms around her, soothing away the black past and offering comfort for the present. Her heart pounded with the need.

But the afternoon would not leave her, and she would not beg. She needed nothing from him. Nothing at all.

She swallowed hard, and she held his gaze. She said distinctly, "But I am not yours."

Simon lowered his eyes, and the moment was gone.

His voice was heavy, and seemed to be laced with defeat. He said, "No. You're not." And slowly drew his hand away.

He got up and walked to the door. The beat of Storme's heart measured his every step. At the threshold he stopped, and she thought he would come back.

But he did not. He merely looked at her, and in the shadowed light Storme thought she saw regret, or even pain. She waited for him to take that first step toward her.

He turned and walked away.

* *Chapter Twenty-two* *

It was two days before Augusta collected the courage to put her feelings into thoughts, much less speak those thoughts aloud. If in that time her behavior was somewhat less than normal, no one seemed to notice. Simon was distracted and preoccupied, Storme kept very much to herself, and Peter . . . Peter made a point of not noticing her at all.

Augusta very badly needed someone to talk to. Circumstances being what they were, there was only one person in the house in whom she could confide. She did not for a moment deceive herself into thinking Storme would be very sympathetic, for when matters of sentiment were concerned, Storme O'Malley was blatantly matter-of-fact, nor did the mere fact that she was a woman guarantee understanding. But Storme was the most sensible person, male or female, Augusta knew, and she at least could be relied upon for discretion.

In the afternoons Storme liked to sit in the cool of the grape arbor and watch the river. Augusta, good hostess that she was, knew when to leave her guest to her privacy, and did not like to intrude into Storme's solitary meditations.

Today she made an exception, and hoped she would not be sorry for it.

Storme barely glanced up to acknowledge her presence when Augusta, sewing basket in hand, sat down upon the bench beside her. "I do believe it is cooler out here," commented Augusta pleasantly. "How right you are to come here."

Storme replied shortly, "It's still as hot as Lucifer's backside."

Storme sat with one foot propped up on the bench, her hands looped around her bended knee, her skirts draping gracefully around her. Her neckline was, as usual, bare, and her hair caught in a plain black ribbon at the nape of her neck. She looked cool, relaxed and comfortable, despite her most unladylike posture and attire. No fashion, however outrageous, and no mannerism, however vulgar, ever managed to show Storme to disadvantage. Augusta felt a brief and not uncommon twinge of envy for her friend. *Perhaps*, she thought, *if I were as pretty, or as daring, it would make a difference. . . .*

Augusta took out a handkerchief to be hemmed, and Storme stared fixedly at the river. The two ladies sat in silence for some time, and then Storme said abruptly, "For a plantation as big as this, not too many ships stop here."

Augusta was distracted from her own nervous tangle of thoughts, but was relieved Storme seemed in a conversational mood. "Well, it's the wrong time of year, you see. Shipping is done in the spring and fall. However, I do believe a transport of some sort will be calling soon—Simon mentioned the other day that he had held back some hogshead of tobacco in hopes of a better price, and means to get them to market before autumn. Was there something you needed? A message you'd like to send, perhaps?"

Storme shot her a quick look, but what it might have conveyed Augusta could not guess. Storme turned back to the river.

Augusta couldn't stand it any longer. She blurted, most ungracefully, "Oh, I do so despise people who burden others with their troubles, but I don't know where else to turn! I've been in the most awful despair and Simon—I dread to think what Simon would do if he knew!''

Storme looked at her, quick with interest. The distress which was now afflicting the usually placid Augusta was genuine and most unusual, but even more intriguing was the suggestion of Simon's displeasure. Storme said, "If Simon knew what?"

"About Peter and me." It was barely above a whisper, and Augusta's cheeks were flame-red. Her eyes were lowered miserably. "Oh, Storme, I am quite in love with him, and he with me—and I don't know what to do!"

"Oh, is that all." Storme's disappointment was obvious, and she gave a dismissing shrug. "What's so troublesome about that?"

"Only—only that I don't know how I can live without him." Augusta lifted eyes to her that were shy and dark with misery. "I do love him so desperately."

Storme gave a snort of laughter that was neither gracious nor sympathetic, but she did not know quite else what to do. So many of the ways of women were still strange to her, and she had never had to deal with female vapors before. "You'll pardon me a-saying so," she commented dryly, "but it don't sound like it's giving you much pleasure, lovin' him. I should get over it, was I you."

"Oh, but you're wrong!" The pain in Augusta's eyes was mitigated by something more intense, the color in her cheeks pinkened to a glow, and she seemed momentarily transported. "It's—it's the most wonderful thing in the world. He makes me happy just by entering the room. The sound of his voice makes me feel alive—as though I never had been before I heard it. He makes me feel beautiful, and slim and graceful, just by looking at me. There is nothing more wonderful than being in love."

Storme watched her, fascinated. When Augusta talked of Peter, her eyes softened and her skin glowed and she looked almost beautiful. Plain, tranquil Augusta, whom Storme had never thought of being anything more than diverting company, suddenly seemed transformed.

There was a sparkle to Augusta's voice as she continued,

"But it's more than that, don't you see? With Peter, it's even more. He's my very best friend. I can say things to him I would never dream of saying to anyone else, and he understands. He's the only person I've ever known who likes me just for what I am, who never expects more of me—who lets me just be *me*. I've known him all my life. I can't imagine a day without Peter. He's always been there for me. Simon . . . he is my brother and I love him dearly, but I think sometimes his responsibility—and his ambitions for me—get in the way of allowing him to really *see* me. . . ."

She smiled a little, and her voice gentled with reminiscence. "When I was very small, I found a nest of orphaned fox cubs whose mother had been killed. I brought them home but Simon said they should be drowned, that it would be a less cruel fate than what awaited them in the wild. Oh, I cried until I thought my heart would break. But somehow Peter spirited them away to the barn and the next morning he took me to them. We raised them in secret until they were old enough to fend for themselves, and I think Peter was the only one who ever really understood that I was thinking of those orphaned cubs as myself, knowing how it felt to live without a mother. . . ."

Storme glanced at her, surprised. "I know that feeling," she said softly. She looked at Augusta with a new respect, and a sense of kinsmanship. She had never thought there might be others in the world who shared her feelings, her sense of loss and emptiness. She asked the question that had been a great deal on her mind lately, but she spoke slowly, and thoughtfully. "Do you ever wonder what it might be like—if your mother had lived?"

"All the time," Augusta replied without hesitation. She smiled a little, as though in embarrassment. "I used to think she would make me pretty and graceful and witty, all the things I simply don't know how to be . . . that if she were here everything would be magically changed. Now I only know that if she were here today, she would know what to tell me, and what I should do. . . ."

Augusta's voice trailed off and Storme thought wistfully,

Yes. How different it all might have been if her own mother had lived. If there had been someone to teach her womanly things, and explain to her the mysteries of a woman's heart . . . someone who could tell her what she must do, and how she must feel, now.

Augusta looked at Storme curiously. "What became of your own mother?"

Because yearning was a futile endeavor, Storme shrugged sentiment away. "She died birthing me. She's probably better off not knowing what her daughter grew up to be." But there was an unexpected lump in her throat when she said that, and she couldn't help adding softly, "Sometimes I wonder what she would think if she could see me now."

Augusta smiled gently, understanding. "I wonder, too, sometimes, and I suspect my own mother would be rather disappointed. She was a beautiful woman, and very courageous. She left her home to travel to the wilderness against her family's wishes and built a home here with my papa. She followed her heart," Augusta finished softly, and her eyes took on a musing, almost wondering expression. "Against all odds, she risked all for the man she loved. I wonder if she would not wish me to do the same."

Storme said, "My own mother was a brave lady, they say. She followed my father to her death." Her tone took on a note of bitterness. "That's the way of women and men. He commands, she follows, and little matter what is lost on the way."

"No," Augusta insisted earnestly. Her eyes began to shine with quiet conviction. "That is the way of love. I love Peter," she said quietly, as though discovering a new wonder within herself, "enough to follow him anywhere."

Storme turned back to the river, and said stiffly, "I know nothing of love. I don't even know why you're telling me this."

Immediately chagrin weighted Augusta's tone. "I know— it's very wrong of me, and I truly never meant to impose upon our friendship . . . it's just that I felt I would go mad if I couldn't talk to someone, and you see how I could never confide in Simon . . ."

"Why not?" asked Storme with no more than desultory interest.

Augusta's cheeks paled a little with the very thought. "Why—he would never approve!"

Storme scowled. "What business is it of his?"

Augusta was rapidly retreating back into her timid shell, and looking more horrified by the moment. "Don't—don't you understand, Storme?" Her voice was low and tight. "Peter is a servant—indentured to Simon for life. Simon could never sanction such an allegiance, and Peter—Peter feels as though he's betrayed Simon already, so that he hardly can even bear to look at me."

Suddenly her face crumpled, and she brought her fingers to her eyes. Her voice was muffled through choked-back sobs. "It must be wrong, what we feel for each other, for there is no future for us, none at all! Yet how can it be wrong when it is the only good thing I've ever known in my life? Oh, why must life be so cruel?"

Storme looked at her in helplessness and impatience. Her own inner turmoil was clawing at her composure, and she wanted to make Augusta feel better, but she didn't know how. She said shortly, "There's no need to carry on blubbering so. What the bloody hell do you care what Simon has to say about it? It's your life."

Augusta looked at her with eyes that were wet and red. She didn't look at all pretty now, but at least she had been shocked out of her crying fit. "But—Simon is my brother. And Peter's—*owner*. How can you say it doesn't matter?"

"Because it don't. If he's so meanspirited he won't even let you love who you please, I wouldn't give a fig for what he says!"

Augusta's eyes widened with dread at this perfidy, but her voice was low and earnest. "No, you don't understand. Simon—is the head of the house, and it's his responsibility... I know at times he's a little high-handed, but he only means the best for everyone. He—wants me to marry well, and learn my place in society, and—he's not meanspirited at all!"

"As long as you do what he says," pointed out Storme.

Augusta looked at her helplessly. "He would never permit this! I could never make him understand—I can't even persuade him to let me stay away from all those wretched balls and parties he drags me to, nor make him see how—how *ridiculous* I look in all those stylish gowns he insists I wear. How can I possibly expect him to understand how I feel about Peter? He wants so badly for everything to be perfect for me. How could I disappoint him so?"

Storme got to her feet in a sudden burst of impatience and anger. "Let me tell you something about your brother," she said sharply, and then she stopped. Augusta's eyes, so full of distress and trust, were turned up to her, and Storme wondered what the gentle woman would think if she knew that Simon was not so perfect as he pretended. That, far from coming to the gallant aid of a lady in distress, he was keeping Storme a prisoner here against her will? That he had taken her in savage lust on the floor of his own library and left her with no more than a stiff apology for her efforts? That he, too, was prey to human weakness and had no right to sit in judgment upon anyone.

But Storme turned away with a soft hiss, and she was never sure why she did it. Was it a reluctance to hurt Augusta ... or Simon?

She finished only, tightly, "Was I you, and the overseer meant so much to me, I'd fight for him. And I'd stop letting a mortal man tell me when to eat and sleep and breathe, for the love of God. Don't go to his blasted parties if you don't want to! Stop trussing yourself in them foolish-looking frocks! *You've* got to wear them, not him!"

That brought a soft and surprised chuckle from Augusta, and when Storme looked back she was relieved to find all signs of tears gone. "Oh, Storme," Augusta said warmly, "you *do* make me feel better." And then her face clouded. "Although I could never do as you suggest, of course. Simon is my brother."

Storme gave her a hard look. "Your brother," she said firmly, seriously, "is keeping you a prisoner, just as much as any African on this place, as much as Peter, or—" *Or me*, she thought, but she didn't say it. She finished instead, simply, "That's not right, no matter how you look at it. Every man—and woman—has got a right to live their own life the way they see fit. And if it don't say that in the Scriptures, it should."

Augusta smiled, but it seemed a rather absent gesture. Her eyes were dark and thoughtful. And she said quietly, almost to herself, "I think you may be right."

And then, without any warning, she got to her feet and kissed Storme on the cheek. "What a dear friend you are," she said, misty-eyed. "I don't know what I should do if you hadn't come to us this summer!"

With another quick, shy smile, she gathered up her sewing basket and left Storme.

Storme brought her fingers lightly to the place Augusta had kissed. No woman had ever done that before. It made her feel . . . strange.

But then, embarrassed and impatient with herself, she shook off the foolish sentiment. What did she care for Augusta and her ill-fated romance, or Simon and his inexplicable temperament, or the complex and unreasonable emotions that wound through everyone on this place and ensnared Storme in their wake? On ship the rules were simple, the duty clear. She was in command, and no one questioned her, no one confused her. She had to get back where she belonged, and the sooner the better.

She turned back to the river, and this time her gaze was a little desperate. She stood there a long time, watching, waiting, and planning.

Across the river at Edenhouse Governor Charles Eden watched the carriage draw up in the courtyard and its passenger disembark. With a measure of trepidation mixed with satisfaction, he turned away from the window and went to pour a glass of sherry for his visitor, ready for whatever news he might bring.

The governor had retired to his country home for the hottest months of the summer, as was his custom. This year it seemed more imperative than ever that he be at home on the Chowan. Now at least, Storme O'Malley could not move without his knowing of it.

Governor Eden was growing somewhat desperate. He had had a profitable allegiance with Storme O'Malley for some years now, as he had with most of the pirate captains, and he saw nothing wrong in it. By bringing pirate goods into Carolina he afforded its citizens the best of merchandise without the exorbitant prices charged by British ships, and avoided paying the absurd taxes the British thought were their due. In addition to material profit, the arrangement afforded the citizens of North Carolina protection from invasion, for the captains would fight to insure their free harbor safe from any threat. It was a mutually agreeable situation for all concerned, and only a fool could find fault with it.

Yet Eden was not unaware of the danger. The pirate masters were a curiously independent lot, and given to treachery at the slightest provocation—witness only the notorious letter of Blackbeard for proof. And O'Malley, Eden had long suspected, was the most dangerous of them all. Perhaps it was because she was a woman, easily the most deadly and treacherous gender, or perhaps it was because she possessed a certain passion and determination for her work which other captains, who had gone into the business only for sport or easy profit, lacked. Eden knew above all things she was not to be crossed, and he had walked a fine line since she had inherited that cursed letter.

He would put nothing beyond her. Perhaps she had already negotiated an amnesty with Spotswood for possession of the letter, in which case every moment Eden lingered on Carolina shores shortened his life expectancy. Perhaps she intended to use the letter to entrap Eden into some folly, or schemed to put Eden and Spotswood against each other's heads with herself the only victor. Whatever the plan, Eden's very life depended upon staying one step ahead of her, and not knowing what lay in store was slowly driving him mad.

Tobias Knight came in, and Eden turned to him expectantly.

With a formal bow, Knight made his greetings, and Eden dismissed them impatiently, thrusting a glass of sherry into the other man's hand.

"What news?" Eden demanded.

Knight relaxed his manner somewhat, and his face shadowed with regret as he replied, "None, I'm afraid, my lord. At least none to our advantage."

Eden's lips tightened grimly, and he half-turned away.

"Inquiries among the other captains are much as we expected—none of them admit to knowing the whereabouts of the letter, but we must think whether they would tell us if they did know. As for the exact nature of the circumstances that brought O'Malley to Carolina—again, we are no further ahead than when we started. Spotswood, naturally, places the responsibility for her escape at the door of roaming pirates and has vowed vengeance. The pirates claim that York acted alone, but I think we must agree that seems unlikely." He paused to take a sip of sherry, his tone laced with apology. "It appears the only one who knows the truth of it is Captain O'Malley herself. We have nothing to work with but conjecture."

Eden was silent for a moment, scowling into his glass. Then he demanded abruptly, "Any chance of getting to her at Cypress Bay?"

"None," replied Knight flatly. "Extra guards have been posted at all accesses to the house, and their vigilance is around the clock. A raiding party could be mounted by night, but its chances for success are slim. Even then, we must consider whether or not she would come with us willingly—or even, once we had her, whether she might not prove more dangerous than if left alone. We must take into account that she—or York—would expect us to do just such a thing, and may, in fact, be counting upon it. As for trying to approach her openly, on pretense of a social call to York—your pardon, my lord, but you surely must see the inadvisability of that. Any untoward expression of interest in Cypress Bay by the house of Eden at this point can only be condemning and, again, precisely what they expect. I see no alternative except to do exactly what we have been doing—nothing."

The governor spent a long time whirling the amber liquid in his glass, studying it thoughtfully. Then he said slowly, "I see an alternative."

He turned to face Knight. "There is, after all, the river."

Knight looked uncertain. "And if that fails?"

Eden smiled. "My annual ball is coming up in less than a fortnight. Simon York has never yet failed to attend, and should he do so now, it would only start all sorts of gossip he can ill afford, unless I miss my guess. We shall simply make certain that his invitation this year includes his houseguest."

Knight looked skeptical. "That's hardly a guarantee that she will come here, my lord. She could be prevented, or unwilling. If we have misguessed York—"

But Eden's face was placid, his eyes shrewd with confidence. "If she does not come, so much the better. The family will be away from the house, the servants will be lax, and she will be alone." And he looked directly at his assistant, leaving little room for doubt about his meaning. "In any case," he said firmly, "we will know what to do. And we will do what we must."

* *Chapter Twenty-three* *

Storme awoke early, as she always did in this godforsaken place. She heard Simon leave the house to go about his farming duties before the sun was even well in the sky, and the servants began to stir around downstairs. Fretfully she turned in bed and tried to sleep again, but it was no use. She flung back the covers and pulled on her clothes.

There was no point in going downstairs. There was no one to talk to, nothing to do. Augusta required hours, instead of minutes, to dress, and breakfast wouldn't be served for some time yet. Simon had already departed and the servants were truculent and suspicious, hardly even any fun to torment anymore. Storme thought that if she did not soon go mad from frustration, she surely would do so from sheer boredom.

Restlessly she pushed open the door to the gallery and stepped out. It was an ugly, dismal day. The weak rays of the sun barely penetrated the thick gray sky, and a low fog rose up from the river. The air was thick with the heavy smell of rotting vegetation, and Storme wrinkled her nose, offended. She started to turn and go back inside. But then she stopped.

Simon had designed this house like any good fortress, with an eye toward invasion. As commander in chief he could stand upon the galleries and have a perfect view of the surrounding land in any of four directions. If he had been here now, he would immediately have seen what Storme had seen and would have taken measures to deflect it.

But Simon wasn't here. No one knew but Storme.

She gripped the rail, hardly daring to breathe, peering intently through the low-lying mist, afraid her eyes had deceived her. But no. There was no mistake. The fog began to lift from the river by slow inexorable degrees and she saw it plainly now—a small, sleek shallop nestled securely in a cove, hiding . . . waiting.

Her heart slammed and began to pound. It wasn't a barge bringing trade goods; it wasn't a canoe bringing visitors. It was a small swift ship designed for hiding and running, and there was only one possible reason for it to be lurking in the mist at the edge of Cypress Bay.

Pirates.

On feet as swift and as silent as a cat's, Storme left the room, stole down the stairs and out into the gray, soupy day. She engaged a few curious looks from the servants she passed, but it did not matter. By the time anyone thought to question her departure, it would be too late.

It didn't matter whether the pirate ship was friend or foe, whether it had come to rescue her or to plunder Simon's warehouses or merely to hide from pursuit. Once Storme was aboard she would be master, she would be free. All she had ever needed was a ship, and she had always known if she waited long enough, the opportunity would be hers for the taking.

She moved swiftly across the lawn, concealing herself as well as possible in patches of mist and shadowy yews. For something over a week now Storme had remarked the absence of the guards and could only assume that farming duties at this time of year took manpower away from security. The timing couldn't have been more perfect, and Storme congratulated herself on the ease of her escape.

Once she reached the grape arbor she abruptly turned left onto a pathway through the wood which would, she knew from many hours of silent observation and study, eventually lead to the river. The path was dark and damp, crowded with cloying vegetation and earth smells. Though urgency pounded inside her head, Storme made herself stop every few minutes to listen for signs of pursuit.

There was nothing but the crunch of her own soft footfalls on the leaf-covered ground and the distant sounds of the plantation going about its morning business. The muffled creak of wagon wheels, the workers' voices, the fog-smothered low of oxen. When she realized she was hearing those sounds, smelling the smells, and seeing the sights of farm life for the last time, she was filled with such elation that she was almost lightheaded from it.

Her heart was beating very fast, and there was a tight thrill of excitement in the pit of her stomach. It had been so long since she had used her wits and her daring against an enemy, and now, within moments, freedom would be hers. Her mouth was dry as she paused, before emerging from the wood, to look and listen one last time.

Her eyes turned back, without her being aware of it, the way she had come. She could see through a break in the trees an expanse of lawn, a stand of well-ordered flowering hedges, and beyond the brown and green sweep of a field. The rising sun glowed pink on the bricks of the house and turned its windows to mirrors. How familiar it all was. How tranquil and predictable and . . . safe.

Is this what you wanted for me, Papa? she wondered

absently, and the thought, treacherous and unbidden, came from nowhere. *If you had lived, would this have been your life? Planting and reaping and raising a daughter very much different from the one you have now....*

But with a convulsion in the center of her throat, she cut the musing off, angry and alarmed that it had even intruded. Nothing but the Farmer's foolishness had put such ideas in her head, and it was the Farmer who had gotten her into this mess in the first place.

But she had outwitted him. Through patience and perseverance, cunning and courage, she had endured his captivity and triumphed over it. Now she would return to her own life, fighting her own battles and engaging her own victories, and he would be little more than a whisper of memory in the shadows of her life. In moments now, only moments, she would be away from this place and from him, and if he were wise, he would take care their paths never crossed again.

With a satisfied nod of triumph and determination, she squared her shoulders and turned away from the house. Victory was within grasp, and victory was all that mattered. She swooped up her hampering skirts with one hand and moved at a greatly quickened pace through the woods.

The wooded path gave way to a gentle clearing, surrounded by huge ancient oaks, that overlooked a sharp decline toward the riverbank. From this approach, no one could see her slide down the bank and make her way stealthily toward the waiting ship some two hundred yards away.

She stepped out of the cover of the woods.

"Good morning," drawled Simon's voice behind her. "You're a long way from the house, aren't you?"

Storme's heart lurched, stopped, and throbbed painfully again. A swift hot rush of rage and denial swelled up inside her and she wanted to scream with frustration; she wanted to pick up her skirts and run. So close. A few hundred yards. How could she be so close and fail now?

But, of course, she did not scream, she did not run. She was much too wise for either of those courses. She turned slowly to face him. "You followed me."

He gave a small apologetic smile. "I couldn't resist, I'm afraid. I saw you enter the wood and thought some harm might befall you all alone."

Storme looked at him carefully. Had he guessed her intentions? Did he know of the ship skulking in his cove? No, he couldn't know of the ship, or else he wouldn't be wasting time talking to her. There was still a chance.

He was dressed for the day's work in homespun and jackboots; his only weapon was a broadsword strapped to his waist. He had removed his hat and he stood before her casually, droplets of mist clinging to his hair, his eyes lazy and unaware. If ever she were to escape him, now would be the time. But she must go about it very carefully.

Deliberately Storme kept her eyes from cutting toward the river. She could feel the presence of the ship like a tangible thing. If only she could distract him for a short time, lull him into complacency, and then move quickly, she would be down the bank and within sight of the ship before he could stop her. She could feel her heart pounding, but she kept her face perfectly blank, and walked toward him as casually as though that had been her destination all along.

She said, "You've called off your guards."

"That's right. By now you've had a chance to realize there's no place for you to go even if you could escape, and it seemed unnecessary to waste my men that way."

She shrugged. "So you waste your own time following me around instead. Whatever suits you, Farmer."

A shaft of sun filtered through the opaque sky and momentarily caught in his eyes. He said, "I've given orders that you're not to be allowed near the river, you know."

She met his unreadable gaze levelly. "Do you really think that would stop me?"

He gave a small lift of his shoulders. "Perhaps not. But first you would have to get past me."

Her heart was beating fast, but her face was impassive. And her voice was careless. "Why go to so much trouble, Farmer? Why not just let me go and have me off your hands?"

Still, his sun-bronzed face revealed nothing, and his eyes

were like mirrors reflecting a screen of sunlit gray. He replied simply, "Because I am afflicted with a very inconvenient appendage known as a conscience. And I would not like to see you die."

Storme gave a little snort of laughter, tossing her head back to look at him askance. "Oh, mighty Farmer! Always taking care of the whole world, aren't you?"

"No," he answered evenly, "just that part of it that is my responsibility."

She flared quickly, "I am not your responsibility."

He only smiled, and Storme had to turn her eyes away. Something strange happened to her throat when he smiled at her like that.

She could hear the sounds of workmen in the fields nearby. The sun was growing stronger, slowly dissipating the mist upon which the shallop relied for cover. But it didn't matter. No one could see the ship from here. No one knew it was there except Storme. Impatience shuddered within Storme like a wild thing straining against the leash, and she forced it into quiescence. She could wait. The one thing she could not afford to do was alarm Simon, or make him suspicious.

Surprising him, Storme dropped to the ground, folding her legs beneath her. "Rest easy, Farmer," she tossed back up at him negligently. "I'm not going anywhere."

After a moment's hesitation, he sank down beside her, a speculative half-grin playing with the corner of his lips. "No," he agreed, "I don't suppose you are."

He rested his forearm on his upraised knee, giving Storme a good view of the sword in his belt. It was a sturdy weapon, handsome and sure. The breadth of his body separated Storme from it.

He watched her with an odd expression on his face—a mixture of wry speculation and sober reflection. "Don't you ever get tired of it, Storme?" he asked after a moment. "The running, the fighting, the uncertainty of the life you lead?"

What a peculiar frame of mind he was in today. His voice was reflective, almost tender, and he looked at her in a way that she had never seen before . . . too perceptive, gently curious. It unsettled Storme even as it intrigued her, and she wondered whether she could use it to her advantage.

She forced a dry smile she did not entirely feel. "Still trying to save my soul, Farmer?"

He plucked a blade of grass and carelessly tossed it away. "A useless exercise, I admit. But then . . ." And he surprised her again with that rakish half-grin, the crinkling of the eyes. "I wouldn't keep trying if I didn't think there was something there worth saving, now would I? That should be of some comfort to you."

She was caught for a moment in the sparkle of those eyes, the lazy teasing in his voice, and then she jerked her eyes away. *God, I'm going to miss you*, she thought, and it hurt. But the hurt made her angry, and she returned tersely, "Save your bloody preaching, Farmer. I'd rather spend an eternity in perdition regretting what I've done than even one day of harp-playing counting all the things I *wish* I'd done!"

His eyes lightened and danced with amused appreciation. "Ah, a philosopher! You see, I told you there was something worth saving."

Storme affected a scowl, but in fact her ears were sharply attuned to the sounds from the river. Could that be a movement in the water, a footstep in the mud? How long would the pirate ship stay at anchor? Had they indeed come for her or were they even now preparing to push off?

Her eyes fell on the sword at Simon's side. Could she use it against him?

She had no choice. She had come too close, and this was her last chance. She would *not* be defeated now.

She said, knowing only that she had to keep him talking, and keep his attention away from her plans, "It's more than I can say for you, at any rate." And as she spoke she moved, on pretext of rearranging her skirts, a fraction closer to him, and the sword. "A life as boring as yours isn't even worth living, much less saving."

His smile remained in place, but a shadow seemed to come over his face. His voice was light, but seemed to be a little strained as he answered, "But I've worked very hard to keep my life boring. I like it that way.''

Storme made a great show of brushing off her skirts and moved a fraction closer to the sword. Still she could not reach it without stretching over him, but if she could catch him off guard...

And abruptly it no longer mattered. The day erupted in a fierce cacophony of hoarse yells and glinting steel as from the riverbank below pirates came swarming toward them.

Storme caught a glimpse of the shock on Simon's face and in an instant he was on his feet, his sword drawn, crouched for battle. But Storme was even swifter than he. In a single leap she was out of his reach, running for the invading forces and the river beyond.

Wild exhilaration filled her as she made her dash for freedom. Images flashed by in brilliant color and roaring sound. A horse broke through the clearing and its rider bent as though to scoop her up. Vaguely she recognized Peter and with a growl she whirled in the opposite direction. Someone else caught her arm and propelled her toward the river, shouting, ''Run, girlie! We've come for you—get to the boat!''

For just an instant Storme stood still, staring at him. He had called it a boat, not a ship, and any self-respecting seaman—even a river pirate—would know the difference. In a flash she noticed other things: shod feet, clean-shaven faces, clumsy swordsmanship. There couldn't have been more than a half dozen of them, screaming and waving their weapons like lunatics, but none of them were pirates. On that she would have taken an oath.

But she had no time to contemplate the matter, for before she could barely register it there were more sounds and movements from behind her; the very earth seemed to spew forth chaos. A legion of men broke through the woods and swarmed in from the fields—horsemen swinging swords, Africans carrying wooden spears, fieldworkers wielding picks and hoes. Their faces were ferocious, their cries bloodthirsty, and it was plain to see a massacre was in the making.

It was evident the small complement of pseudo-pirates

were unprepared for anything of this sort. When they had begun the attack only one man had been visible; now they were facing two dozen, and the blood began to flow. The men from the ship were poorly trained as soldiers and even less skilled in valor. Most began to retreat immediately; a few, trapped in defeat, fought desperately. Storme wasted no sympathy on any of them. It mattered not who they were nor whence they had come—they had brought with them a ship, and her only mission was to reach it.

While the sounds of battle and the clash of steel rang around her, Storme ran toward the ship. She shoved and pushed and leaped over fallen men; she struck out with her arms and her feet at anyone who got in her way. She heard shouts, running footsteps behind her, the pant of labored breath. Someone tackled her and with a breath-robbing thud she hit the ground, locked with her assailant and rolled over and over until her shoulders hit the trunk of a tree, hard. She bit down viciously on a fleshy arm and drew blood; the man screamed and abruptly she was free, up and running again.

She waded into the water. Most of the pirates had been driven down to the waterfront; some of them still made a show of brandishing their swords while they scurried for the safety of the ship; some abandoned pretenses and swam for it. The lines had already been cut, and the ship was casting off. Storme fought against the dragging weight of her wet skirts as she struggled toward the ship. A strong hand was reaching out to her, an urgent voice commanding, "Hurry, woman! On board!"

Storme grabbed the hand and leaped aboard.

She stood there for a moment, her breath coming in gasps, her head spinning with triumph. She had made it! She was free! Below her were the shouts and splashes of men scrambling on board, behind her were the few remaining grunts of battle; someone was calling to raise the sails, someone else was gripping her arm joyfully and trying to tell her something. And Storme never knew what made her do it. She looked back.

Simon was standing on shore, not twelve feet away from

her. His chest was rising and falling visibly with the exertion of battle, his sword held slackly by his side. He was simply looking at her, and what was in his face she could not tell. She only knew that when her eyes met his something seemed to hold them there, the sounds and sights of chaos faded away and there was a twisting deep within her that felt like sorrow, or regret.

But it was no more than an instant. Abruptly she jerked her eyes away and started to turn, and something caught in her peripheral vision. She whirled back to him.

Simon was still standing there, looking after her. His impromptu troops were busy at the edge of the shore, hurling insults and flashing weapons at the sailors who were scrambling toward the boat. And two men were rushing Simon from behind, swords drawn.

Storme screamed, "*Simon!*"

Simon pivoted and deflected the descending blow with his half-raised sword. But the movement sent him off balance and he stumbled backwards directly into the path of the second assailant.

"Damn you, Farmer!"

Storme didn't think about it, she didn't hesitate. She grabbed a sword from the hand of an astounded sailor and, with a throaty battle cry, she leaped on shore.

With a single swift slash she drew the attention of the one man while Simon engaged the other. For an endless series of thrusts and blows, slices and parries, she and Simon fought side by side. Her head roared and her blood thrummed as she pushed her opponent inexorably back toward the river and then, with a skillful upward slice, disarmed him entirely. He turned and leaped into the water, swimming for the ship that was already filling its sails and speeding down the river.

Storme stood and stared, her breath coming in ragged gasps, as her last chance for freedom sailed grandly away. The sounds of cheering on shore, the sporadic splashing as one more victim made for the river, the victorious activity around her faded away and she stood very still, watching. It was gone. After all this time . . . it was gone.

She heard a step beside her, and she turned. Simon stood there, his face dirty and smeared with sweat, his hair tousled, his shirt torn. His blade was bloodied and his opponent was scuttling toward the water. The pace of his labored breathing matched her own and for a long time neither of them spoke. They simply looked at each other.

Then Simon said quietly, "You had your chance. Why didn't you leave?"

Storme felt a knot of pain and self-disgust rise up inside her that was almost choking. *You are a fool, Storme O'Malley. A fool.*

But she hardened her face and squared her shoulders, refusing to give him an answer. She flung down her sword and turned away. Her back was straight and her head held high, but her eyes were burning hot with tears as she walked back toward the house.

Simon did not return to the house until almost twilight. He had dispatched messengers to warn the other plantations along the Chowan, and he and Peter had ridden as far as Queen Anne's Town to try to find out what they could about the marauders. No one had any information about a band of river pirates running the Chowan, nor even so much as a rumor, and this discovery only confirmed Simon's grim suspicions. Eden had made his first move. And he had almost won.

Simon returned to the house tired and dispirited, and more shaken by the events of the morning than he cared to admit. *Eden had almost won.* Simon, who had taken such pride in his elaborate precautions against invasion, had been caught totally unprepared. Simon, whose job it was to protect Storme, had failed utterly. In the end she had protected him, and the whole of it was a disaster from which he wanted to cringe in shame and hide.

A frantic Augusta met him in the hallway. "Simon, I have been beside myself with worry! The servants have been gossiping of an attack and you've been gone so long—"

Simon mustered the last of his energy to smile at her

reassuringly and brush her cheek with a kiss. "A mere drill, my dear, greatly exaggerated."

But Augusta's distraught gray eyes reflected little faith in his assurances. She gripped his hands. "But Storme! Simon, what happened to her?"

Simon felt a surge of alarm rush through his veins and his voice sharpened. "What do you mean? Isn't she here?"

Augusta nodded distractedly. "She came in with her clothes torn and dirtied, and I was terrified she was hurt, or ill—but she wouldn't speak. She went to her room and refuses to answer my calls, or even take nourishment. Simon, something terrible must have happened, and you weren't even here! How could you desert us at a time like this?"

Simon frowned and looked toward the stairs. "She is in her room? You are certain?"

Augusta faltered. "I—I think so. As I said, she doesn't answer my knocks and I haven't seen her, but where else would she be?"

Simon swore softly and took the stairs two at a time, leaving an astonished Augusta staring after him.

Augusta might have been too polite to enter a room without an invitation, but Simon had no such compunction. He flung open Storme's door without hesitation and at first he thought his worst fears had been correct. She was gone.

The room was in shadows, illuminated only by the faint gray light from the open window. His eyes searched quickly, his heart pounded—and he wasn't sure whether it was from relief or regret. After all he had been through, was he to lose her now? And wasn't it better to do so?

But then as his eyes adjusted to the dimness, he looked more carefully. And what he saw caused a chill to go through him. Storme was lying on the bed, as still and as lifeless as the humid evening air that surrounded them.

He said cautiously, "Storme?"

She made no reply.

He went over to the bed. She was awake, but she did not look at him. Her eyes were dull and tired. He sat down carefully on the bed beside her and lightly touched her forehead. "Are you unwell?"

She did not move or look at him. Simon counted off the moments of her silence in heartbeats. At last she spoke, in a quiet, conversational tone. "They weren't real pirates, you know."

Simon felt something tighten in his throat and spread slowly to his chest. It was an effort to speak. "I know."

At last she turned her eyes to him. The bleakness within them dragged at Simon's heart. She said, "But I still could have gone. I could have been free."

Simon knew then just exactly what it had cost her to stay. He knew it as clearly as he had ever known anything, and the knowledge filled him with a hollow, empty ache that surely was as great as her own. He reached down, and gathered her to him. His hand stroked her hair, and his shoulder cradled her head. "Ah, Storme," he whispered, and he closed his eyes. "I am so sorry."

Her arms crept slowly about his neck. Her voice was tight. "I don't *know* why, Farmer," she said fiercely, her face buried in his neck. "I don't know anything any longer. . . ."

He turned his face to hers and kissed her. It was a slow kiss, filled with gentleness and comfort, and giving it was the most natural thing in the world. Receiving it, for Storme, was like filling the shadows of emptiness with warmth and light. He took her pain and shared it and, with the sharing, lessened it.

She did not know why. She did not understand the madness that had propelled her off the ship to fight upon the side of the enemy. Words like responsibility and conscience meant nothing to her. Her only loyalty was to herself, and to the men who served her. Should the death of one farmer mean so much to her? Was his life worth the trading of her own?

The moment she had taken sword in hand, something inside her had changed. She didn't like it, she didn't understand it, but it was so. And now, clinging to her captor for comfort and strength against forces she could not even comprehend, she began to wonder if it really mattered.

He lowered her to the pillow, leaning over her. His hand stroked her hair away from her face, and his eyes were dark and beautiful in the grainy light. She should hate him. She should strike out at him. She lifted her fingers to trace the gentle planes of his face and she whispered, "Will you lie with me, Simon?"

His voice was shaky as he replied, "Yes."

The flames of passion did not roar, the fires of urgency did not consume. His touch was so gentle it made her ache, his kisses so tender she could have wept from them. And yet none of this surprised her. For this space in time they were strangers meeting for the first time; they were lovers from times of old. There was no anger, no scorn, no betrayal or imprisonment. They were simply a man and a woman, knowing each other, needing each other, giving and taking with no thought of the past or the future.

He removed her clothes and kissed each part his hand uncovered. He lay naked beside her and she explored with her fingertips his body, which was now as familiar to her as her own. She had never known it could be like this: so silent, so lingering, so intense. It was as though no other world had ever existed outside the one they created in this time, and no others had ever populated it besides the two of them.

When he was inside her she knew a measure of fulfillment that was beyond physical pleasure. She looked into his eyes and she saw tenderness, adoration, and joy. She saw herself there, because his feelings were her own, and she had never before guessed a man and a woman could be a part of one another in such a way. Yet it seemed only natural.

Fiercely she clung to him, for suddenly it was more important than anything in the world that it should always be like this—that she should hold him, and he should always be there for her to hold. She needed him with an intense and desperate longing like nothing she had ever known, and she thought, *Is this it, then? Is this love?* She knew only that she was no longer sorry that she had come back to him.

As his rhythms quickened so did hers, each of them

fueling the other in familiarity and discovery, and both striving for something beyond themselves and far greater than themselves. When she closed her eyes and clung to him in a single eternal moment of blinding fulfillment, it seemed as though the entire world stopped and everything she had ever been, or hoped to be, expanded from her soul and blended into him.

Afterward they lay together, very quietly, damp limbs entwined, hands clasped. Storme was shaken inside, confused to her very depths, for what had just happened between them she had not expected. A familiar act that should have been for pleasure only was somehow much, much more. A carnal coupling that was not new to her seemed like the most important thing that had ever happened. She was different inside. Everything was different.

And she knew, with no surprise, why she had come back for him. Because she did not want to leave him, ever.

Her head was resting on Simon's chest, the sound of his heartbeat pulsing in her ear. She turned now to look at him. And she knew he was different too. He said softly, "I wish I could stay with you, all night. I want to sleep with you."

The words seemed to swell in Storme's heart, contentment edged away the shadows of uncertainty. *Yes*, she thought. *That is what I want. What I want ... always.*

But even as he spoke, even as her heart answered, she knew it could not be so. His arms tightened around her; his lips touched her hair. There was tightness in his voice as he whispered, "I wish we lived in a different world."

But they did not. Beds and men who slept in them belonged to the civilized world. Storme and her like belonged ... somewhere else. Simon was bound to the conventions of his world, and Storme was bound to be free.

She looked up at him and the sorrow that was in his eyes broke her heart. Everything had changed this night, but nothing had changed. What she said was no more than a simple statement of truth, but saying it seemed the most courageous thing she had ever done in her life. "I still have to leave this place."

He looked at her for a long time, sadly, quietly, and the

moment bound them in understanding and acceptance. He said simply, "And I still have to stop you."

Storme turned her head against his chest and closed her eyes. They stayed that way, holding each other, while the sun sank from the sky and darkness enfolded them both.

PART THREE

*

The Betrayal

* Chapter Twenty-four *

It took three days of traveling, by water and by foot, before Squint and Pompey arrived in Bath. There, at the notorious Green Parrot Inn, they could be assured of finding one or more of the pirate captains at any given time. This was the safest and surest way to learn the latest news of Storme O'Malley.

It was early afternoon, and the tavern room was not very busy. A scullery boy was sweeping up the remnants of last night's high spirits, and several sailors were snoring against shadowed walls. A merchant was haggling with a sailing master over a bolt of silk, and in the back room the innkeeper could be heard beating his cook. Squint and Pompey sat at a corner table with Mad Raoul Deborte, sipping ale and thinking over what they had learned. Squint did not know whether to be relieved or dismayed at the news.

Raoul shook his head sadly. "No, *mon ami*, there is no way to retrieve the *Tempest* from Spotswood's guards. Do not think we have not all considered it, but he holds the ship as though it were a treasure beyond price. Long ago I realized it would be madness to risk the *Petite Morte* on a mission doomed to failure."

Squint set his mug on the table with a decisive thump, scowling fiercely. "Storme could get her out. Storme O'Malley be not afeared of Spotswood, nor any man living. Where be this place she's imprisoned?''

Raoul laughed lightly. "Ah, my foolhardy friend! You would have even less chance there! Only last week a rescue was attempted, and the cavaliers were driven into the river like rats with a fire on their tails. This Simon York is a general to be reckoned with, and his Cypress Bay a fortress well-held.''

Squint fixed him with a long contemptuous look. "You were her friend. Would you leave her there to rot?''

A measure of shrewdness passed across Raoul's eyes as he lifted his mug to drink. "Some of the captains think it best. Not many are willing to risk life and limb for a woman who'd put them out of the business with her skill. I, of course,'' he assured Squint gallantly, "am not one of those. Never let it be said that Mad Raoul Deborte would turn his back on a friend in need. It is merely a matter of approaching the problem sensibly.''

Squint frowned. "What do you mean?''

Raoul examined the dregs in his mug. "There is only one thing that can free Storme O'Malley now—the same thing that has kept her free all these years.'' He looked at Squint. "Blackbeard's letter. If we had it, we would have the power we need.'' Though his tone was casual, his eyes seemed to sharpen a fraction as he inquired, "Do you know where it's hidden?''

Squint laughed sharply. "And if I did, do you imagine I'd be living to tell the tale? Nay, not I, nor anyone save Storme herself.''

Raoul nodded thoughtfully. "*C'est dommage*. Now the task will be more difficult, *oui*? But not impossible.'' He leaned forward confidentially. "Impossible to get Storme away from Cypress Bay,'' he reiterated, "but not impossible for you to go to her, *n'est-ce pas*? One''—he glanced at Pompey—"or two men alone could perchance slip past the guards, and speak to Storme. Find from her where the letter is hidden, and then retrieve it. *La Petite Morte* and I will then be at your disposal, *mes amis*. We will go to Eden with the letter as our weapon, and he will have no choice but to

raise an army to free her! Do you see?'' His voice grew
animated with excitement. "It is the only way!"

Squint nodded slowly. "Aye. I see."

Raoul's eyes glowed confidently, and he reached across to
clasp Squint's arm. "*Eh bien!* We shall triumph, the three
of us, when all the other cowardly dogs cringe in their
shelters! And how proud Storme will be of her clever
friends, eh?''

Squint smiled mirthlessly. "Aye. It's proud she'll be to
hear of this.''

Raoul lingered awhile longer, discussing plans for getting in and out of Cypress Bay, savoring their victory. He
left with an admonition to let no other captains share
in this noble plan, and to be certain to return to Raoul as
soon as they had the whereabouts of the letter. Squint
promised.

When Raoul had gone, Squint lingered over his ale,
looking at Pompey as though reading the big man's thoughts.
His face was dour. "Aye, my friend, I agree. That scurvy
bastard's a mite too interested in that letter for my liking.
Upon my oath, he'll never see it, nor us, again." He pushed
grimly away from the table and Pompey stood beside him.
"Well, we got what we come after, let's be away. Our girlie
be a-waitin'.''

For two days it had been raining, sweeping the lowlands
with a low, soggy mist, muddying the river, filling the house
with a dismal dampness and a musty chill. Storme sat at her
bedroom window, her cheek resting against the pane, and
the landscape within her was as bleak and disconsolate as
the grayness outside.

For the first time in her life she felt fully and completely
trapped—not just in body, but in spirit as well. Memories of
her last encounter with Simon haunted her and pinned her
down, and she thought now, bleakly, *I must love him. How
else could I be so miserable?* Escape was more imperative
now than ever before, yet her will to fight was seeping away
as inexorably as the summer rain pushed the land, particle
by particle, into the river. Soon there would be nothing left

inside her but hurt and wanting things she could never have.

Storme did not even hear the soft tap on her half-open door, nor see Augusta enter. She barely glanced up as the other girl stood in the center of the room and inquired nervously, "Well? What do you think?"

It took Storme a moment to realize Augusta was referring to the new gown she was wearing. It was a fancy dress frock of lavender tulle which Storme had never seen before, and she wondered briefly why Augusta was wearing such a thing in the middle of the day. She commented tonelessly, "Very pretty," and she turned back to the window.

Augusta went over to Storme's pier glass, examining her reflection with some trepidation. It was a lovely gown, and very costly, even somewhat flattering to her complexion. But the tight corset flattened her ample bosom grotesquely and the wide hoops made her look like she was hiding two pumpkins under her skirts. The cascades of expensive lace that sectioned the stomacher and petticoat were so lavish as to be almost overwhelming, and she looked, in short, like a child dressed up in her mother's clothes.

Dismay crossed Augusta's face. "I hate it," she said. "It's a hideous gown and I look awful. Oh, if only I didn't have to go!"

Storme roused herself enough to inquire, "Go where?"

"To the governor's ball next week."

"Eden?"

Augusta nodded glumly, tugging at her bodice. "The invitations only arrived yesterday, but my dressmaker's been working on this monstrosity for a month—and this was the best she could do! Oh, it isn't her fault, I know, it's only that I am not suited to any of it—the gown, the company, the high manners . . ."

But Storme let her voice fade out. Eden. Now that would solve everything, wouldn't it? If only she could get to Eden. And how ironic that Augusta, who detested the thought, should be dragged into his presence kicking and wailing, while Storme, whose very life depended on that good man, hadn't a chance in beggar's hell of ever seeing him.

Storme spoke out loud, without meaning to speak at all. "I'd give my eyeteeth to go."

Augusta sighed, turning from the glass and sinking heavily onto a low hassock. "I would gladly trade places with you. If only you knew how horrible it was. Standing about with all those strangers, waiting for someone to ask you to dance and knowing that no one ever will except out of pity or obligation to Simon—"

Storme turned back to the window. "It couldn't be that bad." Not as bad, she thought, as what would happen to her while everyone else was off enjoying themselves at the party. She would be locked in her room with guards stationed at every egress, for she knew the way Simon thought now too well to expect less.

Unless . . . unless there was some way she could get out of the house that night. Surely she would be able to outwit Simon, to connive somehow. . . .

Augusta smiled weakly. "No, it wouldn't be bad for you. You're so pretty, everyone would want to dance with you."

Storme studied the view from the window, her eyes narrowed with cunning. "If I was at the ball, the last thing I'd be worrying about is dancing."

"But you have to dance," Augusta insisted earnestly. "That's the worst part, especially when one is as clumsy and graceless as I . . ." And her face crumpled with distress. "Oh, I simply can't bear the thought. I don't think I can go through it one more time—my stomach is ill with dread even now. What am I going to do?"

Storme was too involved with her own problem to give much concern to Augusta's. She said absently, "Don't go."

Augusta got up and began to pace distractedly. "How can I not go? I always go, I'm expected to go. I can't simply decide not to go. Simon would be so angry." And she turned to Storme uncertainly. "Wouldn't he?"

Storme shrugged.

Augusta began to pace again, her hands clenched tightly before her, her lavender skirts waving and swishing. Storme didn't understand the reason for such intense agitation and didn't particularly care. She wondered briefly if it would be possible to entrust a message to Eden with Augusta, then dismissed the notion. No, it all would be pointless unless she, Storme, could get off this plantation and see the governor in person. . . .

"Of course," Augusta was saying, her voice tight with distress and uncertainty, "Simon has been angry before. And I'd almost rather face his displeasure than the governor's ball. The only reason he drags me about to these things is so that I may find a suitable husband, and how can I marry anyone when I love Peter so desperately?"

Love, thought Storme dully. *What an awful lot of misery it brings*.

To Augusta she said, without looking around, "You'll do what your brother tells you to do. You always do."

Augusta looked at her in despair. There was no scorn in Storme's voice, just a simple statement of fact. Augusta recognized the truth in her words with a sinking feeling of defeat. "But must it always be that way?" she said softly, and her voice almost broke with the powerful treachery that seemed to underline those words.

Storme said, "Company's coming."

Augusta went to the window, peering over Storme's shoulder at the coach that was bouncing down the muddy drive. She was almost relieved for the distraction. "Cousin Christopher," she said. "He's come for the ball, too, and no doubt Simon will browbeat him into being my escort." She sighed and smiled wanly as she straightened up. "I suppose I'd best change out of this absurd costume before we go down to greet him. At least he'll be some amusement for Simon. He has seemed rather fierce lately, don't you think, and perhaps a visit from Christopher will improve his spirits."

Christopher did not bother to change his damp and travel-stained clothes, or even remove his muddy boots. He knew the house as well as he knew his own and did not wait to be announced. Leaving a trail of wet footprints upon Simon's highly polished mahogany floors, he strode into the library.

Simon sat at his desk, his fingers templed at his chin, a brooding scowl upon his face. He did not look like a man who needed more bad news, and Christopher took perverse satisfaction in the fact. He stopped before the desk, flung down the letter, and announced, "You presume a great deal upon our friendship, Cousin. May this missive bring you as little pleasure as it brought me in getting it."

Simon responded mildly, "Welcome, Cousin. I trust you had an enjoyable journey."

"Abominable." Christopher flung himself into a chair beside the fireplace, stretching his hands and feet toward the cheery blaze that had been lit against the room's dampness. "One would think that with all the revenues piracy brings into this dreary province, you could afford better roads."

Simon broke the seal upon Governor Spotswood's letter and scanned its contents silently. Christopher watched alertly, but Simon's expression remained immobile as he read. Abruptly he crumpled the parchment in his fist and stood up.

Christopher inquired, "What does it say?"

Simon tossed the paper into the fire. His shoulders and his neck were very stiff. "It says," he responded tightly, "I must be patient."

Christopher gave a snort of disgust. "For that earth-stirring bit of advice," he drawled sardonically, "methinks you could have entrusted a lackey with your dirty work."

Simon's hands were folded behind his back, obviously in a restraint against the urge to strike or throw something. As Christopher watched, his carefully controlled expression began to darken, his brows lowered, his eyes began to churn. "Patient, hell!" he swore at last, sharply.

Simon turned abruptly and stalked back to his desk. "Look at this." He snatched up an embossed card and with a twist of his wrist sent it spinning across the few feet that separated him from Christopher. Christopher leaned forward to catch it in midair.

"An invitation to the governor's ball," he said, not comprehending.

"The name," snapped Simon.

Christopher glanced at it again, and the puzzlement on his face slowly cleared into amazed understanding as he read, "... Requests the honor of the presence of Mistress Storme O'Malley at Edenhouse..." He looked up, and Simon nodded curtly.

"I am going to allow her to go. And you, my dear boy, will be her escort."

Christopher lifted an eyebrow, leaning back. "I'm honored, to be sure. But am I to take this to mean I'll be abetting her escape? For you know the moment she sets foot over Eden's threshold that is exactly what she'll do."

"I know she will try," corrected Simon. "And that, sir, is where you and I come in."

"I hardly see the point in all this trouble," replied Christopher with a shrug.

"The point is," returned Simon shortly, "that the quickest way to end this debacle and achieve Spotswood's aim is to take her to Eden personally. I've no more time—or patience" —he practically spat the word out—"for games."

Christopher was thoughtful for a long moment, possibilities and probabilities clearly moving through his head. Uncomfortably, Simon looked away.

"Indeed," murmured Christopher softly at last. "I've always suspected more to this scheme than you would confess. A trap for the pirate girl, is it? And you're caught in the middle."

"You don't know the whole story," began Simon tiredly.

Christopher lifted a lazy hand for silence. "Nay, nor do I want to. I might feel compelled to make a speech in the Assembly and that, I'm afraid, would show neither of us to good accord."

Simon smiled, but the expression did not touch the bleakness in his eyes. "You're a wise man, Christopher. If I had your sense, I wouldn't be in this trouble now."

Christopher regarded him soberly for a moment. He knew his cousin too well not to recognize that Simon was in pain. And it was a distress that went deeper than the inconvenience of this intrigue, whatever that might be. Christopher knew that what he must tell Simon now would not improve his spirits much, but he would not be a friend if he kept silent.

"I'm afraid," Christopher said at last, carefully, "that you are in more trouble than you know."

Simon looked at him alertly.

"Matters have been most—unsettled in Williamsburg since you last visited. Rumors are flying, and none of them to your credit. It's no secret you helped the pirate escape, and they're saying you're in league with Eden. There's a call for you to be brought to trial in Virginia for treason, and your good friend Spotswood, by remaining silent, has all but denounced you."

A dry smile touched Simon's lips. "As a politician, what else could he do?"

Christopher kept his expression mild. "And it's not all just politics, either, I'm loath to say. I happened to stop by the Trelawn household on my way here, and they're all aflurry with the gossip over your keeping a mistress—a savage pirate wench, so the tale goes, whom you keep naked and chained to serve your perverted pleasures. I'm afraid, dear boy, your reputation is in shreds, and you have been stricken off the lists of every mama with a daughter of marriageable age."

For the first time a genuine sparkle broke into Simon's eyes, and he laughed out loud. "Well, then, that's one good thing that came out of this, I would say!"

Christopher grinned reluctantly. "I shouldn't congratulate myself too soon if I were you. The mamas are appalled; the daughters seem to find you more fascinating than ever. Bless me if I can fathom why."

Simon chuckled, but the humor faded from Christopher's eyes. He regarded Simon intently. "I say again, I do not wish to know the details of your scheme with Spotswood. But I suspect already the situation has proceeded otherwise than you were at first led to believe. In all truth, doesn't this give you pause to wonder what other surprises might lie in store?"

Simon turned toward the window, his gaze absently fixed on the distant, fog-shrouded river. His face seemed to tighten by measures, though whether this was from dread or determination Christopher could not tell.

At last Simon turned back to Christopher. He said simply, "I would not be involved if I thought harm would come to anyone because of it. I have matters well in hand. After the governor's ball, Spotswood will have what he wants, and Storme O'Malley will be pardoned to go free. That is the beginning and the end of my participation."

Christopher said, "A pardon? Is that what he promised you?" And he shook his head gravely. "I should be less than dutiful if I did not warn you again that Spotswood is deadly. Be careful he does not hang her anyway... and you alongside her."

Simon looked at him sharply and might have spoken, but just then there was a sound at the doorway. Simon smoothed his expression and turned to greet his sister... and Storme.

Two days had passed since the twilight evening he had lain so passionately entwined in her arms, but even now Simon could not look at her without a constriction in his chest that felt like a swift knife thrust to his heart. Was it passion only? Or was it something more... something that had begun the moment she had leaped off the ship, sword in hand, to fight by his side. Simon knew only that something had changed inside him, something tenuous and powerful that seemed to have been building without his noticing for a long time and was about to reach its full growth. Simon didn't understand it; he didn't want to understand it. But it frightened him.

He looked at her now and, as with all such moments lately, time seemed to be suspended in the pulse of a heartbeat while the impact of her presence washed over him. Her skin had grown paler since she had been here, so that now it was almost ivory, delicate and translucent. She looked at him with eyes that were solemn and unrevealing, a striking blue against the clearness of her skin. There were slight mauve circles under her eyes, and Simon, noticing them, felt a wrench of concern. Had she known the same sleeplessness he had suffered these past nights? Could she be feeling the torture of uncertainty and confusion as well?

But her head was tilted proudly, her gaze cool and defiant, and nothing in her demeanor suggested she was any more vulnerable than she had ever been. She was controlled, defiant, and beautiful.

She was wearing an old gown of Augusta's that had been cut down for her, and whereas Augusta had always looked rather frowsy and overblown in the dark purple bodice and magenta-striped petticoat, Storme looked brilliant. She had draped a turquoise shawl over her shoulders, and her hair, which had earlier been pinned into a careless knot atop her head, was now escaping its confines in tousled swaths and tendrils around her face and shoulders. As usual she wore no hoops or padding, and when she moved her skirts draped around her thighs and hips, revealing a few inches of bright yellow stockings above the tops of her red slippers. Everything about her, from the way she wore her clothes to the way she held her head, was striking and arresting, charging the room with the vibrancy of her presence. And if ever Simon had had doubt of that, he had only to look at Christopher's face the moment she walked into the room.

Immediately Christopher was on his feet, but like the gentleman he was bred to be he went first to Augusta. "Gussie, my dear!" He clasped both her hands warmly and brushed her cheek with a kiss. "How sweet you look. I do believe you grow more charming every time we meet."

Augusta curtsied and made the requisite murmured welcomes, but already Christopher was turning to Storme. No one could have missed the light in his eyes as they swept over her, nor the change in his tone as he said, "Mistress O'Malley. How delightful to see you again. And, if I may say so, you've changed almost beyond recognition. Quite an improvement since the last time we met."

Storme regarded him speculatively. "Like the goose fattened for the slaughter?"

Christopher laughed. "What a charming metaphor! I can see your disposition has improved as well."

Augusta looked confused. "The two of you—have met?"

Storme did not reply, and Christopher barely took his eyes away from her. "I had the rare opportunity of playing host to Mistress O'Malley as she passed through Williamsburg. A most—er—memorable occasion.''

"As I recollect," replied Storme flatly, "you tried to drown me."

Christopher's eyes were dancing madly. "And I can't say how pleased I am to see you've made a full recovery. Country life must agree with you."

"It might agree with you," retorted Storme, "if you like the smell of pigs and manure and rot and rain. As for me..." And over Christopher's shoulder she sought and held Simon's eyes coldly. "I'd rather take my chances in perdition."

Again Christopher laughed with unabashed delight and appreciation. "My sentiments exactly, my dear! I can tell already you are a woman of exacting taste. This dreary countryside is no place for free-spirited adventurers such as you and I, is it?" He caught her hand, holding it dramatically in both of his, and suggested in a loud stage whisper, "Perhaps you and I should run away together."

Storme was utterly unimpressed. "Name the day," she answered flatly.

Christopher shot a twinkling, challenging look toward his cousin. There was no humor at all on Simon's face. "Perhaps Simon would have something to say about that."

Storme stared directly at Simon. "I doubt it. He'd probably thank you for it."

Abruptly Simon spoke up. His tone was smooth but his eyes were hard. "I had no idea you grew so restless under our hospitality, Storme. If you're so anxious to go somewhere, perhaps this will cheer you."

He bent toward the chair Christopher had vacated and picked up a card. "A letter from an old friend," he said, handing it to her. His face was completely without expression. "You have been invited to the governor's ball."

Augusta exclaimed softly, "Oh, Storme, how wonderful for you!"

Storme took the stiff parchment with uncertain fingers, staring at it. "For me?"

Christopher bowed to her. "And I, my dear, will be honored to escort you, if you'll have me."

Storme raised her eyes slowly to Simon. The disbelief and hesitant joy she felt widened her eyes. "And you're going to let me go?"

Simon stretched his mouth into a smile that seemed to pain him, so great was the effort. Everything about him was stiff and his eyes were churning, but he answered mildly, "Why, Storme, you'll have my cousin think I'm keeping you prisoner! As we will all be attending, of course you will accompany us."

Storme's heart beat with slow suspicion, but Simon's face was unreadable. A rescue from Eden! Just what she had been waiting for, hoping for . . . and Simon was sure to know it.

Storme knew Simon too well to suspect this sudden generosity was anything but a clever trap waiting to be sprung. But she had no choice. She had been waiting for this, and this time she would succeed. Whatever Simon was plotting, she would be more clever, more daring, more inventive. She would have Eden and his power on her side, and this time she would succeed. Also, this time she would not look back.

Simon looked at her, and read her thoughts. She looked at him, and knew it. The challenge had been laid down and she had accepted. Only one of them would emerge victor from this last game. For a moment Storme thought she saw regret in Simon's eyes, and a wave of bleakness touched her. This was what they both wanted . . . wasn't it?

Abruptly, Simon spoke, and the moment was gone. "Augusta, I suggest you set your dressmaker to work on a gown for Storme without delay. There's very little time, you know."

Augusta took Storme's hand, her eyes shining with excitement for her friend. "I have the most exquisite fabric I've been saving for a special occasion. It will be perfect for you!" She led Storme away, chattering enthusiastically, and Simon went forward to close the door firmly behind them.

He turned on Christopher, his eyes churning and his voice icy. "What was that all about?"

Christopher lifted a perceptive eyebrow, his suspicions confirmed. "My little flirtation with your pirate wench? I simply couldn't resist. What a delightful minx! Utterly charming, and as refreshing as a summer breeze."

"She is a viper," returned Simon shortly.

"And you, my dear chap," commented Christopher mildly, "are jealous."

Simon stared at him. "You're insane!"

He strode over to the desk and made a great show of rearranging books and papers. Tightly repressed anger radiated every move. "It's been hell since she got here. She's turned my household upside down, terrified my servants, corrupted my sister—"

"Gussie never looked better," interrupted Christopher, greatly amused. "You take life a great deal too soberly, Simon."

Simon shot him a glowering look. "Some things require sobriety—but I hardly expect you to understand that!"

Christopher lifted his hand as though in self-defense. "There's no need to take my head off! I'm just an innocent observer in all of this."

Simon stared at him for a moment longer and then, with a sigh, let his anger dissipate. "I'm sorry. You're right, of course. It's only that I have a great many things on my mind at present, and Storme O'Malley is only one of them."

"Indeed? I should think that would be enough. What else is troubling you?"

"Augusta." Simon walked across the room and uncapped a decanter of brandy, carefully formulating his approach to the subject he had been postponing too long. "She's reached the age of womanhood, and it's long past time she was married."

Christopher accepted the glass Simon offered and resumed his seat by the fire. "I couldn't agree more. She's a sweet girl, very modest and capable. She'll make someone a fine wife."

"Do you think so?"

"Without a doubt," Christopher assured him with a decisive nod. He sipped his brandy. "I tell you what. Bring her to Williamsburg in the fall, if you like. I'll make some introductions and take her about. We'll find a suitable match in no time."

Simon took his brandy over to the window, gazing studiously out at the rainfall. "As a matter of fact," he said carefully, "I already have someone in mind."

"Who?"

Simon turned. "You."

Christopher paused with his glass halfway to his lips, his eyes flying wide with astonishment. Quickly and adamantly he exclaimed, "I think not!"

Simon looked at him sharply. "Why not? You're fond of her, aren't you?"

"Well—well, of course I am! That's hardly the point!" He had to take a restorative gulp of brandy, and in a moment continued more calmly, "I can't imagine why you'd think I would suit at all. You don't want a scoundrel like me for your sister! Besides," he explained simply, "she's like my sister, too, you know. I like her well enough, but I could never love her."

Simon made a hissing sound and turned away, pretending a disdain he didn't feel. He hadn't really hoped Christopher would agree, but he had to try.

"You are a romantic fool, Christopher," he said, and took a short taste of the brandy. "Love, indeed. Notions like that will bring you nothing but trouble."

Christopher regarded him mildly over the rim of his glass. "You should know."

Simon's gaze swung to him sharply. "What does that mean?"

"Storme O'Malley," returned Christopher mildly. "It's plain to one half-blind you're in love with her."

Simon felt color creep up his neck and his hand tightened around his glass. He gave a harsh bark of laughter. "Now I *know* you've taken leave of your senses! What would I want with a she-dog like that? She's a half-tame savage with the manners of a goat, as treacherous as Eve and just as dangerous. I can barely tolerate her presence in my household, much less—!'' And he broke off with another curt and mirthless laugh, raising his glass again.

Christopher regarded him in silence for such a time that Simon, growing uncomfortable under his scrutiny, turned away. Then Christopher said quietly, ''Sometimes, Cousin, you are a pompous ass.''

Simon's nostrils flared with a short breath, but he did not look around. He sipped his brandy.

''You are in most ways an outstanding man,'' Christopher continued mildly. ''You've built this godforsaken patch of swamp and forest into the finest plantation in Carolina, you've raised your sister by yourself and turned her into a gently bred young lady, you conduct your commerce with dignity and honor and have never lost sight of your goals. Many's the time I've wished to be more like you.''

Simon bowed sardonically. ''I'm flattered, to be sure. But pray save your gentle pontifications for the Assembly floor. I can't help but be suspicious of the intent of your generous words.''

''Indulge me. For, as I was about to say, at present I am most profoundly grateful I am not the least like you.''

''Aha,'' observed Simon humorlessly, and turned back to his brandy.

''You have one outstanding weakness, Cousin, which almost casts all your other laudable qualities into shame. You cannot tolerate that which you can't control. With my own eyes I've seen you wrestle with a stubborn rock or boulder until your hands were bloodied, and slice a path through a deadfall with your knife when it would have been much simpler to go around. Why? Would it harm you to let that boulder lie there for another hundred years or so, or to let nature take its course with a deadfall in the forest?''

''I presume,'' said Simon dryly, ''there is a point to this discourse.''

''Quite correct. The point is that what you cannot control, you either ignore or destroy. You can do neither with the lady Storme, and that causes you no end of frustration.''

''I grow bored, Cousin.''

''Storme O'Malley,'' stated Christopher flatly, ''is elemental, honest, unfettered, and wiser in her own way than you or I will ever be. She is also a fierce and violent savage, knowing no rules except basic gratification . . . all those things,'' pointed out Christopher shrewdly, ''that you have worked so hard to disguise in yourself, and have labored so long to control. That frightens you.''

Simon fixed his gaze on the contents of his glass. ''You are on dangerous ground, Christopher,'' he warned in a low voice.

Christopher shrugged. ''Beat me for it. I'm feeling reckless. It is all painfully simple, at any rate. You love her for things you cannot understand, you despise her for things you cannot control. From such do the grandest of passions thrive, for the lady pirate is, my fine-feathered friend, precisely what you need to bring some blood into your oh-so-very-proper life.''

Simon drained his glass. ''The only thing I need,'' he responded stiffly, ''is to get her out of my life.''

Christopher smiled and shook his head sadly. ''You never were one to know what was good for you. If I were in your shoes, I assure you I wouldn't make such a mistake.''

''But you are not in my shoes.'' Simon strode over to the table and refilled his glass, and when he turned his face was very composed, his tone mild. ''Now,'' he said with purpose, ''let us discuss our plans for the ball. I want you to know what you're getting yourself into, for it's not an undertaking entirely without danger.''

Simon drew up a chair and began to explain. But for the next hour Christopher noticed that the haunted look never quite left his friend's eyes, and he was sorry he could do so little to help.

* *Chapter Twenty-five* *

Having lived all these years with a sister, Simon was accustomed to being the first down on any formal occasion. Usually he was irritated with Augusta's unwavering tardiness, but tonight he was grateful for the solitude.

He made an elegant figure as he stood before the fireplace in the lamplit library, resplendent in his court dress. His coat was gold brocade, his waistcoat peacock blue embroidered with heavy scarlet threads. Silver garters buckled his white satin breeches above red silk stockings, and a dress sword was fastened around his waist. His hair was drawn back in a neat bag at the nape, and stiffly starched lace adorned his cravat and cuffs. As always, he wore the elaborate attire with the air of one completely unaware of how exquisitely it complemented him, and if anyone had told him, in all honesty, what a striking—indeed, breathtaking—figure he made, his astonishment would have been genuine.

He stood straight and tall, as befitted a gentleman of formal manners, and his long fingers held a delicate glass of pale sherry. Upon his face was a slightly preoccupied, almost brooding, frown, and he sipped the sherry absently, hardly tasting it. He had a great deal on his mind.

He did not know what would happen tonight. That Storme—or Eden—would make some sort of move he was certain, but what it might be he could not tell. Perhaps she would reveal the whereabouts of the letter to him this very night, in which case arrangements must be made to apprehend Eden in the act of taking it. Perhaps the two of them would arrange a second meeting, or formalize plans for her escape, and Simon must be very careful that whatever passed between them did not remain secret for long. After this night, Storme—and Eden—would have to be watched with the vigilance of a hawk, for whatever was to happen, it would begin now. This was the turning point for them all. After tonight, nothing would ever be the same.

It was all a very risky business, Simon was aware, but what choice did he have? Was he to keep her prisoner here forever, waiting and hoping? Or worse, let her escape as she had almost done the other day to return to her life of crime upon the high seas with nothing having come of this but wasted time? And yet, it was more than wasted time. What she had brought into his life since she had been here could never be thought of as a mere waste of time. . . .

And therein, perhaps, lay the real source of Simon's uneasiness. After all they had shared, he could not help feeling a twinge of conscience when he thought of what he was plotting against her this night. From the moment of complete unquestioning trust when he had lain in her arms to this act of betrayal . . . was it so easy for him, then? Could he pretend it had never happened? Yet what choice did he have? He must do his duty, for his sake . . . and hers.

He heard a step behind him and turned, expecting Augusta. What he saw took his breath away, and left him momentarily speechless.

Storme was wearing a ball gown of ivory satin, all of a color, without a fichu or a strand of ornamentation to detract from the stark elegance of the garment and her own loveliness. The tightness of the stomacher nipped in her waist and lifted her bosom to a daring décolletage, where a simple bow of the same material drew the eye inexorably to the swell of her breasts. The petticoats draped gracefully over wide hoops, parting in the center around an apron of cream-colored lace. The sleeves ended at the elbow in a fall of lace, and in her hand she carried a pair of Augusta's white evening gloves.

Her hair was upswept in a luxuriant twist of pale honey, ornamented by gold pins. Her lips were slightly rouged and her eyes were as clear and as stunningly blue as the day he had first looked into them beneath a blazing Caribbean sky.

She held herself with all the regal grace of one born to it and moved with a floating whisper of motion he had never seen her use before.

Through the fog of enchantment her unexpected appearance had cast about him, Simon thought slowly, *Why . . . she is beautiful*. Not just the beauty he had known before, the feral untutored beauty of an animal in the wild, but the civilized beauty of elegance and charm. No one, looking at her now, would ever guess who she was or where she came from. She was as composed and elegant as a drawing-room portrait, as ladylike as any daughter of society. In her world or his, Storme O'Malley was mistress of all she surveyed.

And Simon, looking at her, suddenly lost all doubt over the rightness or wrongness of what he was doing tonight. He saw in the vision who stood before him only a glimpse of all that Storme could be, and nothing could have persuaded him at that moment to abandon his plan. Could any man with conscience turn this beautiful, elegant woman back to a life of crime? Having seen her as she was this night, could he countenance her return to a world filled with blood and violence? No, what he was doing was right. Spotswood would have his letter, Storme would have her amnesty, and she would be free to live the life she was meant for. She might not thank him for it now, but Simon knew this was the only way. He would save her despite herself.

And upon the resolution he stepped forward, a sweet elation warming him like liquid light. And he did the only thing that was appropriate under the circumstances: He bowed over her hand and lightly brought her fingers to his lips. "Storme," he murmured. "How lovely you look."

Her eyes widened, and an enchanting trace of pink color touched her cheeks. She replied with her customary disarming frankness, "So do you."

Simon laughed softly.

For Storme it had been like a game, dressing up like the gentry, donning a disguise to infiltrate the enemy's stronghold. The corset constricted her uncomfortably, the horsehair-padded hoops were scratchy, and Augusta's velvet slippers were much too tight. She had muttered and complained throughout the process, for the hairpins dug into her scalp and she could hardly take a breath for the cinch around her waist. And though she liked pretty things she thought the dress designed for her was colorless and plain, badly in need of some red or purple to liven it up. But when she looked at herself for the first time in the pier glass she hardly recognized the image there, and she thought, *So this is what it is like to be a fancy lady.*

And when she saw the look in Simon's eyes she thought, *So this is what it is like to have a man think you're beautiful.* And she liked that feeling, very much.

Simon turned and walked over to his desk. "Your attire is lacking only one thing to make it complete."

She watched as he unlocked a drawer and withdrew a strongbox. Curiously she came over to him as he opened the box and took out a necklace, holding it for a moment in his hand.

It was composed of three strands of pearls fastened with a diamond clasp, quite among the finest she had ever seen. She looked at him hesitantly. "You want me to wear them?"

A corner of his lips deepened with a smile that seemed to light up his eyes, and he replied, "I would be honored."

He moved behind her and draped the necklace around her neck, and Storme's heart began to beat very fast. She had to talk to try to rid herself of the peculiar, quickening emotions that were evoked by the touch of his fingers upon the back of her neck as he worked the clasp.

"Where'd you come by such a fine piece of work?"

"They were my mother's."

"She must have been rich."

"My father gave them to her on their wedding day. It's traditional."

She could feel the warmth of his body close behind her, and the whisper of his breath on her neck. She had known his closeness before, and it never failed to excite her . . . yet this time it was different. This time she was beautiful; this time he was an elegantly dressed gentleman bestowing upon her a gift of pearls, and the breathlessness she felt, the tingling of her skin and the thump of her heart seemed somehow forbidden, and even more delightful for it.

She said, "Will you give them to your bride?"

Simon fumbled with the clasp and almost dropped it. His voice was husky. "I suppose...the pearls will go to Augusta."

"Don't you intend to take a wife?"

His tone was somewhat brief as he replied, "I suppose so. Someday."

The thought of Simon with another woman caused a hollowness in the pit of Storme's stomach that was elemental and unpreventable. And before she even planned the words she said, "And will you teach her, too, the way you taught me?"

Simon's throat convulsed and his hands fell still. He looked at the graceful curve of her neck, the slim white sweep of her shoulders, and an ache swelled up inside him that left him momentarily still and helpless. A wisp of light hair nestled against her neck and he could see it stir with the release of his breath. He wanted to touch that curl, to bend and lightly kiss her neck. He wanted it so badly that it hurt.

He steeled himself; he replied quietly, "Yes. I will."

He fastened the clasp with a final firm movement, and then he took her shoulders and turned her around. He looked into her eyes and all his noble resolve melted.

He thought, *No*. If he lived to an ancient age, if he knew a dozen women or more, if he married or remained celibate, there would never be anyone like her. No one and nothing would ever touch him so, move him so, burrow into the private place of his soul and rearrange all he held dear the way she had done. Storme, a multitude of women in a single form; innocence and wisdom, strength and vulnerability, surprise and delight, frustration and anger...what more could there be that Storme was not? How could he imagine that anyone could come close to filling the gap she would leave in his life?

Wanting her was madness, but letting her go would be the hardest thing he had ever done.

His fingers tightened on her shoulders; he tried to keep himself from pulling her close. He said hoarsely, "Storme..."

She saw the intensity in his eyes, searching, needing. She felt the ache of wanting that was as much hers as his, and she thought helplessly, *No*. Not now, not ever again. Tonight she must leave him, and how could she leave with the taste of him on her lips, the ache for him in her blood? Yet how could she leave without having known it, one more time?

The moment that they looked at each other was still and alive, throbbing with awareness and poised upon the edge of danger. Neither could move away; neither dared move closer.

Then there was a small sound at the door; a footfall, a clearing of a throat. The moment was gone, and Storme was swamped in relief—and regret. Simon did not turn around, but she saw it in his eyes, too. An ending of something he could not quite accept.

Peter said awkwardly behind them, "Pardon me, Simon. But there's something outside I thought you'd want to see before you left."

Simon's hands left her shoulders reluctantly, but the gentle sadness in his eyes held her still. He said softly, "You *are* lovely, Storme."

And then he turned to Peter, his manner brisk. "Yes, of course. What is it?"

Storme watched him leave the room, knowing it was best, glad he was gone. But very, very sorry as well.

Simon walked across the yard with Peter, his hands linked behind his back, his stride purposeful, but his mind only half on Peter's words. He was thinking of Storme, and wondering if she would ever forgive him for what he must set in motion this night; wondering whether, if he tried to sit down and earnestly reason with her, she might see it was for the best and cooperate. Perhaps she would even tell him where the letter was and save them all the trouble. Then it could be dispensed with, and fear and suspicion would stand between them no longer. . . .

". . . Couple of poachers," Peter was saying as he led the way toward the grain barn. "Wouldna have troubled ye wit'it, but your orders were to bring all intruders to you, personally. The big one, he gave us a spot of trouble afore we took him, that he did. Took six strong bucks to get him down and tie him up, but he's quiet enough now.''

"Did you find out anything from them?'' asked Simon absently. "Who they were or what they were doing here?''

"Nay, not a word.'' Peter nodded to the guards outside the barn door and they stepped aside. He pushed open the barn door and lifted a lantern.

Simon stood there looking at the two men in a long and heavy silence. The one-eyed man he was not certain of, but he could never forget the black giant. Storme had called him Pompey. She had cried real tears and said he was dead. . . .

Simon said quietly, "Well, I know who they are, and exactly what they're doing here.''

Peter shot him a quick astonished look. "Not the girl Storme?''

Simon nodded grimly. "They were on her ship. And now they've come to take her back.'' His voice sharpened as he turned to Squint. "Isn't that right?''

The two men were bound hand and foot and lashed securely to the support beams. Squint stared at Simon through his one contemptuous eye and said nothing.

Simon looked at Pompey. "She told me you were dead. Yet another of her many lies.''

Fury was rising, slow and bilious. No wonder she had not been anxious to contact Eden. She knew her men were coming. A girl as clever as she must have arranged this long ago. And as for her noble gesture of leaping off Eden's ship the other day. . . small sacrifice indeed when she must have known her escape would be delayed by only a few days.

Simon turned on his heel and snapped shortly to Peter, "Keep them tied up here tonight, with an armed guard. I'll deal with this in the morning.''

Just how he was going to deal with it he was not sure, but that was the least of his problems as he strode back to the house. He should have expected this, and he did not know why he was so angry. Except that he had *not* expected it, that twice in a little over a week his impenetrable fortress had been invaded and he had been caught unprepared.

Storme had lied to him, but that should come as no surprise. She had schemed and cheated, and everything she had done from the moment she came here had been guided toward this moment, but why should he have expected better of her? She was playing the game by the only rules she knew, and it was he who had been a fool. And that was why he was furious. Because he had lain with her and believed that inside that lithe pirate's body was the heart of a woman. Because he had looked into her eyes and seen innocence there, listened to her voice and trusted in her lies, because he had allowed himself to hope, even for a moment, that she might have changed. . . .

No matter, he assured himself grimly. The veil was lifted from his eyes, and now he was ready to fight with her choice of weapons. Tonight would be the turning point, and whatever happened, he had no more room for regrets.

She was in the front parlor with Christopher when Simon came in. They made a striking couple, she in her satin and pearls, and Christopher in his red velvet coat and knee breeches, as dashing a young swain as ever any European court could produce. Christopher was apparently teaching her to curtsy, bending over her hand and delivering laughing instructions as she sank to the floor. Bitterness boiled in Simon's throat and he thought, *Look at her. As ladylike as you please, but beneath all that finery and glitter as corrupt as the black heart of Satan . . .*

And then, as he watched, Storme lost her balance and stumbled against Christopher with a colorful oath. Christopher caught her to him in something very near an embrace, laughing with delight, and when Storme looked up at him her eyes were dancing with the same mischief and amusement she had so often turned on Simon. Simon felt a wrench of hateful emotion inside his chest that was almost choking.

He stepped forward abruptly. "Where is Augusta?" he demanded shortly. "We'll be late."

They turned to him, Christopher still holding Storme's hand possessively in the crook of his arm, as innocent and unconcerned as a new day. "She hasn't been down," he answered easily. Then, with an affectionate glance at Storme, "What do you think of our pirate girl, Cousin? Is she a vision? I think I shall marry her after all."

Simon turned and took the stairs at a furious pace, leaving Christopher to watch after him for a moment with a careless shrug before turning back to Storme.

Simon knocked sharply on Augusta's door. "Augusta, we're waiting. Come along."

He received no answer, and knocked again, more loudly. "Are you in there? We'll be late." Still no answer, and his patience was at a limit. "I'm coming in, whether you're decent or not. I've no time—"

He opened the door and found Augusta standing calmly before the window in her dressing gown. Not even her hair was dressed, and her maid was nowhere in sight. Simon stared.

"What in the name of all that is holy do you think you're doing?" he demanded. "I've already sent for the carriage. Where's your girl? Why aren't you dressed?"

Augusta's decision was almost as much of a surprise to her as it was to Simon. Until this very evening, until her maid had begun pressing her gown and laying out her undergarments, Augusta had believed she would be able to go through with it. And even now, until this very moment, she had not been certain she had the courage to defy her brother.

Tonight was a turning point for her in more ways than one, and she knew nothing would ever be the same after this moment.

She pressed her hands tightly together, she strengthened her voice, and she met his eye. She said as calmly as she could, "I'm not going."

"Don't be absurd." Simon barely paused to hear her. He strode over to her wardrobe and began looking through her gowns. "Is this what you're wearing? Call your girl. For the love of God, woman, you're seventeen years old. I shouldn't have to preside over your toilette like a nursemaid!"

Augusta squeezed her hands more tightly together; she closed her eyes briefly. She said clearly, "I am *not going*."

Then Simon stopped, and looked at her. Forceful restraint backed the impatience in his eyes, and he regarded her as though she were a child indulging in a particularly inconvenient temper tantrum. "Augusta," he said sternly, "I will not tolerate this. Not tonight of all nights. Now, dress yourself and be downstairs in a quarter of an hour and we shall not speak of this again." He turned to go.

The quiet pressure Augusta had been exerting on her timid nerves cracked. To be intimidated was one thing, to be commanded another, but to be ignored . . . "No!" she cried. Her face crumpled and her voice went shrill as she took a single determined step forward. "No, Simon, you cannot force me! I will not be ordered about like a servant, and I *am not going!*"

Simon turned, nothing but outright astonishment in his eyes.

"For years you have been dragging me about," she went on, her voice cracking with wild emotion. "From this fête to this gala to this tea—and I hate it, I've always hated it, but you refuse to listen to me! I simply cannot bear it anymore, Simon; you can't make me bear it!"

Simon seemed to require a moment to collect his thoughts. He looked at Augusta as though she were on the verge of madness and must be dealt with very, very carefully. "Augusta," he said quietly after a moment, "surely you can see I only do it for you—"

"That's just the point!" she cried. "I feel like a runt sow on market day! You all but invite prospective suitors to examine my teeth!"

Simon's face colored darkly, and he drew himself up. "That will be quite enough," he said stiffly.

And then, with a snap of incredulity in his eyes, Simon exclaimed, "Can you really think it is *my* heart's desire to go to Edenhouse tonight? To play chaperon to that—that—!" Words seemed to fail him, or else he thought better of what he was about to say, and he continued tightly. "The only reason I accepted the invitation was for your sake, and now I'm in the blasted thing too deeply to reconsider. You *will* accompany us to Edenhouse and act the part of the well-bred young lady you were brought up to be!"

Augusta threw back her head in despair. "Oh, Simon,

how long must you continue deceiving yourself? Can't you see you are only making fools of both of us?''

"I see nothing foolish in attempting to find a suitable husband for my only sister," replied Simon stiffly.

"No one is going to marry me!" she cried. Her eyes were wide and distressed, yet intense with conviction of an unvarnished truth. "Can't you see that! I am fat and ugly and clumsy and no one wants to marry me!"

The confusion in Simon's eyes was genuine. "But what a foolish thing to say. Augusta, you are lovely. You know that."

Augusta closed her eyes briefly, touched by his honest appraisal of what he genuinely believed. Love, Peter had said, was blind. Simon would always be blind where she was concerned, and Augusta would always love him for that, but he was wrong.

She came forward and lightly touched his arm, pleading. "Simon, don't you see—"

But Simon could not deal with this tonight. He thought of Storme, the treacheries she had already performed and those she yet planned; he thought of the two throat-cutting pirates tied up in his barn and of what lay ahead of him this night, and he had no time to play the compassionate sibling. He face tightened impatiently and he said, "I see only that you've spent too much time in the company of that pirate girl. These are her words I hear from your mouth, and I will not abide it. A disobedient female is one thing I will not tolerate. This is no night to engage my temper, Augusta," he said firmly, and turned toward the door. "We will await you downstairs."

Augusta cried loudly, "*No!*"

Simon turned with his hand on the door handle, fury and helplessness churning. Augusta stood before him, her arms wrapped tightly about herself, her eyes blazing hurt and defiance, and Simon saw in that moment everything spinning out of his control. How well he had deceived himself into thinking he was the master! How long had he lulled himself into believing destiny was his to command? He had grown soft and lazy, allowing emotion to overrule judgment. Now his home was invaded by pirates, his peace of mind destroyed; Spotswood commanded him, Eden threatened him, and his own sister defied him. He had been gentle long enough.

The muscles in Simon's jaw tightened, his eyes grew dark. He said quietly, "Very well, Augusta. Short of throwing you over my shoulder and carrying you by force across the river, I see there is no way I can make you attend the governor's ball. You shall have your way tonight. And on the morrow we shall discuss plans for your departure for England."

He saw her eyes grow wide with horror, and he steeled himself against it. "You were right about one thing, my dear. I have been deceiving myself. I have allowed you to run tame about this place, with nothing but livestock and servants for your playmates; I have placed you under the influence of a cut-throat criminal and sheltered you in this backwoods society and convinced myself that from all this you will find a husband. Well, no more. I will do what I should have done long ago.

"You will go to your Aunt Sybil in London on the next ship," he stated flatly. "I will endower you in such a way as to make you the catch of the town, and I promise you *will* be married before the year is out."

And without another word he turned and left the room.

Christopher and Storme were waiting at the foot of the stairs. Simon had no doubt but that they had heard every shouted, hysterical word, but he hardly cared.

Christopher said politely, "The carriage is waiting. Will Augusta be joining us?"

"Augusta has a headache," Simon said tersely. "I insisted she remain at home and nurse it." And, glancing at neither Storme nor Christopher, he swept up his cloak and hat and strode out the door.

* Chapter Twenty-six *

Edenhouse was grandly decked out for the occasion. The windows glittered with a hundred candles, festoons of roses lined the arched doorways, and fragrant bunches of sweet shrub banked the walls. The floors were strewn with crushed mint and juniper, and the air was thick with the cloying scents of hot tallow, perfume, and human sweat.

String musicians plucked out a lively tune, and the guests were splendidly clad in silks and velvets prominently sprinkled with jewels. Though most of them wore worsted and homespun—or even buckskin—by day, this was a very elegant affair and the closest any of them were likely to get to an evening at Court.

Storme made her entrance into the reception hall between the two strikingly handsome men as though she had been doing such things all her life. Her skirts were lifted just the proper degree to manage the stairs, her steps were light and graceful, her head was high. She paused under a chandelier, regally surveying the room, allowing everyone a chance to notice her. And notice her they did.

The buzz of laughter and conversation almost audibly paused, then resumed a noticeably altered, and considerably more excited, tone. This was what they all had been waiting for, as rumor had been rampant that she would be attending tonight. Quick darting glances were shot her way, whispers were hidden behind fans, wide eyes and craned necks turned for a better view of the notorious lady pirate. Some were scandalized, some were awed. She was a living legend come into their presence, and this would be a night no one would soon forget.

Christopher took it all in with a sweeping glance of amusement and delight, and he turned to Storme. "Well, my dear, what do you think of all this finery? I must say," he added gallantly, "you seem right at home."

Storme gave a small sniff. "You think I've never been to a party before? Some grander than this."

"Perhaps another time," Simon said coolly, looking straight ahead, "Mistress O'Malley will be kind enough to regale us with tales of the parties given by Captain Blackbeard, who, it is reported, served his guests human blood in golden goblets."

Storme shot him a sharp, indignant look, but just then a

familiar figure caught her eye, a movement parting the crowd toward them. She felt every muscle in her body tense, and exhilaration flooded her veins.

"Master York. How good of you to come."

Simon bowed low to Governor Eden. "So kind of you to ask us, my lord. You remember my cousin Christopher Gaitwood?"

"Yes, indeed, from the fair land of the James. My best to your father, sir. I trust he is well?"

Christopher made his bows and murmured the amenities, and then Eden turned to Storme. All eyes were upon them now, and conversation had all but ceased with the intensity of the drama.

Governor Eden bowed low over Storme's hand. His voice was clear and distinct for all who might hear. "My dear Mistress O'Malley. How long I've waited to welcome you to my humble home. You do me honor."

Storme gave a small, arctic smile. "Yes," she replied. "I do."

The governor straightened up, his eyes reflecting perhaps just the slightest bit of uncertainty. Then he turned quickly back to Simon. "But your lovely sister, Simon," he said. "Will she not be joining us?"

"Augusta is, unfortunately, indisposed," replied Simon smoothly. "She sends her regrets and asked to be remembered to you."

"And I to her as well. What a great pity. She always brings such a spark of light to my dreary little gatherings, and her presence will be most sorely missed. But you have made grand compensation with this lovely lady." He turned back to Storme with a liquid smile. "Perhaps you will allow me to take you around, my dear? Sir, you don't mind?"

There was the briefest moment's hesitation, and Storme's eyes met Simon's. Would he really do it then? Had he gone to all the trouble of taking her prisoner, placing her under guard, and fighting off her rescuers at the risk of his own life only to deliver her personally into the hands of his enemy? Did all his noble words about justice and criminality mean nothing? What *was* he planning?

But Storme could not guess, and nothing in Simon's face gave a hint of his motives as he bowed to the governor. "Your pleasure, sir. I'm sure the young lady couldn't be in better hands."

Eden offered his arm, and Storme took it.

Simon said quietly to Christopher, "Don't let her out of your sight."

Christopher, smiling to someone across the room, nodded and moved off.

So far, all was going according to plan. These few moments alone with Eden would be all Storme needed; all that remained for Simon was to keep his eyes and ears open. This thing could be over, tonight. His heart began to pound in slow, steady anticipation of the challenge.

Simon began to move around the room, circling toward a better vantage point of Eden and Storme, trying to look as at ease and relaxed as any young gentleman planter whose only purpose here was to enjoy the ball. He smiled and bowed to his acquaintances but made it a point to look distracted so no one would stop him. Then he spotted Mistress Abigail Trelawn and made the mistake of nodding to her.

She advanced upon him like a man-of-war, her eyes flashing, her chins jerking. Simon had no choice but to stop and greet her.

"Mistress Trelawn," he said, bowing low. "I was hoping to see you again. I must deliver my most abject apologies for being absent when last you visited Cypress Bay—"

"You have more to apologize for than that, sir," returned the good lady sharply, and Simon straightened up, one graceful brow lifted inquisitively.

"I will have you know," continued Mistress Trelawn in a low, cold undertone, "that the only reason I did not cut you dead is because I felt compelled by Christian charity to tell you why: I have always looked upon you as a favored son, and I would be less than dutiful if I did not speak aloud of the mortification your shameless behavior has brought on me. I took to my bed for three days when I heard the news, and though I staunchly tried to defend you I soon found it an impossible task. I have never been so appalled..."

Simon, sensing a discourse of some length coming on, looked anxiously past her toward the direction in which he had last seen Storme and Eden. At last he caught a glimpse of her, her head bent close to Eden's, engaged in intense conversation. Simon chafed to be close enough to know what they were saying. Christopher, he saw after a moment, was not too far away, but he, too, was busily engaged—with both the Trelawn girls. Blast it, had he forgotten his mission already?

"... And I will have you know, sir," Mistress Trelawn was saying heatedly, "that you needn't bother ever calling at my home again, for you will not be received. No, nor your sister either. I should certainly have thought that, however little regard you have for your own reputation, you might at least have given care to that of that poor dear child who has no one to depend upon for her career but yourself! Her chances are completely ruined in Carolina—yea, I venture to say the Colonies over!—for a scandal such as this spreads far and wide, and she will have no one to blame for it but you . . ."

Simon's jaw tightened with impatience and bitterness, for there was a ring of truth to the old matron's words he had not bothered to consider before. How, by all that was holy, had things ever gotten so out of hand? He had worked all his life to enhance his family name and keep his sister secure, and now it was all falling down about his ears. And why? All for the sake of Storme O'Malley, the treacherous, ungrateful wench who would kiss him one moment and stab him in the back the next.

For half a crown he would walk away and leave her now. It would be no less than she deserved, and he would be well rid of her. Let her pillage the seas if she would; it was no concern of his. Let Spotswood capture her again if he was so desperate to have her, and this time hang her on the spot . . .

But no. Even as the thought crossed his mind it was dismissed. Storme had made it clear their first order of business would be to assassinate Spotswood, and whatever Simon's feelings for the man at the moment he could not be a party to that. And Storme, for all her cleverness and skill, was bound for a violent death if she went through with her plan. Simon had gone too far and sacrificed too much to let her meet that end now. There was nothing for him to do but wade in deeper, and hope that somehow it would all come out right.

And on that grim resolution he lifted his eyes and began to search the room again for Storme.

"Enough of this blather and nonsense," Storme said. "I didn't come here to pretty up to your high-flying friends or be paraded about like a trophy on a cart."

Governor Eden had maneuvered her slightly away from the crowd and toward a curtained alcove, where they might not be overheard so easily. He inclined his head toward her respectfully. "And just why did you come here, my dear?"

Storme looked at him coldly. "That's what I'd like to know. I never heard of such a duck-brained scheme in all my days—sending an engraved invitation to a prisoner! Is that your notion of being clever?"

Eden chuckled lightly. "It accomplished its purpose, didn't it?"

Storme scowled. "I wouldn't be so bloody sure. That one"—she jerked her head toward the general direction in which she had last seen Simon—"has got something up his sleeve, you can bet your wild hairs on that."

"I think you overestimate his cunning, my dear. He is just a simple planter who finds himself in an awkward situation and would do almost anything to alleviate it. So he brought you to me. That is what we both wanted, isn't it?"

Storme's scowl lingered a moment longer, but she had little time to waste on trying to outguess Simon York. For now, at least, she did have what she wanted—an opportunity to meet in private with Eden—and she would deal with Simon's tricks when the time came.

She said, "All right, then. I've a bargain for you, so listen close."

Eden looked interested. "What sort of bargain?"

"I'll not be made a fool of by that prancing goose

Spotswood,'' Storme said fiercely. ''I don't like it any more than you did when he did it to you. This is our chance to strike and strike hard.''

''Indeed,'' murmured Eden. ''An opportunity long-awaited. What is your plan?''

''Get me to the *Tempest*,'' Storme pronounced without further ado. ''Give me four more ships with guns and men to outfit them. I will personally lead the fleet against Spotswood, and before the year is out what remains of him and his fair colony will be nothing but a smudge on the map.''

''You're speaking of war,'' murmured Eden. There seemed to be a touch of reluctance in his eyes. ''Risky business. Not to mention expensive.''

''Not as expensive,'' pointed out Storme sharply, ''as it would be if a certain letter should fall into the wrong hands.''

Eden's eyes lit upon her thoughtfully. ''Indeed,'' he admitted, after a time. ''Perhaps your idea is a sound one after all. We could be rid of Spotswood once and for all.''

Storme could hardly keep the contempt out of her voice. ''I thought you'd see it my way.''

Eden looked at her a moment longer, his expression unreadable. And then he seemed to come to a decision. ''First,'' he pronounced briskly, ''we must get you away from your jailor.''

''The sooner the better.''

''Very well. Then it will be done tonight.''

Storme gave a small nod of satisfaction. ''Right beneath the Farmer's nose.''

Eden smiled. ''Exactly. The last thing he expects is that you would do something so foolish. Why else would he have let you come?''

Storme thought about it for a moment. ''The Farmer is smarter than that. He never would have brought me here if he did not have a plan of his own. I half-think he wanted me to try to escape, and we must be careful of a trap. We shall simply have to be more clever than he is . . . and very wary.''

"Of course, my dear," Eden murmured. "But whatever York may have in mind, *you* will be the victor this night."

A tight smile touched Storme's face. "I promise you that."

"Do you know the wine cellar?" Eden demanded, all business now.

Storme gave him a look of disdain. "Of course." There was a tunnel beneath the cellar floor that led to the river, whereby Blackbeard had often smuggled goods. Storme, too, had visited that tunnel on more than one occasion.

Eden nodded. "My emissary, Tobias Knight, will await you there. He will take you by river to a safe place, and from there we'll make plans to recapture the *Tempest*. Do not delay," he warned, and bowed over her hand just as though he were doing nothing more treacherous than thanking her for a dance. "The sooner it is done, the less likely York will be to expect it."

Storme watched him move away, and then she lost no time. She slipped behind the curtained alcove and began to move toward the wine cellar.

This time she did not look back.

* *Chapter Twenty-seven* *

Simon looked up, and Storme wasn't there. One moment she had been across the room, standing in conversation with Eden, the next both she and the governor had disappeared. Abigail Trelawn's voice faded to a thin high screeching in his ear as his eyes swept the room. He saw Christopher, laughing with Darien Trelawn as though he hadn't a care in the world, and then he saw Governor Eden smiling and bowing to the daughter of a wealthy planter, but Storme was nowhere in sight.

"And I assure you, my dear man," came Mistress Trelawn's

voice, "that there is not a matron in this room who doesn't agree with me. Your precipitous and unconscionable behavior has rendered your status in this community—"

Simon said abruptly, "Mistress, I do humbly beg your pardon for all my sins." He bowed to her deeply but with some haste, and left her before she could even draw breath for a huffy reply.

Simon pushed his way quickly through the crowd, and his hand clamped around Christopher's arm in what could have been perceived as a friendly gesture but was in fact a grip of iron.

Darien Trelawn curtsied to him, her eyes wide with excitement. "Why, Simon York, you sly hawk! I thought you'd never come over, and I've been making such a dreadful spectacle trying to get your attention—"

"Your sweet cousin has been regaling us with tales of your exploits," interrupted her sister with a pout, "but I dareswear they would be much more convincing coming from you. You have been a naughty, naughty boy, you know, and it may yet be too late to redeem yourself by asking me to dance!"

But her provocative tone and inviting eyes were completely lost on Simon, as was her sister's catlike glare. He bowed absently to her. "You flatter me, my dear, but I am quite out of favor with your mother, and I hold you in too high respect to taint your reputation by going against her wishes. Ladies, please excuse us while I have a word with my cousin."

And without waiting for leave, he tightened his grip on Christopher's arm and pulled him out of hearing range. "I told you to keep an eye on Storme," he accused furiously.

Christopher was nonplussed. "Precisely what I was doing, dear chap. And quite a pleasant task it was, if I may say so—"

"You fool! She's gone!"

Christopher lifted an eyebrow in mild reprimand for Simon's tone. "Now, now. The situation is well in hand. She only just this moment walked behind that curtain, as I would have told you if you'd given me a chance—"

"Why didn't you follow her?"

"Why, I felt it only sporting to give her a head start."

With a furious hiss Simon released Christopher's arm. "Damn it Christopher, this is not a game!"

But Christopher's eyes were alight with mischief as he replied, "Such a display of passion for a woman you only recently referred to as a viperous savage! Calm down, sir, she can't have gone far. I've made inquiries, and there are only two exits from this house, neither of which can be reached from the passageway she took, which leads only to the wine cellar. Doubtless she plans to hide there just to see if you will come for her."

But Simon was far from sharing Christopher's amusement as he made his way as inconspicuously as possible toward the alcove Christopher had indicated. His heart was beating fast and panic was beginning to tighten his chest. For him it was a desperate chase, and he was not about to lose her now.

The stairway that led to the wine cellar was twisting and steep and lit by pine-knot torches at every bend. Storme moved as quickly as she could in the hampering hoop skirts, knowing that it was not unlikely that some lackey could be along any moment for another cask of wine to assuage the thirsty guests upstairs.

The walls of the lower room were lined with bottles of wine turned on their sides, as thorough a collection as that of any old-world peer. The dirt floors were stacked with barrels and casks of other smuggled goods, and the whole of it had a damp, sour, underground smell. Storme looked around for a moment, and then Tobias Knight, bewigged and decked out in his ballroom attire, stepped from the shadows.

"Mistress O'Malley," he said, and gestured toward a small doorway in the wall. "This way, please."

"I know the way," Storme snapped, as he took a torch from the wall, bending low to enter the door.

"Did anyone see you leave?" he inquired over his shoulder as Storme followed him through the door.

"Of course not."

"Then hurry, please. A ship is waiting to take you to safety."

Governor Eden rose a small notch in Storme's esteem. He had evidently planned it all to the last detail, and so far it was almost too easy.

If Storme had not been so desperate, so excited and greedy for her first taste of freedom—if, in fact, her wits had not been so muddled by the months of confinement in the Farmer's presence—she might have paused to wonder *how* Eden could have planned it all so perfectly. She might have been given pause by the fact that nothing genuine was ever this easy, for she had enough experience to know that. But as it was, her heart was pounding and her senses were soaring, and all she could think of was the sweet taste of victory.

The tunnel was narrow and slick with the collected moisture of the river toward which it wound steadily downhill. Storme cursed the foolish shoes that slid in the mud beneath her feet and the fancy skirts that hampered her movement. She had to hold on for balance against the wall and her hoops kept catching against the rough surface on either side of her. The satin snagged and tore and she barely noticed. She kept her eyes on the circle of Knight's torch, a few feet ahead.

"Watch your step, here," he said, waiting for her. "There's a sharp turn and the path is slippery downhill."

Storme gave him a quelling glare as she drew up. She had been in and out of this tunnel more times than he ever would, and knew the paths by heart.

She rounded the turn and took the heart-pounding course downhill. She could see a patch of light gray, which was the mouth of the tunnel, and she could smell the river. Elation soared. She was free. . . .

She stepped outside, and two men moved briefly into the light of Knight's upheld torch. It all happened so quickly Storme could not have prevented it even if she had had warning. One of the men grabbed her and pinned her arms behind her back, wrapping them with strong rope. Another thrust a cloth into her mouth, which was opened for a cry of fury and surprise, and began to bind it around her head. Her eyes went wild; she struggled, but in an instant she was thrown to the ground and her ankles were bound tightly together.

In the flickering torchlight Tobias Knight's face was pale and cruel. He smiled coldly. "So, Captain O'Malley, you are not as clever as we were led to believe. I'm sure you'll understand, my dear, that we can hardly allow you to continue your subtle blackmail of this government with that letter of Blackbeard. It's become far too inconvenient. And, unfortunately, as long as you are the only one who knows the whereabouts of the letter, the easiest way to deal with the entire matter is to dispose of you. It will solve all our problems, you see."

Storme struggled wildly, but to no avail. The night spun and blurred as she was lifted roughly and dragged toward the river.

Christopher's voice echoed with a note of excited awe on the damp tunnel walls. "So the rumors are true. Eden does have a secret passage to the river. By Jove, this is rich."

"This is no time to be planning your next House of Burgesses speech," Simon snapped. His chest was tight with urgency and his throat was dry, and Christopher's insistence upon regarding this all as a grand adventure grated on his nerves almost to the breaking point. He lifted his torch to survey the dripping walls around him, impatience and dread mounting. "If she gets to the river, we'll never stop her."

"And you're quite certain she came this way?"

"The bloody door was standing wide open." Simon increased his pace, careless of the hazardous jagged walls and slippery floor. "Who else would have come in here?"

Behind him, Christopher paused. "You're right," he said slowly. "Here's a footprint. In fact, several."

Simon turned, lowering his torch to blend with Christopher's, and then swiftly swinging around to examine the ground before him. The tracks were clearer there, though still not particularly distinguishable. And one of them belonged to a man.

The anxiety in Simon's chest leaped and tightened, and he moved faster.

Before they even reached the end of the tunnel, they heard the scuffle and the voices outside. Simon's eyes met Christopher's in a single swift moment of alarm and consent, and they began to run. They burst out into the moon-washed night with their swords drawn and their eyes swiftly searching, and what they saw warned them they were almost too late.

Two men were dragging Storme's bound and writhing body toward the river. A third, leading by torchlight, was shouting orders. Hardly allowing the incredible scene to register, Simon and Christopher shouted and lunged forward.

The man with the torch cried, "Throw her in!" And, flinging his torch in the path of the two approaching swordsmen, he ran. Simon and Christopher were four paces behind when Storme's body hit the river with a splash.

With a fierce battle cry Christopher struck out before either of his opponents had a chance to draw a weapon. He sent the first man to the ground with a single powerful slice to his midsection and turned to meet the raised sword of the other. Simon flung his sword to the ground and without even a pause for breath, dived into the water.

Though in fact the whole of it took less than a minute, for Simon it was a lifetime of black, whirling water, bursting lungs, and panic rising and gathering speed and threatening to choke him with helplessness. Over and over it played before his eyes—Storme, bound hand and foot, plunged into the water. Helpless in the hands of her enemies. Storme, brilliant in jewels and satin; Storme in torn and bloodied clothes, her eyes flashing at him from the depths of a prison cell. Storme, fierce and undefeated, innocent and curious, gentle and quiescent as she lay within the circle of his arms . . . Storme, struggling in a watery grave. Had he gone through all of this only to lose her now?

He flailed beneath the water, blindly searching. Desperation pounded behind his eyes, defeat clawed at him with raking fingers. And then he brushed against something. His hand tangled in her gown. The surge of relief almost burst his lungs. He got his arm around her waist and fought his way toward the surface.

Simon floundered onto the bank, gasping and struggling to hold onto Storme's heavy body, in time to see Christopher's second assailant staggering away, his bloodied arm hanging uselessly at his side. Christopher slid down the bank and relieved Simon of his sodden burden, gripping Storme under the arms and dragging her forward.

"Is she alive?" he demanded. The light of battle was still high in his eyes, but the tautness of his voice reflected his own very real appreciation of the seriousness of the situation. "My Lord and Savior, what the hell happened?" His breath was short and his face gleamed with perspiration as he worked the gag loose from Storme's mouth.

Simon, on a new surge of desperate energy, turned Storme over onto her side and slapped her back. She began to gag and cough, and the relief that went through Simon was so great it left him weak. He sat back for a moment, struggling to regain his own breath.

Christopher unloosed the ropes from Storme's hands and ankles, and she pulled herself onto her elbows, coughing furiously and spitting water. Christopher looked around quickly. "I don't know about you," he said to Simon, "but I'm not inclined to wait for the second round."

He placed Simon's sword in his hand. "I'll bring the carriage around to the riverfront. Perhaps it would be best if we left with as little fuss as possible."

Simon nodded, gulping air. "Hurry!" he commanded, and on the word Christopher scrambled up the bank and disappeared into the night.

Storme's face was white and drawn, streaked with underwater slime and scratched by submerged brush. Her lips were blue with cold and her eyes dull with shock. Her hair was plastered to her head and her lovely gown sodden and muddied. She gasped and coughed, shuddering helplessly, and Simon's heart swelled to melting with the sight of her.

Simon helped Storme to a sitting position, and then he

couldn't let her go. He held her against his chest while her shoulders shook with weak gasping coughs; her hand wound itself into the material of his shirt, clinging to him, and for a moment everything that had gone between them was forgotten. The betrayals, the secrets, the anger, and the hurt were swallowed up by the great gulf that separates life from death, and all Simon could do was hold onto her. She was alive. That was the only thing that mattered.

Then she turned her face up to him, looking at him. She said weakly, "I thought—you wanted me to escape. Yet you followed me . . . you saved my life."

And as though the steel jaws of a trap slammed down, Simon hardened himself. Nothing had changed. She was still a criminal, and he was still her jailor. She had almost died tonight because of her own treachery . . . and he had led her to it.

He said briefly, "You saved my life the last time you tried to escape. Now we're even."

Storme felt the chill come over his voice, and she pushed slowly away. She looked at him closely. "Is that all?"

Simon looked away. "What the hell happened?" he demanded tersely. "Who were those men?"

Wearily, Storme pushed her wet hair away from her face. "Eden's men. The bastards tried to murder me."

Simon looked at her sharply. "I thought Eden was your friend."

"I thought so too. Turns out I'm worth more to him dead than alive."

"Why?"

There was a sound in Storme's throat that might have been a strangulated laugh. "Blackbeard's treasure."

"What?" Simon demanded, certain he had not heard correctly. His head was reeling with this new turn of events.

Storme's lips twisted into a dry smile that was wise and weary. "There's this letter that Eden wrote to Blackbeard. Tells all about their arrangement for smuggling in goods and protecting the pirates in Carolina, enough to put Eden in a pretty fix if it ever got into the wrong hands. As long as

Blackbeard had that letter, he sailed free in Carolina. Now I have it.''

Simon's heart was pounding slow and steady. His voice was careful and controlled. ''And they were going to kill you for that?''

She shrugged. ''Seems like as long as that letter's around Eden's nervous. Especially now that Spotswood's after it too. And since I'm the only one that knows where it is, all they have to do is kill me and their troubles will be over.''

Her face went bleak, and her voice was low. Only now was she beginning to realize the full implications of what just happened here. Eden, her last hope. He had turned on her like a vicious dog, and she had been a fool to trust him. But what choice had she had? What was she to do now?

''The secret will die with me,'' she repeated, very lowly, ''and then Eden figures he'll be safe.''

Simon's fists tightened slowly, and slowly the anger, the tension, spread to every muscle in his body. How could he have been so stupid? He should have realized . . . Spotswood should have realized . . . He had delivered Storme into the hands of her enemy for nothing more than expediency's sake, and she had almost died. Even now she was not safe, for if Eden had tried once to kill her, he surely would try again.

He turned to Storme quickly and on a breath of decision. This foolish game had gone on long enough. He refused to play chess with human lives as pawns, and he had never planned on this.

He said firmly, ''Storme, listen to me. There is only one possible end to this madness. And I think you know what it is.''

She stared at him, not comprehending.

''As long as you are the only one who knows where that letter is, your life is in danger. Unless you give up the secret and now, you will, I'm very sorry to say, take the secret to your grave. Is that what you want?''

''So what am I to do?'' she tossed back at him. ''Give it over to Eden? He'd kill me anyway, the traitorous varlet!''

Simon said quietly, "Tell me. Tell me where the letter is."

Her voice rose in incredulity. "I should trust you? You, who can't let a day pass without preaching at me about my sins on the seas and would as soon see me hang as—"

He interrupted simply, "What choice do you have?"

For a moment Storme was silent. Simon held his breath. And then Storme laughed, softly, tiredly. "All this bloody mess," she said, shaking her head.

She looked up at Simon. Her eyes were brittle with stress and her expression was composed and humorless. "All right, Farmer, I'll tell you, for all the bloody good it'll do you. Ain't no one can get in and out of Teach's Hole alive except me or another one of the Brethren, and that's where it is. Buried 'neath a cypress tree and marked with a yellow stone." She laughed again. "Blackbeard's treasure. That's all in hell it ever was."

In the shadows of a rolling hillock Tobias Knight crouched, trying to still the frenetic rasp of his own breath, straining to listen. There would be hell to pay for this night's work. His one and only chance at Storme O'Malley foiled . . . one man dead and another injured . . . Simon York appearing out of nowhere to unravel the scheme . . . How could it have gone so wrong? How would he explain it to Governor Eden?

The words of the two below came to him in snatches and phrases, carried by errant currents of the breeze. He had delayed long enough. There was nothing to do but go back and face the governor's wrath. At least now that Gaitwood was gone, he might have a chance to creep back through the tunnel unnoticed. He started to pull himself away. And then something caught his ear.

"Tell me," came York's voice. "Tell me where the letter is."

Knight froze, his heart leaping and thudding. What incredible fortune! If she told York . . . if he, Tobias, could overhear . . . then all might not be lost. Something could be redeemed of this catastrophe if only he could hear . . .

But the breeze fluttered the words away, slapping them

into the sound of the river striking the bank. Inwardly
Knight cursed, straining, and then he heard Storme O'Malley's
voice . . . "All right, Farmer. I'll tell you."

But that was all. Murmurs, snatches of phrases. "Buried—
cypress—treasure . . ." And then there was the distant clatter
of approaching carriage wheels and Knight knew he could
linger no longer.

Cursing himself and Simon York and Storme O'Malley
with all that was in his soul, he melted into the darkness.
Tonight should have been the end of it all, but all he had
succeeded in doing was making it worse. Now there were
two people who knew the secret worth killing for, and
matters were more complicated than ever.

* *Chapter Twenty-eight* *

For two hours Augusta had paced the floor of her room,
fighting back horror, her hands and her lips pressed tightly
together to repress the gulping sobs that wanted to break
through. Simon was serious. Had it been an idle threat
delivered in anger, Augusta would have taken it in stride,
confident it would all be forgotten when her brother came
out of his temper. But she had seen more than anger in his
eyes; more, even, than disappointment. Behind the cool
words that he uttered had been a quiet, unbreachable acceptance of fact, and Augusta knew there was no hope for her.

He would send her away. He would send her to a faraway
place in the care of a relative she had never met, and she
would never see home again. She would never see Peter
again . . .

All her life she had been a coward, a passive and obedient
servant to Simon's greater wisdom. She had never dared to
fight or object or state her rights, for in her own mind she
had believed she had none. Perhaps, after a fashion, she had

even enjoyed Simon's stern rule over her, for it was much easier to be an extension of a man as strong as Simon than to struggle for an identity of one's own. And as she knew this she was ashamed of herself and her own lack of courage, but she was also frightened. For the time for cowardice was past. If she did not act now, it would be too late, and she would lose the only thing in the world worth fighting for. . . .

She stopped at the window and looked down. The light from Peter's office was a thin yellow glow, a beacon of hope in a world turned dark and stormy. And suddenly she knew what she had to do. She did not stop to think, or even to change out of her dressing gown. She ran down the stairs and out of the house, toward Peter.

Peter was preparing for bed. He had changed the guard on the two prisoners in the barn, secured the perimeter of the plantation, and closed his ledger books for the day. He had stripped down to his breeches and bare feet and was turning down the covers on his cot in the back room when the outer door to the office burst open. Almost before he could turn Augusta appeared at the door of his bedroom.

Automatically he reached for his shirt. "Gussie! What on God's green earth—"

"Oh, Peter!"

Peter's heart lurched with alarm as he saw her wide, distraught eyes, her tear-streaked face. He let the shirt drop as she rushed toward him, and he caught her up in his arms. His voice was thick with concern as he murmured, "What, little darlin'? What has got you in such a state?"

"Peter you mustn't let him do it! Please help me!"

His arms tightened. "What—"

She lifted her face to him, pale and lined with distress. She was trembling. "Simon," she whispered. "He's going to send me away—to London, to find a husband. He's going to send me away and I—I'll never see you again! Oh, Peter, how can I marry anyone when I love you so desperately?"

Peter felt his heart twist with a shaft of agony that tightened every muscle in his body. "No, love, please. You mustn't—"

But she lifted her small, unsteady hands to his face. Her eyes were dark with the depth of her emotion and seemed to swallow him alive. "We've got to go away, Peter, to leave Cypress Bay. No, I know what you'll say, but I've thought of it and there is no other way. It's the only way we can be together, our only chance . . ."

"Gussie, that is madness you speak—"

"Peter, please . . . hold me. I need you to love me. Please let me be yours tonight. . . ." Her lips lifted to his.

She kissed him with the innocent sincerity of a child, and the desperate passion of a woman. She kissed him as though it were for the last time, and Peter, with a surge of desperate need, kissed her back. Reason fought with instinct and reason was losing, until with a sudden surge of strength he lifted his mouth. He looked down at her searchingly, his breathing hard, his blood thrumming. "Gussie," he whispered hoarsely, "you mustn't do this thing—"

But he saw in her eyes not the pliable, easily confused child of his youth, but the quiet certainty of the woman who loved him. Her arms tightened around his neck, and she kissed him again. And nothing else mattered.

Augusta knew it was wrong, and she knew it was right. She knew nothing but the desperation for all they would never share beyond this moment. Waves of need washed over them and drew power from them, and they were helpless beneath its force until finally all else faded away and Peter lowered her gently to the bed.

The bouncing, jostling progress of the carriage through the night was a mundane conclusion to the frenetic events of the evening, but for Simon it was a greatly welcome respite. His damp clothes were cold and uncomfortable; he was dull with exhaustion, but could not rest. His head throbbed out demands, questions, anxieties, and there were no answers for any of them.

It had started out as such an easy thing, simple and clear-cut. Save Storme O'Malley from a gallows-hungry mob while Spotswood searched for evidence against Governor Eden. A matter of days, the man had said, or a mere week. But if that plan failed, all Simon had to do was keep the girl under guard and wait for Eden to contact her.... Well, he had waited. And matters had steadily deteriorated until they had concluded in tonight's tangled nest of lies and betrayals and escape from a near death.

What a fool he had been. He had warned Spotswood from the outset that he was no match for intrigue and espionage, and he had proved it at every juncture. He had failed abominably, not only in procuring the evidence Spotswood needed but in the simple task of keeping Storme O'Malley safe. And what was he to do now?

The irony was that, for all their pains, they had accomplished nothing. He knew the whereabouts of the letter, but the information was useless to him. No one but a pirate or a fool would venture into Teach's Hole and expect to return alive. He knew he should turn the information over to Spotswood and be done with it, but what good would it do? Simon would only be setting himself up for more involvement in this dastardly game of endless check and checkmate, and all he wanted now was a way out.

But a way out was the one thing he could not appear to find at present.

He looked at Storme, who, as always, appeared little the worse for wear. She was wrapped in Christopher's cloak, her wet hair clinging to her cheeks, her head upon his shoulder. Christopher's arm was around her comfortably, and no dreads or worries disturbed her rest. Indeed, Simon must worry for all of them.

Simon did not know whether it was the cozy scene she made with Christopher, leaning upon him so confidently and completely oblivious to the dark consequences of this night's work, or whether it was the residual tensions of the evening's events, but irrational anger stabbed at him and the only vent he had for it was to lash out at Storme. He said coldly, "You are certainly very quiet, Mistress O'Malley, for one who is usually so quick with boasting and bravado. Could it be that the great pirate captain has finally been outwitted by a man of lesser character? Your fine friend

Governor Eden hardly turned out to be all you expected, did he?''

If it was a fight he was looking for, he had succeeded. Storme, exhausted to the point of numbness, was shocked out of her lethargy by the sarcasm in his tone and a fire born of hurt and anger kindled in her eyes. ''Don't try to make me think it surprises you, Farmer,'' she spat. ''You were Johnny-on-the-spot when it all started, weren't you? You knew exactly what was planned for me tonight and I wouldn't be afraid to wager you'd conceived the whole plan! You've wanted to be rid of me from the start and—''

''So naturally I plunged into an icy river to save your worthless skin!'' Simon's eyes narrowed and his muscles went tight. He did not know what he had expected, but this outrageous accusation was not it.

''That only goes to prove you're not as damn clever as you thought!'' Storme knew there was no logic in her words and she did not believe any of it, but hurt clamored with confusion and all she knew was to fight back. ''You're a fine one for running people's lives, Farmer, planning this and scheming that and ordering the other thing, but you didn't do such a flawless job this night, did you? Something went wrong with your little scheme and—''

''Oh, for the love of Jesus,'' Christopher said tiredly, shifting his weight as Storme stiffened in his arms. ''Cannot you two leave it be? Must we have a duel tonight?''

Simon barely heard him. Something wild and explosive was still battering at him, singing through his nerves and shattering his composure. He wanted to grab Storme by the shoulders and shake her senseless. He wanted to shout at her, he wanted to throttle her, he wanted to clutch her to him and kiss her until she wept. . . .

He leaned forward tensely, every muscle in his body straining against the urge to do any of those things. His eyes were churning and as much as he tried he could not stop the words that he knew from the beginning he should not say. ''I have laid my life on the line for you over and over again,'' he pointed out. ''I have saved you from prison and mob lynching and murderous pirates and your own foolish determination to escape my protection. I have bloody well risked everything I have for you! Are you such a selfish, ungrateful wench that you can't see—''

He broke off abruptly, on the verge of making a startling, emotion-driven declaration here in the carriage with Christopher looking on and Storme regarding him with hate in her eyes. The quick enlightenment in Christopher's eyes embarrassed him, and the stubborn defiance in Storme's eyes infuriated him.

Storme said sharply, ''I'll thank you to make no more grand efforts on my behalf, Farmer! I can take care of myself.''

Simon sank back slowly, the anger gradually taking second place to a sense of defeat, and a sorrow he could not quite understand. He said quietly, ''That's the trouble with you, Storme O'Malley. You don't need anyone.''

For a moment Storme hesitated. She did not understand his words, but the sadness in his eyes spoke to her, and hurt her in some indefinable way. He had saved her life tonight. When all else had betrayed her, Simon had been there, wielding his sword for her, pulling her into the safety of his arms. . . .

Yet now he turned on her. She did not understand why, or what she had done to provoke him, or why he looked at her with such weariness and loss now. She knew only that he had hurt her, and it wasn't fair, and it was much easier to fight with him than to try to comprehend him.

She fumbled with the clasp on the pearls he had given her earlier in the evening. ''You're damn right I don't need anybody. Not you, not your fancy words or your pretty promises or your baubles!'' She released the clasp and flung the necklace across the carriage at him. ''There!'' she declared, her eyes glowering. ''Now we are even, Farmer! I owe you nothing, nor you me!''

He caught the necklace automatically, his expression darkening again. ''Are you so sure, my fine pirate queen? Just what do you expect to do with yourself now that your avenues of escape are closed? How do you plan to go on living without depending on me?''

Storme drew a sharp breath through her nostrils and clenched her fists. She kept her tone deliberately cool, purposefully taunting, as she replied, "Just what do *you* think I should do, Farmer? You're the one with all the clever plans."

"You can go straight to blazes for all I care," Simon growled, turning to stare out the window.

"I'll see you there," she assured him with a mirthless smile. "Eventually. Meanwhile, it looks like we're stuck together, don't it?"

Simon jerked his head around for some quick retort, but Christopher interrupted dryly, "As a member of the court, I have the power to join you two lovely souls in wedlock. Perhaps that would be the most efficient way to stop this ceaseless bickering."

Simon's eyes met Christopher's sharply, but he saw nothing in his friend's expression except a weary attempt to put an end to the tension. He turned again to stare out the window, oblivious to Storme's fixed and furious glare, and the remainder of the journey passed in stony silence.

The carriage swayed down the Cypress Bay drive, and lurched to a stop before the front door. Two servants quickly appeared with lamps to light the steps.

"Quite an evening, hmm?" murmured Christopher, as Storme leaned forward to fumble impatiently with the door lock.

Simon was ashamed of his earlier behavior and tried to remember his manners. "I appreciate your help, Christopher," he said.

The footman opened the door and brought up the carriage block, and Storme climbed out. Christopher and Simon followed.

"I haven't lost my touch since our bouts in the schoolyard, have I?" agreed Christopher gamely. "But I must say, I'm looking forward to a warm brandy right now."

Simon noticed the lamp burning in Peter's office, and a new concern was added to his burden of troubles. It wasn't Peter's custom to be up and about this late, unless something was wrong. Abruptly Simon remembered the pirates tied up in the barn and cursed himself inwardly. He had left his sister alone without a thought of the cutthroats that had been captured on his premises. Would it never end?

"Storme," Simon said shortly, "I'd like to talk to you as soon as you've changed."

She looked at him, but said nothing.

"You're soaked," Christopher said. "Aren't you coming in?"

"In a minute. Pour me a brandy. I have something to check on first." He started across the yard toward Peter's office.

Simon stepped into the office and looked around. It was empty. He told himself not to overreact, but after all that had happened this evening why shouldn't he expect the worst? He felt his chest tightening again.

He called out sharply, "Peter?" And, without waiting for a reply, he strode across the room and opened the door to the sleeping quarters.

Afterwards he would remember only a collage of impressions; quick frozen vignettes that superimposed themselves upon his mind with ever increasing rapidity, freezing for a split second of horror before moving on again. Peter's face, shocked and stricken. Augusta's soft cry. Peter's naked chest. Augusta grasping for the sheet, pulling it to cover her breasts. Peter's arms shielding her.

It seemed forever that Simon stood there, blood draining from his veins, his lips growing numb. He couldn't move, he couldn't take a breath. Even his heart was suspended to bursting between beats, and all he could do was stare.

And then it struck him with the force of a gunshot; he almost staggered beneath the blow. He said hoarsely, "Augusta, clothe yourself." He spun and left the room, closing the door behind him.

He went perhaps two steps and could go no further. He leaned against the wall, shaking with shock and horror and a dozen other things he could not yet define, fighting back bile and trying very hard not to be ill. Augusta. And Peter. Naked. Wrapped in a carnal embrace like two heated animals. *His sister*. Peter . . . and *Augusta* . . .

The door opened, and Peter came out. He was dressed only in his breeches; his hair was tousled and his eyes were drawn with pain. Simon stared at him. For what seemed like the longest time all he could do was stare.

Peter said quietly, "I love her, Simon. I know what you must be feeling, but I would never mean her harm..."

Peter, whom he trusted. Peter, a *servant*, with his sister...

"I deserve your hatred, but you mustn't blame the lass. Do what you must with me, but be gentle on her...."

In a rush the black hatred inside Simon gathered, spun, erupted in a single surge of blinding, violent rage and no power in heaven or earth could keep it back. His eyes went wild, his face went dark. He roared, "*You bastard!*" And he lunged at Peter, his hands fastening with a murderous power around the other man's throat. "You bastard!"

* *Chapter Twenty-nine* *

Storme had stripped down to her bare legs and her corset and chemise. The horrible padded hoops, the painful slippers, and the ivory satin gown lay in a heap upon the floor, spreading a wet stain across the polished wood. Storme could not find the bird-witted maid who had gotten her into this outfit and was too impatient to try. She began to tug at the wet laces of the corset herself, making little progress.

She stank of foul river water and was chilled to the bone. Muscles long unused ached from the recent exertions, and her throat and lungs burned with the streams of water she had inhaled. Yet her wits were not dulled a fraction, and they attacked the new problem that assailed her with perseverance and fury.

She was more angry with herself than with Eden. She had always known he had the cunning of a weasel and wasn't to be trusted much beyond view, but murder... He had been her protector, they had had a bargain, he had been her last resort. Anger and disgust churned within her. Eden was a fool for the attempt, for her vengeance would be sure. But she was even more the fool, for she had stepped right into his trap.

And what about Simon? How was she ever to comprehend the man? He had taken her to the ball knowing she would try to escape, but when her life was endangered by doing so, he had come to her rescue. He had saved her life, yet a moment afterward turned as cold as a nor'wester on the open sea. She wanted to despise him, for she had not deserved his treatment of her in the carriage, but even more she wanted to understand him. That sad look in his eyes haunted her. "You don't need anyone," he had said, as though it were a crime. And that had hurt her, because deep inside she was struggling to admit how much she did need him. . . .

Abruptly her thoughts were cut off by a clamor in the outer yard. Every muscle tensed with alertness and she flew to the window. She saw torchlight and men running, a small knot of them converging near an outbuilding at the side of the house. There were shouts and excited gesticulations and Storme could tell nothing from this distance. Had Eden launched another attack? Had his spies been waiting for them when they got home, and was Simon even now fighting them off?

She whirled and snatched the first garment she saw from her open wardrobe. She jerked on the skirt and tied it at the waist, not bothering with a bodice. Distantly she heard the clatter of footsteps on the stairs and a woman's sobbing, running breaths, but Storme was halfway to the door herself when Augusta burst in.

She looked like someone escaped from an asylum. Her hair was tangled and streaming down her back, her face was white, her eyes wild with hysteria. She cried, "Peter— Simon! He's killing him!"

Augusta was almost incoherent, her voice broken and shrill with sobs, and Storme did not pause to question. She pushed past the other woman, and snatching up her skirts in one hand, she ran down the stairs. On her way out she paused to grab the only weapon she could find, a sturdy cane in a stand beside the door.

The corset cut off her breath, her heart pounded painfully against its constraints. Servants were streaming in from their quarters, their faces gleaming in the swaying light of torches, their voices babbling. Storme ran toward the crowd that had gathered near the side of the house, and as she got closer she distinguished other sounds—murmurs of horror beneath shouts of excitement, and the unmistakable crack of a whip.

Storme pushed through the crowd, using the cane when necessary, until she caught a glimpse of what was happening. And then she stopped still.

Simon stood in the center of a cleared circle, his coat off, his hair tousled, a whip in his hand. His chest was heaving, his face was hard, and his eyes were like burning coals. Peter, stripped to the waist, was bound to the whipping post. Already the red welts of three crisscrossing lashes scarred his back.

In all the time she had been here, Storme had never known Simon to beat his servants, nor had she even heard of it—though she personally thought that a few lashes would have done some of them a great deal of good. No, it wasn't the act itself that shocked her, but the fact that it was Peter, whom Simon hardly regarded as a servant at all. And it was the look on Simon's face—a look very near to madness.

Storme pushed forward, and someone grabbed her arm. "Go back to the house, Storme," Christopher advised in a low, strained voice. His face was drawn and his eyes were grim. "And try to keep Gussie there too. There's nothing—"

"What the bloody hell is going on?" Storme demanded, staring as the whip whistled through the air again.

"I don't know," Christopher answered hoarsely. He flinched as leather bit into flesh. "He won't say. All I know is I can't control him—I can't talk to him—it's as though he's lost his mind . . . I fear to God for this night's work."

Storme knew the value of discipline. She also knew that a good leader never administered it in anger, for to let one's emotions control the whip was as dangerous and as foolhardy as going into battle blinded by rage. And that was what Simon was now: blinded. He was a good leader; he would not make such a mistake. But what Storme saw in Simon's face now was nothing she had ever known of the man before, and Christopher was right. Murder would be done before the night was over.

She let the cane fall to the ground; she jerked away from Christopher and moved toward Simon. "Farmer!" she shouted, trying only to get his attention, to break that awful spell of madness that gripped him. "How many lashes? What is his crime?"

Simon appeared not to hear her. His face was white and shiny, his eyes focused grimly on the task before him. He lifted the whip again.

"I'll tell you his crime!" Augusta screamed. She broke through the forefront of the crowd, her face smeared with tears, her eyes flashing desperation. "He loved me, that was all! Peter loved me and bedded me and for that he must die!"

It happened in an instant. Simon whirled on his sister, his eyes dark with loathing, his face contorted with rage. With a low animal roar in his throat he drew back the whip and snapped it forward.

Suddenly Storme lunged to catch the strap in midair, using its forward impetus to jerk the weapon from Simon's hand.

There was absolute silence. In the flickering glow of the torches the crowd stood as though frozen. Peter, with his eyes squeezed shut against a pain more than physical; Augusta, her hysteria suspended in horrible disbelief; Simon, the sound of his harsh breathing echoing clearly in the still night air. And Storme, standing between the two of them, her breasts heaving with exertion, her muscles taut for further action.

Slowly the cloud of madness cleared from Simon's eyes to be replaced by a creeping horror and shock as he realized what he had almost done. The pain that stiffened his face was awful to behold. He took a halting step forward, his hand half-lifted toward his sister. Augusta shrank back, her face buried in Christopher's shoulder.

Simon stood there for a moment longer, looking at her with his eyes full of useless words he could not say, of horrible truths he could not face. And then all the life seemed to go out of him. His shoulders slumped, he dropped his hand. He turned and walked away.

For the longest time no one said anything. The crowd shuffled restlessly and looked away. Then Christopher, with the authority of a legislator and the competence of a planter's son, stepped forward. "Get back to your quarters," he ordered shortly. "You—and you—" He pointed out two men with a terse jerk of his head. "Help me cut him down and take him to the guardhouse."

The crowd dispersed quickly and eagerly, for all had seen more this night than they wanted to. Christopher escorted Peter, held up between two strong Africans, across the yard. And Storme stood there, looking the way that Simon had gone, her head reeling, aching with something indefinable inside for him.

She was surprised after a time to notice that Augusta was still standing there. The two of them were the only ones left in the yard. Suddenly weary, Storme dropped the whip in the dust and turned toward the house, assuming Augusta would follow. The other woman's quiet words stopped her.

"I'm leaving this place," Augusta said. "Now. Tonight."

Storme stared at her. Augusta's face was strangely quiet, her eyes calm and determined. More than one thing had changed this night. Augusta, too, was a woman Storme had never known before.

But Storme had little patience for the complexities that were being heaped upon her with such unfailing rapidity. She said shortly, "Don't be a fool. Where would you go?" And, not even waiting for a reply, she turned for the house again.

Augusta replied simply, "It doesn't matter. But I must leave."

Storme stopped. "You're serious," she said slowly.

Augusta turned to her. "I have to get Peter out of here

before morning. I've never seen Simon like this; I don't know what he'll do. But neither of us can afford to stay and find out."

"True enough," murmured Storme, and she was thinking, *If only it was that easy for me, to just pick up and leave . . .*

If the two of them were going anyway. . . with all the excitement and in Simon's current state, what better time to effect an escape? And almost before the hope was even life it died an undistinguished death. After what had happened at Edenhouse, any attempt to leave this place would be suicide. For where would she go? Two governors were after her head; there was no safe harbor. On land, burdened by a runaway servant and a cumbersome woman, Storme wouldn't have a chance. But. . . .

A spark ignited in Storme's brain and swiftly kindled into a full-blown idea. She looked alertly at Augusta. "I can help you," she said, "if you will do something for me."

The heavy bolt screeched loudly as Storme lifted it, and the two women held their breath. The heavy block guardhouse was windowless and impenetrable except by the door that was bolted from the outside, and Christopher, either through distraction or overconfidence, had not thought to post guards.

It was three o'clock in the morning. The servants' quarters were silent, and Christopher had gone to bed. A single dim candle burned from a window on the far side of the house, where Simon had shut himself into the library. He could neither hear nor see what went on this far away, and in his state Storme doubted whether he cared. After a moment, when nothing moved, she cautiously pushed open the door and she and Augusta stepped in.

They had dared not bring candles, and for a moment one dark shadow was indistinguishable from another. Then something stirred in the corner, and Augusta, with a soft cry, rushed across the room.

Peter was bound hand and foot, and he struggled to a sitting position. As Storme's eyes adjusted to the darkness she could see the lashes on his back, and the surprise and concern on his face. "Lassie!" he exclaimed softly. "Mistress Storme—"

"Hush." Augusta knelt beside him, while Storme stood close to the door, cracking it a fraction so she could watch the outside. "I've brought an unguent for your back. Be silent, we must hurry."

"You shouldn't be here—"

Storme interrupted tersely, "Your horses are waiting by the side of the road, along with your clothes and all the coin we could scrape together. You've got to be well away before dawn breaks the sky or you won't have a chance."

Peter gave an involuntary gasp of pain as Augusta began to smooth unguent on his back, and Augusta bit her lip. "I'm sorry," she whispered shakily and let her hands fall. "Oh, Peter, your poor back—"

"Untie his hands, girl," Storme snapped, turning briefly from her vigilance at the door, "or it'll be more than his back that's cut up if we're found here."

Peter said through an obvious haze of pain and confusion, "Wait a minute—what can you be thinking—"

"We're leaving." Augusta, after her one lapse into weakness, recovered quickly. Her voice was strong and she efficiently began to undo the rope that bound Peter's hands and feet. "Tonight, the two of us."

"You must be mad!" Peter's hoarse whisper broke on incredulity. "We can't run away—"

"We have no choice," Augusta said firmly, tugging off the last rope. "You can't stay here to be sold or executed on the morn. And I will not stay another night under this roof."

"Lassie . . . love . . ." Peter's face softened with pain and adoration, and he took both her small hands in his, holding them gently. "You must understand. Your brother has the right to do with me as he likes. What I did was wrong, vastly wrong, and I am bound to him. Ye needn't fear for my life, lovely, for it was a fever that overtook him tonight and on the morn will be forgotten—"

Augusta drew her hands away, and her jaw set in a way that was strongly reminiscent of Simon's. Her eyes were cold and her voice was clear. "*I* shall not forget," she avowed quietly. "Nor shall I ever forgive what I saw tonight. Nothing will ever be the same between myself and my brother, Peter, and I *cannot stay here*. If you won't come with me, I cannot force you, but mark this—I go. Tonight. Would you have me be alone?"

Impatiently, Storme moved away from the door. "Enough of this blather. We've no time to waste."

She dropped to her knees in the straw and pressed a folded paper into Peter's hand. "Listen to me. Go to the Green Parrot Inn in Bath. Seek out Mad Raoul Deborte of the *Petite Morte,* or any of the other captains whose names are on this paper. Give over this note from me. It will vouch for you and assure you passage to the Indies."

Peter looked uncertainly from Storme to Augusta. His face was a mixture of dread and hope. He said slowly, "You are determined to do this thing?"

Augusta replied, "I love you. Have I a choice?"

Peter's hand gripped hers hard, and for a moment the emotion that radiated from the two was palpable. Storme, watching them, felt a weakness—almost a hurting—inside her that was embarrassing. She looked away.

Peter turned to Storme. "Lassie, I never thought you was as bad a sort as they made you out. You've been a good friend to my Gussie, and now to me. I'm in your debt."

Storme drew her brows together uncomfortably. "I'm not doing it for charity," she said gruffly. "That note you bear will bring my freedom too. Now go. It might already be too late."

Peter got to his feet with Augusta, her face creased with concern, supporting his arm. At the door Peter hesitated, and turned back. "There is one thing I can do for you now," he said.

"You can get out of here," Storme replied impatiently, checking the door. "The way is clear. Hurry."

"Two mates of yours are tied up in the granary," Peter said. "They won't be able to help you now, but you'll want to know it." He looked at Storme soberly. "Simon is a good man, and he means you no harm. Don't make me sorry I told you, lass.''

And then, without another word, Peter and Augusta slipped through the door and disappeared into the night.

Storme lost no time in investigating Peter's story. It could be a trick, she realized, but knew human nature better than to suspect Peter would have wasted precious time after she'd saved his life to set up a trap for her. Likely it was more of Eden's men sent under the guise of befriending her, and if there were enemies on the property she needed to know it.

Two burly English bondsmen guarded the door to the barn. As she approached they lifted their swords to bar her entrance.

Storme stood straight a few feet before them; she looked the biggest one straight in the eye. She said clearly, ''If you challenge me I'll carve up your liver with your own knife. Let me pass.''

Storme's position on the plantation had become somewhat nebulous these last few weeks, and evidently Simon's orders for this night had not included denying her entrance to the barn. After a moment of uncertainty, the men lowered their weapons. She pushed open the door.

A covered torch burned low in a corner; two more guards, armed with long rifles, stood just inside. They swung their weapons up as Storme entered, watching her suspiciously, but Storme was motionless, staring beyond them.

Sitting on the floor, bound back-to-back against the support beams, was Squint and—''Pompey!'' she cried. Exultation spun through her head, surprise and disbelief left her weak. The big man's head jerked around and he saw her. Though his dignity would never allow him to smile, his eyes filled with liquid joy and Storme cried again, ''Pompey!''

She flew across the room, taking the guards so by surprise that they hadn't a chance to stop her. One of them exclaimed, ''Say there, woman, you can't—''

''Be quiet!'' Storme shouted back. Her face was radiant and her eyes snapped brightly from Squint to Pompey, hardly daring to believe it was true. ''I'm allowed to talk to them!''

The guards muttered among themselves, "He didn't say nothing about talking—"

"Just said hold them till morning—"

"Can't see how it'd do no harm."

Storme sank to her knees, closing one hand about Squint's arm and another around Pompey's. "You're alive! God's bones, I thought—"

"Storme, my girl! Ye're lookin' fine! We've been some worried about you— "

"Squint—Pompey!" She had to say their names again, just to assure herself it was true. She filled her eyes with them. "I thought you were dead!"

"Hey, now, lass, we couldn't die without making sure you were all right. Taken us a while to get here, that's all." Then Squint's face went sour. "Appears we didn't do too fine a job o' it either. I'm sorry we got caught, girlie. Now 'tis only more trouble on yer head."

Storme's fingers tightened on their arms, hope and triumph soaring. Squint and Pompey, here, come for her. It was going to be all right now. Everything was going to be all right.

"Have you heard of the *Tempest*?" she demanded eagerly.

"Aye, that I have." But Squint's voice didn't sound particularly encouraging. "She's at anchor on the James, under the governor's guard."

"It doesn't matter. We'll get her back—aye, and the rest of the crew, too." Nothing could stop her now that Squint and Pompey were here. This was the beginning of the biggest victory of her life; she knew it in her bones.

She went on swiftly, "That eel-eating Eden has turned on us. Tried to kill me tonight."

Squint's face was grim. "Aye, and that I'm not pleased to hear. He was one o' the few friends you had left."

"Bah! Who needs him? For you haven't heard the best of it." Her eyes were alight with victory as she went on lowly, "I've only this night sent a message to the Brethren in Bath. They'll be here soon enough to free us all!"

But Squint's reaction was not at all what she expected. He shook his head slowly, chafing his hands against their bonds. "Nay, lassie, I fear not. There's been talk around, and most of them are happy to have you out of the business. Ye can expect little help from that quarter."

Storme sucked in her breath sharply, her eyes narrowing. "Bastards!" But, in the height of her excitement, this minor hindrance seemed hardly worth considering. "They'll change their minds right enough when they hear my plan," she determined, her eyes beginning to glow again. She looked at Pompey, then at Squint, squeezing their arms swiftly. "Not one among them can resist the prize I'm offering."

Squint looked at her warily. "What prize?"

"The Colony of Virginia!" she exclaimed triumphantly. "We are at war! We'll raise an armada the likes of which won't soon be seen again. The Brethren will sail against Spotswood in force, we'll take his treasure for our own, we'll leave a trail of blood along his coast that will feed the gulls for years! We'll—"

"Nay, lass!" Shock was swift and stern in Squint's features, obstinacy underscored his voice. "Are ye out of yer bleedin' mind? I didn't risk me neck to save you just for the pleasure of seein' ye carved up for shark bait!"

Storme's eyes went dark, her face hard. Determination clenched in every muscle. "I'll *not* retreat from the fight!" she swore lowly. "I will rule again!" Her eyes narrowed with cunning. "And along with Spotswood, I will take care of Eden, too. We'll make certain word gets back to the King that Eden was behind our raid, and that slimy bastard will be destroyed. He'll die a thousand times before he breathes his last, and I'll take pleasure in every gasp!"

Squint looked as though he would object again, and more forcefully, but the gleam in Storme's eyes was fierce and the set of her jaw intractable. He said nothing, but the unhappiness on his face, if only Storme had been willing to see it, spoke volumes.

Storme made herself relax. She gave their arms one last brisk squeeze, and released them. "Enough for now; we'll make plans later." She hesitated, a small frown troubling her brow. "I can't release you; you'd be captured again before dawn and likely shot. Mad as it seems, for now this bloody plantation is the safest place to be. Until I get word from the Brethren, there's nothing to do for any of us but to lay low and wait."

And then she smiled, the joy and relief that flooded her face only a reflection of the triumph that was swelling inside her. "At least," she said, "we're all together."

Squint tried to muster some enthusiasm for her plan, if only out of loyalty, but he failed miserably. "Aye," he agreed glumly, for that was the best he could do. "That we are."

* *Chapter Thirty* *

Dawn was just breaking on the horizon, painting one-dimensional streaks of lemon and peach across a pale sky. In the wooded shadows just outside Bath two men sat in a darkened carriage, and the stillness of night still lingered.

Tobias Knight had lost no time. After the governor's rage at this latest disgraceful failure concerning Storme O'Malley, Knight had seen only one option left, and had chosen it without hesitation.

An urgent message to the Green Parrot Inn had found Raoul Deborte upstairs asleep between two whores. Never one to let carnal pleasure stand between himself and the smell of coin, Raoul had met Tobias Knight as instructed on the outskirts of town. And he could tell already he would not be disappointed.

Knight said, "You've always been one we could count on for a favor."

Tobias Knight had a habit of gazing directly ahead when he spoke to Raoul, as though he found his presence and the reason for it too distasteful for notice. Raoul did not mind. In fact, he found the other man's discomfiture rather amusing. He answered modestly, "I do my best to be a true friend to the ruler of Carolina."

"We have a favor to ask of you now."

"Of course," drawled Raoul, "even friendship has its price."

Knight stiffened. "We'll make it worth your while, I assure you."

"I'm listening."

"We want you to kill Storme O'Malley," stated Knight flatly.

Raoul's smooth brow lifted in mild surprise. "*Eh bien*, my friend, no small task. I hear that the last who tried to get to her failed most miserably."

Knight gave a small disgusted snort. "They were fools and braggarts. This time I choose true fighting men. And this time . . ." He cast a swift, sly glance at Raoul. "We will not waste time trying to get her off the plantation. I care not where the murder is done, only that it is finished."

Raoul was hard put to disguise his own elation. What an incredible turn of events. Raoul Deborte was definitely moving up in the world, and he had every intention of playing this game to its end. He said, pretending reluctance for the sake of the price, "It is no small thing, to risk my ship and my men on a mission that has failed once, but I shall consider it. Is that all?"

"No." Knight took a sharp breath. He spoke without looking at Raoul. "Simon York must be disposed of as well."

Now Raoul's surprise was genuine. "York?"

"Unfortunately Simon York is the only person living besides Storme O'Malley who knows the whereabouts of a certain document that could destroy us all. We will dispose of them both and put this wearisome matter behind us."

Raoul was thoughtful, busily absorbing and arranging this incredible turn of events. Simon York *and* Storme O'Malley. This put an entirely new complexion on matters and required a great deal of contemplation.

But for now he would take advantage of what was offered. A smile of satisfaction curved his lips as he extended his hand. "Perhaps," he suggested smoothly, "a little show of faith?"

Without hesitation, Knight placed a small bag of gold in Raoul's open hand. "There will be more when the job is done, along with the undying gratitude of Governor Eden."

Raoul fingered the gold, smiling to himself and plotting. The game was becoming very interesting now. Very interesting indeed.

The sun had been up almost an hour, but the candle was still burning, sputtering low in its dish, in the library. Simon sat behind the desk, hollow-eyed and haggard, leaning back in his chair, gazing dully at the opposite wall. His cheeks were stained with the overnight scruff of a pale beard, and the room reeked of liquor. Storme, when she opened the door, was shocked, and for a fleeting moment even afraid— not for herself, but for Simon.

She did not know why she had come in here. She had not been to bed either. She had spent an hour or more with Squint and Pompey, then crept up to her room just before dawn. But with all that had happened during the night, how could she possibly sleep?

She kept thinking of Simon, dragging her out of the water, and the look on his face as he took her into his arms . . . the coldness in his eyes as he told her they were now even. She remembered the madness that had seized him as he wielded the whip against Peter, and the pain that tore his expression when he walked away from his sister. She had seen so much of him that night she had never known before, so much she did not understand . . . and perhaps did not want to. But as dawn broke the sky and there was no sound of his footsteps climbing the stairs to his chamber, she had come here, in search of him.

She said now, keeping her voice very flat and disinterested, "You said you wanted to talk to me."

He turned slowly and looked at her for a long time as though without recognizing her. His mind seemed to come back from a great distance to focus at last on the pain of the present. Storme thought she had never seen anyone so weary, or so filled with sorrow. And it twisted at her heart to see him so.

He said at last, in a voice so low she had to strain to hear, "Dear God. What have I done?"

Storme stiffened herself against the pain—his, and her own. She replied briskly, "Acted like a damn fool."

A tired smile touched his lips briefly, and faded. "And you, my dear Mistress O'Malley, never make a mistake, do you?"

Storme came slowly into the room. She answered, "I've made my share, or I wouldn't be here today."

He looked at her with eyes that were quiet with understanding, old with resignation, and something within Storme was touched, and bound. The shadowed room, the gutted candle and the stillness of the dawn seemed to wrap them both in an insular seclusion. He sat before her in naked despair, the barriers gone, the defenses down, and she was drawn to him. She couldn't help it.

Simon looked away from her slowly, gazing again toward the opposite wall. "I used to be so proud of the way I had everything under control," he said heavily. "My home, my business, my family... my life. There were no surprises, no mistakes. I simply wouldn't allow them.

"Now... nothing is in control, and everything I've done is wrong. I've made one drastic misjudgment after another, and everything is falling apart. Eden, who was supposed to be so predictable. Peter, whom I trusted with my life. Augusta, my own sister, whom I never knew. Even myself. Nothing has happened the way I planned."

Through the thick silence that echoed in his last words, he turned to Storme. Perhaps, far back in his eyes, a sad sort of smile ghosted. "It seems as though the only person I've ever really known is you. You are the only one who can be counted upon to behave consistently."

Storme swallowed hard, visions of her most recent treachery against him stabbing briefly. She lifted her chin, and she said firmly, "You cannot control people, Simon, like you do your farm animals. You were foolish to try."

He looked at her, tired and sad. "I know no other way," he said simply.

His suffering was painful to watch, and Storme's heart wrenched for him. Strong and arrogant, angry and laughing . . . now bowed with defeat, she knew all of him, and all of him touched her. How great had been his burden all these years, how strong he had had to be to bear it. Simon, who was responsible for all the world, who protected what was his own with iron resolve and flaming sword, who would make any sacrifice to keep his world safe.

She had never understood before the complexities of his world, the things that had both intrigued and irritated her about the man called Simon. For Storme the rules were very simple: Might makes right, the strong survive. But Simon was guided by a very different set of rules—strength tempered with tenderness, power balanced by vulnerability. Those were the things that made greatness in a man. She looked at Simon now, and she understood.

She came close to him; she touched his arm. Her throat was unaccountably thick. She said, "You should get some rest."

He shook his head slowly. "Ah, Storme," he said heavily. "The last thing I need from you is pity."

Storme's chest tightened, aching with something she could not define. "It's not pity," she said. "It's . . ." But she had no words. She looked at him helplessly, unable to say it, afraid to try.

He turned his eyes to her, his gaze quiet and clear and strangely understanding. The time for secrets was past. He reached up and touched the hand that rested on his arm, closing his fingers about it. "What?" he said softly, looking at her with eyes that were tired of the game. "What is it, Storme O'Malley, that we are so persistently reluctant to say to each other?"

Storme knew that she was balanced on a dangerous precipice from which, should she take that one step over, there would be no turning back. She both yearned and feared to take the step.

But she was never to have the chance. The door burst

open and Christopher stood there, disarranged and distraught. Storme quickly moved away.

"Simon, I'm sorry," Christopher said without preamble. "I was just out to check the guardhouse and—he's gone. Peter's escaped."

Simon was out of his chair in an instant, his eyes dark with alarm, his face taut and alert. "What do you mean? How did he get past the guards?"

Christopher looked startled, then wretched with guilt. "I didn't think to post—"

"You just left him unguarded with Augusta out of her mind and likely to do anything?"

"I didn't think—"

Simon drew in a swift breath that seemed to stifle a reply forcefully. He said tensely, "It doesn't matter. It was my responsibility, not yours."

Simon strode to the door and called out sharply, "Bessie! Go upstairs and wake Mistress Augusta—I want her down here now!"

Storme said quietly, "She's not there."

The eyes of both men riveted on her with such force that Storme was hard put to it not to flinch instinctively from them. And Simon demanded, "What do you mean?"

Storme stood straighter; she looked him in the eye. "She left with Peter."

Nothing on Simon's face changed. His voice was quiet, his words infused with a cold deliberation that was more alarming than a tirade of shouting would have been. "Why," he demanded of her, "didn't you stop them?"

She answered calmly, "I couldn't have, even if I'd wanted to. And I didn't."

The horror of betrayal began to mount in his eyes, the fury darkened his face. His hands clenched by his sides and he took a step toward her.

Storme said sharply, "Have you learned nothing, Farmer? You can't rule their lives! Let them go. They've a right—"

And Christopher interrupted tersely, "They can't have more than a few hours on us, and there're only two ways they're likely to go—west to the mountains or south toward

Bath, and the sea. I'll take a crew and start combing the area."

Simon was looking at Storme, and for just a moment he looked uncertain—almost as though he had heard her words, and attended them. But then he turned swiftly and brushed past Christopher. "I'll saddle my horse."

Christopher caught his arm. "Look at yourself, man. You're in no condition to go anywhere."

Simon stared at him as though he had just uttered a blasphemy, and tried to jerk his arm away. "Get out of my way!"

But Christopher held firm. "Listen to me. With Peter gone, one of us has to stay here and mind the plantation or there'll be nothing left—"

"You can't seriously believe I would stay behind while my sister—"

"You're the one she's running from," Christopher said. Simon winced as though struck, and Christopher's own face reflected the pain it cost him to speak the truth out loud. "I'm sorry, Simon," he continued, more gently. "But it's true. Even if you can make her come back with you, she'll only run away again. I can reason with her, make her see the foolhardiness of what she's done. You won't have a chance, Simon."

Simon hesitated, and Storme, watching him, could sense his struggle. But slowly the self-control of which he once had been so proud reasserted itself. His jaw set, his shoulders stiffened. He said, "You're right, of course." Then, briskly, "We'll need two search parties. Gather volunteers in Edenton, and take five of my men and go to Queen Anne's Town. Comb every inch of the countryside. Someone will have noticed them. There's no time to waste—"

Christopher was already moving toward the door. "I'm on my way."

"Christopher—"

Christopher stopped and looked back, and a silent message of trust and understanding passed between the two men. Christopher said quietly, "I'll find her. I promise."

Simon nodded, with difficulty. And he said simply, "Godspeed."

* * *

* *Chapter Thirty-one* *

The following two days were the most tortured of Simon's life. He went through the hours in a haze of anxiety and anguished self-examination, eating little, sleeping little, resting not at all. And as each successive moment put more distance between the search parties and their quarry, the flame of hope died a little more.

Over and over he reviewed the events of the days—even the months—that had led up to this nightmare. At first the veil of bitterness obscured his vision and he found it all too easy to blame Storme, with her flamboyant ways and treacherous ideas, for his sister's defection—or Peter, who had insinuated himself into Simon's trust while plotting to destroy him, or even Augusta herself. But time and despair brought the inevitable truth: Simon had no one to blame but himself.

He tried to imagine what he could have done differently, and he thought of many, many things. Though those were the most confused days of his life, strangely, Simon saw many things more clearly than he had ever seen them before. All his life he had seen in people only what he expected to see, allowing little or no room for individual variances that grated against his concept of perfection. Augusta was his adored little sister, sweet, lovely, obedient. Peter was his strong right hand, loyal and reliable. He had never allowed himself to imagine that either of them could have feelings or thoughts or actions that did not relate directly to Simon and what he expected of them. He had tried to remake them into his own image, and this was the price he paid for his selfishness.

Like a fever that had peaked and broken, he awoke on the morning of the third day with a strange serenity and the strength of a quiet resolve. Today if he heard nothing he would go to Bath himself. He would find Augusta and Peter, and he hoped they would return with him. But if they did not, it wouldn't matter. Because everything was different now.

As he was coming downstairs a sharp voice from the hallway below caused him to pause and look over the landing. Storme was standing in the hallway, her brow drawn formidably, her wrath directed at two cowering servants.

She was in her element, full of power and command, her eyes snapping, her voice reverberating. "Now get back to work, you lazy toads, or I'll lay a strap across your hides. Where the bloody hell do you think you are—a market fair? And you tell that filthy galley crew I'll be out for inspection in a quarter of an hour, and I'd damn well better find things shipshape! Now, move!"

The servants scurried off, and Simon, torn between amusement and astonishment, came slowly down the stairs. Over the past few days he had barely noticed what was going on around him, and had given no thought whatsoever to the running of the household or the plantation. Yet unfailingly the meals had been served on time, the fires lit, the candles trimmed . . . and it had been Storme who had kept it all together.

She looked up as he came down, and Simon could not prevent a surge of unexpected admiration. She was wearing a red gown and yellow apron, and the fiery colors were only a reflection of the proud flame in her eyes. Her hair was tied back at the nape, her face flushed with energy, her bearing strong with confidence. She was full of life and spirit, and after the self-imposed exile of his own dark dungeon of the soul, she was as welcome as the breath of life itself to Simon.

He said, "Good morning."

She looked at him, seeming to perceive some change within him, and nodded a curt approval. "So, you've decided to show yourself. Your breakfast is on the table."

He couldn't help smiling, however faintly. He jerked his head to indicate the scene with the servants he had just witnessed. "You did that quite well. I never imagined you a woman of domestic talents."

She seemed embarrassed and shrugged to cover it. "Running a house is no different from running a ship. You've just got to let them know who's in command."

She turned to go, and when she did Simon noticed the keys attached to a string around her waist. They were the chatelaine's keys, customarily worn by Augusta, and with them every lock in the house and beyond could be opened. For the first time Simon realized how many other things he had given no thought to these past days. Storme, who was supposed to be his captive, the two pirates held prisoner in the barn . . . yet how little it seemed to matter.

He said only, and with little emotion, "I'm surprised you haven't used those keys to open the weapons cabinet. This would be the perfect opportunity for you to escape."

She turned back to him, and met his eyes calmly and without shame. She answered simply, "Where would I go?"

With that quiet statement of unabashed truth Simon felt a weary sort of pathos sweep over him, and he shook his head slowly. "Ah, Storme," he said softly. "I never planned it to be like this."

She looked at him unwaveringly. "Neither did I."

There was so much he wanted to say, so much he wanted to express to her. Only recently had he come to see the danger in squandering time, the tragedy of moments passed and words unsaid. How much he had been through with this woman. How he had despised the fate that had thrown them together, and how he had fought against its bonds. But now, in the darkest moment of his life, she was here. It seemed only right.

Storme, with all her passions and contradictions, was the one person in the world about whom he had never been able to deceive himself. Storme, made of fire and light, demanded attention, demanded acceptance, refused to be changed or cowed. She had challenged him, she had defeated him, she had made him see things within himself he had never guessed at before. And, because of her, he would never look at anything in the same way again.

He stepped forward and took her hand. He saw her surprise and felt a small involuntary movement to withdraw her hand, but he held it gently. Her hand was strong with a woman's strength, and soft with a woman's beauty. It felt right, enclosed in his grasp.

He said, "Do you ever wonder what would have happened if we had met differently?"

Storme swallowed. Her pulse had begun to speed the moment he touched her; the gentle solemn look in his eyes caused her throat to tighten. But she answered, firmly, in the only way she could. "I am who I am, Farmer. I could never be different."

"Yes, but look at you. You told me once you could never live on land. You are not only doing it, but thriving at it."

His hand was warm and rough around hers, and he was so close she could smell the sunshiny fragrance of his hair. It was difficult to deny anything he said when he looked at her like that, when the linking of their hands was like a bond that touched her very thoughts.

Besides, there was truth to what he said, and that both startled and confused her. She had thought she would die the slow wasting death of a beached fish in the sun when he had first brought her to this place. But she hadn't died. In fact, the days at sea seemed further and further away as life on land became a habit.

But she lifted her chin stubbornly. "I'm still me inside," she said. "I'm still a pirate and a savage and a barbarian and all those other things you're always calling me."

He smiled, and a spark of admiration joined with the gentle amusement in his eyes. "Yes," he admitted. "You are. But those are the very things that have allowed you to survive in an uncivilized world—both on sea and on land. Perhaps," he added quietly, "those are the things that all of us need to survive."

Everything about him—the clasp of his hand, the look in his eye, the tone of his voice—was gentle and intimate, different in many ways from all she had ever known of Simon, bringing him closer to her than she had ever felt before. The closeness both frightened and intrigued her, and the strangeness of it made her voice husky. "You've never talked to me like this," she said.

He lifted his hand and touched her face. His eyes were serious. "People can change, Storme. You've changed— and God knows the past few days have changed me."

He dropped his eyes briefly, then looked back at her. His hand curled against her neck in a single lingering caress. "I was wrong," he said quietly, "about a lot of things. I know now I can't rule other people's lives, or change them to suit myself. All I ever wanted was for Augusta to be happy. She found someone and because it wasn't my choice I wouldn't let it be. But I was wrong, desperately wrong. And I drove her away.

"Love is a precious thing, Storme," he said softly, "and so very rare. When two people find it, no one—not even they themselves—should be allowed to destroy it."

Storme could no longer meet the gentle intensity of his gaze, and she shifted her eyes away. Her heart was pounding very fast. Why did she feel as though Simon were speaking of someone other than Augusta and Peter? And why should he say such things to her?

His hand dropped slowly from her neck, caressing her shoulder and her arm, and then leaving her entirely. He still held her hand. He said, "All I want to know now is that Augusta is all right. As soon as I locate them, I'm going to have Peter's emancipation papers drawn up, and they will be free to live as they please."

Storme's eyes flew to him, startled. This kind of change she had never expected from him, and she half-suspected some trick. He saw her skepticism and smiled. But the smile was sad, and it faded soon.

"That's what I want for you, Storme," he said. His voice was low and his face was serious. His thumb gently stroked the back of her hand, soothing and reassuring. Storme felt the muscles of her stomach tighten, and she was caught by the quiet sincerity in his eyes, the gentleness of his voice.

"It's what I've always wanted," he said, "for you to be free. That's why you must take the amnesty from Spotswood."

Slowly Storme pulled her hand away, staring at him. "What amnesty?"

Simon cast his eyes down briefly, as though frustrated with her wariness and his own inadequacy with words. When he looked back at her, his face was taut with conviction, his eyes dark and determined. "You may hate me for this," he said, "but you have hated me for less. The game has gone on too long, Storme, and too much has been lost—can't you see that?"

She said nothing, watching him. Her heart beat slowly and steadily, waiting.

"Certain death awaits you in Virginia," Simon said. "Eden has betrayed you. You have been held a prisoner of your own power, and all because of a single document that you possess and others want. Don't you understand yet, Storme?" he insisted tightly. "Spotswood will pay for that letter; Eden will kill for it. Turn over the letter to Spotswood and Eden will be powerless to harm you; you will be pardoned to live your life the way you choose. Cannot you see the reason in that?"

There was tightness in Storme's chest that refused to allow air to pass. Her head reeled for a moment in an effort to assimilate what he had said, and yet strangely, there was little shock, and no anger. She should have known—and perhaps, on the deepest level, she had known all along—that Simon's motives since the day he had brought her here had been connected to Spotswood, and the letter. Now he had revealed it, and there was no surprise.

What he was suggesting was preposterous. What he divulged was a treachery of the grandest sort, in which he had conspired with Spotswood to obtain the document that meant the difference between freedom and captivity to her. And yet . . . beyond all this, what he said was reasonable. What had happened to her, that she could see reason before she felt outrage?

A month ago she would not have reacted so calmly—even

a week ago. But so much had changed in that time . . . everything had changed.

She looked at Simon; she worked hard to keep her voice steady. "You want me to turn over to the hands of my enemy the one thing that keeps me free?"

Simon said quietly, "Is Spotswood your worst enemy, Storme?"

And then, with a short, tight breath, Simon reached for her hands again, holding them both in a strong, warm grip. This time Storme did not pull away. Perhaps she was too stunned. She simply stared at him.

"Storme," he said quietly, "we are all, I think, the sum total of our choices. I have made many choices in my lifetime, and some, I now come to see, were the wrong ones. But the one thing I can never regret was in bringing you here, though I have cursed the decision and called myself a fool a thousand times over in the past for doing it. Perhaps I have sometimes acted for the wrong reasons and I have made mistakes, but you must believe that all I wanted was the best for you. For you to be safe."

His hands tightened, his eyes darkened with intensity. "I believe so strongly that Spotswood is your only hope that if I had learned the whereabouts of the letter a week ago I would have tried to take it from you, and deliver it to him. Perhaps it's just as well I didn't," he admitted softly, and he dropped his gaze briefly before returning it to her again. "Because now I see that you, too, must be allowed to make your choice.

"You have known the sea, Storme, and a life of piracy. Now you have known the land . . . and me." He looked at her solemnly, a quiet gaze that held no secrets. "You will choose, but it must be of your own free will."

Her breath was shallow, her heartbeat heavy. His hands were like the grip of life on hers, infusing her with his presence, the essence of all he was and all they had known together. But she held steady, and she said, as evenly as possible, "And if I choose the sea?"

A sorrow came over his eyes; slowly he released her

hands. "Then I shall be sorry," he said quietly. "But I won't stop you."

Storme stood there, the pulse of her heart marking the course of her thoughts, anxious, restless, unsure. What was he saying to her? Would he have her stay here . . . with him? In his home, in his bed, by his side? If he asked, what would her answer be?

Like a recurring melody it came again to haunt her. Outside a rough waterfront tavern, on the deck of the *Tempest*, during the long dark hours in the gaol . . . the warnings had been given to her; she had known she was fighting a losing battle, and the same choices had been hers. Hadn't she wished even then, in a small secret part of herself, for a chance to choose differently? For a brief moment after the first night with the Farmer, hadn't she known what it was she was missing, and what she wished for? A man to hold and love at night, gentle laughter, and quiet times. A woman's hopes and dreams, and even the freedom to know a woman's fears . . . then, such had been impossible. But now . . .

And for a moment she allowed herself to consider it. Life by his rules—quiet, simple, reasonable. Surrender. Comfort. It would be so easy.

She said softly, without meaning to speak aloud at all, "The sea is all I've ever known."

She saw hope in his eyes, and a renewed determination that bordered on desperation. Though he did not touch her, he seemed to move toward her, gripping her with the force of his plea. "No," he said firmly, "it's not. Not anymore. You can put an end to it now, Storme. Your choice is simple. All you have to do is—"

"Surrender." She spoke out loud the word that had been haunting the back of her mind, and once it was said the moment of indecision, of foolish wavering was gone. She looked at him and a spark of anger kindled in her eyes—though not with him, but with herself, for having considered, however briefly, what he proposed. "That is all you ask of me, Farmer. Surrender!"

"You had rather die?" His voice grew tight with the frustration of a man who knew he was fighting a lost battle.

Contempt laced her tone. "I don't fear death, Farmer. I have no immortal judgment awaiting my soul. You think you are so clever, but that is one thing you have never understood about me, and never will. I am no white-faced coward who shrinks before the blade of the sword—I thrive on it! Do not think to frighten me with talk of death!"

"Damn it, Storme, it's over! Can't you see that? Why do you persist—"

"No, Farmer, it is not over!" Her color was high and her eyes snapped with the fire and power that led men into battle and commanded them to follow her to their deaths. "It will not be over as long as I have a breath left in my body, for *I* will not go down in history as the lily-livered woman who betrayed Blackbeard's trust! I will fight to the death before Eden or Spotswood ever lays a hand on that letter!"

She took a breath, her eyes flaming. "Fie on all your pretty words and grand ideas! You call me a savage, but I know more of honor than you will ever fathom. For that's what it is, Farmer—a matter of honor, and I will not be defeated!"

"What is honorable about setting two powers against one another over a scrap of paper?" he demanded incredulously.

She looked at him, and pity, worse than the anger of a moment before, crept into her eyes. "Nay, Farmer," she said softly, "you would not understand. You, who make your own rules and care for naught but what is your own—you have so much else, you don't need honor, too. I live by a code, the only one I've ever known, and if I betray it now, I'd just as well be dead, for there'd be nothing more left of me."

Her muscles tightened and her voice grew taut with intensity; desperately she tried to make him understand. "Don't you see?" she insisted. "It is more than my fate that is in the balance here, more than a single letter or a feud between two powers . . . it is a whole way of life! I fly the last banner, I sail the flagship of all the Brotherhood! I am the legacy of centuries of freedom fighters, and if the Queen of the Pirates goes down, so does all of piracy. I hold a sacred trust, and I *cannot betray it.*''

He looked at her in helplessness and defeat. ''Then that is your choice?''

She replied without a trace of hesitation, ''It's the only one I can make.''

''Then you go to your death.''

''Perhaps,'' she agreed calmly. Her stance was proud, her head held high. ''But I will die fighting, and unashamed. I wish you could say the same, Farmer.''

''There is nothing I can say to persuade you?''

''No,'' she replied simply. ''Nothing.''

For a moment longer they faced each other, she in quiet resolve, he in heavy sorrow. And then she said, ''I've got things to do.'' She started to turn, then looked back at him, her words distinct and her eyes holding a trace of challenge. ''The prisoners have to be fed.''

If Simon felt any surprise for that new evidence of her authority about his household, he hid it well. Storme left the room without another word, and he watched her go.

* *Chapter Thirty-two* *

He stood in the hallway for a time, unmoving, weighted down with all he had learned, and all he felt. Through the window he watched her leave the kitchen with a tray of food and stride across the yard toward the barn where Squint and Pompey were held. Amazement threaded through his confusion and he shook his head slowly. She was right. He didn't understand her at all. And he wasn't even sure he wanted to.

The sound of hoofbeats on the drive drew him out of his heavy contemplation, and he moved closer to the window.

The rider was moving hard, spraying up dirt beneath the hooves of his mount, and Simon's heart lurched with relief and tightened with alarm. Such urgency could mean only one thing. Christopher, and word from Bath.

By the time he had flung open the front door and stepped onto the gallery, he could tell the rider was not Christopher. By the time he descended the steps to meet the rider at the hitching post, he saw his visitor was Lawson Beecher from the neighboring plantation. Simon tried to suspend his anxiety as Beecher dismounted and he hurried forth to greet him.

"Lawson." Simon gripped his hand firmly. "You've ridden hard. Come inside and ease your thirst."

Beecher removed his dusty hat and drew his forearm across his sweat-streaked face. "Aye, my friend, I've ridden all night and your offer is welcome, but I cannot linger. I've been away from my own too long."

Everything within Simon tensed. The man did not look like the bearer of good news. "You were with my cousin Christopher?"

Beecher nodded. "Me and my men were covering the woods and backtrails between the river and Bath. We were to join up with Christopher's party yesterday morning."

Dread flowed through Simon like ice water. "You found nothing?"

Beecher shook his head. "Nary a trace. And..." His face was grim. "Christopher wasn't in Bath. His men said he'd disappeared sometime in the morning. It doesn't look good, Simon."

The dread in Simon's veins congealed into a cold lump in the center of his stomach. His breath was constricted, his muscles locked. All he could think was, *Christopher. Not Christopher, too...*

Slowly, Beecher withdrew a leather pouch from his coat; he held it for a moment by the drawstring, away from his body, as though it were poisonous. "While we were inquiring on the waterfront about your sister, an urchin gave me this. Said it was to be delivered to you personal."

Simon took the pouch and opened it with leaden fingers.

He felt the touch of something silky inside, and illness went through him that left him dizzy. Slowly he withdrew the object.

The lock of Augusta's hair glistened in the morning sunshine, curling around his finger as though it had a life of its own. The silence that hung between the two men was as powerful as the thunder of doom.

And then Beecher said awkwardly, "I'm sorry to bring such news. I'll send a message to Bath. What shall I tell the search parties?"

As though galvanized by the other man's words, Simon reached into the pouch again and withdrew a folded paper. His movements were still slow and numb as he opened the paper and read the words. The color drained from his face, and his lips went tight.

His voice was hoarse when he said at last, "Nothing. Tell them nothing."

And, like a sleepwalker, he turned and went into the house without another word, still clutching the pouch and its ominous contents in his hand.

In the past days Storme's authority over the prisoners had become unquestioned. Though the guards stayed posted, she had had the prisoners unbound and they lived in relative comfort within the confines of the barn. For a time the guards had been understandably wary of Pompey, and quick with their weapons. But as time passed and no effort was made to escape—and as Simon did not bother to amend their orders or even check on the prisoners—diligence was relaxed. Storme passed the door with no difficulty.

"Well, now," Squint greeted her from the dusty interior of the barn. "Don't ye look like the proper little lady? Yer pa would sure be proud to see you now."

Storme scowled and set the tray on the hay bale in a corner. Her head was still full of the encounter with Simon and she was in no mood for Squint's nonsense. "Listen," she said abruptly. "I've been thinking about how we can get the *Tempest* back."

Pompey squatted beside the tray and began to eat; Squint came over more slowly. He said, "I been thinkin', too."

Relieved that the resolution to their problem was not going to be left entirely to her, Storme sat cross-legged on the floor and waited with interest. Squint had always been good for an idea in a tight spot, and suddenly things were looking much brighter.

Squint took his time, sitting on his haunches and helping himself to a slice of ham. "They sure have some vittles here," he commented. "Aye, and not a bad life."

Storme scowled sharply. "For a pig!"

Squint looked at her soberly. "Now I'm gonna say somethin' hard and you're gonna listen. I always steered ye a true course, ain't I? Always told ye the right of it?"

Storme looked at him warily.

Squint said, "Ye'd be a fool to give all this up. I been watchin' and I been listenin' and this is what I know: ye're doing yerself fine here. That farmin' man, he ain't a bad sort, and ye've got him under yer thumb. Here ye be, prancin' around in skirts and sleepin' in a feather bed and eatin' like a princess and he not begrudgin' ye one whit— 'twouldn't surprise me none if ye was to get him to marry ye, bein' as clever as ye are. Why—"

Throughout his speech Storme's eyes had grown wider, her incredulity stronger, and now she could contain herself no longer. "Have you got worms in your brain? What the bloody hell—"

Squint said firmly, "This is the life fer ye, lass. Ye've got a chance here, at what yer pa wanted for ye, and what ye deserve. This is where ye belong, and I can't let you go back."

Storme's head reeled. Had the whole world turned upside down? Even Squint, echoing the Farmer's words, turning against her when she needed him most . . . She said furiously, "And just how do you think you're going to stop me?"

He replied firmly, "By doin' whatever I have to do. But I ain't going to stand by and bury the bloody pieces of ye, after swearin' on yer pa's grave to see you growed. I'll not follow ye to yer death, lass, and that's exactly where ye're goin' if ye proceed with this mad scheme o' yo'rn.''

Storme stood slowly, her heart pounding with heavy outrage and hurt. It was a conspiracy. First Simon, and now Squint; from all sides she was being bombarded with treacherous notions and outrageous suggestions, and it was more than she could absorb all at once. They were all plotting to confuse her and make her weak. But from Squint she had expected it least of all.

She said, ''I thought you were my friend.''

''I am,'' Squint replied. ''And that's why I'm sayin' this.''

''You're a foolish old woman!'' she cried, shaking. ''If we were on the seas, you'd be flogged for this!''

''But we ain't,'' he answered implacably. ''And mebbe it's about time you stopped livin' yer life like we was. It's a whole different set o' rules here, lassie, and you ain't the captain anymore.''

Storme stared at him for a moment longer, impotent with hurt and rage. Then she said abruptly, ''I'm *your* captain, you insolent slime-eating dog, until you're strong enough to prove I'm not! I'm still giving the orders, and you will follow me or by God I'll leave you here to rot in the manure where you belong!''

She turned and strode out of the barn, bolting the door behind her.

Simon was surprised to find himself in his own library, sitting behind his desk; to look up and see that the sun had barely lifted an inch in the sky. It felt as though an eon had passed since he had taken that rough leather pouch in his hand and felt the texture of Augusta's shorn hair.

He looked at it now, focusing with difficulty, and then at the letter in his hand. The words were a meaningless jumble of marks to him; pain was like a tight band that wound around his chest and closed up his throat. With a furious, determined effort, he made himself concentrate. He read the letter again.

Your sister is my prisoner. Her price is the
document held by Storme O'Malley, to be
brought to Alligator Cove on the Sound before
sunrise Tuesday, eleven September. Until then,
she lives.

He read it again, and a third time, and then, without his
being aware of closing the muscles of his hand, the note
began to crumple between his fingers. He watched his
knuckles turn white; he listened to the anvil-like pounding of
his heart. A thousand questions, thoughts, and horrors
plummeted through his brain, but he had no time for any of
them. One thing only stood clear: urgency.

Eden had won after all. If not one way, then another. For
all of Spotswood's cleverness, for all of Simon's efforts,
they had failed. Now Eden had Augusta, and there was no
more room for failure.

With a sudden surge of desperate clarity, he knew what
must be done. Simon could not sail into Teach's Hole
himself to retrieve the letter; neither could Spotswood, even
if he could be persuaded to do so or if Simon could afford
the time it would take to gather troops. Simon had less than
a week to obtain the letter that had eluded two of the most
powerful men in the colonies for years; he then had to
deliver it to a cove on Albemarle Sound without arousing
suspicion or doing anything that might jeopardize Augusta's
safety. It must be done quickly, quietly, and efficiently. He
could afford no mistakes.

And the only person in the world who could help him
now was Storme O'Malley.

He thought of her as he had seen her this morning, brisk and
efficient and in charge of his household. Carrying his keys and
using them only for what they were meant for. Taking charge of
the prisoners, but not aiding them to escape. She had changed
since she had been here. She had proved herself trustworthy.
For a moment—a wild brief moment only—he considered
telling her the truth of it, and asking for her help.

But the notion died almost before it was born. Only

moments ago she had made it clear that some things about her—the most important things—would never change. If he told her the truth, she might agree to help, but in the end there would be some trick, some small deviation from the plan that could mean the ruination of all. She had sworn to die before relinquishing that letter . . . that damn letter.

For a moment he was almost overwhelmed with despair, with the horrible irony of what this had come to. For a paper, a few scrawlings written by a criminal who had died a horrible death for his crimes—for a scrap of parchment even now rotting in the ground—two colonies were ready to go to war, Eden was plotting murder, Spotswood was stooping to blackmail, and Storme was willing to die rather than relinquish it. Simon had lied, conspired, betrayed his own conscience, and now must be ready to do even more for the sake of a single piece of paper. And Augusta . . .

"Dear God," he whispered out loud. "Augusta . . ."

He closed his eyes against the pain, tightly, briefly, and then he forcefully pushed the weakness aside. He tensed his muscles, he tightened his jaw. He would do what had to be done. And this time the game would be played by Storme O'Malley's rules. He could chance no other way.

He heard the front door slam behind her, and her footsteps in the hall. He called out to her.

Storme came into the library impatiently, her mind still in turmoil and her temper shortened by the demands of her confused thoughts. She had harsh words ready but they died on her tongue. She had only to look at Simon to know something was wrong.

He stood slowly. "I've had news," he said. "Bad news."

Storme took a step into the room, curious.

"Augusta has been abducted." He spoke in brief, clipped tones. His face was hard and his eyes were like glass. "Doubtless she will be sold in the Indies or murdered before she gets there."

A soft sound escaped Storme, and her eyes went dark. "By one of the Brethren?" The words were out before she knew it, filled with outrage and astonishment. "That's not possible! I gave her a letter of passage! I—"

Simon's eyes went dark; his voice was like a knife. "You sent her to pirates?" His fists clenched and it seemed as though he took an involuntary step forward, then forcefully restrained himself. "You sent my sister into a den of throat-cutting, murderous renegades where the least that might befall her was rape for sport? You did that?"

Storme stiffened; she swallowed hard. But she held his gaze unflinchingly. "I did no such thing! I sent her to safe harbor. If some hooligan got her before she reached my friends, or if she didn't do like I told her, are you blaming me?"

Simon's nostrils flared; Storme could see color, dark and hateful, creep into his pallid face. But his eyes were very strange—cold, almost, and detached, yet with a ferocity she had never glimpsed there before. He reminded her of a hunted animal who had suddenly decided to turn and fight, caring not how the fight went because he had nothing left to lose.

He said quietly, "No. I do not blame you. You acted in the only fashion I could have expected." He held her for a moment longer with those strange eyes, and then abruptly he turned away.

For a time he looked fixedly out the window, his hands clasped behind him, his back straight. And then he spoke without looking around. "A while ago I asked you to make a choice. I take it you have made it."

Storme said nothing. Her muscles were like tight wires drawn between the framework of her body, and her mind was racing, trying to make sense of this new development, trying to understand how it had happened, what had gone wrong, and what could be done now. And Simon—what was he thinking? Was he hating her? His calm, matter-of-fact tone was unsettling, even frightening, and she no longer knew what to expect from him. This morning, in the hall-way, for a moment she almost thought she knew him, and each had touched something within the other that was as wondrous as it was confusing. But now...now everything had come tumbling down, and nothing made sense anymore.

Simon said, with no emotion in his voice whatsoever, "I see by your silence that you have chosen." He turned, and looked at her. "Now I, too, must make a choice."

Perhaps, for a moment, Storme saw sorrow in his eyes, but then she thought she must have been mistaken, for when she looked more closely there was nothing there. Nothing but firmness, and decision.

He said, "I can help you, Storme. I will get your ship back, and your crew." And over her astonished breath he went on briskly, "All I ask is that you use them first to help me rescue my sister from her captors. After that you will be free to do as you please."

"But how—"

He made a short dismissing gesture with his wrist. "My men in Bath have learned her whereabouts, and how a rescue may be effected. But it must be done quickly, and I'll need a ship like the *Tempest* to get in and out of tight spots, and a ready fighting crew. I haven't time to look elsewhere, and even if I did I couldn't find anyone better qualified than you. Will you help?"

Storme was stunned, and for a moment she did not know how to react. Her emotions were a wild tumult of incredulity, joy, anxiety, and . . . yes, strangely, far below the surface, a measure of hurt. He had spoken so convincingly this morning of his wish for her to renounce the pirate life, had even gone so far as to make her believe—or perhaps only hope—that he wished her to stay here, with him. Now he was not only giving Storme her freedom, but he was supplying her with ship and crew to return to the seas and the life he claimed would be her certain death. Was it so easy for him, then, to let her go? After all they had been through . . .

But there was his sister. He would do what he must to protect those he loved; Storme had always known that. In his position, would she have done otherwise? In fact, she had been doing exactly the same thing since he had brought her here—scheming, plotting, and fighting to return to those who were her responsibility: her crew, and her ship. Now for once she and Simon must fight on the same side, and afterward . . . afterward they would return to their separate lives, their own responsibilities. It was as it was meant to be.

But Storme could not dismiss a small lingering echo of sadness, not entirely.

"How will you get the *Tempest*?" she demanded. "It's being held under guard."

"Spotswood will cooperate when I tell him what is at stake," Simon replied tersely.

"And send a detachment of redcoats with you!"

"No." Simon's eyes were hard, and looking into them Storme found it impossible to believe that he would not accomplish whatever he set his mind to. "We go alone. And our bargain remains between you and me. I've had enough of governors and politics," he said bitterly. "This I handle on my own."

"She'll have to be reoutfitted," Storme said, thinking rapidly. "After those bastards were done with her—"

"She'll be ready to sail by the end of the week," Simon interrupted. And he looked at her closely. "Will you?"

Something about the question, or perhaps it was the way he looked at her, caused Storme to hesitate. She did not know why. This was best, it was right, it was the only thing to do. Then why did she feel that moment of wavering uncertainty, that sadness that she could not seem to make go away?

Regrets were foolishness, and sentiment was futile. She had no choice. Neither of them did.

Storme met his eyes. She said firmly, "Yes."

Simon nodded, as though satisfied, and turned away.

That night, after Storme was in bed, Simon crossed the darkened yard, nodded curtly to the guards, and lifted the bolt on the barn door. The two men sleeping in the hay scrambled to an alert position as he entered, staring at him warily. When the big one started to get to his feet, he was stilled by a cautious gesture from the other. Both men looked at him with alert, snakelike gazes.

Simon was dimly amazed by the man he had become in one short afternoon, by the ease with which lies had come to his lips, the ruthless, precise way in which he plotted, the conscienceless manner in which he went about breaking every rule of civilized behavior he had ever known. He was amazed, but he felt no remorse. He could not afford it.

He could only guess at the agonies Augusta must be undergoing now, and the fate that awaited her, should he fail, was too repellent to be imagined. Christopher... Christopher was most probably dead, and Simon had to face that. He was completely alone.

He knew now he had made the right decision. Could he expect a woman who had deliberately sent his sister into a nest of murderers to willingly aid in her rescue? Could he, in the short time left to him, have bridged the gap of thought and culture that separated his world from Storme's in order to make her see the importance of what was at stake? He had spent months trying and had been rewarded with nothing but treachery. The treachery he now performed upon Storme seemed a small thing indeed in comparison to his sister's life.

Storme spoke of a code of honor he did not understand and did not care to. He had no time to try to combat it, nor could he risk failure. If nothing else, he had learned the art of deception well from Storme O'Malley, and now he would put it to its best and final use. For the lies he had told her were only the beginning.

First he must persuade Spotswood to release her ship. He had no doubt it could be done, if Simon convinced the governor that that was the only way to retrieve the letter he so desperately coveted. Spotswood would, of course, assume Simon was going to turn the letter over to him, and by the time he found out it had been given to Eden for Augusta's freedom, it would be too late.

The matter of the crew might be more difficult, but Simon had not entirely lied when he told Storme he needed good fighting men. More than that, he needed a crew familiar with the *Tempest* and in a position to be easily bought off. For the promise of wages and freedom they would take his orders, and not Storme's, and what Spotswood thought of the bargain would not matter once they were under way.

But for any of this to be brought about he needed leverage. And the quickest way to obtain that was through these men, Storme's friends.

Simon held the candle high for a moment, examining them in its uncertain glow. Then he placed the candle on a shelf and dropped down onto his haunches beside them. "I have a bargain for you," he said abruptly. "My sister is being held prisoner. I need a crew of strong fighting men to free her. You can help me."

"Might be," said Squint expressionlessly. "But I ain't heard nothin' in the bargain to interest me yet."

Simon took a breath. "I know where Blackbeard's letter is. I can retrieve it and give it to Spotswood in exchange for a pardon for Storme and every man who helps me. That is my part of the bargain."

There might have been a flicker of interest in Squint's eyes. "And what does the lassie think of this plan of yourn?"

Simon held his gaze. "She knows nothing of my plans for the letter."

"And when we done the deed," Squint said at last, "and get the wench back, we sail away free?"

"It makes no matter to me," Simon answered brusquely. "You will do what you please. No one will stop you."

"And ye'll pay?"

"Each man who swears loyalty to me will get five pieces of gold the minute he boards the ship, and twice as much when the deed is done."

There was another silence. Squint looked at the black man and they seemed to share a kind of silent communication which Simon could not fathom.

Simon waited for a reply.

"Will you turn her back to Spotswood?"

Simon replied without hesitation, "No."

For a long, long time Simon was victim of the little man's unnerving single-eyed gaze. And then Squint said slowly,

"Ye know somethin', Farming-man? Ye've got an honest face. I think I'll throw me lot in with ye, for whatever else that be, I think ye can be counted on to do right by my lass."

Simon couldn't meet his gaze any longer. He stood and turned away, his throat tight with dread and self-loathing. He said, "We start for Williamsburg in the morning. Be ready."

Squint replied with a low chuckle, "Aye, cap'n."

Simon left the barn with steps that were purposeful and a heart that felt like lead. There would be no turning back now.

* *Chapter Thirty-three* *

Peter slept the dull sleep of exhaustion in the dank, humid hold of the *Petite Morte*. His hands and feet were bound, forcing him to sleep in a semisitting position, his back wedged between two kegs of stolen molasses, his head lolled back against a bolt of stolen silk. He was filthy, ragged and somewhat weak from his days of confinement, but otherwise he was physically unabused. He was fed and watered more or less regularly, and had been told that as soon as the ship reached the high seas, he would be freed to join the crew.

It wasn't physical misuse that forced Peter into such exhaustion, but mental anguish. Augusta had been taken from him, and he did not know what had become of her. Many times over the past few days he had wished for death—he had even tried to goad his captors into killing him—rather than living without her, and living with the awful truth that he had been responsible for her fate.

The creak of the hatch did not disturb him, nor did the brief white square of light that flooded the compartment below. The pirate climbed stealthily down the ladder, crept soundlessly across the littered floor, and Peter did not stir. He knelt beside the sleeping man and touched his arm.

Peter jerked awake, every muscle tensing, his hands automatically straining against their ropes. His head swung around and his eyes narrowed against his captor and then he stopped, and stared.

"Master Christopher!"

Christopher lifted a quick hand for silence and began to work the knots that bound Peter's hands.

Peter lowered his voice, still staring, still disbelieving. "How did you—"

"I've been aboard a few days," Christopher answered in a low, excited whisper. "This is the first time it's been safe to check on you." Then, quick to answer the only question that was on Peter's mind, he added, "Augusta's safe. She's been kept in a cabin quite comfortably, and the captain has threatened the manhood of any man who molests her. But just in case . . ." And a small, incredible smile flashed across Christopher's features. "She's stolen a fruit knife from her tray and hides it in her garter."

Peter leaned back against the silk, weak with relief, strong with admiration. "That's my lass."

"She's quite a girl," Christopher agreed. "I've seen her, and except for worry about you, she's in good spirits. She knows everything is going to turn out all right."

Now that the first shock and anxiety had passed, Peter had a chance to look at Christopher more closely. There was very little to remind him of the fine young gentleman he had previously known.

Christopher was shirtless and barefoot, his face covered with a scruff of beard, his hair unbound. Grime stained his hands. He wore a broadsword strapped to his waist and a dagger in a belt across his shoulder. A short, vicious-looking knife was tucked into his waistband, and he looked more like a pirate than any of the pirates Peter had previously seen. From the gleam in Christopher's eye and his quick, energetic movements, he seemed to be enjoying every moment of the charade.

Peter said wonderingly, "How in the name of the dear Virgin Mary did you get on board?"

Christopher grinned, leaving the ropes on Peter's hands and going to the ones at his feet. "Quick thinking, sir, and an incredible talent for theater. The good gentlemen aboard this vessel believe me to be nothing but a clever pickpocket fleeing the local constabulary and were more than happy to take me on as crew when I asked for sanctuary.

"I arrived in Bath only hours after you and Augusta," he went on, a bit more seriously. "A few inquiries and some generous bribes led me to the Green Parrot, and the innkeeper was more than cooperative when he saw the size of my purse. A great many nefarious things transpire in that room, I've no doubt, but it isn't easy to forget a young man and woman who were drugged and dragged in broad daylight from the place."

Peter frowned, moving his head back and forth worrisomely. "I don't remember much about it. We went there with a note from the girl pirate. She said we'd be safe. I didn't like the looks of the place, but we hadn't much choice. We found a man—a captain . . ." His frown deepened, trying to remember.

"Deborte," Christopher supplied. "They call him Mad Raoul."

Peter nodded. "That's it. And he seemed right enough. We gave him the letter, and he had someone bring me a tankard and some tea for Gussie. . . . Then it goes a wee bit fuzzy. Seems like I remember Gussie swooning, and . . ." He shook his head helplessly, at a loss.

Christopher nodded grimly. "He took you prisoner. The note must have told him who Augusta was, and he plans on a ransom. At any rate, I didn't know any of that then, only that I couldn't let you out of my sight. It was quite simple, really. I roughed up my appearance a bit and ran to the ship as though all the demons of hell were after me." He grinned again, remembering the pleasure of that first adventure. "I got there just as the *Petite Morte* was preparing to cast off, so you see there wasn't a great deal of time to waste. Since then, I've been watching and waiting."

Peter looked at him soberly. "And now the three of us are here, on the seas, on our own. What will we do?"

Christopher's reminiscent pleasure faded somewhat, and he gave his attention to the ropes. "There," he said. "I've loosened them just enough so that a good snap will free you. But you mustn't do anything until I give the word. Stay here, lie low, pretend to be a prisoner. And here." He removed the short knife from his waistband and hid it carefully inside the bolt of silk. "Use that when the time comes."

He stood and looked down at Peter for a moment, his hands on his hips, his brow thoughtful and concerned. "I am not certain," he admitted at last, "what we shall do, or when our chance will come. I must get word to Simon, for it's certain we cannot take the ship on our own. One thing gives me hope, however. We are not on the high seas, and I don't think that is our destination. I heard orders, in fact, to steer a course down the James, so we must make landfall soon. When we get to Virginia, where I have friends . . ."

He smiled, and reached down to clasp Peter's arm bracingly. "Never fear. We *will* get out of this. We've come too far to know defeat now."

Christopher's opportunity came sooner than he expected, but like everything about this incredible journey, it was not in the least what he expected when it came.

By sunset he could tell the *Petite Morte* had indeed entered the mouth of the James, and if he had not recognized landmarks for himself, the grumbling and tension on board would have confirmed it. These were not safe waters for a pirate ship. Christopher's excitement increased as they moved further inland, for he was on home ground now; his father's plantation could not be more than a day's sailing away. Would Fate be so kindly disposed as to deposit him virtually on his own front doorstep?

Evidently, it would not. At sunset there was a great flurry of activity aboard, with orders to lower sails and drop anchor for the night. The James was not a waterway that offered many hiding places or natural docks for a ship the size of the *Petite Morte*, and they were forced to lie at anchor in the middle of the river, not more than a few miles inland at most. The ship was a perfect target for marauding bandits or vigilant patrols, but worse—at least as far as Christopher was concerned—it was anchored too far away to swim for shore against the strong current. Even if he were willing to leave Augusta behind and go for help, he was not at all certain of his chances for survival in the dangerous waters.

All his life Christopher had relied upon his wits and a certain sort of reckless courage, and it was those two traits that came to his aid now. Though he never lost sight of the extreme gravity of the situation, he looked upon the entire escapade as a challenge, an exercise in cleverness and daring, and had he been asked he would have been forced to admit that he derived a certain amount of enjoyment from his charade. Had he not, in fact, approached the problem with the enthusiasm of a born gamester, he doubtless would not have succeeded half so well in bringing it off.

Christopher had some skill as a seaman, having spent his youth upon the Chowan and the James and having learned at an early age to navigate his father's yacht, so he was not completely lost. More than that, his ability to deliver a convincing performance—indeed, his passion for such—served him as well on the decks of a pirate ship as it did in the courtroom, and the captain of this particular vessel was well impressed with his new crewman.

As darkness fell and rumors began to circulate about speeding away from Virginia on the morn, Christopher knew something important was in the making and that his opportunity would have to be well used. Part of the persona he had adopted was that of a cocky, ambitious young man anxious to prove his worth, so when Raoul announced his need for two strong men to accompany him ashore it was no surprise to anyone that Christopher stepped forward. And so convincing had he been in his performance that it was even less of a surprise when Raoul, with a gleam of approval in his eye, accepted the newest crewman into his landing party.

They rowed through the darkened waters in a small launch, tied up, and disembarked on a wooded bank.

Christopher and his companion remained near the launch, their swords at the ready, while Raoul walked a little way into the woods.

After a long time of night sounds and river smells in which absolutely nothing happened, Christopher's anxiety was at a boiling point. He spat upon the ground, and spoke to his companion in the Cockney accent he had adopted and which, he thought, suited him quite well. "What the bloody 'ell d'ye think is going on?"

The other man leaned back against a tree, his arms crossed, his eyelids drooping. To all appearances he looked half-asleep, but his sword could be in his hand in half an instant and his flabby body held all the alert power of a coiled snake. Christopher had learned that for himself a short while ago, when, on the pretense of answering nature's call, he had tried to move out of sight. With his first crunching footstep the other man had his sword drawn and his eyes boring holes into Christopher's back. That was when Christopher realized that he had not been endowed with quite as much trust as he had been led to believe.

The other man answered now, "None o' our bizness, mate. Our lot is to keep our eyes open and our mouths shut."

Many things about life aboard a pirate ship had disappointed Christopher. For the most part it was hard work and dull routine; his fellow companions were dirty, slovenly, and ill-mannered. As far as he could tell they possessed no particular cunning or daring, and were no more vicious than any other group of lower-class seamen. But in one area he could not help being impressed: Loyalty was absolute, and discipline was harsh. He knew if he tried to make a run for it now, he would be run through before he was an arm's length away.

Panic began to gnaw at him. He was so close, yet so helpless. Tomorrow, if the rumors were true, they would set sail for the open sea and might never see Virginia again. If ever he was to act, it must be now. His only chance, slim though it might be, was to disable his companion, swiftly and silently, and then go for Raoul. Even if he succeeded in killing the two of them, the odds were enormous against his returning to the ship and spiriting off Augusta and Peter safely. But it was a risk he must take. He saw no other choice.

He eyed his companion warily, beginning to make his plans. If he made even one small misstep, allowed the slightest cry to warn Raoul . . .

Suddenly there was a sound in the undergrowth— approaching hoofbeats and the jingle of a bridle. Christopher tensed, waiting for the sound of the horse to cover any noise he might make as he attacked the other guard. Then the hoofbeats stopped; leather creaked as the rider dismounted.

Raoul said, *"Bon soir, monsieur le gouvernant."*

"Good evening, Captain. I see you had no trouble with our rendezvous."

Christopher's head snapped around, peering into the shadows, and even then he recognized the voice long before he recognized the man—or before he could believe it. It wasn't until a fitful shadowed moon cast a wavering light over the face of Lieutenant Governor Alexander Spotswood that the full impact of what he was witnessing struck Christopher.

Christopher sank back into the shadows, concealing himself as well as possible, and his companion glanced at him suspiciously. Christopher barely noticed. His head was roaring so loudly that he could barely think. Forcefully he made himself concentrate, and listen.

"So you've got the girl," Spotswood was saying, "well and safe."

"Aye, *mon ami*, as fresh as the day she arrived."

"I must confess, I was baffled when I first received your message. It seemed insanity to me to hold York's sister hostage when he had nothing of value to trade for her. But as it happens, you were right." A note of admiration came into Spotswood's voice. "Simon York arrived in Williamsburg only yesterday with a plea for me to release Storme O'Malley's ship and crew. He claimed to have learned the whereabouts of Blackbeard's letter—which, if your information is correct, must be the case . . ."

A pause indicated a nod of agreement.

"And concocted some tale of retrieving it for me." Spotswood chuckled. "Of course, I know he has intentions of doing no such thing, plotting instead to deliver it to the hands of my enemy for the sake of his sister. But his betrayal does not disturb me, for little does he know he will in fact deliver it into the hands of the man who is *employed* by me, which is all the same." He chuckled. "A well-laid plan my friend. I grow more impressed with your cleverness each time we meet."

"So you released the *Tempest* to him?"

"Of course. For such a true and trusted friend, what else could I do?" Spotswood chuckled again.

"Aye," agreed Raoul. There was a note of avaricious pleasure in his voice. "What else?"

"But now I must know one thing. How did you learn that York could lead us to the letter?"

"*Bien sur, monsieur le gouvernant*, I should not stay in this business long if I told all my secrets, eh?"

"No, I suppose not. And the girl? How did you come upon her?"

Now Raoul laughed, a full and lustful laugh that sent shivers down Christopher's spine. "That, *mon ami*, was—*comment dit-on?*—a stroke of fate? The gods of the sea smiled upon poor Mad Raoul and delivered her straight into my hands. It was a sign from above! Our partnership was meant to be, *mon ami*, and we must not question such a gift."

"Indeed. You have served me well, Captain, and more than earned my gratitude . . . and this." There was a muffled clink, as of a bag of coins being passed. "There will be more—much more—when you deliver the letter into my hands."

"You are too generous, *Monsieur*," demurred Raoul, but there was more clinking, the counting of coins. "We meet the *Tempest* at Alligator Cove on Tuesday. You will have your package within a week."

"Very good. I'll await your word."

There was again the creak of leather and the jingle of bridle, and the hoofbeats grew fainter through the woods.

Raoul Deborte sauntered back to the bank, his hands tucked jauntily into his belt, his face split with a jubilant smile. Unexpectedly, he clapped the two men exuberantly on the shoulders. *"Voilà, mes amis!"* he exclaimed. "You see before you the most clever man who ever sailed the seas! I have outwitted not only two royal governors but the great Storme O'Malley herself. You sail in the presence of greatness. I deserve to be King of the Pirates, and that is just what I shall be before this week is out!"

Raoul was laughing as he climbed into the boat, and Christopher rowed silently, thinking hard.

Chapter Thirty-four

It was Storme's second morning on the deck of the *Tempest*. The day was fine and clear with a strong wind, and the little ship skipped and glided across the smooth waters of Albemarle Sound as though it were a child's toy being pulled on a string. The breeze whipped back Storme's hair and the sun stroked her face; the rail beneath her hand was warm and silky, and Storme caressed the smooth strong wood as though it were a living thing. For a time she simply stood there, in solemn communion with it all.

Simon had kept his promise. The *Tempest*, though it still bore the scars of savage swords and its inner compartments had been literally torn from stem to stern, was as seaworthy as ever. Horror had seized her when Storme first saw the violations that had been performed upon the ship—even the wheel showed signs of having been dismantled and hastily thrown together. Once she recovered from her initial shock, she felt much as a mother might who, in welcoming home a lost and battered child, is grateful only that it is still alive. Her cabin had been ransacked, her trunk and few personal possessions stolen or destroyed, and the crew's quarters and galley similarly ravaged. But the *Tempest* herself had required only a few repairs, a good scraping, and new rigging, and she was under way.

But everywhere Storme looked there were reminders of the abuses the ship had suffered at strangers' hands, and she could not escape the fact that her beloved *Tempest* was not the same ship she had left.

Storme had slept on deck the night before beneath the stars and the sea breeze, reveling in the exhilaration of an impossible dream come true. For that was what it had been from the moment she had set foot upon the decks that had been the only home she had ever known—a wild and joyous dream. She had known nothing except she was free, home at last with those to whom she belonged, and nothing else mattered. Strangely, this morning everything seemed different.

"The first thing I'll be doin' is buyin' me a female—nay—two! And when they be used up, I'll set out to git me more!"

"Ye'd have to ransom the king afore a woman would look at you, ye barnacle-eaten sea worm!"

The voices went back and forth over Storme and she tried to ignore them, but they irritated her somehow. Only eight men had survived imprisonment, and though they were sailing with a short crew, Storme had assured herself that it was the best of all possible crews. Now she wasn't so sure anymore. They were a sorry, ill-nourished, lackadaisical lot with very little on their minds except how to spend the coin Simon was paying them for this cruise, and every time Storme looked at them, her disappointment—and confusion— rose. Had prison affected them so, or had they always been this way and she had never noticed before?

Out of the corner of her eye she saw a line whip free of the mast and drift downward. She whirled, shouting, "Avast there! Secure that line!"

But the heavy line struck a crewman on the head, knocking him off his feet, and the inner sail began to droop. She reached the scene just as the injured seaman was struggling to his feet, holding his head and cursing profoundly.

"You lazy dog!" She grabbed the line, eyes flashing.

"Who was responsible for raising this line? If you've forgotten how to tie a knot, why the hell did I waste my time getting you out of the gaol?"

"Beats the bloody 'ell outa me," the other man growled insolently, glaring at her. "At least back in the straw I didn't have to risk me bleedin' noggin' fer me three squares!"

Storme stared at him, dumbfounded and speechless with fury. Then she thrust the swaying line into the hand of a passing seaman and commanded, "Straighten that sail! And swab down this deck before somebody else falls and breaks his bloody neck!"

The crewman pulled on the line, beginning to tie it off, but barely glanced at Storme as he replied, "Ain't got no time for polishin' up, Missy. Got all we can do to keep 'er on course."

Missy. He had called her *Missy*. Storme stood there for a moment, churning and impotent, then turned and strode away. A tongue-lashing would be futile, and physical abuse would be self-defeating. She couldn't forget the urgency of their mission or the restraints of a short crew. But what had happened to the noble fighting men who once had sailed under her flag? What had happened to the fierce loyalty, the courage, the aptitude that had made them the finest on the seas?

Everything was different now, and none of it was right.

When she looked around her—really looked—what she saw caused a hollowness in the pit of her stomach that nothing seemed able to fill. A motley, ragged group of men who, far from being grateful to her for their freedom, accepted her orders sullenly or not at all, or who—even worse—regarded her with lascivious grins and ribald comments when they thought her back was turned.

Her family, her stalwart, loyal crew—the men about whom she had fretted and worried every day and night for the past three months and for whom she had been willing to risk her life—were more concerned with the easiest way to line their pockets than with the freedom she offered them. She realized with a start that they had always been up to the highest bidder, and the only loyalty they had ever held to her was for the sake of the prizes she had taken. The moment those prizes stopped coming, they would desert her without a backward glance.

And the *Tempest*. Her beloved, her lifeline, her home ... Even it was changed, and from more than the ravages made by Spotswood's soldiers. It was a ship, tall and beautiful, sound and fleet, but the memories it held for her were no longer powerful and sure. It didn't feel like home anymore.

Such a realization was treacherous and disturbing, and the knot in Storme's stomach only tightened. What had gone wrong? Why wasn't anything this morning the way she had expected it to be?

Squint was at the helm, and the crewmen had their orders. Her presence on deck was superfluous, even a distraction. She couldn't stand there anymore, bombarded by uncertainties and confusing, treacherous notions. She needed to be where she belonged, to find something that would remind her of who she was, and why she was here. She went below, to her cabin.

But even there she found nothing that would connect her to the woman she once had been. Maps had been ripped rom the walls, sextant and compass were missing from their usual places. The table had been ripped from its bolts, long with the chair. Great holes were gouged in the inner bulkhead. Her bed remained, but its mattress and linen were slashed. Only one thing was the same.

Simon was there, sitting on the bed, pulling on his stockings. He was shirtless, and his hair was rumpled in soft auburn waves that gently shadowed his face. He was apparently just arising from sleep, and he was as breathtaking, as certain, and as right as the first time he had entered this room, when he stood before her in Pompey's grip, his eyes flashing and his shoulders proud. Something within Storme wrenched with the memory.

Simon stood as she came into the room. "This was the only bed onboard that was still intact," he explained, gesturing. "You didn't seem to want it, so I thought you wouldn't mind."

Storme looked around slowly. "It's all so different," she said.

But for Simon it was an extreme case of *déjà vu*. The rolling of the ship beneath his feet, the musty taste of seasoned wood and sea air, the spartan cabin with its row of windows washed in blue sky . . . and Storme.

Her hair was long and loose, tangled by wind and lightened with sunshine. She wore tight knee breeches and no stockings or shoes, and a big white shirt belted at the waist. He could see the shape of her breasts beneath the material, the curve of white skin against the open laces at the throat. It was as though he had been suddenly thrust back in time and the intervening summer months had never happened. His pulse quickened and his muscles tightened, from no more than looking at her.

He said, with a slight huskiness to his voice he had not expected, "Is it so different, Storme?"

She wished she could put it into words, the uneasiness she felt, the aching and confusion inside. She was like a child flailing in the dark, and instinctively she focused on the one thing that was familiar to her, the only thing that was right. She came toward Simon.

"So much has changed," she said.

He looked at her for a moment, then dropped his eyes. He turned to retrieve his shirt. He answered only, "Yes."

He gathered the folds of the shirt to pull it over his head, but Storme laid her hands upon his, stopping him. His eyes met hers and she could see the light there, the surprise and the wanting and the urgency that was a bond with hers, even though he fought it. Her heart was beating powerfully, and she needed him with the blind instinctive hunger that was as old as time.

She said, "One thing hasn't changed. Not since the minute I laid eyes on you."

She took the shirt and pulled it from his hands, letting it drop to the floor. She saw his muscles tighten, and the struggle in his eyes. When she would have touched him, he caught her hand. "Storme . . ."

It was a low and husky protest that carried less conviction

than it should. She entwined her hand with his and, leaning forward, lightly touched her tongue to his nipple. She tasted salt and flesh; she felt his breath quicken and the skin quiver. His hand tightened on hers.

She moved her mouth across his chest, to the other nipple, around the curve of musculature and across the hard frame of bone and sinew. He tugged his hand away from hers and she thought he would push her away, but he only drove both hands into her hair, holding her, and the release of his breath was shaky and powerful.

Storme's hands cupped around his waist and tightened there. His fingers curled around her scalp as her lips and tongue explored his chest, his ribs, the flat planes of his stomach and the indentation of his navel. When her fingers moved to the buttons of his breeches, he caught his breath and he whispered, "Storme . . . we mustn't. We cannot—"

She looked up at him solemnly, her eyes brilliant and alive with wanting. "Why? Is there a rule that says we cannot end as we've begun? You know all the rules, Farmer," she whispered. "Tell me this one. Tell me how we should say good-bye."

Simon closed his eyes against a surge of pain, a twisting emptiness that gripped his heart, and he thought, *Not at all. We should not say good-bye at all. . . .*

His hands drifted down to her neck, tilting her face to his. He looked at her with all the tight, helpless longing in his soul and he said, "It's not that simple, Storme. You know that."

"No." She dropped her eyes. "Nothing is simple anymore."

His fingers tightened on her neck. His voice held a low note of desperation and she could feel his muscles strain with need. "What do you want, Storme?"

She raised her eyes to him. Her voice was thick but her eyes held no secrets. Sorrow, confusion, wanting—all were there, clear and unashamed, for him to read. She answered simply, "You."

He drew in his breath, and his eyes flared with something powerful and helpless and right. Storme's arms wound around him and his mouth covered hers.

With her mouth and her tongue Storme caressed him, greedy to taste every part of him, to imprint the memory of her on his brain and of him on hers. Boldly she crossed the borders of intimacy and fiercely he welcomed her until the pleasures she gave him became a test of endurance. With a soft cry, he caught her shoulders and reversed their positions, pinning her beneath him, and began to explore her body as she had his, showing her depths of need and pinnacles of power she had never imagined before.

There was a measure of madness to their lovemaking, an intensity and a magnificence that wiped away reason. He took her with flames in his eyes and passion unrestrained, and Storme responded with a ferocity that was more powerful than any unleashed at the height of battle. There was greed and there was hunger, but behind it all there was desperation, for each of them knew that what they felt now they would never know again. Not with anyone. Not ever.

And when the power between them peaked and exploded, Storme locked her arms and her legs around him, holding on as though to never let him go, and she thought, *Is this good-bye?*

Then, slowly, *No. It cannot be. . . .*

For suddenly it was very clear. Her surrender had begun in this cabin, many months ago, and in that time she had begun to know the meaning of victory. Today she had surrendered all of herself, but she had triumphed over more than she had ever expected to know.

They lay in each other's arms, their sticky bodies twined together while hammering heartbeats quietened and breaths came more easily. The ship gently rolled beneath them, and the sun grew higher in the sky.

Simon kissed her face tenderly. "Storme," he whispered. "My lovely child." And then he looked at her, stroking a damp strand of hair away from her face, and though he smiled his eyes were sad. "But you're not a child any longer, are you?"

"No," she replied somberly.

Simon rested his shoulders against the mattress again, his head turned toward the ceiling. There were lines of pain around his eyes which should not have been there. His hand drifted down her arm and stroked her fingers, then closed about them. He released an unsteady breath. "I shall miss you," he said.

Storme kept her eyes, too, upon the ceiling. "Once you said you wished things could be different."

She felt his head turned to look at her, and the muscles in his arms seemed to tighten.

"You could never live on the sea," she went on.

"No." The reply was hoarse, barely audible.

Now she turned her head, and their faces were close, almost touching. She said softly, "I'm not certain I can anymore, either."

His breath stilled, his eyes were quick and intense upon her. "What are you saying?"

Gently she extricated her hand from his, and sat up. She said, "You asked me to make a choice, before. And I didn't realize it had already been made for me."

She stood and began to gather up her clothes, dressing to keep her hands busy and because these words were the hardest she had ever had to say, and words were so important to Simon. She knew only truths, feelings, and inevitabilities, but Simon needed the words. She could count her heartbeats, they were so loud.

When she turned Simon was dressed, too. He finished pulling on his last boot and he watched her with eyes that were alert and cautious. Storme said, "I thought this was what I wanted." She gestured vaguely to indicate the ship. "In my life I have loved only a very few things. My father, my ship . . . Squint, and Pompey. Those were the loves of my girlhood," she said simply. "Now I am a woman, and I know what it is to love a man."

Simon stood slowly. Every muscle was aware, every cell was flooded with life. All of him was caught in the quiet, solemn depth of her calm blue eyes and all he could think was *Yes* . . . It came to him like a glimmer through a fog, something he had waited for all his life and never expected to find, and he welcomed it home with wonder and joy. It began as a whisper that grew and expanded to every part of him, filling him with certainty. *Yes . . .*

She said, "This is not my life anymore. You are the one I love."

The emotion that went through him left him weak. Joy, pain, wanting . . . how could he have questioned what was so simple, and so sure? How could he have thought, for all they had been through, that they could ever be separate again? And there was turmoil, for all he had done, all she did not know, and anxiety for what yet might come. He had to make her understand, and forgive, and he did not know where to begin. All he could say, for that moment, was, "Oh Storme . . ."

She saw the look in his eyes, pain and reluctance, but beyond it even more—a certainty and a need that matched her own. She said sharply, "Don't try any of your fancy words with me, Farmer, about how we don't match and how we wear on each other, for haven't I lived with you long enough to know it for myself? You said it was my choice. Well, here it is. You think you can just cast me off when this deed is done? You think you can go sail back to your big fine house and live out your days just fine in peace and quiet?"

Her eyes snapped and her hands clenched into fists, though even she did not realize it was anxiety as much as determination that strengthened her tone. "Why, you can't even keep your banks safe from a bunch of scurvy river pirates without me there to lend you my sword! And who's going to keep your meals on time and get that lazy band of cheese-eaters you call servants to give you a full day's work? You'll be gray-haired and muttering to yourself inside a year. You need me, Simon York, and you might as well face it. I'm not letting you go back to that place alone!"

His face softened with an intensity of tenderness and joy that was a reflection of the opening of his heart. He said thickly. "Yes, Storme. I need you." And he opened his arms to her.

She flew to him; they embraced in a long breathless moment of straining muscles and aching hearts. And then

Storme said into his shoulder, "Don't worry about Augusta. We'll get her right enough; you went to the right person for the job and you know I won't let you down. And after that— we'll get that blasted letter and take it to the bastard Spotswood. I can live without his bloody amnesty, but you need to do things right. So we'll do it."

Simon's breath caught, and twisted in his chest so that he could barely speak. He closed his eyes against the pain, and he tightened his arms around her. He said, "Storme, I must tell you—"

But suddenly Storme stiffened in his arms; she pushed away. Her brow was knit with alarm and her gaze swung sharply to the window. "What was that?"

The creaking, scraping sound of the anchor being lowered was clearly audible. Simon's heart lurched. "Storme—"

"We shouldn't be making land this soon! What the bloody hell—"

He reached for her, desperately, but she was already rushing from the room.

* *Chapter Thirty-five* *

There was more activity on deck than Storme had witnessed since the journey began as sails were lowered, a longboat dropped into the water, the rope ladder secured. Squint was barking out orders as though it was his place to do so, but what was happening on board blurred in comparison to what Storme saw around her.

They had drawn into a cove, dark with swampy branches and thick with insect life, and long before she could believe it Storme knew instinctively where they were. On a far shore she could see the tendril of smoke from a campfire, and the shadowy figures of several men moving warily close to the bank to get a better look at the ship that intruded into their territory. The upturned hull of a ship rigged for scraping partially blocked the foreground.

From that shore there was a single musket shot, and the faint cry, "Ahoy, the *Tempest*!"

Squint shouted back, "Ahoy!" and the pirates on shore, reassured that the *Tempest* was on legitimate business, waved them past.

For a moment Storme stood gripping the rail, staring about her with stunned disbelieving eyes while the dark truth gathered like a leaden cloud over her head. There was no mistake. This was Teach's Hole, a full day's sailing away from their destination. But it couldn't be...

She whirled on Squint. "You bleedin' half-blind turtle! What the hell's the meaning of this? Have you forgotten how to read a compass?"

Even before he spoke, she knew what he was going to say. She could tell by the sober, quiet look on his face. "We're right where we're supposed to be, girlie."

But still Storme fought it. Horror, betrayal, and disbelief rose up inside her like a scream of rage, and a tremor began in her muscles as she shouted, "These were not my orders—"

Simon said quietly behind her, "I gave the orders."

Storme whipped around to face him. His face was tight, his eyes dark with pain. "I tried to tell you, Storme. There was no other way. Augusta—"

"You lied to me." She meant it to be a scream, but it was barely a whisper. She felt ill inside. "You *lied*—"

And then a scream escaped, low and primal and wild. She lunged at Simon, blind with fury, and someone grabbed her from behind, holding her out of his reach. Simon turned and walked away.

Storme struggled wildly as she watched Simon climb down the ladder and into the longboat. Pompey—her own Pompey—held her fast. She screamed, "Let me go, you fool!" Then, whipping her head around for aid, "Stop him! To arms, you yellow sniveling bastards! He's betraying us all!"

No one moved.

As she lurched wildly against Pompey's iron grip her

lungs felt torn by a single gasp of pain and defeat. She watched helplessly as Simon made shore and walked unerringly to the yellow stone beneath the crooked cypress tree.

"*Stop him!*" she screamed once more, helplessly, and not a single head turned toward her.

Squint said quietly, "They're workin' for 'im, lassie. They won't listen to ye."

She looked at him, her eyes wide with agony and denial, and he touched her arm awkwardly, briefly. "It's for the best, me girl, ye'll see it. Once Spotswood has that letter, we'll all get pardon—"

"Spotswood!" She spat out the word in rage and bitter mockery for his naïveté. "You fool! It's Eden that's behind this! He's taking the letter to Eden to free his sister and we'll all *die*! He's lied to you—he's betrayed us all!"

For a moment Squint looked uncertain, and his gaze traveled worriedly to the shore. But even if he had believed Storme, there was little he could do—he was one man against an entire crew, and all of them were at the mercy of Simon York.

He looked back to Storme, and said with certainty, "Nay. He'll not harm ye, lass, I know it in me bones. D'ye think I would've agreed to this if I thought it wasn't so? Besides," he added grimly, "if I ever find out differently, I won't lay down me head till I've slit his yellow-coated gullet and he knows it a-sure."

Storme stared at him for one last moment of frustration and denial, and then she let her head sag. "By then it'll be too late," she said. "It will be *too late*."

Storme did not raise her eyes again, nor did she hear anything that went on around her. Slowly Pompey's grip on her arms relaxed, so that he was, in fact, supporting her, rather than restraining her. Briefly she thought of options. The pirates on the opposite shore were too far away, and too disinterested, to be of any help to her, and even if they had known what was going on they would only rise up in arms against the *Tempest* and take the letter for themselves. She had no weapon, and her own men had turned against her. She was helpless.

But it was not the lack of loyalty or manpower that defeated her; it was not even Simon's manipulations or the defenselessness of her position. It was his lies. She could have borne up under anything except that. Now there hardly seemed to be anything left worth fighting for.

She lifted her head when she felt his presence, but there was nothing in her eyes, and very little in her soul—except a coldness, a dull and empty blackness that it seemed nothing could ever fill. Pompey released her arms but stood close behind her, and Storme did not move.

In his hand Simon carried the flat oilcloth pouch Storme had buried almost two years ago. In his face was sorrow. He said, "Storme, there was no other way. I couldn't let my sister die."

She responded dully, "I believed in you. I truly did."

A shaft of pain crossed his face. "You told me you would never surrender the letter. I wanted to be honest with you, but I couldn't risk my sister's safety on your sense of honor—"

Something twisted through Storme that felt like amusement. Perhaps even a ghost of a sharp and bitter smile touched her lips. "Honor," she repeated, as though marveling he could speak the word. But her voice was tired, and her face held no emotion at all. "Ah, foolish Farmer, how little you know of me, after all. There would have been no dishonor in saving a life. I would have fought for you, had you asked."

He took a step forward. "Storme," he said intensely, "I would fight for you, too. Haven't I done it often enough? You must trust me now. I won't let any harm befall you, I swear it. Only . . . trust me."

She stared at him for a long time, and the rage that swelled inside her was like an ice lock, huge and horrible, but paralyzed by its own weight. She wanted to strike him, to spit upon him, to pummel him with her fists and make him bleed—but the depth of his treachery made such gestures seem pale and futile.

She held his gaze in cold contempt, and at last she said

only, very quietly, "You bastard. I shall hate you till the day I die."

She turned and walked below.

The *Tempest* sailed throughout the night, and Storme remained in her cabin, locked in thought, weighted down by sorrow. Memories, as brief and nebulous as fog-demons, danced across her brain. Her father's face, laughing in the sun as he lifted her for the first time to the wheel of the *Tempest*. Screams of battle, the clash of swords. The snap of the black flag as it was raised on the mast, the surge of triumph as grappling hooks snared their mark.

An auburn-haired man, swinging his sword with fire in his eyes while his companions cowered and begged quarter. And Simon, standing here in her cabin, his chest bared and his head proud while she held a knife to his throat.

Like tired soldiers the pictures marched across her mind and faded in defeat. Blackbeard, Jack Rackham, Raoul Deborte . . . campfires and drunken brawls, squalid island hideaways and blood in the dirt . . . such were the times of her life. And all for this.

She did not know what would become of her now, and it seemed to matter very little. For so long Blackbeard's legacy had been her passage to freedom, the difference between life and death to her. It had been a sacred trust, a symbol of power, a crown of glory. And now . . . it was nothing more than a scrap of paper, for it had cost her far more than it had ever been worth.

Prison in Virginia, or death at Eden's hand—it mattered little. Already she had lost the only thing worth fighting for, and the rest was no more than idle words to fill the history books.

She was standing at the porthole when the *Tempest* pulled carefully into Alligator Cove, but the fog was so thick she could see nothing. Vaguely she remarked Squint's navigational skills, but even that most graphic reminder of her uselessness on board provoked little emotion in her. She gazed absently at the thick gray moisture that encased the porthole, and she felt nothing.

The door opened behind her, and Simon stepped in. He wore a sword and a knife and carried another sword in his hand. The tension for what was to come was evident in his bearing, but he stood tall and proud, and for a moment Storme could do nothing but look at him. Simon. The beauty of his features, the sternness of his frown, the laughter in his eyes, the tenderness of his touch. Fierce and protective, quiet and reflective, angry and sad . . . she knew all of him. And that, at least, no one would ever take from her. Those memories of him would be with her the rest of her life.

He said, "It is time."

Storme nodded. "I wish you luck."

He came over to her. His face was very quiet, and so was his voice. The inevitability of the moment hung between them like a shroud. He said, "I was asked to choose between you and my sister. That's a choice no man should ever be faced with. I love you, Storme, for right or wrong and for all time. You are a part of me, and I could no more harm you than I could carve out my own heart. So the choice was never mine to make."

She looked at him, nothing but the quiet pulse of her own heart marking off the moments between them. She was silent.

Simon glanced down at the sword in his hand. Slowly he handed it to her. "This is yours," he said quietly, "to use as you will."

For another moment their eyes met and held, without question or denial, a final solemn acceptance of what must be. Then Simon turned and left her.

Storme slid the sword into her belt and followed him on deck.

The deck was swathed in an eerie misty glow as lanterns from the wheelhouse and the bulkheads absorbed the fog and gave back light in miserly measure. The *Tempest* glided through the waters like a ghost ship, occasionally scraping a branch or skirting a sandbar. Dampness enfolded them all like a blanket, smothering sound, blotting vision.

From ahead came a distant muffled cry. "Ahoy, the Tempest!"

Simon's voice returned, "Ahoy!"

Storme stood against the rail, peering intently through the fog as orders and directions were shouted from the other ship and the crew of the Tempest blindly went about obeying them. Her heart was pounding loud and hard until the fog began to break and the shape of the other ship became distinguishable. And then her heart stopped entirely.

The Petite Morte stood like a great black beast in the mouth of the channel, blocking entrance and exit.

"Lower your sails!" came the command from the deck of the Petite Morte, much clearer and closer now. "Come around and prepare to be boarded!"

Storme looked around wildly as sails were lowered and the Tempest maneuvered into position. She heard the creak of grappling hooks and stepped backward quickly as a huge iron hook sailed over the rail and dug into the deck of the Tempest a few feet from where she stood. The ship lurched and listed starboard as the lines were tied off.

The fog was snatched away in slices and patches, and the first thing Storme saw was the deck of the Petite Morte, lined with men—twenty or thirty, she could not be sure—all of them armed and ready. The second thing she saw was Augusta, standing at the bow in the grasp of a bearded blond man who held a cutlass at her side.

Simon moved quickly to the bow of the Tempest, his voice hoarse with relief and sharp with concern. "Augusta! Are you all right?"

"Yes!" Her voice was strong, yet shrill with what might have been the onset of hysteria. "I'm unharmed! Simon, be care—"

The pirate clamped his hand over her mouth, cutting off the words.

Storme whipped her head around toward the sound of Raoul's laughter. "And so she shall remain, mon ami, if you have come prepared to fulfill our bargain."

He stood on the deck, his hands on his hips, his teeth flashing, and in an instant it was clear to Storme. Raoul, who never was one to do anything the hard way, who would not work if he could cheat, who had tried for years to wheedle, steal, or insinuate himself into Storme's good graces so that he might grasp her power ... who carried a crew of thirty for a job six could have done ...

The thud of the plank hit the deck, bridging the short gap between the two ships. Raoul sauntered across, and Simon went forward to meet him.

"Bring my sister aboard," Simon commanded harshly.

"All in good time, my friend, all in good time." Raoul turned to Storme, a delighted grin twisting his features. "*Eh bien, ma petite,* you seem not surprised to see me."

"I always knew you were a whimpering, scuttling dog," Storme replied with cool contempt. "Nothing you would do surprises me."

He chuckled. "Didn't I tell you it was time to get out of the business, *chérie*? If it were not me, 'twould be someone else. Time has passed you by, *petite*, and left victory to the strong."

Storme stepped forward to within striking distance of him. She saw wariness in his features and his hand moved stealthily toward his sword. Storme filled her mouth with saliva and spat on his boots.

For a moment no one moved. Raoul's eyes locked with hers and she saw the fury there. Then, slowly he grinned. It was an ugly, humorless expression. "What a great lot of trouble you have caused, *chérie*," he said. "You and scribblings from Blackbeard. But trouble is what I hold dear, my very stock in trade, *n'est-ce pas?*"

He shrugged. "Eden pays me well to kill you and keep the secret of the letter. Spotswood pays me to take the plump sister and trade her for the letter. But Raoul ..." he chuckled again. "Raoul, he works only for himself, eh? So this is what I do. I have my gold; I let you live. I have the letter, I return the charming sister. As for me—I will take the *Tempest* and the letter and ply my trade upon the seas forevermore with no one to stop me. A clever bargain, eh? And who will say Raoul Deborte is not a fair man!"

He turned to Simon with a small bow. "I have been most

generous with your sister. Not a hair on her head is harmed. You have the price of her freedom?''

Stone-faced, Simon reached into his pocket and withdrew the parchment. It was creased and yellow and ragged at the edges, and it held all their lives in the balance.

Simon said, ''Here is the letter.'' He held it up for inspection but just out of reach. ''Take a careful look at it. Think how much has been lost for it. Think of how many people have died for it. Think how many lives will now be ruined for the sake of it. Look closely, and remember. For now it ends.''

And he lifted both hands and tore the letter in two.

Storme released an involuntary cry; she lurched toward him. ''Simon, no! He'll kill her!''

But he tore again, and again, and the pieces fluttered to the deck. Simon said clearly, ''I am tired of making deals. Now I fight.''

And at the very moment Raoul recovered his shock and reached for his sword, Simon's sword was in his hand. Steel met steel, shrill cries of challenge resounded from the surrounding crew, and the deck thundered with the swarm of invading forces from the *Petite Morte*.

The air was filled with the clash of metal and the cries of battle, from every direction man surged against man and blood began to flow. Raoul, a clever fighter and a determined survivor, retreated behind his men, shouting orders and forming a living barricade between the *Tempest* and the *Petite Morte*. Simon, supported by a small band of his own who fought only to protect themselves, advanced determinedly, wielding his sword like a battleax, shouting for Augusta.

He felt himself grabbed from behind and he whirled with a thrust that would have killed had not his opponent deflected the blow at the last minute. Simon found himself staring into an oddly familiar bearded face and Christopher cried, ''God's blood, man, quarter!''

Simon had no time for astonishment or questions. He shouted, ''Augusta—''

''She's safe, with Peter!'' He swung his sword toward the water, and through the surge of bodies Simon could see a man and a woman in a longboat, rowing close to shore. "We haven't a chance!" Christopher shouted, grabbing Simon's arm. "We've got to get off this ship!"

Simon swung his head around and knew there was no denying what Christopher had said. They were outnumbered three to one, already the crew of the *Tempest* were flinging down their swords or leaping overboard, Augusta was safe . . . and then he saw Storme. With a single strangulated cry, he lunged toward her.

Storme knew she was fighting her final battle. Her sword arm felt as though it were filled with shards of glass, her breath came in heaving, burning gasps, and the enemy was everywhere. Halfway up the mast Raoul clung, laughing and brandishing his sword, shouting, "Surrender, you cowardly girls! Surrender or die!"

Desperately Storme looked around and saw how hopelessly outnumbered they were. The wisest of her crew had already deserted, others clung to combat only long enough to make their escape, and she knew they were lost. But Squint and Pompey were still by her side, fighting valiantly, and Storme seized on one last slim hope.

"The lines!" she shouted to Squint. "Cut the lines! It's our only chance to save the ship!"

Squint heard her, and, with Pompey, he fought his way to the grappling hooks that bound the *Tempest* to the *Petite Morte*. Storme, with a savage cry, gripped her sword in both hands and lunged forward, striking back an attacker who would have gone for Pompey, then turning to fend off another on her right.

Her strength was failing, her muscles quivering. Perspiration blurred her vision and spots danced before her eyes. With every lunge she made she was forced two steps backward and she did not know how much longer she could hold on. But the battle was spread across two decks now; if they could free the *Tempest* it would cut the number of assailants in half. If she could buy enough time for Squint and Pompey to cut the lines . . .

She felt the cold solid pressure of a bulkhead against her

shoulders; a barrel of oil against her knees. Blindly she looked about and saw she had no place left to retreat. Before her face was an evil, black-toothed grin and the glint of a cutlass. She swung her weapon viciously, and fire slashed through her arm; her sword sailed from fingers that were slippery with her own blood.

Storme went to her knees, groping desperately for her sword. And just as her numbed fingers closed about the hilt, her attacker dropped to the deck beside her with a heavy thud.

Simon knelt beside her, his bloodied sword in hand, his face white and his breathing heavy. His eyes were stark with fear and concern for her. "Storme—my God, you're hurt!"

"I'm not—what I was," she answered him through dragging breaths. "I've—grown soft on land."

He jerked off his neckcloth and began to knot it around her arm, but Storme pushed him away, lunging shakily to her feet.

"Storme, this is madness!" He caught her around the waist as she swayed, trying to drag her away. "Augusta is safe—our mission is done! We must get away!"

Storme tightened her grip on the sword and gritted her teeth against the pain. She pushed away from Simon with a sudden surge of desperate energy as she saw the glint of a sword coming their way. Gripping her weapon in both hands she swung out, and suddenly she had an ally, a dirty blond-bearded man who shouted to Simon, "Get her to safety! I'll hold them off as long as I can!"

Dimly Storme recognized Christopher's voice, and then another was upon them. Simon lunged forward to stop the swing of a cutlass across his sword and leaped forward, striking out blindly at whatever crossed her path. "Save yourself, Farmer!" she cried. "She's my ship and I go down with her!"

"Look around you, woman!" Christopher shouted above the sharp ring of blade against blade. "There's nothing left to save!"

"*No!*" She thrust forward with the last of her strength; her blade met flesh and her opponent staggered backward.

But everything about her told Storme it was over; the fiery
pain in her arm, the shaking of her muscles, the burning of
her lungs. No one remained to fight but Squint and Pompey,
Christopher and Simon. Everywhere she looked the crew of
the *Petite Morte* swarmed across her decks. Raoul cackled
from the mast like a mad demon, shouting, "I give you
quarter, Storme O'Malley! Surrender while you can!"

Storme stood still; she turned her face up to him with
eyes blazing and she shouted, "I take no quarter from you
or any man living, Raoul Deborte!"

"Storme, for God's sake!" It was Simon again, his hand
gripping her arm, his face raw with pleading. "Let it go.
Don't do this thing—"

"Save yourself, Farmer, I beg you! I stay with my ship!"

"*I will not leave you!*"

She looked at him, she heard the sounds of battle and
smelled the scent of death; her eyes swept around to those
who remained to fight for her, and she knew what must be
done. Tears mingled with the perspiration and the sea mist
that blurred her vision and she stood still; she cried in a
loud, clear voice, "Abandon ship!"

She pulled away from Simon and flung down her sword.
With both hands she grasped the heavy cask of oil and
began to drag it forward. Simon saw what she was doing
and lent his strength; in an instant they had pried off the lid
and sent a flood of oil across the decks.

From his perch above Raoul watched in horror as Storme
grabbed a lantern from the bulkhead. She held it aloft for a
moment, a torch of triumph, and she shouted, "No quarter
taken, Raoul!"

She swung her head around; she cried a last warning.
"Abandon ship!" And she tossed the lantern into the oil.

A wall of flames exploded upwards as Simon grabbed her
hand and together they jumped into the water.

The survivors were strung out along the shore. Peter and
Augusta stood with their arms around each other while
Simon made his way over to them. He paused, and they

turned to him. Silently he drew them both into a fierce embrace.

Crewmen from both sides lay gasping on the bank, glad to have escaped with their lives, while the *Petite Morte*, with Raoul at the helm, cursing and swearing vengeance, limped out into the sea toward an uncertain fate. Christopher stood with Squint and Pompey, their faces bathed with an unearthly glow, watching in awe as the flaming skeleton of the *Tempest* crumpled and tumbled bit by bit into the water.

Storme sat upon the ground, her knees drawn up to her chest, her face turned toward the flames. Embers sparked and sizzled on the water, timbers groaned and cracked and crashed as they fell. The sails floated away in ashes; the bow dipped and sank. Tears coursed silently down Storme's face.

Simon, across the way, saw her sitting alone. He left Augusta to Peter and walked slowly back to Storme. He dropped to his knees beside her and then, without hesitation, pulled her into his arms. "Ah, my love," he whispered. He stroked her wet hair; he kissed her forehead. His own body ached with her pain. "I am so sorry."

Slowly Storme looked up at him, and through the sorrow in her eyes there was courage, and peace. She moved her eyes back to her ship, watching it sink slowly below the waterline. "She lived a proud life," she said softly. "But her time was over... just as mine is, and soon, probably, the Brotherhood's."

She looked back to Simon. "You were right," she said solemnly. "You and all those who said it before. The days of sailing free upon the seas with no one to call master are dying. I fought the good fight and went down with honor, but the defeat of the Brethren did not begin here today with me... it began long ago. Before Blackbeard, perhaps, even before Woodes Rogers and his crusade in the islands. It's in the spirit of things, I think. The world is changing, becoming—civilized. There's no room for the life we once led, and those that can't change with the times will die." She lifted her chin. "I do not intend to die, Simon."

Simon loved her then with a fierce and proud intensity that filled his soul. He touched her face, and his hand trembled with emotion. "No, my love," he said huskily. "You are too fine and brave for that kind of defeat. You will master this new world just as you did the old."

She turned her face into his palm, and closed her eyes. He bent his head and kissed her gently, lingeringly, atop her damp hair.

And then he lightly stroked her face, turning it back to him. A shadow of sorrow crossed his face, and his eyes were anxious and reluctant as they searched hers. "You could have fought alongside Raoul," he said. "I would not have thought less of you had you used your sword against me."

She shook her head, slowly, but with force. "No," she said hoarsely, lowering her eyes. "That I could never do."

His hand dropped; he let his gaze wander bleakly over the landscape, resting in turn on each of the ragged survivors, and at last on the sinking ship. "I never wanted it to be like this, Storme," he said heavily. "I never wanted you to hate me."

She lifted her face, surprise and denial quick in her eyes. She tried to hide both by shifting her gaze away. The next words were difficult. "It was a brave thing you did, Farmer. And clever. And..." She made herself look at him. "Right."

His eyes were searching hers; he even tried to smile, weakly, and failed. "Perhaps. But somewhat foolish as well. There will be a price to pay when Spotswood hears of this."

Storme said cautiously, "It looks like we're in this thing together, now."

Then Simon's smile strengthened, and spread to his eyes. His hand closed over hers. "For better or worse," he said huskily.

Storme looked into his eyes. It was easy to let go now, for he was there. And that, in the end, was all that mattered.

She lifted her arms and encircled his neck. She pressed her head against his shoulder, and she smiled. "For better, I think," she said.

EPILOGUE

*

1722

St. Thomas, the Virgin Islands

The white sands spread around the little cove like a crystalline shawl, separating jewel-blue Caribbean waters from the rich dark tangle of green on shore. Brightly colored birds flitted back and forth from treetop to bush, arguing vociferously over the tastiest of the tropical fruit. In the distance dark-skinned fishermen waded waist high into the ocean, casting out their nets, and naked children chased the gulls away from the catch.

Upon the high bluff stood a sprawling gray stone house, its windows winking like merry eyes in the sun. Beyond the house richly furrowed fields curved, tall rows of sugarcane waving as far as the eye could see. One hundred fifty stone steps were carved into the bluff from the house downward to the sea, and halfway down a woman paused and waved her arm in greeting. Behind her, an everpresent shadow, a big black man, stood guard, almost as much a part of the landscape as was the woman herself. The wind combed back her honey-colored hair and tugged and molded her skirts against the shape of her legs, and she began to descend to the beach, her movements lithe and graceful, her steps carefree.

On the beach below Simon watched, his heart caught and filled, as always, by the simple beauty of her. He held his coat by one thumb over his shoulder; his shirtsleeves were pushed up and his neckcloth discarded. He had left his shoes and stockings somewhere along the beach, and the sand was warm against his bare feet. Every part of him warmed, simply watching Storme approach.

"What news from town?" she called as she drew near.

Simon waved the paper he held in his hand. "The ship from the Colonies is in. We've a letter from Augusta and Peter."

Storme slipped her arm around his waist, looking up at him eagerly. "What do they say?"

"They're well. Augusta plans to bring the baby for a visit in the autumn."

Storme laughed out loud in delight. "And you thought she'd be afraid to sail! There's not a cowardly bone in that girl's body and my namesake will grow up just the same! In the autumn you say?" Her eyes grew thoughtful with making plans. "None too soon to get the young one used to the sea."

Simon laughed. "Madame, I beg of you, one sailing woman in the family is enough. My niece may bear your name, but please, if God is good, my sister's temperament!"

"Fie on you, Farmer!" Storme stepped in front of him, looping her arms about his neck and tilting her head back to examine him. "Living with the sea hasn't done you a mite of harm, I will say. You never looked fitter." She traced the lines of laughter around his crystal-gray eyes, and feathered her fingers over his deeply bronzed skin. The sun had lightened his hair to an almost coppery hue, and days of working shirtless had darkened his chest and arms so that the hair upon them was golden-red in contrast. His muscles were long and hard and his step was light. More than ever, just looking at him was enough to take her breath away.

"You would've withered away to a stump in that swamp-infested piece of ground in Carolina," she told him firmly. "And died of fever or madness before you were gray. I told you I'd take care of you, didn't I?"

His eyes crinkled with amusement and affection and he squeezed her waist hard, lifting her a little off her feet. "That you did, wife. I was wise to put my faith in you.

"I also," he continued as they resumed their walk, "was wise to turn Cypress Bay over to Peter. It was always as much his as mine, and he reports a good profit this year. It shan't be long before they're able to buy me out."

"And then we'll be rich and lazy. What shall you do then, Farmer?"

"Exactly what I'm doing now," he returned, and planted a kiss on her rich, sun-washed hair. "Or maybe I shall buy something pretty for my wife."

She cast an enticing glance at him. "Like what?"

"What do you want?"

She thought about that for a moment, then leaned her head back contentedly against his shoulder. "The sun, the sea, and you," she said, and looked up at him. "What more could I possibly want?"

He smiled at her.

"There's word of Christopher, too," Simon said, after a moment. "It seems he eloped with Darien Trelawn only last month."

Storme glanced at him suspiciously. "Ain't she the one that set her cap for you?"

"One of several," Simon admitted modestly.

Storme gave a satisfied bark of laughter. "Then may she lead him a merry chase. Sounds like a she-cat to me."

"My cousin will not have a dull life," Simon agreed. "But he always was one for adventure."

Storme stopped, then, and looked up at him soberly. "Tell me true, Farmer. Are you ever sorry?"

Simon gave his answer the consideration it deserved, but Storme could see the truth in his eyes long before he spoke. And it filled her with lightness, and joy.

"Perhaps I have taken a lesson from my cousin," he said, "and from you. Life soon grows old without challenges, and I am among the most fortunate of men. I've a chance to start over again, and build from nothing. That's what I love—the building. And look at what we've done."

His eyes grew avid and his tone animated as he gestured toward the bluff and the rich full fields there. "Already we have a harvest as fine as any in the islands, ready to ship within the month—''

"And the ship will be ready just in time,'' Storme interrupted excitedly. "Squint has a crew working 'round the clock to build her and she'll be a fine piece of work. Not as swift as the *Tempest*, of course, but sturdy, and we'll pack her to the gunnels. Of course,'' Storme added with an impish grin, "I don't suppose I'll be having to outrun any British frigates, so she can be as heavy as you like. There's something to be said for being a respectable merchant at that, I guess.''

Simon chuckled, bringing his hand up to caress her neck beneath her hair. "Just don't become too respectable, if you please. I'm beginning to like being a fugitive.''

Storme frowned a little. "Is that what we are?''

"Not really.'' Simon smiled. "I rather doubt that either Governors Eden or Spotswood are much concerned with what goes on in St. Thomas, or what became of us. As far as they are concerned, you were defeated utterly, never to rise again.''

They looked at each other, and as one they laughed, tossing back their heads to the sun like children sharing a delightful secret. Storme looked at him, her eyes sparkling, and declared, "They always were a pair of fools! We haven't lost at all—we've won!''

Simon's face was etched with tenderness, and his fingers tightened around her waist. "Ah, yes,'' he said softly. "And how we've won!''

They turned and, arm in arm, walked slowly toward home.

* *Historical Note* *

Although the character of Storme O'Malley is purely fictitious, there is historical precedence in the piratical careers of Anne Bonney and Mary Read, who proudly sailed and fought alongside Blackbeard, Stede Bonnet, and Calico Jack Rackham.

The strife between Charles Eden, governor of North Carolina, and Lieutenant Governor Alexander Spotswood of Virginia is well documented. Spotswood accused Eden of giving refuge to pirates, and it was Spotswood who was responsible for capturing and killing Blackbeard in the waters of North Carolina in November of 1718. Even after Blackbeard's death, Spotswood continued to search for evidence proving Eden's collusion with pirates. Though he finally obtained both written and spoken testimony against Eden and his secretary, Tobias Knight, both were cleared of all charges by Eden's own Council. Colonels Moseley and Moore, two North Carolinians who joined with Spotswood in searching for evidence against Eden, were taken to trial before the high court and found guilty. Spotswood was frustrated once again by Eden's wiles.

In 1717, when King George I sent Woodes Rogers to the Bahamas to rid the Caribbean of pirates, many were driven north to the Colonial shores where they flourished for a while. But by the mid-1720s, because of political and economic pressures, the age of piracy was virtually at an end.

Even today Blackbeard's treasure is sought in vain along the coast of North Carolina, but the true legacy of Blackbeard—and indeed, all of the pirates—lives in the legends that have endured through the centuries.